Daughters of Havah Volume One
Copyright © 2024 by Ellen Hooge

Published in Canada by Sparrow House Collective
www.sparrowhousecolective.com
jehooge@shaw.ca

All rights reserved. No part of this book may be reproduced by any means without the prior written consent of the publisher, other than for brief quotes for reviews.

Scripture taken from the Holy Scriptures, *Tree of Life Version**. Copyright © 2014, 2016 by the Tree of Life Bible Society. Used by permission of the Tree of Life Bible Society.

Cover design by Joyelle Komeirowski

Praise for Daughters of Havah

"Although this story has been retold many times over the years, this version adds something extra to the tale."
- The Word Guild

"*Daughters of Havah* will challenge your sanctified imagination and stir your heart. For women who today also live demanding and complex lives, these stories will build your confidence in a God who has a tender heart for the overlooked and sometimes forgotten."
- Marilyn Elliott, M.A.Theology, D. Min, Vice President Asbury Seminary (retired)

"It was such a good read - a novel and an in-depth Bible study all wrapped into one. How incredible it was to see these well-known Scriptures from a woman's view point."
- Dr Jean Barsness, author of *Anywhere, Anytime, Any Cost*. Professor of Missions, Briercrest Seminary (retired).

"Surprising, unexpected, and quite simply genius. Rather than impose modern-day values onto these familiar characters, the author presents a fresh and possibly more accurate perspective. It made me stop and consider my own cultural biases and how I have probably inserted them into these familiar stories without even realizing it. Bravo!"
- Tracy Krauss, award winning and best selling author & playwright

"*Daughter's of Havah* is a set of lovely stories that creatively explores the lives of some of the great women of the Bible. Hooge's retelling of these stories will draw readers deeper into the Scriptural text, through a contemplative imagining of the very human and spiritual pressures these great women encountered."
- Rev. Dr. Dane Neufeld, Rector, St. James Anglican Church

**for
Alana, Elyse, Lara and Joyelle**

A NOVEL

Daughters of Havah

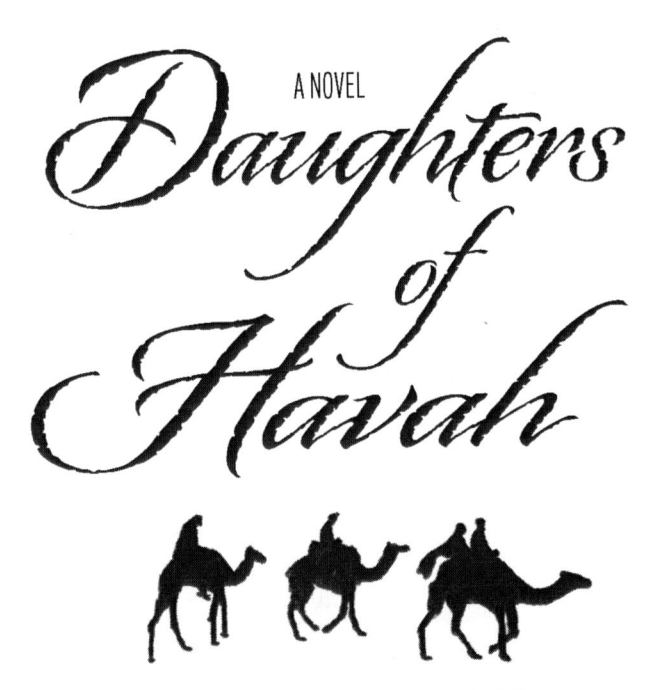

MATRIARCHS OF ISRAEL VOLUME ONE

ELLEN HOOGE

TABLE OF CONTENTS

8	**MAP**
10	**FAMILY TREE**
11	**GLOSSARY**

SARAH

14	UR OF THE CHALDEAS
20	HARRAN
22	OAK OF MOREH
25	BIET-EL
28	EGYPT
34	THE ALMOND GROVE
38	OAKS OF MAMRE
42	WASTELANDS
45	TENTS OF AVRAHAM
51	G'RAR
58	DESERT PLACES
60	MORIYYAH
62	BE'ER-SHEVA
63	HEVRON

RIVKAH

66	THE CAPTIVE
71	THE ENGAGEMENT
78	THE JOURNEY
89	THE WEDDING
93	THE RIFT
97	THE CAVE
99	THE PRAYER
101	THE PROPHECY
103	THE BIRTH
105	THE TWINS
107	THE BIRTHRIGHT
111	THE VISITATION
113	THE LIE
119	THE BLESSING
126	THE GARDEN

LE'AH

132	FAMILY
136	BRIDAL AUCTION
138	BETROTHAL
143	WAITING
147	NUPTIALS
151	DAWN
154	COUPLINGS
160	BIRTHINGS
182	FLOCKS
183	FLIGHT
191	BROTHERS
195	REST
196	VIOLATION
204	MOURNING
210	PARTINGS
214	JOURNEYS

TAMAR

220	ACCUSED AND CONVICTED
224	STORIES AND STARS
231	TRUTH AND LIES
236	DISHONOUR AND DESTINY
240	JUDGMENT AND MERCY
245	ACQUITTED AND ACCEPTED
247	BIRTHS AND BEGINNINGS
249	GRIEF AND GROWTH
253	FAMINE AND FAREWELLS
259	MEMORIES AND MOONLIGHT

272	**STUDY NOTES**
297	**ABOUT THE AUTHOR**
298	**ACKNOWLEDGMENTS**
299	**BIBLIOGRAPHY**

Map

MOUNT HERMON

The Great Sea

Yarden River

- Sh'khem
- Biet-El
- Shalem
- Biet-Lechem
- Hevron
- G'rar
- Be'er-Sheva
- S'dom?
- Be'er-Lachi-Ro'i
- Hallab
- Hamath
- Quatna
- Dammesek

Nile River Delta

- Avaris
- GOSHEN
- EGYPT

THE NEGEV DESERT

UTZ?

MOUNT SE'IR

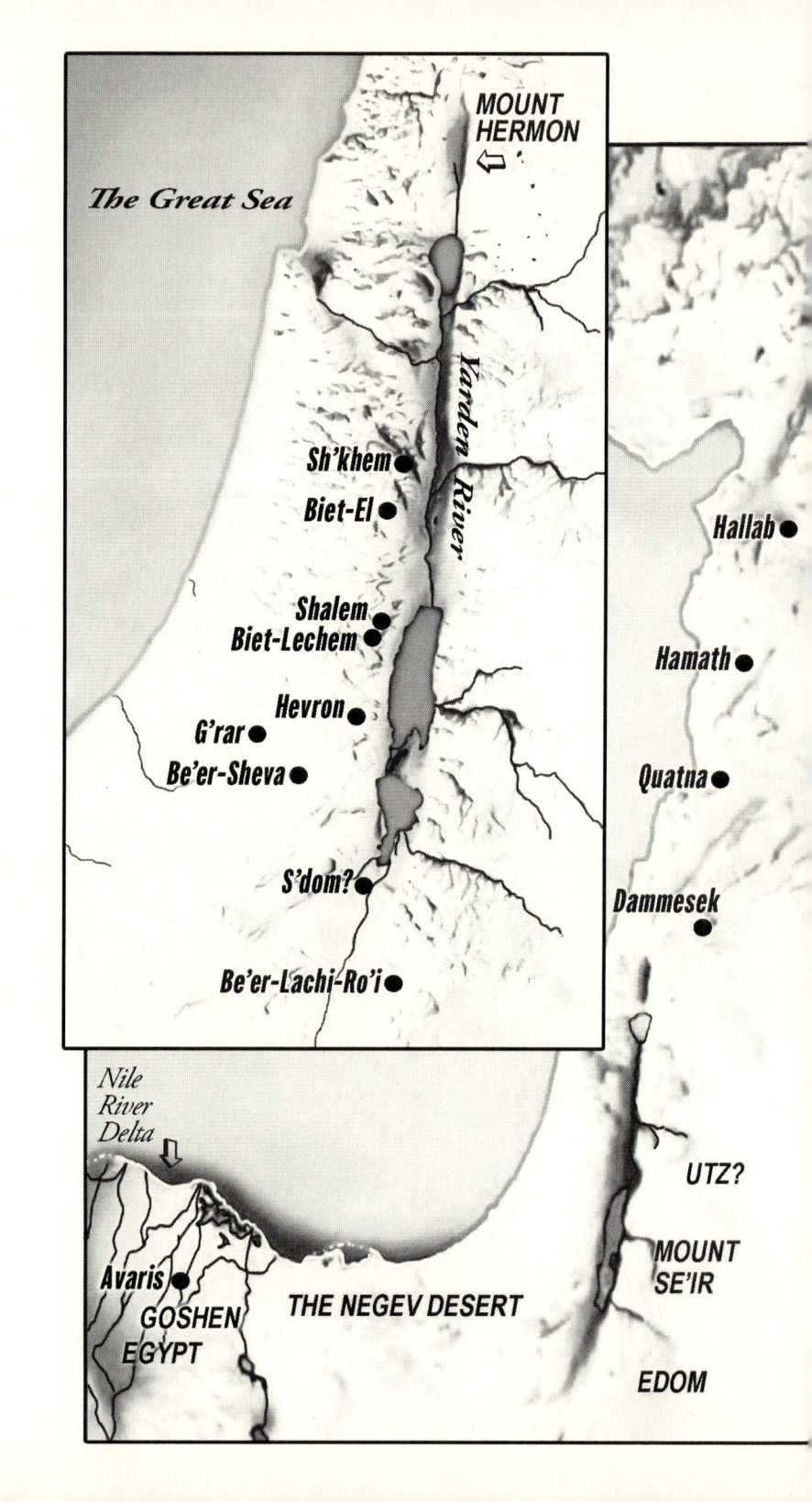

EDOM

Follow the Daughters of Havah on Their Journeys

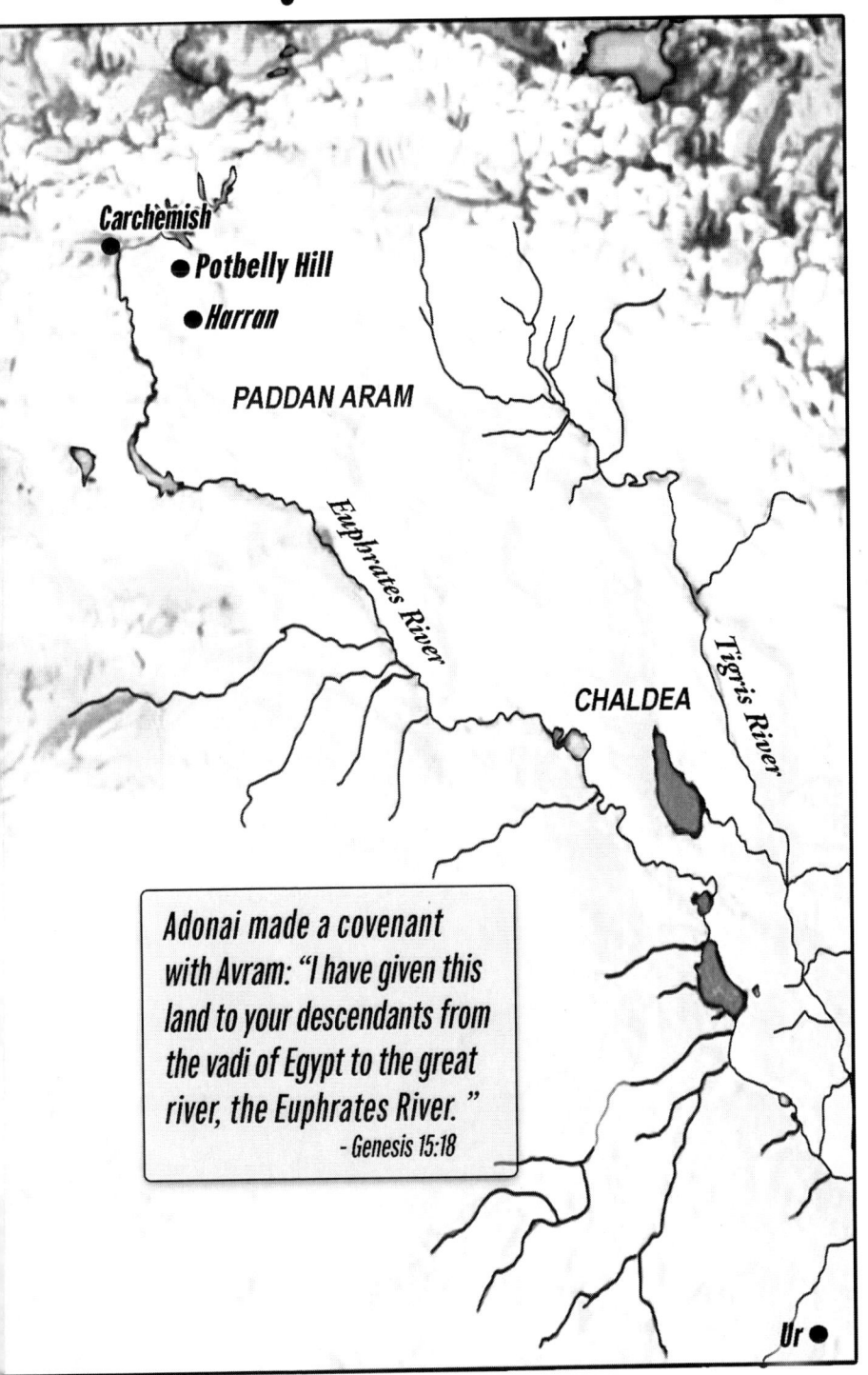

- Carchemish
- Potbelly Hill
- Harran

PADDAN ARAM

Euphrates River

Tigris River

CHALDEA

Adonai made a covenant with Avram: "I have given this land to your descendants from the vadi of Egypt to the great river, the Euphrates River."
- Genesis 15:18

Ur

The Redeemer of the World

Efaryim
M'nasheh
↑

Peretz
Zerach
↑

Bin'yamin
Yosef —m— **Osnat**
↑

|— m ——————— **Dinah**
| **Z'vulun**
| **Yissakhar**   **Asher**
Tamar —m—— **Y'hudah**   **Naftali** **Gad**
| **Levi**   **Dan**
Iyov | **Shim'on**
| **Re'uven**

Korach
Ya'lam
Ye'ush
Re'u'el
Elifaz
↑
'Esav →   **Shabar** ← *Leah*   **Rachel**   **Bilhah**   **Zilpah**
Son of   ↑   **Lavan** ← *Rivkah* → **Ya'akov** —m
Yitz'chak   **Lot**   **B'tu'el**   ↘m
& Rivkah   ↑   ↑   **Yitz'chak** — *Sarah*
                  Haran   Nachor   **Avraham** —m— *Sarah*
                  Terach ————————————————————
                  Nachor   m
                  S'rug   ↓
                  Re'u   **Hagar**
                  Peleg   ↓
                  'Ever   **Ishmael**
                  Shelach
                  Arpakhshad
                  Shem
                  Noach   **LEGEND**
                  Lamech   ———→ direct offspring of
                  Methusela   —m—   wife or concubine
                  Enoch   *Cursive* daughter of Havah
                  Jared   ---→ distant lineage
                  Mahalalel
                  Kenan
                  Enosh
       Adam → Seth ← *Havah*

Daughters of Havah Family Tree

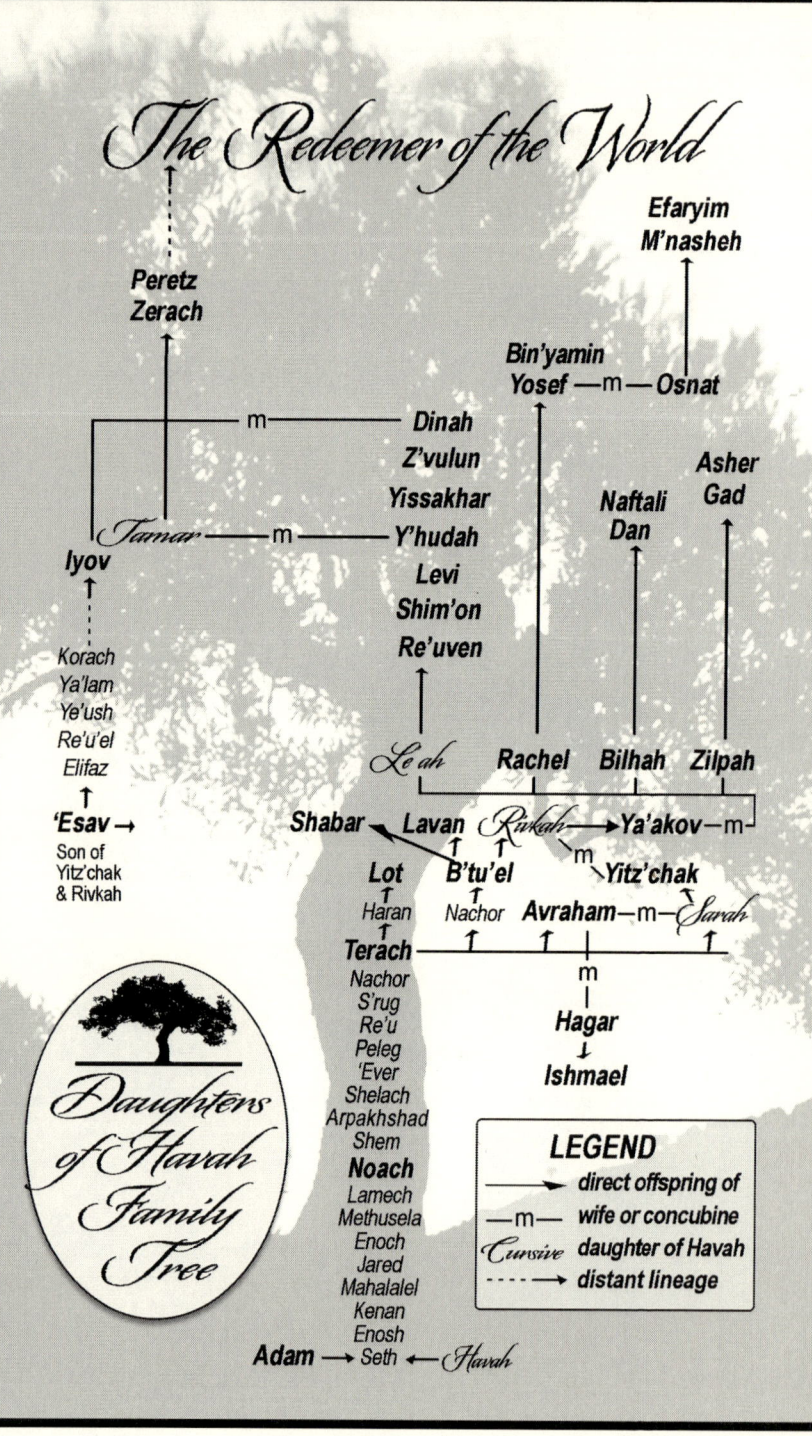

GLOSSARY
Hebrew and Mesepotamian names listed in the order they appear in the book

SARAH

Avram	Abram
Abba	Father
Ima	Mother
Terach	Terah
Kena'an	Canaan
Nachor	Nahor
Sh'khem	Shechem
Ba'al	Baal
Biet 'El	Bethel
K'turah	Keturah
Yarden River	Jordan River
S'dom	Sodom
'Eden	Eden
Eli'ezer	Eliezer
Hevron	Hebron
Moriyya	Moriah
Biet-Lechem	Bethlehem
Shalem	Salem
Malki-Tzedek	Melchizedek
Havah	Eve
Yishma'el	Ishmael
Avraham	Abraham
G'rar	Gerar
P'lishtim	Philistine
Avimelekh	Abimelech
Yitz'chak	Isaac
Be'er-Sheva	Beersheba

RIVKAH

Cig Kofte	regional meat dish
King Nimrud	Nimrod (perhaps)
Lavan	Laban
Saj Bread	unleavened flatbread
Rivkah	Rebecca
D'vorah	Deborah
Hitti	Hittites
B'tu'el	Bethuel
Carchemish	Jerablus, Syria
Dammesek	Damascus, Syria
Hallab	Aleppo, Syria
Hamath	Hama, Syria
Chadouf	Irrigation tool
Quatna	Qatna, Syria
Be'er-Lachi-Ro'i	Beer-Lahai-Roi
Mount Se'ir	Mount Seir
'Esav	Esau
Ya'akov	Jacob

LE'AH

Le'ah	Leah
Dolmas	meat wrapped in grape leaves
Keskek	traditional Turkish wedding stew
Ayran	savory yogurt drink
Water-Bearer stars	Aquarius
Baba-ghanoush	eggplant dip
Re'uven	Reuben
Sea-Goat stars	Capricorn
Shim'on	Simion
Scorpion stars	Scorpio
Fish stars	Pisces
Lion stars	Leo
Y'hudah	Judah

Noach	Noah
Hanokh	Enoch
Archer stars	Sagittarius
Weigh-Scale stars	Libra
Scarab stars	Cancer
Virgin stars	Virgo
Yissakhar	Issachar
Ram stars	Aries
Z'vulun	Zebulun
Bull stars	Taurus
Yosef	Joseph
Twin stars	Gemini
Bin'yamin	Benjamin
Iyov	Job
Land of Utz	Land of Uz
Elifaz	Eliphaz

TAMAR

'Einayim	Enaim
'Er	Er
Molech	Moloch
Peretz	Perez
Zerach	Zerah
Sh'ol	Sheol
M'nasheh	Manasseh
Osnat	senath
Potu-Fera	Potiphera

Sarah

Just as Sarah obeyed Avraham, calling him lord, you have become her daughters by doing what is good and not fearing intimidation.

I Peter 3:6

SARAH

UR OF THE CHALDEAS

The day was hot, and noisy with the bleating of sheep. Moving among the shearers, I offered ladle after ladle of water from my brimming gourd. My laughter bubbled around us while the shepherds gulped down the life-giving liquid, letting the overflow soak their beards.

And I knew he thirsted for it.

Setting a newly sheared ewe on her feet, he gathered up the fleece and straightened his back. Our eyes met and I could see that every drop of moisture had drained from his soul. "Water for the weary?" I asked.

He bent his head to drink from the gourd but I snatched it away. He reached for the handle but I was too quick. My hand flashed like my smile and liquid splashed in his face. When he reached again for the water I ran away and he found himself chasing me through the crowded sheep pens.

We tore through the throng of bleating sheep and mocking shepherds until my path was blocked by a pile of wool. He pushed me into its soft embrace and asked, "What kind of punishment should be meted out to a Chaldean maiden who withholds water from her lord?"

In mock humility, I replied. "Forgive me lord Avram, I thought your soul seemed thirstier than your throat. I can never bear to see a man take life so seriously."

His face clouded. "There are reasons a man would take life seriously. Do you expect me to forget the grief our clan has suffered? Do you expect me to ever laugh again after watching the horns of a bull gore our brother?" Turning on his heel, he left me lying in the wool and went to shear a nearby ram.

I reached for a handful of pungent wool. Avram intrigued me. Strangely drawn to his stormy countenance, I had watched my father's youngest son throughout the shearing. His upbringing in the city of Ur must have been very different from my country childhood. I had heard how Haran, my half-brother, died. I was no stranger to life's hardships. But laughter always smoothed the rough edges of my day. Perhaps living in the city had soured Avram. Perhaps he needed to be taught to laugh.

I shrugged and smiled. And in an attempt to prevent the desert from stealing its beauty, I rubbed waxy wool residue into my shining copper skin. When I lifted my face from the task, I saw Abba (Father) making his slow way across the shearing floor. Scrambling to my knees, I peered around the hill of fleece to see where he would go. Would he finally command Avram to marry me? It was high time he did. With Ima (Mother) gone, and Abba bowed with age, I needed a new home and a sure future. Holding my breath to hear them better, I crouched behind the pile of wool.

"Not Sarai."

"Why not, Avram? She is by far the most beautiful woman in the land. She works hard. She . . ."

"She is my sister."

"But all our kindred, and the great pharaohs of Egypt, marry their sisters, why not you?"

"I am not a pharaoh."

"Avram, take pity. When these old bones return to dust, my little princess will be alone in the world. Her mother's final illness forced me to give the country home and all its furnishings, to the moon-god's so-called healers. And your brother's jealous wife refuses to welcome your beautiful half-sister into her household. Sarai now lives in a tent with the hirelings. She needs a home, a place to bear children in safety and comfort."

Without a word, Avram left our father standing alone by the pens and went to shear a spotted ram, his face was unreadable.

ఎంకౖ

Avram's gloom still pressed on my soul while the angry rays of Nanna, the-moon-god, penetrated the tent I shared with our servants. I tossed about on my pallet, uncertain whether Avram would comply with our father's request. If he did not, what would become of me? Every young woman has dreams of an ardent husband who sweeps her away on a tide of passionate love. But with Abba's waning health, my main concern was for a home and a provider. Avram was industrious and shrewd in business. He would be a good provider. He was also tall and handsome in a craggy sort of way. Perhaps love could develop over time.

    Calling me toward its glare, the pointed horns of the crescent-moon pierced the sky. With a sigh, I submitted to Nanna's malicious power, threw back the thin wool coverlet, and stepped into the night. Standing in the dark, I sampled the scent of sheep, soil, and the fennel fragrance of olive blossoms. Reluctantly, I raised my face to the god in the sky. Was he angry again? Was he not appeased by the sacrifice offered after the shearing today? Why did I feel drawn to his brooding glow? Why did he call on me? I was just Sarai, a desert girl, a shepherdess. Could Nanna not be satisfied with the oh so graceful ministrations of the ever so lovely Enheduanna? After all, she was his true princess and high priestess, living in the spectacular city of Ur at the base of the fantastical ziggurat.

    I looked back at the worn black tent I was forced to call home. Enheduanna most likely lived in an elaborate two-level house, surrounded by gardens and ponds probably. She would have a grand camel to take her from place to place, complete with an elegant fringed saddle, a bridle tinkling with bells and . . .

    "Young women should not wander about under the watchful eye of Nanna."

    The stern voice made me jump. "Who are you?"

    "A worshiper," he said from the shadows.

    "Oh. Greetings, Avram. I also came out to pray."

    "And what do you ask of the great Nanna, in the middle of the night?"

    My temper flared. "I ask Nanna to let me go. I ask

him to call someone else from their bed to meet with him."

My outburst surprised me, so I stopped to consider the situation and could not help but smile a little. I shrugged. "Perhaps you are the answer to that prayer."

"Or perhaps we have the same prayer, Sarai."

My bitter laugh barked into the darkness. "You? The same prayer? You are from the favoured limb of the family tree. You have all the advantages. You live with our father in a brick house deeded to him by the great king Nimrud—in gratitude for the sacrificial death of our brother Haran.

I, on the other hand, am the product of a lowly country wife. I live in a patched tent and have nothing whatsoever to thank Nanna for. He ignored my prayers and the sacrifices offered for my Ima's healing. Now she is dead. He also ignores my prayers for a place to call home. So I am here in the night, trying to escape the stink and snoring of our father's servants, wanting to be free of Nanna."

"You do not fear to speak this way, under the observant eye of the moon-god?"

"What have I to lose? He has taken everything already."

"I am surprised to see you take your life so seriously."

I snorted—then laughed. "I deserved that. What exactly is your petition of the great Nanna?"

"I have come into the night to bid him farewell. I will no longer serve a deity who demands human blood."

"Haran? Because of Haran's death?"

"Yes, and Yiskah's." He noticed my silence. "You do not know about Yiskah, Haran's daughter? She was Milkah's twin, sacrificed the day she was born. I was forced to watch that gruesome ceremony. So, we agree, our family has lost enough to the bloodthirsty moon-god."

I gathered my garments close to my body and shuddered in revulsion at the thought of the ritual Avram had witnessed. To speak with Avram about such things was dangerous. Heretics were punished severely for saying much less. But I had never heard anyone dare to voice my same thoughts. Perhaps he would also share my questions. "Are there really other gods beside the ones we know—Nanna the moon, his wife the sun and his daughters the stars?"

Avram stepped out from shadows and into the pale light of the crescent-moon. He did not glance at the leering Nanna. His face held no fear. "After the shearing, I will leave Ur and travel along the rivers to search for a new deity. I want to find the Mighty One the ancients worshiped, the One who created the sun and moon and wrote a story of earth's redemption in the stars. Do you want to come?"

I frowned. Was this all I could expect from the stoic Avram? Just a vague proposal of marriage with no declaration of love? How would my life unfold with this stone-faced man? I sighed and spoke a veiled assent. "We would live in tents I suppose."

☙❧

The setting sun announced the end of the shearing festival, and my soul churned with turmoil. Relieved of their winter wool, the flock grazed contentedly in the fields. Evening fires invited revelry and I was pestered with requests. "Come Sarai, sing for us, favour us with a song." I shook my head and made sure my duties took me within earshot of my father and half-brother.

After our moonlight conversation Avram agreed to marry me, but our future was still uncertain. And I would be the last person consulted about where we would live, or how our lives would progress. Eavesdropping was my only hope and I saw that Avram was finally side by side with Abba. They were ready to talk about something while I stood nearby, pretending to be unaware, heaping almonds, dates, and figs onto huge platters.

"Not the city of Harran."

"Why not, Avram? My sacrificed son was named for it. It is the most beautiful city in the land. I know you can no longer abide living in Ur so I will accommodate you. I sold our house there, and sent a servant ahead to purchase a dwelling in Harran. It will be a fine one, with gardens and a fountain. You know how Sarai longs for a home and..."

"Harran is the city of Sin—the moon-god of the north. How will our lives be any different if we are not free of his cruelty?"

"But all our kindred, and the great pharaohs of Egypt, worship the moon. Why not you?"

"I am not a pharaoh."

"Avram, take pity on your aging father. Every day my infirmities slow me further. I need a resting place, and Sarai should live in a permanent dwelling. She has suffered great turbulence of soul due to her mother's illness and passing."

"Nachor and Milkah now trade their wool with the wealthy merchants of Egypt. Would you not like to live with them, closer to the great River Nile? You could go there..."

"I am not a pharaoh," said Terach.

HARRAN

"Hagar! Hide it in that jar. Perhaps he will forget the whole thing if he cannot find the way. Quick child! He is coming!" Our laughter bounced off the archways and dissolved in the splash of the fountain. We tried to stifle our giggles as Avram came around the bend of the hall—as serious as ever.

"Sarai, have you seen the papyrus map of Kena'an? I left it on my writing table. It seems to have disappeared—again." Avram's arms were crossed and he glared down on me like the moon-god. Then my slave girl, Hagar, gave away our plot with a wayward snicker. "Give it to me!" Avram reached over Hagar's shoulder and snatched the scroll from its hiding place behind her back. "We are leaving tomorrow," he said.

I could see that my husband's thoughts were aimed like an arrow—at Kena'an. He seemed blind to my desire for a settled life. So, one last time, I tried to sway him. "Avram, I love our house in Harran. We have spent five happy years here. I want to stay. Where will we live in Kena'an, and what kind of people dwell there? How do you know they will welcome us?"

"We have discussed this, Sarai. I will buy you a house in Kena'an when we find the place our God will lead us to."

"Are you sure you heard the voice of this nameless god? Are you sure this god told you to leave Harran? Are you sure this god promised to bless you and make a great nation from your seed? Despite the bloody sacrifices our family made, the fertility gods of our youth have not favoured us with a child after many years of marriage. Can this nameless god do what our gods cannot?

"Sarai! Watch your tongue! The Almighty will keep the Promise if we obey the Voice. We must go. Our father, Terach, has departed to the realm of the dead. Our brother, Nachor, has been recalled to the city of Harran to claim his birthright. We are now free to leave. Make your final preparations."

I knew I had lost the battle to keep our comfortable

home in Harran, so I swallowed my disappointment and decided to continue a fight on another front—my struggle to gain Avram's love. Perhaps submission to his plan would help, and a few feminine wiles maybe... "Avram?" I looked up so he could see tears glistening in my eyes. "May I at least make the journey on one of your new camels? That pretty white one is very elegant..."

He stepped closer and looked down at my upturned face. His eyes softened as he traced the curve of my cheek with a gentle finger. "Yes, my princess, and for this grand occasion I have purchased a fine fringed saddle for you."

"... and a bridle tinkling with bells?"

He nodded and drew me close. "Yes, silver bells that sound like your joy. Perhaps in Kena'an, the Promise will be fulfilled." Then he kissed me and melted my resolve to fight for anything.

OAK OF MOREH

The tree stood in the distance, a lone guardian on the hillside where it watched over the town of Sh'khem. Haran's son Lot, and his eternally peevish wife, lagged behind us while my husband rode up and down beside the caravan urging everyone forward with his customary intensity. I could not understand Avram's hurry to reach an unknown destination, and hoped we could soon pitch our tents in the shade of a nearby hill. Not that I ever had a say where we went or when we stopped. That was decided by Avram — and his god.

We had journeyed for weeks by then, and I longed to dismount the fancy camel Avram purchased for me. She turned out to be an ornery beast that could land spittle squarely in a person's face from ten paces away. My lovely fringed saddle was caked with the dust of the road, and the silver bells on the bridle had turned as black as my mood.

"Sarai, organize your women and set up the camp. We will stay on this plateau until God appears." Avram turned from me to gaze at the great tree, his face dark with apprehension. "The Presence is near, I feel it. Have our tents erected under the oak."

At this suggestion, I felt my heart constrict. "The servants say the tree is sacred, the navel of the earth. It has strong magic and people are afraid of it. No one ever camps there."

He wheeled around at my words. His eyes flamed with anger that burned into my soul. "We are not ruled by the gods of this land and we pay no attention to the fears of these people. The Almighty One protects us. Make haste, woman. Set up camp. I feel the Presence."

Twisting in my saddle, away from Avram's wrath, I surveyed the small plateau and planned how the tents should be arranged. Secretly, I did love this part of the journey, so I set to work hollering out impudent orders to the servants who carried each part of our living quarters. Dust swirled, tents unfurled, posts were erected, fires lit, lanterns hung, water drawn and cushions placed—in a flurry of insults, laughter, and song. This was a task I was born to, and I saw it through by the time a pink dusk descended onto the city of Sh'khem in the valley below.   We were busy beside the cooking fires when the men came back from penning the animals in for the night. The air was crisp and cool, and the pottage warm and savory with lentils and spices brought from Harran. Our people filled their bellies, then rolled onto their pallets, asleep in moments.

Wakeful under the glare of the menacing moon, I waited for Avram's visit. I had perfumed my bed with jasmine and adorned my body with the sheerest Egyptian linen. Hagar worked her Egyptian arts to paint the outline of my eyes with kohl, and I knew they glowed, green and gold, in the pale radiance of the oil lamp. Where was he? I did not possess his love but I saw the hunger in his glance. His flaring anger could not hide it. What was that? Did I hear a step outside my tent?

A deep shadow slid over the moon. It sharpened the lines of the curtains in the glow of the oil lamp. A stillness crept over the encampment, not even the night crickets chirped. The flame of the lamp flickered wildly in the motionless air—and went out.

My heart raced as I raised myself on an elbow, straining to see through the darkness. Who was out there? Not Avram. The Presence was deep and vast. It passed my tent, lingered for a terrifying moment, then dissolved into the night. I scarcely dared to breathe as I waited—tense and expectant.

"Sarai," Avram's whisper was strange and trembling. His breath caressed my throat as he settled onto the night cushions. My arms went around him and drew him in. Was he shaking?

"Avram, what happened?"

"God appeared."

"Yes, I felt the Presence. Was anything said? Did you receive a message?"

"The Eternal One promised to give this land to

my offspring, to make a great nation from my seed — to bless me."

"Then perhaps your god will open my womb. Perhaps tonight I will become the Woman of the Promise."

☙❧

"Not this tree."

"Why not, Avram? It is by far the most beautiful tree in the land and your god visited you here. You built an altar in this place and sacrificed a lamb on it. Why would we leave? Is this not the land your god promised you? We could build a house in the shade of The Oak of Moreh. If your god keeps the promise and gives us offspring, we could raise them here. You know how I long for a home, and the Kena'ani . . ."

"No! Sh'khem is a city of Baal — a storm-god who demands human sacrifice. How can we bear to gaze down from here upon that grievous practice? The One will show us another tree. I will buy a plot of ground in that place and build you a home."

I knit my brows together as fiercely as I could, but he knew I would comply. He also knew I would search for concession. "This house you will build me when we finally find that mythical tree . . . will it have ivory doors and golden pillars and windows draped with red silken hangings that billow in the wind like flowing streams?"

"I am not a pharaoh," he said.

BIET-EL

Avram may be vexing at times, but he does take me to wondrous places. In the morning, I bid a reluctant farewell to the great Oak of Moreh, and that very evening, made an exotic new discovery.

A distant song beckoned me. Its strange music rose above the clatter of setting up camp. I left my servants, Hagar and K'turah, in charge of the supper pottage. Then I followed my curiosity down the path and around the breast of the hill to search for the source of the song. When I walked around the bend, what met my eyes, my ears, and my nose, dropped me to my knees in wonder. Gazing in rapture at the scene before me, I raised trembling hands in worship. "Surely, oh Great God of Avram, this is the place where you dwell. This is your house, the home you have called our people to."

My eyes took in soft white archways of flowering trees, stretching to the horizon. The intoxicating fragrance was like honey, with a slightly bitter twist. The music came from bees gliding from blossom to blossom, collecting nectar for their young—for God Most High—and for the pleasure of our people. Tears filled my eyes as my voice joined their song. How long was I lost in the bliss of that lovely place before I became aware of another presence?

While wiping at tears with the corner of my veil, I turned to see him. He stood in the dappled light of the grove, his face glistening with the sheen of his own tears. "Avram, what is the name of this place?"

"I have heard it called Biet-El, The House of God."

I laughed with delight. "The Presence dwells here, with the song of the bees and the fragrance of the flowers. Can we stay, Avram? Will you build our house next to The House of God?"

Avram reached down and lifted me to my feet. He kissed me and encircled my waist with his arm. We strolled in silence through the scented tunnels, taking pleasure in the cool green carpet, and breathing in the Sacred Presence.

"This is a place of promise," Avram murmured. "In this place we will wait for the blossoms to fall like snow and for the fruit of the tree to grow into nourishment. Take heart, my princess. All good things come to those who wait. This is Biet-El, a place where God will meet with us and our offspring for years to come, but is it is not the place to build our home."

The grove spun around me while I stared at my husband and all my joy fled. "What is it you seek Avram? Where will all your wandering lead? Do my desires mean nothing to you? We passed by many beautiful cities, built with golden stones and carved gates. Are none of them good enough? What do you seek?"

Was it my imagination? Did Avram grow taller in the filtered light of the grove? Did the hovering bees weave a halo of gold around his head? Did my heart stop completely the moment he said, "I am seeking an eternal city, whose architect and builder is God."

୫୬୦୧

Our people worshiped at the altar Avram built in the grove. And from the generous bees, we gathered great quantities of golden honey to use for trade and sustenance on our journey south.

On the first night, our treasure unbolted the gates of Biet-Lechem, a strange little town southwest of the ancient city of Shalem. After trading there, we set up camp in an open field on the top edge of the town, where there was plenty of grass for our animals and a cave for us to shelter in. I had an unearthly feeling in that place—almost a feeling of home—a sense of belonging. But it was just a way-stop on our journey and we moved on.

The roads and people became rougher and meaner as we journeyed south. Welcome was begrudged. Not even a gourd of water was offered. If not for the stores of honey and wool we pulled from our trade packs, we would have been chased away or murdered. Avram trained all our able-bodied men to fight and carry a weapon. Even our effeminate nephew Lot was taught to fight—but I would never hire him as a bodyguard if I came to need one.

As the famine became severe, we found no grazing land to support our flocks. The people of Kena'an glared menacingly at us from their hovels, so we only stopped to rest for the night and to barter. I began to doubt my husband's good judgment. Had he heard the voice of his god correctly when he prayed for direction at Biet-El? If so, what kind of deity would lead pilgrims into famine and peril? Avram's god seemed to make great demands on his followers— and leave promises unfulfilled.

EGYPT

"Sarai. Leave preparations for the evening meal to Hagar and come with me. There is something I wish to say." Avram's face was like thunder again. What was he brooding about this time? Turning on his heel, he stalked off, without a backward glance, toward a tall sand dune. I shaded my eyes with my hand and watched him go, his neck was taut with determination. I sighed.

I said to the child at my side, "If the pot boils dry before the beans are tender, add more water and sprinkle in a few fennel seeds for flavouring." After sitting in a rocking saddle all day, I was certainly of no mind to climb a hill of hot and shifting sand. But I strode toward the distant dune, steeling myself to avoid being overpowered by my husband's black mood. When I reached Avram at the summit I was too breathless to speak, so we gazed in silence at the valley below.

Egypt! Its fabled river, a glinting silver cobra, writhed through a green and verdant valley. And the Nile's shining delta, a poisoned hood, was unfurled to strike intruders like us. The blazing summer sun melted the kohl around my eyes and I tried to wipe it off with the edge of my robe—which was gritty and sweat-streaked. I glanced at my husband, wondering when he would start the conversation. Travel-worn and weary, I knew I was not the dewy young bride he had married many years before, so his opening words shocked me.

"I know that you are a beautiful woman."

I turned to stare at him and I am sure my mouth hung open most unattractively. In all the years of our marriage he had never said such a thing. I knew I was beautiful. Everyone knew. And though other people made comments all the time, Avram avoided the topic. Did he think it would put him at a disadvantage if he referred to my dark exotic beauty?

Avram kept his eyes on the Nile and continued, "so when the Egyptians see you they will say, 'This is his wife'..."

I stared at his face, trying to read it. His sun-bronzed skin had gone pale and he stood motionless, arms crossed, refusing to look at me. What did he struggle to say? He had never declared his love for me but I knew he was protective of his family. Was he afraid my beauty would cause me to be captured in Egypt and forced into sexual slavery? To what lengths would he go to keep me from that fate? Would he dare turn back into the famine-ravaged desert and force a slow starvation on us all? His words broke into my thoughts.

"... and they will kill me; but you they will let live."

A blast of scorching wind blew sand against my perspiring skin. I tightened my veil and stared at Avram. I had never before heard fear in my husband's voice. But now, he feared for his life. What would become of us? Were my husband's fears a prophesy? Would I be left alone to face an unknown future? His next words shattered those thoughts.

"Please say that you are my sister so that I will be treated well for your sake, and my life will be spared because of you."

I stood in suffocating heat, struggling to comprehend what I had heard. And as understanding emerged, my heart grew cold—so cold a fiery furnace could not warm it. Was Avram's regard for me such a shallow thing? Was my welfare not a priority? Did he plan for Egypt to have its way with me if it would save his life?

I swallowed the lump in my throat and furiously blinked back tears. Our marriage had been our father's idea—a duty. And though I had always harboured hope that Avram would truly love me one day, I knew his dilemma. I had failed to give him a child. By law he was free to divorce me or to take a second wife. But as his sister, our customs mandated that I would continue to live in his household—underfoot. Was Egypt Avram's best chance to be rid of me? A stab of pain cracked and splintered my frozen heart. Then he confirmed my fears by saying it all again.

"Please say that you are my sister, so that I will be treated well for your sake, and my life will be spared because of you."

As I stared at the land of the pharaohs, imagining what would greet me if abandoned to its legendary pleasures, my heart-wound opened into a great crevasse of fear. It grew deep and grasping, crumbling under my feet and dragging me toward its depths. But at the very moment I thought I would lose myself—in a rush that left me gasping—the gaping pit of my fear was filled with hot and searing fury. I looked up into my husband's stony face but he would not meet my eyes. So, I took a fortifying breath of anger-soaked air. Then let it be, I thought. If he will abandon me, I will gladly abandon him—and his god.

"Very well my lord," I said aloud. Then I turned away from Avram, slid down the shifting dune, and began to prepare for my future. If I was to be bartered to the men of the land, I would prefer to go to a high bidder who could build me a grand house with glistening pools for bathing, surrounded by fragrant flowers and flitting birds.

My lovely copper skin would be smoothed with honey and bathed in water that was scented with dried rose petals. I would ask Hagar to spend the evening applying intricate Egyptian henna designs to my feet and hands. And . . . oh yes, I would rinse my hair in henna to cover a silver thread or two that had appeared recently. I would also need to tell my man-servants, Mishin and Balack, to wash my camel and oil my saddle until it shone and . . . yes, the bells needed polishing too.

In the morning, I would wear the green veil that drew such attention to my eyes, which I would paint with kohl, spreading crushed blue lapis lazuli above them in the Egyptian way. Then I would swell my lips with the oily red weed we collected from the sea.

I heard Egyptians loved women with eyes and lips as large as mine. If Avram wanted to trade me to save his life, I would make it worth his while—and mine.

※

"Sarai!" He stood alone in anguish while the crowd swarmed around him and Pharaoh's servant led my camel through the teeming bazaar toward my new life. Yes. I was sold to Pharaoh himself. And I did not give Avram a backward glance. After all, he should have been well satisfied with the bride-price of sheep, cattle, donkeys, slaves, and camels. And I was glad to see the last of a man who would sell me. I decided to make the best of my circumstances. I had no wish to go back to a man who traded me for cattle.

As we entered a heavily guarded gate, I gazed around in awe. Pillars of gold framed ponds of blue and palaces of ivory. Children played with painted toys on grassy carpets of green. Women lounged in intricately carved chairs, while servants fanned them with large white feathers. So, I determined to make the best of my new life in a house built of stone, the life Avram refused to give me.

※

"Sarai, cover yourself."

Because I wore a linen skirt, as sheer as the wings of a dragonfly, a red-faced Avram focused his eyes on the rooftops. And my ample breasts, exposed in the Egyptian way, caused no small stir in the daring court of Pharaoh.

"I have no veil my lord."

Young Hagar—who had slipped effortlessly back into the ways of her people—sauntered over to the vine-shaded porch of the eunuch house. I could see her laughing with the eunuch, Ahmes, head-keeper of the wives. She gestured toward Avram and me as we stood uneasily together in the blazing sun. Ahmes looked thoughtful, then strode across the expansive lawn to the harem's treasure house. He vanished into the room that stored jewels, clothing, and all manner of adornment the women of Pharaoh were entitled to.

Hagar ran back and asked us to wait for Ahmes' return. I shrugged. I was in no hurry to return to my old life of swaying in the saddle all day and putting up with my husband's moods all night—but my future in the court of Pharaoh had also turned sour.

It seemed they blamed my presence in the harem for diseases that broke out among them after my arrival. When diviners were consulted, the lots fell on me as the source of the trouble. More inquiries were made and it was discovered that Avram was my husband as well as my brother. So, my welcome was gone and hostility reigned. That was why Avram was abruptly dismissed from the land and bribed with sumptuous gifts in a plea to take me with him. That was why I was about to be tossed out of Egypt, half naked.

"I sinned against you Sarai," Avram blurted out. "I cast you away. But I hoped that in the courts of Pharaoh, your dream to dwell in a house of stone would be fulfilled."

Ignoring his last statement, I addressed the former. "Because I am barren, you cast me away. Without a child to start your nation, I am worthless to you. You do not believe me to be the Woman of the Promise."

My words hung, suspended, in the dry air. I had voiced the source of our unhappiness, the pressure we were struggling to stand up under. It was true. In my barren state, I could not fulfill the Promise and I could not win Avram's love.

Willing my tears to stop at their source, I held my head high and straightened my shoulders. I would not make an exit from this place with kohl streaking my face. Turning from Avram, I saw Ahmes striding purposefully across the lawn, carrying a bundle wrapped in fine white linen.

He placed the parcel in my hands and knelt at my feet in a posture of homage. "Exalted Princess," Ahmes said, "You are the one chosen by the gods to receive The Cloth of Redemption."

Taken aback, my lips opened in astonishment. Ahmes was an arrogant eunuch who bowed to no one. What game was he playing? Was he trying to save me from my tears? Was he toying with Avram's pride or making some kind of statement to the hostile women around me? It all seemed ludicrous.

Untying the string that bound the parcel, I decided I would follow Ahmes' lead and make a show of opening it. With care, I folded back the delicate wrapping and fingered the newly exposed cloth. I drew in a breath. I had never felt anything like it—so cool and smooth—like a mountain spring. I glanced questioningly at Ahmes who remained on the ground, on his face.

Hagar stepped forward to help me unfurl the cloth. Shimmering red and silver in the sun, it danced for joy in the breeze. Light as air, it took on a life of its own, soaring up to God in a song of worship. Had I not anchored it in my grasp, it would have escaped to the clouds. The court women flocked to it with fascination. Even Avram was entranced. And Ahmes rose to his feet to watch.

"It came to Egypt long ago, as a gift for queen Neferu," said Ahmes. "Before she died, she bid me keep watch for a woman who would one day be redeemed from the court of the pharaoh. She purchased my promise to give that woman this cloth. Forgive me Lady, for not recognizing you sooner. You are the woman of that prophecy. The price has been paid. You have been redeemed."

Gathering the cloth in from the sky, I tied one corner to my golden belt and wrapped its great length around me in lavish loops of crimson that shimmered and bubbled like a water-brook in the sun. As I draped the edge around my face, it flowed gently over my body and cooled my skin. I turned back to Avram.

"I am covered," I said.

THE ALMOND GROVE

Misery multiplied as we wandered day after day through the unforgiving Negev Desert. Neither Avram nor I could reach across the gulf to heal our rift. And because the pharaoh's extravagant gifts for my redemption had enlarged our flocks and herds, we were constantly moving to find enough pasture for them. We stayed deep in the wilderness, avoiding the hostile Kena'ani who were ravaged already by famine. We wanted no war.

Lot and his herdsmen chaffed us daily with their bickering over pasture. You would think my husband would lose patience with our nephew — like he so often did with me. But, no. With Lot, he was a model family patriarch, always looking out for the son of Haran, always making allowances and excuses — while my concerns were ignored. I took to avoiding them both by riding into the hills on my little brown donkey. She and solitude were my only friends while we journeyed north and I lost track of distance and time.

֍

"Sarai, leave the preparations for the evening meal to Hagar and come with me. There is something I wish to show you."

It was a painful echo. Similar words had led to heartbreak, so I put another stick on the fire and made no move to obey. He must have sensed my reluctance for he softened his tone and leaned close to my ear.

"Sarai, come with me. I have saddled your donkey."

I looked up in surprise. "My donkey?"

"The journey I will take you on is short, but I know you are tired from the travels of the day. Please come."

It was true. He had thrown a soft sheepskin onto my donkey's bony back and was holding the bridle. Bewildered, I mounted the little beast and rode around the breast of a hill, led again into Avram's plans.

As we came around the bend, he helped me dismount and silently cautioned me not to speak or make a sound. I followed his lead as he placed one foot in front of the other, careful not to disturb a rock or a twig on the pathway. Intent on watching the path, I jumped when he touched my hand.

"Look up," he whispered.

First, I looked into his eyes. They were filled with delight. Then I turned to see the scene before me. It was Biet-El—the almond grove. How had we arrived there? Lost in a fog of anger and grief, I had not known we were close by.

The white blossoms of spring had given way to clusters of hairy fruit that swelled into rough nuts. The air smelled of dried grass and fallen leaves, the musty aroma of autumn. Avram's finger touched my lips in a plea for silence and patience.

We waited.

Then they came, one at a time, cautious, flitting down from branch to branch in flashes of amber and blue. Hundreds of small birds descended to feast on the waiting fruit. Their soft, chittering, and the crack of almond husks, filled the air with peace. I smiled.

Avram held my hand in his as we watched. I do not know how long we stayed, soaking in the pleasure of the moment—and the sacred Presence. But I do know my wounded heart was strangely healed by the time Avram spoke again.

"I came here to call on God," he whispered. "I want you with me this time." He still held my hand.

"Why?" I murmured. "What have I to do with your god?"

"Perhaps you are the Woman of the Promise. Because of you, the One has blessed me with abundance. Without you, we would be wandering in the Negev Desert ragged and hungry. I know now that you are precious to our God who redeemed you from the court of the pharaoh. I will not again discount your worth."

Never before had my husband spoken so many kind words to me. I knew their truth and longed to open my heart to him, but past hurt made me as cautious as the feeding birds. So, I took flight and spoke aloud. "Can your god fill my womb like an almond pod? Will I bear your seed in the autumn of my life? Will this god find me a place to call home? Will you ask those questions when you call upon the One?"

In a sudden flurry of amber and blue, the startled birds escaped to the treetops and disappeared—leaving silence behind.

Avram's craggy face was awash with regret. "You are a garden locked up, my sister, my bride. You are a spring enclosed, a sealed fountain."

My heart lurched with regret when he turned to leave the grove, so I clutched at the edge of his robe and smiled at him. "Let my beloved come into his garden and taste its choice fruits."

All that night I stayed with Avram in the grove—to seek the Eternal One—and we departed from there in harmony. But in the pre-dawn light, as Avram led my donkey back to our encampment, I braced myself for conflict in the valley below. Perhaps Avram's God could give him wisdom to deal with the constant unrest we lived with, as our servants and Lot's, squabbled over pastureland.

༄༅

They climbed a mountain at dawn, misty figures in flowing robes. They stood on the highest peak. My husband was tall and stern and motionless. Lot was short and animated with broad gestures. I laughed at the contrast. I knew they negotiated peace in the form of divided territory. I knew Lot would cast a bid for the fertile Yarden River valley. And I knew Avram would indulge Lot, as he always did, leaving us to scavenge on the barren hills.

Lot stumbled down the hill in excitement. He gathered up his people herds and strutted off toward the city of S'dom with minimal farewells. I watched from my tent door, musing at the parting. We did not hold a feast and I was not sad to see their dust. But Avram watched from the summit until the last soul disappeared around the bend of the last knoll. Then he became very still on the mountain and I knew he was in the Presence.

While serving Avram a supper of roasted almonds, honey, and freshly baked bread, I asked, "What was said this time?"

"He said the plain of the Yarden River is as well watered as the Garden of 'Eden and he wants to live there."

"No. Not Lot, it was obvious what he said. What did Adonai say?"

"'Lift up your eyes, now, and look from the place where you are, to the north, south, east and west. For all the land which you are looking at, I will give to you and your seed forever.'"

Avram would not look at me as he spoke, so I knew there was more—and I knew I would not like it. "What else?" I asked.

He tore a loaf of bread apart, releasing its aroma. He dipped a morsel in the golden honey. I waited. He was infuriatingly slow. Then he spoke. "'Get up! Walk about the land through its length and width—for I will give it to you.'"

So, we walked the length and width of the land. Neither my husband nor his god could settle on one specific place, it seemed.

OAKS OF MAMRE

"Not these trees."

"Why not, Avram? You built an altar here and sacrificed a lamb on it. This is the most beautiful grove in the land. Why would we leave this place? Is this not the land your god promised you? We could build a beautiful house here in the shade of the Oaks of Mamre. You know how I long for a permanent home where we will raise the children God has promised. And the Kena'ani made a peace treaty with you, and . . ."

Catching my hand, he tried to sooth my anger, but his fingers began to wandered over the gathering of gray in my hair and the creeping lines on my face. Did he think I would never age? "We will pitch our tents under the oaks until we need to move the flock to new pastures," he said.

To avoid his eyes and my longings, I turned away from him and looked toward the horizon. "There is a runner approaching from the north," I said.

The news involved our exasperating nephew Lot who had been captured (with all his goods and his people) as a prisoner of war. He was taken north beyond Dammesek and Avram could have left his foolish nephew to his fate. But no, while abandoning me to the whims of our new Kena'ani allies, he gathered up all his warriors to attempt a rescue. Did he leave to avoid the reproach in my eyes when he refused, again, to build me a dwelling? Of course, he knew nothing of my growing desperation.

With Avram away, trustworthy Eli'ezer of Dammesek was left in charge of the camp, and I saw a window of opportunity. According to custom, I retreated to my tent just before the new-moon—to wait out my period of bleeding. For some months, though, it had been an act. I had always hoped that I would conceive a child and gain Avram's love, but that hope was drying up like my moon-flow. And I feared what would happen if Avram guessed. Would he desert me again? I knew what he was capable of.

I would not plead my case with the fickle moon-god, nor would I call on the Ba'als of Kena'an—and their disgusting fertility rituals. But I knew of a seer in Shalem who worshiped my husband's God. Perhaps he would bless me and resurrect my life-spring.

    Sworn to secrecy with threats on her life and a great many bribes, Hagar would stay in Hevron and continue bringing food and water to my tent. To carry on the ruse that I had retreated there for my monthly week of recluse, she would eat her portion of food as well as mine. And I knew Eli'ezer could be trusted with my secret plan. He would think up a story to cover Mishin's and Balack's absence from Hevron—so they could attend to my safety on the journey. If all went well, I would return with renewed hope.

    My night travels ended in the mountains of Moriyyah, and I sheltered in the cave on the outskirts of Biet-Lechem. Once again, I was enveloped in a strange sense of home. So much so, that I hesitated to leave the cave and complete my uncertain quest in nearby Shalem. Dread and expectation struggled within me. Each vied for supremacy. I tried to squelch my internal conflict by engaging my servants in song and laughter, and by reminding myself of my miraculous redemption in Egypt. Then at daybreak, in a final preparation, I donned The Cloth of Redemption and approached the gate of Shalem's king—Malki-Tzedek.

    Soft and unassuming, he greeted me at the door. He was of medium height with nothing in his appearance to draw attention to him. His eyes held mine for a moment. Like mine, they were green and gold. I felt a spark of kinship.

    "Welcome, Exalted Princess." I stared into his eyes. They were full of compassion and seemed to see so much. Did he already know my desires? Would he hear my entreaty?

    And then it happened. The pressure of my longings became so great that the vial of my sorrow shattered—leaving me completely speechless. I sank to the ground in a heap of sobs. While Mishin and Balack presented Malki-Tzedek with a tribute of almonds and honey, my tears formed ragged patterns on the stone tiles at his feet. As my courage, and all of my words, disappeared into the cracks of the paving stones, I could not find a way to voice my petition.

Was this the same unspeakable grief that the first mother of all the earth experienced, when she knelt in the garden of 'Eden at the feet of God? Was the very first mother, Havah, also unable to make a plea on her own behalf? There in the Garden, was she so terrified as she looked into her future, that she too became dumb? Did she feel as helpless as I? By the power of God, I was redeemed from the court of the pharaoh, but I could not imagine being redeemed from the curse of barrenness. I had no faith for that.

"Have patience, daughter of Havah. The hour has not yet come for your redemption to be complete. That day will arrive in its time. It will dawn with joy and you will laugh at its announcement. But I must leave you now. Another calls."

From my place of prostration, I saw Malki-Tzedek gather bread and wine into a basket. Then he gently touched my shoulder in consolation before he closed the door on my pain.

Mishin and Balack stood guard while I wept and the seer's prophecy took no root at all in my heart. I do not know how long my grief drained into the stones of that place. I could not say exactly when dread gained the victory. But finally, I rose to my feet, smoothed my hair, and began to fold The Cloth of Redemption back into its linen casing.

On returning from his errand, Malki-Tzedek entered the room and caught me at my task. "Daughter of Havah, pride is crouching at your door and you must master it. Your desire will be toward your husband, but he will rule over you."

I nodded. I knew what he referenced. After the act that changed their world, pride had driven an ugly wedge between Mother Havah and Father Adam. Each wrestled with it. Did Mother Havah ever right her wrong? Did she humble herself and close the gap? Or was she unwilling?

Is that why Father Adam insisted on ruling over her? As a daughter of Havah, I longed to close the gap between my husband and me, but knew I was too proud to bare my soul to him. Would we also choose to live out the ancient pronouncement and seek to rule each other? Would we too reap a deadly consequence?

Malki-Tzedek's eyes met mine a final time, pleading silently that I would lay aside my pride and trust in God's redemption. I bowed my head. I could not meet his eyes. His prophecy made no sense to me. The situation looked impossible. As I resigned myself to the only future I could see, Malki-Tzedek stood aside and let me pass into the night.

Back in Biet-Lechem, I curled up in the inner depths of the cave and shut myself away from life. I desired no light and lit no fire on that dark and moonless night. I persuaded Mishim and Balack to sleep at the gates of the town, leaving me wrapped in desolate solitude. But slowly . . . I became aware of another presence.

As it had for so many years, Avram's musk drifted toward me in the darkness. I saw his form in the mouth of the cave and almost called out to him but he seemed deep in prayer. Then suddenly, he lurched to his feet and ran out into the field. "My Lord Adonai," he screamed into the wind, "what will you give since I am living without children and the heir of my household is Eli'ezer of Dammesek?"

Creeping closer to the mouth of the cave, I witnessed the full force of Avram's grief. He had always put up a bold pretense, cloaked in anger. But now in the dark of night, his soul was naked and raw while he shouted hoarsely into the abyss.

"Look! You have given me no seed, so a house-born servant is my heir."

Avram stumbled further into the field, lifting his eyes to the swirling stars innumerable in their majesty. He immersed himself in the mysterious message of the heavens, while I stole away to waken my servants and make a hasty escape to Mamre's great oaks. I could not break into my husband's sorrow or deal with my own. Could anything comfort us?

WASTELANDS

"Not that woman," was Avram's firm reply.

"Why not, Avram? I raised her from a child. She works hard and she . . ."

"She is my slave."

"But all our kindred, and the great pharaohs of Egypt, marry their slaves. Why not you?"

"I am not a pharaoh."

"Avram, God has prevented me from having children. Go, please to my slave-girl. Perhaps I will get a son by her. Her child will fulfill the Promise as my legal son."

When the words were out, they all but stopped my heart. I knew instantly what I had done. I had gone the way of Mother Havah and taken matters into my own hands.

Rage at my grasp for power kindled Adam's fire in Avram's soul. And the consequence was the same for us as it was for our first parents. Avram and I stood under the oaks and watched the gulf between us grow. We felt like strangers. All familiarity fled. I tried to reach across the chasm and snatch back my words — but it was too wide. My hands hung limp while the gap between us broadened and Avram's face turned to stone. Then he walked away from me and entered my tent to seek her out.

ଛର

Gloom pressed on my soul while Nanna's angry gleam pierced the tent I shared with my servants. Tired as I was from the labour of the day, I tossed back the thin wool coverlet and stepped into the night. But where could I flee from what I had done?

Standing in the dark, I lifted my face to the breeze and sampled the scent of sheep, soil, and the fennel fragrance of olive blossoms. I lifted my eyes to the stars. What could they tell me? Could I untangle their mysteries? No. I was just Sarai, a desert woman, a shepherdess. I meant nothing to Avram's God. I had no fertile womb to plant a nation in. The Holy One was only satisfied with the oh so faithful ministrations of the ever so righteous Avram, true prince and prophet who dwelt in the great black chieftain's tent next to mine.

Looking back at the tent I was forced to call my home, I spat in disgust. Ten rootless years had not delivered a house of wood and stone, or Avram's child, or Avram's love. Ten years only brought a drought of unwatered promises from my husband and his god. Ten years had brought a desperate famine to my soul.

"Do you stand here in the night to petition Adonai?" The stern voice made me jump.

"Avram?"

"Perhaps I can join your prayer."

"I did not come out to pray."

"Then what do you seek, in the darkness of night?" My temper flared at Avram's probing so I told him the unspeakable truth.

"I come to seek a moment of peace from the strife in my tent. I come to flee my infertile womb and your god of barren promises. I come to escape Hagar's derision. She is with child—your child."

"You do not fear to speak this way, under the all-seeing eye of the One?"

"What have I to lose? I have lost everything already."

Avram stepped into the pale light of the crescent-moon. His face held no expression. No joy at the news of the child, no compassion for my grief.

So, I lashed out. "The wrong done to me is because of you! I, myself placed my slave-girl in your embrace, but when she saw that she was pregnant she began holding me in contempt. May Adonai judge between you and me!"

"Your slave-girl is in your hand," said Avram. "Do to her what is good in your eyes."

ଅଠଔ

Jealousy is unyielding as the grave. It burns like a mighty flame. In the hope that she would empty Avram's child onto the ground, I poured green-eyed fire onto Hagar. Hellebore and birthwort were administered daily, as were heavy loads, hot coconut shells, and severe kneading of the womb. But the cruel arts of the Kena'ani did not avail. And when she could take no more, Hagar fled my murderous hatred. But she met an angel at a spring and came crawling back, contrite. I shrank into myself then, and let the inevitable come to birth.

༄༅

In the glare of the midday sun, Hagar's screams filled the air. They called him Yishma'el (God Listens). I cried out in pain when I heard his name. He was a child conceived in anger and searing rebellion, a child destined to rage, born to battle us all. What had our folly spawned?

༄༅

Thirteen years of soul-drought followed—while the land flourished and the flocks grew. For thirteen years, from under the Oaks of Mamre, I ruled the women of the camp with justice and wisdom. But laughter and song had died.

For thirteen years, Yishma'el followed Avram's heels like a pup. Hagar moved to a small tent on the edge of camp, and we avoided contact. Avram never went near her tent—or mine. I watched from a distance while his manhood shriveled. For thirteen years Avram could not look me in the eye.

For thirteen years the Presence left us.

TENTS OF AVRAHAM

Awake under the glow of the moon, knowing he would come, I waited. The time of separation was over. Avram's stony heart had somehow turned to flesh. I did not know the reason for the change, but I knew he was ready to reconcile. As they searched out the dark spaces beyond the tent door, my eyes blazed, green and gold, in the pale radiance of the lamp. I heard a footstep in the night. Who was out there?

A deep stillness settled over the camp, not even the night crickets chirped. A shadow hid the moon and the lines of the curtains sharpened in the glow of the lamp. The flame flickered wildly in the motionless air—and went out.

My heart raced as I raised myself on an elbow, straining to see through the darkness. The Presence passed my tent, lingered a moment, then moved into the night. I scarcely dared to breathe as I waited, tense and expectant.

"Sarai," Avram's voice trembled as his breath caressed my throat and he settled next to me on the night cushions. My arms went around him and drew him in.

"Avram, what happened?"

"The Presence was here."

"Yes, I felt it pass by. Was there a message?"

"To walk through the land faithfully and blamelessly, then a covenant will be made between me and God and our numbers will greatly increase."

"But you already made a covenant at Shalem, when you divided the animals and God walked between them."

"In the matter of Hagar, I was neither blameless, nor righteous. I defiled that covenant."

I was suddenly filled with foreboding. "What is the sacrifice this time? What is the sign of this covenant?"

೧⊙೧

Hagar's voice was shrill with anger. "The great pharaohs of Egypt and all my kindred do it that way. Why not you?"

"I am not a pharaoh."

Hagar was furious that the circumcisions were not to be performed in the Egyptian way. I strained to listen as she argued with Avram. Their voices were muffled by the mist, a thick grey cloud that descended just as Avram said something about not worshiping God with half-measures. Hagar stormed off in the direction of her tent, unable to witness Yishma'el's pain if a full circumcision were to occur. When the fog closed in and blanketed our world in eerie expectation, I was busy organizing basins of water and preparing cloth dressings for the coming wounds.

Avram gathered the males of the camp and told them of the sacred visitation. The words of God hung ominously in the dense air. "'This is my covenant that you must keep between me and you and your seed after you. Throughout your generations, every male who is eight days old is to be circumcised. So my covenant will be in your flesh as an everlasting covenant.'"

After Avram's declaration, our women left a basin of water, a pot of mandrake salve and clean dressings — at the feet of each man. Then we retreated to our tents to wait.

Turning back from the doorway of my tent, I peered into the swirling fog. It parted momentarily to reveal the outrage on Yishma'el's face — at the sight of his father's flint knife. I knew he would never forgive the assault on his emerging manhood, and Avram would sacrifice far more than bits of skin that day.

I felt wretched. My heart ached for them both. I knew their rift was partly my doing. With more guilt than I could bear, I crumbled, face down, in the cold stinging tears of the mist. Like Avram, I had failed miserably in the matter of Hagar. As a daughter of Havah, I had enticed my husband to sin and had fallen, with him, into the soul-death of hatred. We all had. We all broke the covenant. Our men and boys now paid the price, but we all needed redemption. Oh, how my pride had railed at my husband and his god for not granting my desires. And now the whole camp suffered.

With tears of shame, I cut off the foreskin of my pride and laid it bloody and pathetic at the feet of the Holy One. I circumcised my heart and begged mercy for my soul, and for the souls of those who groaned and grunted in the churning haze.

༺༻

The required week of healing was busy for the women of the camp. While ministering to the wounds of our moaning men, we kept up our usual duties and also took on the care and feeding of the livestock. We depleted all our stores of wine and paid a great price to buy more from the Kena'ani. It was better than having to listen to constant whimpers and laments. If God had decreed that men would suffer the pain of childbirth, there would be fewer offspring among us, I am sure.

Avram now insisted on a new name—Avraham (Father of Multitudes). He said that God had changed it. In my barren state, the title stabbed me with another blade of pain, but I said nothing.

Avraham also insisted on calling me Sarah (Exalted Princess). He said God chose the name. But in the light of my failures, I felt uncomfortable wearing it.

At the age of ninety-nine, Avraham took longer to heal than his men did, and I could feel his impatience as I nursed his wound. His eyes followed me everywhere. Surprisingly, they were filled with the old hunger . . . and with something else . . .

At the entrance of his tent, I served Avram roasted almonds, honey, and freshly baked bread. "What more was said?" I asked.

"The One said of Yishma'el, 'I have heard you. See, I have blessed him. And I will make him fruitful and I will multiply him very much. He will father twelve princes and I will make him a great nation.'"

"No. Not about Yishma'el . . ." I knew Avraham grieved the loss of his firstborn who, after the circumcision all but abandoned our camp and spent his days in the wilderness learning to hunt. "What did God say about me? My name was changed. Was nothing else mentioned?"

Avram would not look at me as he spoke, so I knew there was more and I would not like it. "What else, 'Father of Multitudes'?" Avraham tore apart a loaf of bread and released its aroma. He dipped a morsel of it in the golden honey. He was infuriatingly slow. I waited.

"God said, 'As for Sarai, you shall not call her by the name Sarai. Rather, Sarah is her name. And I will bless her, and moreover, I will give you a son from her. I will bless her and she will give rise to nations. Kings of peoples will come from her.'"

I shook my head and busied myself at the back of the tent, far away from that doddering old man who lacked the strength to raise his member to fulfill God's Word. I do not know how long I was lost in toil and meditations, but slowly, I became aware of the Presence.

Beyond the grove of Oaks, three men were approaching. One of them had the look of Malki-Tzedek — but I could not be sure. Then Avraham drew my great surprise and concern, when he hobbled from the entrance of his tent to meet them.

Bowing low to the ground, he said, "My Lord, if now I have found favour in your eyes, please do not pass by your servant. Please let a little water be brought to you so that you can wash your feet and make yourself comfortable under the tree. And let me bring a bit of bread so that you can refresh yourselves — then you can pass on."

"Do just as you have said," they replied.

"Quick!" he said to me, "knead three measures of the best flour and prepare some bread loaves!" Then he ran — yes, ran, for the first time in years — to select a choice calf from the slaughter pen. He bid a servant to hurry and prepare it, then brought some curds and milk and set these before the men. While they ate, he stood — without aid for the first time in weeks — near the three men, under a tree. The One who looked like Malki-Tzedek opened the conversation.

"Where is Sarah, your wife?"

"There, in the tent."

"I will most surely return to you about a year's time, and Sarah your wife will have a son."

Inwardly, I laughed at the thought of having a child at my decrepit age. It seemed ridiculous!

Then the One said to Avraham, "Why is it that Sarah laughed saying, 'Can I really give birth when I am so old?' Is anything too difficult for Adonai? At the appointed time I will return to you — in about a year — and Sarah will have a son."

At his words, alarm gripped me! Could the Most High read my inner thoughts? Would I be punished for my lack of faith? Without thinking it through, I blurted out a denial. "I did not laugh!"

Both green and gold, our eyes met. Humour and kindness sparkled in his. "No — you did laugh." Then we both burst into laughter and Malki-Tzedek's prophecy was fulfilled.

ॐ

Awake in the faint light of dawn, I waited for Avraham. Knowing he would come, cousin K'turah prepared my bed with jasmine and adorned my body with sheer linen. I outlined my eyes with kohl and they glowed, green and gold, in the pale radiance of the sunrise. I felt his presence before I saw his form. He walked into my chamber, naked against the rising light, a tall tree in a desert land, ready to bear fruit.

"Like an apple tree among the other trees in the forest, so is my darling among other men," I teased. "I love to sit in his shadow, his fruit is sweet to my taste."

"Sarah," whispered Avraham's familiar urgent voice. His breath caressed my throat as he settled next to me on the night cushions. My arms went around him and drew him in. He was shaking. "How delightful is your love, my sister, my bride. Honey and milk are under your tongue."

Mesmerized by his golden words, I pressed him to me with a renewal of our passion and felt the earth shake at our climax.

Avraham felt it too. He got up suddenly and

stood at the entrance of the tent. Then I saw his stance of victory melt away and he shook his head in sorrow that was mixed with awe. It was a long moment before he spoke. "There is a cloud of dense smoke rising from the cities of S'dom and Gomora. It seems like the smoke of a fiery furnace."

A long silence filled the tent. And later, we would realize that life and death were decreed in the same moment. Redemption and judgment were spoken together.

It felt like a prophecy.

G'RAR

After the destruction of S'dom, our lands lay under a thick shroud of ash. And from the Oaks of Mamre to the plain of Be'er-Sheva, the wells of Avraham turned rancid. With our pastures and water contaminated, we were forced to move westward toward the verdant land of G'rar. We chose a place for ourselves between Kadesh and Shur where Avraham made a hasty treaty with Avimelekh, the wealthy P'lishtim king. He then travelled east to learn what happened to Lot, while I began to put the camp to rights with a true resurrection of my old spirit. Laughter and song once again ruled the people who dwelt in the tents of Avraham.

Until I was taken away.

They crashed in like thunder when they invaded my tent and forced me to mount a swift P'lishtim horse. They only allowed me one veil to wrap myself against the wind. They galloped me through a booming storm without a word. They deposited me at the foot of Avimelekh's throne and backed away while the violence of God shook the palace. They should have heeded the warning.

I tried not to stare at great red pillars and the transparent hangings billowing in the wind like flowing streams. And I tried not to gawk at the wildly painted animals marching across the high stone walls. Instead, I focused my eyes on the man who sat on an ivory throne examining me like a market treasure.

"So, you are the beautiful sister of Avraham?"

Sister? Did he say sister? Too stunned to say a word, I stared at the man on the throne. What was he talking about? Had Avraham reverted to the old half-truth when he made a treaty with this ruler? Had he abandoned me to the king of this land? Did Avraham dare disregard the promise of God—that I would bear him a son?

"I have heard the legend of your beauty," continued the king. "Remove your veil, Exalted Princess."

Making no move to obey, I stared at Avimelekh, trying to stall his request. I was still vain enough to want to avoid the look of disappointment in his eyes when he saw me uncovered. At a distance I did not look my age. My figure had retained the shape of a woman who had not experienced childbirth. I disguised the wrinkles around my eyes with carefully applied kohl, and hid the veins on my hands with intricate henna designs. I refused to stoop with age and kept my skin supple with the waxy residue from sheep's wool. I cleverly wrapped my face in flowing veils to emphasize my youthful eyes and to hide my furrowed neck and sagging chin — but I was ninety years old.

"Forgive me honoured Avimelekh," I said as meekly as I could. "Why have I been stolen from my people in my . . . brother's . . . absence?" Why did I ride through the storm to come to your palace? Does my . . . brother . . . know I am here?"

He answered with a haughty frown. "I have taken you into my household, Exalted Princess, to forge an alliance between my people and yours. Your brother is mighty and I want no war. Perhaps you will find me to be a favourable husband and will convince Avraham to be at peace." Leaning forward, he looked into my eyes. "I can offer you great luxuries in my painted palace." He smiled. "I know you must be tired by now, of your ragged tent."

Fierce guardsmen flanked Avimelekh's throne. They held great bronze axes to their muscled chests. Feeling their menace, I knelt on the pavement at Avimelekh's feet. "Forgive my hesitation, Exalted King. The honour you bestow is great. But in our custom, I can do nothing without my . . . brother's . . . consent. I plead that you wait for his return so he may hear your petition." It felt like an eternity kneeling on the cold stone floor with thunder roaring around us and wind howling through open windows.

"Rise up then," said the king, with a frustrated sigh. "I will install you in the women's quarters where you may pass your days teaching my wives the magic of your people. I am told your camp flows with laughter and song while my courts boil with angry words. Potnia will guide you to your room."

Potnia, his lovely young queen, was tall and statuesque, with elaborately plaited black hair, full red lips, and the large round breasts so greatly admired by the P'lishtim. Her sensual mouth was pursed with disdain as she led me to the women's wing and opened the door to my chamber.

A fire crackled in the hearth, and an elaborately carved wooden bed was layered deep with furs and soft linens. A lovely sleeping shift lay draped on a painted chair. Bread and wine waited on a bronze tray. Exhausted by my adventure, I walked toward the luxuries as if in a dream. But when I shed my veils to don the shift, Potnia gasped with shock and clutched at her neck and chin.

Our eyes met and I grinned. "Now you know my secret. Who will be the one to tell the mighty Avimelekh?"

Our gales of laughter competed with the storm outside. I heard the shuffle of curious feet beyond the closed door, but I paid them no mind as I bid Potnia a fond goodnight. After that, I was a little angry with Avraham for his deceit. Then I recalled my redemption from Egypt and prayed for protection for my unborn child before sinking into the softly pillowed bed and oblivion. And all the while, I praised God for giving a pregnant and travel weary princess a temporary home of stone.

ଔଓ

Avimelekh's blunder was a well-kept secret in the women's court. It made them smile to know of it. The king's women went to great lengths to hide my age and condition with veils and cosmetics. I repaid their kindness with jokes and jests and taught them the playful songs of our people.

As my belly filled with child, my breasts regained their youthful glory and the court women designed a dress for me that showed them to perfection. We wailed with mirth when they caught the approving eye of the king. He was pleased with me and with the mood of his women, but not with himself it seemed. All a-puff with virile pride, he made regular visits to the room of Potnia and his concubines. Then he exited their chambers soon after, looking like a whipped dog. The women kept those secrets too, but I remembered my time in Egypt and wondered . . .

  Despite a runner sent to advise him of my capture, Avraham did not rush to appear before the King of G'rar. Lot, no doubt, was in greater need than me. I just hoped his uncle would return before Avimelekh discovered my pregnancy. And as the months went by, the royal women's moon flow mysteriously dried up. Avimelekh's visits to them also ceased. He looked like a thunder cloud about to burst.

ೞೞ

Dawn broke to a rumbling red storm and the palace was in an uproar of preparation. Amid talk about the king's frightening dream and Avraham's arrival, we were all summoned to the courtroom. After dressing with great care, I went to stand before the throne of Avimelekh while he thundered orders to everyone. Excited women waited between the red pillars of the portico, and court officials stood uneasily around the ivory throne. Then Avimelekh called Avraham in.

  "What have you done to us, and how have I sinned against you, that you brought great sin upon me and my kingdom? You have done things to me that should not be done. What motivated you to do this thing?"

  Avraham glanced from the king, to me, to the gathered court—his face turning as crimson as the rising sun. "I . . . uh . . . I," he stammered.

  The king's face also turned red, but with a tempest of rage, "God came to me in a dream and said, 'You are as good as dead because of the woman whom you have taken—since she is a married woman.'" Avimelekh continued his angry outburst.

  "So, I said, "My Lord, will you slay a nation, even though innocent? Did he, himself, say to me,

'She is my sister'? And even she herself even said, 'He is my brother.' I did this with integrity of heart and the guiltlessness of my hands."

With his next question, the King cast angry bolts of lightning at Avraham's soul. "What was your reason for doing this?"

Avraham's eyes darted around the room but avoided mine. Then he spoke. "It was because I thought, there is certainly no fear of God is this place, so they will kill me because of my wife."

At that, Avimelekh crossed his arms over his chest and glowered at Avraham. But said an eloquent nothing.

Glancing at last in my direction, Avraham took in a shaky breath and continued, "And besides, she really is my sister. She is my father's daughter, though not my mother's. Then she became my wife. So, when God made me wander away from my father's house I said to her, "This is your loyalty that you must show me. In every place we go, say of me, 'He is my brother.'"

Avimelekh scorned Avraham's feeble excuse with a dismissive gesture, then frowned at his women who, highly entertained, were suppressing snickers. Avimelekh leaned forward and looked Avraham in the eyes, "Then God said to me in the dream, 'Yes, I knew that you did this with the integrity of your heart so I prevented you from sinning against me. That is why I did not allow you touch her.'"

Desperately, Avraham looked to me for support. And I shrugged. Was I supposed to respond to this discussion among men? God had defended my honour in the past, and I knew the Almighty could do it again. I wish I had learned that lesson earlier in life.

Avimelekh ended the awkward silence with a snap of his fingers. Like an echo of a former time, servants brought in a parade of sheep, cattle and slaves, to give to Avraham. Then the king moved me across the room with a gesture and presented me to my husband. Another snap of his fingers produced a servant carrying a beautifully decorated bowl that brimmed with silver coins—the symbol of faithfulness. It was placed in my hands.

"I have given your 'brother' a thousand pieces of

silver. It is compensation for everything that happened—
so everyone will know that you are fully vindicated,"
said the king.

Then Avraham somehow recovered his dignity,
drew himself up to his full height, raised his hands toward
Heaven and poured out a blessing of fertility on Avimelekh,
his wife, and his household.

My arrival at the court of Avimelekh was
announced with deafening thunder—the voice of an
angry God. My exit was accompanied by God's blessing,
a cloudburst of applause—a promise of fruitfulness.

I glanced sideways at my husband as our entourage
streamed from the P'lishtim city. Avraham's face dripped
with the liquid approval of God but the rain did nothing to
soften his expression. Though we walked side by side, he
seemed far away. The brimming pot of silver coins that I
clutched to my bosom was another wondrous redemption,
a sign of God's acceptance. It should have been a time of
rejoicing. What could I do to break the tension? Perhaps
with a safe subject—the weather?

"Surely, God has showered us with blessings."
Avraham did not reply so I filled the silence again. "Look,
a mighty downpour announces the favour of God. Let us
praise the Giver of Life for this bounty."

Avraham ignored my olive branch and went
to the root. "Once again I have sinned against you,
Sarah." Repentant tears joined the rain on his face. "I
am a foolish old man. I fell headlong into the waters of
fear. I was swept away by torrents of doubt. I drowned
our love in a flood of self-seeking."

Marveling, I journeyed back through the scenes of
our lives. Avraham had never, not even once, admitted love
for me—until now. Should my response express a lifetime of bitter yearning for that declaration, or should I say
nothing and let grace cover all? While wiping diluted kohl
from my eyes, and laying my ancient face completely bare,
a deep and holy love arose to comfort him. "Many waters
cannot quench love, nor rivers wash it away. Besides, I am
honoured by your belief that my beauty would still entice
a king. But I fear your aged eyes grow dim, my lord. Open

them and look at me. Can you see my face clearly? I am ninety years old!"

Avraham barked out a laugh. He laughed! I had never heard him laugh in all our years together. Had I finally taught him to laugh?

We laughed throughout the deluge all that day, and laughed as we dried off our goods. We fell laughing onto the night-cushions of my tent. We laughed when Avraham finally saw my unclothed body, swollen with child. We laughed many days later when Potnia sent word that the women of her court had resumed their monthly flow, that Avimelekh was healed of impotence and she was pregnant. We laughed when a grand carved bed, complete with pillows and furs, was delivered to my tent dwelling. And my aging body rejoiced that it did not need to lower its growing bulk onto the floor-cushions of a tent. My Redeemer pampers me.

༺༻

The Presence returned at the appointed time, to guide us through the birth of our son. Avraham named him Yitz'chak (Laughter). Yes, God has made laughter for me! Now everyone who hears will laugh with me. Who would have said to Avraham that Sarah would nurse children? Nevertheless, I have born him a son in his old age. Nothing is impossible with God.

DESERT PLACES

But Hagar did not laugh. She became even more sullen. And her son became more distant, preferring to hunt game in the desert. After hours away, he would strut into camp with victory chants and present his kill to Hagar. Now and then, Avraham tried to coax a gift of venison from Yishma'el but failed, wincing at each rejection. I tried to make amends with Hagar, but crashed into high walls of hatred. This anxiety cast a shadow over our joy.

☙❧

Young women danced and musicians played while I sang praises to the God of my soul. Yitz'chak's weaning feast was a jubilant celebration. Guests from all around ate almonds, dates and figs from huge bronze trays while a young bull sizzled, whole, on a spit. It was stuffed with a roasted kid that was stuffed with a roasted chicken that was stuffed with roasted eggs. The feast was a symbol of God's miraculous gift. My babe had become a child, a Promise fulfilled—an heir.

    My voice bubbled up among the people, "I will sing to Adonai as long as I live! I will sing praise to my God!" When the Presence moved into my psalm, a warning jolted my heart. Where is Yitz'chak? I scanned the crowd but could not see his little blue robe. Had K'turah, my cousin-servant taken him to my tent for a nap? Had he wandered off to play with his pet lamb? I stood, led by the Presence, around the side of my pavilion to the dim outskirts of the camp. There he was. My heart froze.

    Yitz'chak was pinned against a tree. An arrow, straight and sharp in the bow, was pointed at his throat. "Come little fawn and bow to me. I am your master, sing praise to me," chanted Yishma'el with a mocking sneer.

    "Yishma'el, lower your weapon and go to your tent. I will speak with you and your mother there."

"It is just an ancient archer's chant," he protested with a grin. "I was teaching it to him. He follows me everywhere, wanting to see my bow. I was showing him how to use it. I meant no harm."

Moving between my son and his brother, I pushed the point of the arrow to the ground. Before Yishma'el dropped his gaze, I glimpsed hatred and defiance in his eyes. I glanced toward his tent where Hagar gloated in the doorway. For her this was a victory, but a small one. I knew she would seek more. Where would it end? What would she demand for the firstborn of Avraham?

Gathering up my son, I swept him to safety and dropped him into the lap of his father. "Keep him close," I whispered. "Yishma'el threatened his life."

We moved away from the crowd and argued under the storied stars. Avraham did not want to hear my warnings but I knew he had not seen Yishma'el's flash of unguarded hatred. Trying to calm me with soothing words, Avraham took Yishma'el's side. But I was a lioness roaring in the dark, defending her cub. "Drive out this female slave and her son! For the son of this female slave will not be an heir with my son—with Yitz'chak."

Avraham stalked off into the hills to cool his rage and I watched him go. I could tell the exact moment the Presence met with him and took my part. When would Avraham learn that in my own way, I also listened to God?

Early next morning, Avraham took Hagar some food and a skin of water. He set them on her shoulder and sent her away with the boy. Why did he supply them so scantily? Was it a test to see if God would provide for them? Was it a message to Hagar and her son, that the blessing of provision would come from the One alone? My husband was tight lipped as he sent Hagar out of our midst to wander the desert of Be'er-Sheva—a bitter woman upheld by the mercies of God.

My heart sank as I watched them disappear behind a pale hill. Their banishment no longer felt like a victory. Hagar's failure reflected mine and would forever blight our future. Our tribes would always be at enmity.

MORIYYAH

While the land flourished and the flocks grew, ten years of tranquility flowed. A water treaty was made with Avimelekh, and Avraham planted a tamarisk grove to shade our tents. From its needles and flowers, I made an ointment that brought some relief to my brittle bones — so crushed by childbirth.

For ten years, from the Tamarisk of Be'er-Sheva, I ruled the women of the camp with justice, wisdom, laughter, and song. For ten years Yitz'chak followed Avraham's heels like a pup — his father's joy. For ten years God was with Yishma'el, who lived in the desert and became a renowned hunter. For ten years Avraham and I lived in harmony — and the Almighty rested in our peace.

Then came the strange request.

"Sarah," whispered Avraham in a stricken voice. His breath caressed my throat as he settled next to me on the night cushions. My arms went around him and drew him in. He was shaking.

"Avraham, what happened?"

"The Presence appeared."

"Yes. I felt it pass. Was there a message?"

"'Take your son, your only son whom you love — Yitz'chak — and go to the land of Moriyyah. Offer him there as a burnt offering on one of the mountains which I will tell you about.'"

"But you said you would no longer serve a deity who demands human sacrifice. Are you sure it was the One who spoke? You are old. Perhaps your mind slipped back into childhood. Perhaps you heard Nanna . . . or thought you did."

Peering wearily across the night cushions at the craggy face of my husband, I saw the turmoil of his mind. But I was at peace. If God had truly spoken, I would comply. The One who gave could also take away. The Almighty had lifted the reproach of my barrenness. The One gave me a child and blessed me in my later years with the love of my husband. Now, the Mighty One was all my desire. If asked, I would give Yitz'chak back. No arguments. Would Avraham do so as well?

Avraham's words broke into my thoughts. "Shall I offer my firstborn for my transgressions, the fruit of my body for the sin of my soul?"

I cupped his face in comfort while Avraham's tears trickled through my fingers and my words flowed around him, words that came from a contrite heart—a heart so weary of doubt. "My lord," I said, "the Breath of Life who quickened our bodies to make Yitz'chak, also has the power to resurrect our son. Is anything impossible for God?"

As the sun broke through the crust of the black horizon, Avraham ceased wrestling with God and trust began to paint a new dawn on the lines of his rugged face. He rose from our bed and loaded his donkey. When he cut enough wood for the burnt offering, he set out for the place God told him about. He took with him, two of his servants and our son, Yitz'chak.

Standing at the entrance of my tent in the glory of the sunrise, I watched in awe as father and son walked toward Moriyyah. Faith had triumphed.

Again, it felt like a prophesy.

BE'ER-SHEVA

"Not another woman."

"Why not, Avraham? Our cousin K'turah is round and ripe like fruit. She works hard. She . . ."

"One woman is quite enough," he laughed.

"But the great pharaohs of Egypt and all our kindred take cousin-concubines, why not you?"

"I am not a pharaoh," he smiled.

"Avraham. Take pity on your old and weary wife. My bones ache from the travail of childbirth and the ravages of age. I do not wish to bear another child, but the Almighty has resurrected the fount of your youth. I would not have you deprived."

I knew he found it hard to consider my words. He must have wondered what lay beneath them. Did he think they were a reaction to his past blunders—his denial of my worth? Did he think I sought freedom from the yoke of our marriage because of past conflicts? Did Avraham not understand that all I longed for was his fulfillment—which I was too old to provide? I tried another tactic, hoping business concerns would make more sense to him.

"My lord, you know our flocks and herds have grown too numerous to keep them all in Be'er-Sheva. We need another home-place. And we need someone to rule it now that Eli'ezer sleeps with his fathers. Perhaps you could be the regent here while I reign under the Oaks of Mamre. Keep K'turah with you here, to care for your needs."

Avraham knew the practicality of my proposal, and he knew my mind was made up about K'turah. So, we grieved our past and our future as we held each other's eyes. "Yitz'chak will be the emissary between us," he said.

HEVRON

I moved my tent and my great carved bed to the Oaks of Mamre, near the town of Hevron. And for a second time, I gave my handmaid to Avraham. But this time she was given in grace, not in desperation. This time she remained my friend though I could not bear to watch her lay son after son onto Avraham's lap. It seemed that Avraham was well on his way to becoming a father of multitudes!

Under the spreading grove of Mamre, God gave me a garland of joy instead of ashes, the oil of gladness instead of mourning, a cloak of praise instead of a heavy spirit. I became a planting of the Almighty, ruling in contentment while our flocks flourished in the land of the Hitti.

Yitz'chak, who had been spared from the sacrifice years before, regularly came to discuss business and to bring me news. He wove such amusing tales of the chaos produced by K'turah's six boys, that our laughter often echoed off the fertile hills.

෫෬

A full-moon pours light into the tent I share with my servants. And tired as I am from the labour of the day, the One calls for me. I toss back the wool coverlet and step into the night. "What is it my God? Why do you draw me into your Presence?"

Standing in the dark, I lift my face to the breeze, sampling the scent of sheep, soil, and the fennel fragrance of olive blossoms. The Presence is near, pleased with the sacrifice I offered after the shearing today. After all, I am Sarah, Exalted Princess, a shepherdess. And the Holy One is mercifully satisfied with the small offerings of my trust, given after a lifetime of failure and regret.

I look back at the great black tent I call my home and fleetingly desire to live in a permanent dwelling. How can I not? The Creator planted such yearnings in every daughter of Havah. But now, in the deep embrace of the Presence, I lay aside all earthly desires to join the One who gives far greater satisfaction than any pleasure.

Joy draws me deeper into the mystery of the swirling stars. And I pray that our people will one day recover the message they long to deliver.

While my heart bursts with the hope of that possibility, my ancient voice begins to sing its final earthly song — the story of redemption — the ballad of the shining stars.

Suspended between two worlds, I stand amazed at the sight before me. With awe I start to move toward my exquisite eternal home. There are ivory doors and golden pillars and windows draped with red silken hangings that billow in the wind like flowing streams — in a city whose builder and architect is God.

Genesis 23:1-5,19,20

Now Sarah's life was 127 years. And she died in Kiryat-Arba (that is Hevron) in the land of Kena'an. Avraham came to mourn for Sarah and to weep over her. Afterward, Avraham buried Sarah his wife in the cave of the field of Makhpelah next to Mamre (that is Hevron), in the land of Kena'an. So the field and the cave that was in it, were handed over to Avraham as a grave-site purchased from the sons of Het.

Hebrews 11:8-11,13,15

By faith, Avraham obeyed when he was called to go out to the place he was to receive as an inheritance. By faith he migrated to the Land of Promise . . . dwelling in tents. For he was waiting for a city with permanent foundations, whose architect and builder is God. By faith, even Sarah herself received the ability to conceive when she was barren and past the age, since she considered the One who had made the promise to be faithful. They died in faith without receiving all the things promised—but they saw them and welcomed them from afar. Therefore, God is not ashamed to be called their God. For he has prepared a city for them.

Matthew 5:5

Blessed are the meek, for they shall inherit the earth.

Rivkah

Pursue shalom with everyone, and the holiness without which no one will see Adonai. See to it that no one falls short of the grace of God; and see to it that no bitter root springs up and causes trouble, and by it many be defiled.

Hebrews 12:14,15

RIVKAH

THE CAPTIVE

Hunched between rows of sweet-smelling herbs, I breathed in their life-affirming scent. The wafting fragrance of my garden soothed my troubled soul. What gods had so disfavoured me that I was born a girl, subject to toil and servitude, excluded from the rank and deference of a male-child?

I shifted my position on the warm red earth. The solid ground beneath me felt protective and my thoughts drifted to happier times—to the bright peace of a small child sitting on my abba's knee, listening to the talk around the trays of savory cig kofte. I loved the stories brought by the merchants who crisscrossed the lands. They gathered up tales like a harvest and shared them in the shade of our courtyard. Even cig kofte had its legend that went back to the time when Great Uncle Avraham lived in Ur.

It was told that Avram—as he was called then—took an ax and destroyed all the idols that King Nimrud the Evil worshiped. Then Avram invited people to follow him in search of the one true God.

In a rage, the wicked king gathered up all the firewood in the land and made a huge burning pyre on which to sacrifice Avram to the gods. But the God of the prophet turned the raging fire into water, and transformed the burning wood into beautiful flame-coloured fish. Since there was no wood left for the people's cooking fires, they mixed raw meat with bulgur and spicy isot—so cig kofte came to be. No one knew if the story was true, but we all knew about Great Uncle Avraham and his fearsome God who protected and prospered him.

For her beauty that captivated kings, Avraham's wife, our Great Aunt Sarah, was a legend in her own right. We laughed around the kofte tray at the proud pharaoh who, not knowing she was married, took Sarah as a wife. But Pharaoh soon humbled himself before the God of Avraham, begging those vile diseases be lifted off his harem. We laughed again when we heard the terrible plight of haughty King Avimelekh who put his treasured manhood in jeopardy when he kidnapped Great Aunt Sarah for his harem. Both he and the pharaoh sacrificed much wealth to restore their honour and posterity.

As a tiny child on Abba's knee, the stories floated above me like winter clouds. Some of them dropped seeds of faith into my heart but they were not watered and did not touch my daily life. We lived in a kumbet village then, built by Grandfather Nachor—who got the idea for our homes while watching desert ants construct their towering round dwellings. Our circular earthen housing was a cool relief from the searing heat of the desert. Traders loved to stay with us, rather than in the grand but scorching houses of nearby Harran.

One room in Abba's kumbet was darker than the rest. It lay sinister and silent behind a dirty veil of woven cloth. Abba entered it twice a day to pray to the gods hidden there. I feared that room. I often thought I saw snakes writhing in the gap between the door-cloth and the floor. Abba went in every morning, laden with barley-beer and food, returning to us later with glazed eyes and an unsteady walk. He never talked about the time spent with the gods and I knew better than to ask questions.

Anyway, communing with the gods is men's work. Women do not participate in such endeavors unless appointed to be a Ziggurat priestess—or unless you are the esteemed Sarah who spoke to her god about the birth of her son. And I did hear about a time long ago, when the Creator walked with Mother Havah in the world's first garden. In the old legends, Havah lived with her husband Adam, in harmony and equality. But those times were gone. As a mere girl-child I did not commune with gods or have equal standing with anyone.

Lowly as a slave, I was kept busy, sweeping the kumbet floor, tidying up after merchants, helping with meals and running messages back and forth between Ima's and Abba's kumbets—which were joined by a mud brick passageway. My brother, Lavan, at our father's right hand, learned to trade goods for a profit. I felt sorry for him as he sat hour after hour on the rugs, calculating sums on the abacus and getting his ear twisted when they would not add up. But even on occasion when he was caught stealing from the storehouse, Lavan was never subjected to the menial labour of a valueless girl like me.

Ima served our father by cooking meals for all the merchants who stopped at our door. She was famous for her saj bread. We were told that the recipe went back to the time before the great flood when Father Adam and Mother Havah were expelled from the Garden of 'Eden and the angel Gavri'el was sent to teach them how to bake. That ancient recipe was handed down from woman to woman—each generation treasuring the sustaining symbol of life.

Ima knew by instinct when a caravan would appear. She started to prepare favourite dishes well before the lines of camels wavered on the horizon. There was laughter and rejoicing when a caravan arrived. Noses were held high to sample familiar aromas, and Abba always joked that it was the saj bread and kebabs that brought in the profits.

When we were younger, our servant D'vorah saw to it that Lavan and I got safely to our beds when Abba and Ima were busy with a merchant's feast. In a gust of cumin and coriander she would gather me up from Abba's lap and carry me to our sleeping chamber where I floated down onto soft cushions while she sang the songs of our people.

I could not tell you when things began to change. It had something to do with a disagreement between Father and Mother. I only heard whispers spat out in shadowy corners. Some debt was unpaid, a responsibility shirked. Father wanted Mother to leave it be. Those times of peace were now a fading memory as I sat huddled between the rows of herbs, watching tears drip down my nose to water their roots.

༄༅

Adad and Enlil are violent gods. Every summer they attack Paddan-Aram with fierce storms of blowing sand, assaulting everything in their path. When I was a child they howled around us, we hid for hours from our raging gods. Our eyes were gritty from their sandy onslaught and our skin chafed in every private place from the rude invasion of their anger. Worst of all, they stole our earnings by erasing our roads, veiling our village with sand and preventing the caravans from finding us.

During the storms, Abba spent time in the prayer chamber pleading for favour. He began to go in five times a day and emerged from its gloomy depths with a scowl and a ready slap if I dared to look his way. In an attempt to do my part, I sacrificed garden herbs to Ninlil, the goddess-wife of Enlil, hoping she could persuade her husband-god to lift his anger and be at peace. But like most husbands, Enlil had no regard for his wife's advice, so the storms continued summer after summer.

As the years passed and business dwindled, Mother grew distant and Father inconsolable. They no longer spoke to each other, and the only words they had for me were orders. "Rivkah, bring some flour from the storehouse. Rivkah, sweep the sand from the courtyard. Rivkah, rinse the pots again. Rivkah, fetch a jar of water from the well. Rivkah . . ." It drove me mad!

Lavan became an irritating echo of their commands, and D'vorah avoided my eyes in their presence. They had named me well, Rivkah, a captive, snared, tied-up. Escape seemed impossible—except in my garden—dreaming of the fabled time when Father Adam and Mother Havah lived in harmony. And I had heard an ancient prophesy about a great Redeemer God who would someday restore our wounded earth and ravished souls. Could it be true?

When our gods flattened my garden with punishing

winds, I tried to urge my bruised and broken plants to live. Long hours in the herb plot kept me well away from my oppressive task masters. It was the only place I had any peace, for the plants did not order me around. They even seemed to respond to my ministrations as I tenderly plucked off battered leaves and repacked the soil around their roots while dreaming of escape from my family . . . but where could I go?

Lavan's plan was to marry me to a wealthy Harran merchant who could enhance our connections in business. But Ima wanted to arrange a marriage with a local tribesman who would join our clan as a labourer. As each lobbied for their own interests, I could hear them hissing out arguments in the dark halls of the kumbet. No one asked me for an opinion so I fled to my garden and let the talk swirl, my anger fueling countless trips to the well and back. Could the thirsty herbs feel my frustration? It almost seemed so. I think we gave each other the will to live.

Sometimes D'vorah joined me in the cool of the evening, and taught me names of the plants. She spoke of a mystical time when the Creator came to the first garden and whispered secrets on the breeze. By the time I arrived on this earth, much of that understanding had been scattered on the winds. But when I breathed in the aroma of rosemary, thyme and all their sisters, I imagined I was with the Creator in a beautiful garden like 'Eden. I longed to gather up the lost knowledge so I pestered merchants with questions when I watered their camels. I begged for scraps of information about the plants of their countries. I peppered them with queries about the conditions their plants grew in. The merchants referred me to their cooks and pack boys, hoping to fend me off like a pesky fly.

The servants knew more than their masters of course. They taught me much about which herbs and fruits liked to live next to each other and what phase of the moon to seed them in. I also learned that, if I seemed to be busy serving the all-important merchants, Ima and Lavan would leave me alone for a while.

THE ENGAGEMENT

The day began like all the others before it. I was dragged out of bed by Ima's high-pitched worship of the dawn. In a sleepy fog I slipped a day-robe over my head and went to start a breakfast fire in the clay oven. It promised to be a hot day and I hoped the sun would draw thirsty travelers to the well so I could serve them there and escape the demands of my family. Meanwhile, I was lost in pleasant thoughts of feeding my new pomegranate tree the goat-leavings I swept up. The tree had only produced two lonely fruits on its shiny green branches and I hoped to coax it to do more.

From there my day dragged on in an endless round of chores as I bounced back and forth between the demands of Lavan and Ima. My head throbbed with resentment and I did not blame Abba for disappearing into the prayer chamber to avoid everyone. I glanced often at the horizon in the hope of seeing a caravan. Finally, one appeared in the south.

"There are ten camels," Ima said. She shaded her eyes with her hand and stood gazing. "Where are they from? They look like Hitti camels, but different somehow."

"And I am sure they will be thirsty," I said, gathering up my water jar and setting off in the direction of the well—which was settled in a palm grove on the outskirts of the village. By the time I got there, the lead merchant had commanded his camels to recline at the outer edge of the grove, and was staring intently at the sky. The low-slung sun would soon paint vivid colours on it, but I saw nothing unusual there this time of day. So, I walked down the steps into the well basin and lowered my jug into the water to begin the familiar process of coaxing the traders to our kumbet village by offering a cool drink.

From the corner of my eye, I saw the head-merchant running—yes running—toward me. I frowned at this undignified behavior usually only exhibited by servants. Something seemed amiss. "Please let me sip a little water from your jar," said the man.

I wore my most winning smile and lowered the jug to give him a sip. "Drink, my lord," I said. Then I saw the pomegranates loaded on the third camel's back. They were beautiful rosy fruit—without blemish and bulging with seeds. Did these people hold the secret of nurturing pomegranates—or know someone who did? Perhaps I could charm some information out of this man. "I will also draw water for your camels until they have finished drinking," I said.

The traveller's eyes widened and he looked at me oddly. Nervous that he would politely refuse my offer, I emptied my jar into the livestock trough and ran back to the well for more water. Eventually, I drew enough water for all his camels. It was no more work than watering my garden every night—in the battle to keep my herbs alive. And all the while, though I slyly watched the man from the corner of my eye, I could not interpret the look on his face. Imagine my surprise when he gave me a gold nose-ring for my trouble. It weighed at least half a shekel. And then, he slid two gold bracelets onto my wrist.

"Whose daughter are you? Please tell me, is there room in your father's house for us to spend the night?"

"I ... I am the daughter of B'tu'el, son of Milkah, whom she bore to Nachor. Uh ... we ... there's both straw and plenty of feed with us, as well as room to spend the night." I fingered the gold bracelets, wondering why he gave them to me. What did he want?

Then the man bowed down and worshiped his god, saying, "Blessed be Adonai, God of my master Avraham."

My mouth fell open. Was the Avraham of legend this man's master? Dropping my water jug on the ground, I ran home to tell Ima and D'vorah about the golden gifts and puzzling words. Thoughtlessly, I left the whole weary caravan standing by the side of the well-spring staring after me.

Upon hearing my astounding news, D'vorah summoned Abba from the prayer room and seated him as the head of the family in the courtyard's place of honour. Shrewd Lavan gave my new jewelry a hasty appraisal then hurried to the spring and said, "Come in, blessed of Adonai. Why are you standing outside when I have tidied up the house and there is also room for the camels?"

So, the camels were unloaded, straw and fodder provided, water was poured for everyone to wash their feet and we set food before them. But the man said, "I will not eat until I have stated my business."

"Speak." Lavan said as he leaned forward, eager to listen.

"I am Avraham's servant. Adonai has blessed my master so that he has become great. Sarah, my master's wife, gave birth to a son for my master after she was old, and Avraham gave him everything he owns. Then my master made me take an oath saying, 'You must not take a wife for my son from among the daughters of the Kena'ani, in whose land I am dwelling. Instead, you must go to my father's house and to my family and take a wife for my son.'"

I glanced around at the faces of my family. Their eyes were focused on Avraham's servant, their foreheads creased with lines of astonishment. The servant was most certainly speaking of the miracle-son that Sarah bore. And his quest to find a wife for that son had brought him to our village. Yes, we were of Avraham's clan but . . .

The servant continued. "So I came today to the spring and I said, 'Adonai, God of Avraham my master, if you are really going to make my way successful, then here I am, standing by a spring of water. And I will say to one of the girls coming out to draw water, 'Please give me a little water to drink from your jug.' If she answers, 'You drink, and I will also draw water for your camels,' then let her be the woman whom Adonai appoints for my master's son."

I drew my head back in disbelief, then leaned forward again, trying to catch more of the servant's strange words. Was he referring to me? My mind recoiled. How could that be?

The servant continued. "I had not yet finished speaking in my heart, and there was Rivkah, going out with her jug on her shoulder—and she went down to the spring and drew water. So I said to her, 'Please give me a drink.' And she quickly lowered her jug off of her and said, 'Drink, and I will also water your camels.' Then I placed the ring on her nose and the bracelets on her hands. I bowed down and blessed Adonai, the God of my master Avraham, who guided me on the true way to take the daughter of my master's brother for his son. So now, if you are really going to show loyalty and truth to my master, tell me. But if not, tell me, so that I can turn elsewhere."

    My eyes grew as large and round as the rising moon. Could this be happening to me? I pressed a hand to my pounding heart. Was this my way of escape from the prison of demands I lived in? Was this the fulfillment of my dreams? Was my fate to be decided in the next few moments by my drunken father and greedy brother? My head whirled and my stomach churned as I furtively glanced around at my family. Lavan was mesmerized by the servant's account and Abba glistened with concentration. Would they allow me to escape their control and become the wife of Avraham's son? What would they value more—a lifetime of my unpaid service or the wealth displayed in the camel packs?

    I need not have worried. The camel packs won and Abba and Lavan burst out together, "The matter proceeds from Adonai. Rivkah is before you. Take her and go, and let her become a wife for your master's son—just as Adonai has spoken."

    I bleated out a nervous laugh that startled Avraham's servant into searching my face. Did he see my need for escape? Did he hear the greed in the voices of my father and brother? Did he catch a glimpse of their cunning ways? If so, he ignored all and bowed down before his God. D'vorah used that moment to escort my failing father to his kumbet, while I clenched my jaw to keep my growing anxiety at bay. Would Avraham's servant truly choose a girl like me from a family like mine to be the bride of Avraham's son?

    When his prayers were done, the servant gave

costly gifts to my brother and my mother, then he presented us with the beautiful pomegranates—a symbol of love and fertility in his country. After that, he and his men ate and drank and spent the night.

The next day began like no other as I lay in bed straining to hear the argument taking place outside the thick mud walls of the kumbet. "You cannot let her go. Who will make the morning fire? Do you expect me to do it myself? Do you want me to die from overwork in my old age? She should marry a local man and bring him into the business." That was Ima.

"Did you see those camels laden with the bride-price? With all that treasure, I could buy you a strong young slave with a much better attitude than hers and we would have plenty of wealth left over." That was Lavan.

"I will go to Harran and make sacrifices for her fertility. I am sure the bride-price includes libations for the gods." That, of course, was Abba.

"Give me at least ten more days with her. What will our neighbours think if we send her away without the proper ceremonies and without an engagement feast? The cooking alone will take days. Besides, you need time to travel to Harran and purchase a slave to replace her." Ima again.

"No! If ten days pass, they will see through her beauty to discover her sullen spirit and clumsy blunders. And we will get no bride-price at all!" Lavan.

There was a long pause before Ima broached her final arguments. "Unless we perform all the proper ceremonies, how will she receive the moon-blessing of the goddess, Inanna? Do you want to curse her with barrenness? You bring shame on me if you rush her off like that. What will people think?" Then Mother launched into an ear-splitting mourner's wail that stopped all conversation.

Numb and confused, I slipped a day-robe over my head and went to start the breakfast fire. My new gold bracelets jingled as I worked, but Ima's screeching lament was the sound that woke everyone and brought the sleepy visitors into the courtyard. They partook of an uneasy meal, not knowing where to rest their eyes. Abba, as usual, said nothing while Lavan scowled at mother, and D'vorah bustled around the courtyard, somewhat too busy.

Finally, Avraham's servant looked up from his saj bread and wiped olive oil from his beard. "Send me off to my master," he said.

Lavan glowered openly at Ima, so she stopped her deafening howl to glare back at him. "Let the young woman stay with us a few days—at least ten. Afterwards she may go," said Lavan.

The servant's expression was unaltered by the tension in the courtyard. He remained calm and polite, but firm in his resolve. "Do not delay me since Adonai has made my way successful. Send me off so that I can go to my master."

Lavan's eyes threw daggers at Ima, but his voice matched the servant's tone in civility. "We will call the young woman and ask her opinion."

I was so shocked at being consulted that I lost my grip on a cauldron of hot soup I was carrying. I screamed when the scalding liquid splashed a nearby camel-boy. He yelped and leaped to his feet, clutching his burning leg. Quickly, I grabbed the first jug of water that came to hand and ran to cool his searing pain. I whispered apologies and coaxed a rueful smile from him while everyone stared.

"Rivkah, will you go with this man?" asked Lavan. I could hear exasperation in his voice. He would be glad to rid himself of me and my fumbles. He was right. Mother would be better off with a less clumsy slave and I would be better off when out from under the burden of their disagreements. If I stayed another ten days so the ceremonial blessing could be accomplished, it would be another ten days of constant conflict.

"I will go," I said.

So, they sent me on my way, along with D'vorah. In lieu of Inanna's moonlit fertility rites, Lavan stood in the middle of the courtyard and declared a blessing:

> "*Our sister, may you become thousands of ten-thousands, and may your seed possess the gate of those who hate him.*"

    Then Ima, still annoyed that her noisy negotiations had failed, grudgingly did her part and sang the hymns of Inanna while D'vorah served the traditional red lentil soup to symbolize the ripeness of my womb. As usual, Abba retreated from family conflict by hiding in the prayer room. He said it was to make libations for my departure.

    During the hasty farewell feast, frantic thoughts ran through my mind. Had I been too quick to leave? Should I have insisted on the full ceremonial season to play itself out? Was the blessing of Inanna on my union? Perhaps the legendary faith of my future husband's clan would make up for the lacking prayers. My head was all a-jumble when I mounted my camel and it lurched to its feet then padded through my childhood village toward my new life.

THE JOURNEY

Day One
Harran and Pot Belly Hill

Eli'ezer of Hevron had served my intended's family all his days. His father, Eli'ezer of Dammesek, was Avraham's trusted servant—and his heir before Yitz'chak was born. With the first Eli'ezer gathered to his fathers, his namesake held a similar place of prominence in the household.

I marveled that a servant could hold such authority that he was trusted to find a bride for the heir. Though I was not a servant, I was not considered equal to anyone in our village. I was very much intrigued with the status of this servant, and eager to find out about my future husband and new homeland. So I peppered Eli'ezer with questions. "How big is the town of Hevron? What kind of crops grow there? How long is the growing season and why are we going north? Does my betrothed not dwell to the south? What manner of man is he? How long will our journey take?"

Eli'ezer's replies were brief and kind. "Hevron is not the size of Harran. We grow wheat and barley there. The crops grow for six moon cycles. Yes, Hevron is south of here but I have business along the northern route and it is an easier road for you and your nurse. My lord, Yitzchak is quiet and kind. Our journey will take one phase of the moon, God willing."

As we entered Harran, a piercing call to prayer sounded from the Ziggurat pinnacle and the faithful fell on their faces in waves. Even the beasts hushed as the merchants who travelled the roads dismounted their camels for worship. I was embarrassed to be late to the service and motioned for a camel-boy to make my mount kneel. But he turned his face away from me and fixed his gaze on Eli'ezer who sat upright in his saddle staring intently at the sky—which, again, was unremarkable and cloudless. He was lost again in thoughts or prayers, so I shrugged and took the opportunity to look around at the wonders of the city.

Abba and Lavan often came to Harran to trade and worship, but I had never been further than the outskirts of my village. From childhood, my head had been packed with titillating stories of the magical Ziggurat.

Every year, the sacred marriage consummation of Inanna and Dumuzi was performed on its sun-kissed top. Everyone knew it was really the king and the high priestess performing the act, but we all hoped that when the vulva of Inanna was spiritually plowed, our fields would birth abundance in the coming season. Not that the ceremony had much effect the last few years.

Ima had been to Harran only once — a year or two before I was born. D'vorah told me how she wore her best veil and sat at the entrance of the temple waiting to take part in a ceremony that was every newly married woman's spiritual duty. Ugly women could wait for days, even weeks, for a man to pass by and throw coins into her lap.

Ima came home the very next day because a tall stranger threw her two full bekas before taking her inside. D'vorah said Ima cried for weeks after visiting the House of Joys. D'vorah said the place stole something precious from her. Was that at the root of my parents' unhappiness?

As I sweltered in the sun, I wondered what my future husband's faith would require of me. While the Ziggurat sacrifice burned itself out, the stench of charred flesh and scorched hair hung heavily in the air. When the service ended, streets again surged with determination as everyone went back to their business. Babble and bartering swirled around us like desert winds. And we were sucked into the teeming masses. I was grateful to be perched above the crowd, high up on my camel which broke away from our caravan, striding purposefully toward the bazaar as she tagged along behind Eli'ezer's he-camel. In a futile attempt to stop her, my camel-boy tugged with all his might at my camel's bridle, yelling frantic words I did not understand. We narrowly missed a cart of green melons, jolted past some colourful spices, and came to a stop at a slave market—where my mount found a prickly thorn bush to munch on.

Eli'ezer dismounted his camel and walked toward a slave trader whose wares were on display. He looked closely at a few of the women and turned to me with a question. "Will one of these fit your service?"

"What?" I looked at the women, aghast.

"Which of these should I purchase for you, Mistress Rivkah?"

I was shocked. Though I knew it was done all the time, the thought of buying someone in a market offended me. D'vorah was our slave, but her grandmother had been born into Nachor and Milkah's household, as she had been born into ours. She was more like family.

"I need no slave but D'vorah," I said.

"My master is a man of great wealth," said Eli'ezer. "One servant is not a proper entourage for his son's bride." Eli'ezer seemed calm but I could feel his tension. I knew I was a dubious selection for the bride of Yitz'chak. I had no dowry to load on the camel's backs and only the one servant. I saw his dilemma. On our long journey ahead, Eli'ezer was responsible to uphold the reputation of his master. At every stop along the way, how would he explain the acquisition of an impoverished bride like me?

Not wishing to shame Eli'ezer or my husband's family, I let my gaze slide over the bodies of the slaves and down onto the dirt at their feet. It was there that I saw her, a broken twig of a girl squatting on the bare earth, her eyes shut tight to close out the world. I thought I glimpsed the tail of a thin black snake disappear in the dust at her feet, and saw a familiar line of despair in the curve of her back. I had just been redeemed from despair like that. I had been released from the oppression of my family by the bride-price Eli'ezer brought. Would I ever have a chance, again, to set another free? I searched Eli'ezer's eyes. They were full of mercy.

"I want her," I said.

She would not speak her name. She would not speak at all. Wilted and silent, she followed my camel, oblivious to the dust and dung she staggered in. By late afternoon she began to faint, so I insisted she ride my mount. I did not mind the walk and wondered what storms the girl up on my camel had weathered. She seemed much like my bruised and broken herbs. Would my chatter and care heal her like it healed my plants? Would helping her, heal me from the bruises of my childhood?

Eli'ezer was no help. Though he had talked at length to the slave seller, I could not harass the girl's story out of him. He was tight lipped and sad, his countenance closed to my pleading. Perhaps he disapproved of the purchase. I shrugged and named her Shabar (Broken).

By the time we ended our journey for the day, the sun was painting long shadows on the ground. I had always viewed the northern mountain range from a distance and could not believe I was standing at its base. We made camp in the shade of an unusual knoll that rose from the ground, looking very much like Abba's pot belly. At its summit, a lone mulberry tree trembled in the breeze. What had I heard about mulberry trees . . . something about a life-giving tea? Yes! Traders from the east once told me about a way to make a paste of its fruit then add hot water. The tea was said to enrich the body and brighten the eyes. Perhaps it would help Shabar.

I called my camel-boy and strode up the hill. He panted behind me trying to keep up. After commanding him to climb the tree, I bade him shake the branches with all his might. Luscious berries fell into my veil and I gathered up their abundance while the boy ran back toward the supper smells with no thought of helping me with my burden.

I was planning to twist his ear over that, when something unusual caught my eye. There was a large, flat, rectangular stone embedded in the ground. It was not a natural shape so I knew it was man-made. Was it a paving stone? Were those chisel marks? Had ancient peoples once lived on this hill? I leaned down to touch the stone and thought I saw a shadow move. But there was no wind.

Suddenly, the earth began to spin and the sky flashed brass. Breath laboured in my chest and my heart raced. I fell to the ground on my face, powerless over my limbs. My nose pressed into the warm, sage-scented earth and I lay overwhelmed by a Presence I could not name. I dared not look up. I knew it could wipe out my life but it did not. I could not tell you how long I lay there, helpless.

"Mistress Rivkah?" Eli'ezer's voice was soft and distant.

With great effort, I opened my eyes and peered up at him. He was concerned, his hand outstretched to help me up. "What is this place, Eli'ezer? Who are the people that lived here? What is the power that dwells on this hill?"

"It was said to be the Garden of God where Father Adam named the creatures and Mother Havah carved their likenesses. Perhaps it was the place where the Creator came in the evening to whisper secret knowledge. The people who dwell in these hills are still called the People of 'Eden."

I surveyed the dry hills. "What happened to the garden?"

"They say that cherubim were sent to cover the site from view, and to guard it with a flashing sword."

I nodded and let him help me to my feet, but I said nothing about seeing the flash. I went to the mulberry tree and scraped back the outer bark. I could not tell you how I knew, in that sacred moment, that mulberry's inner bark could heal burns. I dropped the cuttings into my veil along with the berries, and tore off a piece of my robe to bind the wounded tree. Then Eli'ezer helped carry my precious harvest down the hill.

Day Three
Carchemish

Eli'ezer was right. The journey to my new home took one full phase of the moon as we travelled the ancient trade routes and bought treasures to fill the empty camel packs. At Carchemish we forded the Euphrates River, but Eli'ezer refused to pay the crossing tax to their goddess. "We pay homage to the God of Avraham alone," Eli'ezer said. The ford-keepers frowned but let him pass. I asked him why they did not argue. "The Almighty does not bow to their gods or goddesses—especially not to a drunken alewife like Kubaba."

Day Eight
Hallab

In Hallab we bought sacks of pistachio nuts and heard the famous story of how Avraham gave milk to the poor on his journey through the city. This tale of mercy was my childhood favourite and I was stabbed by a pang of grief for the loss of our peaceful story circle, destroyed by my parents' discord.

Day Fourteen
Hamath

The farmers of Hamath knew how to irrigate dry fields with water ditches. Chadoufs were constructed at intervals, and their long wooden levers lifted water-gourds out of the canals to turn the desert into a garden. I examined them with longing. That invention would have saved me thousands of trips to the well. But Lavan would never have spared a servant to help with the construction. And, could the convenience of a chadouf have kept me from my fateful meeting with Eli'ezer's caravan? I asked Eli'ezer to stop so I could make thanksgiving sacrifices to Asimah, the goddess of destiny, who had a temple in Hamath. But he said, "Your destiny is decided by Adonai. Give thanks to Avraham's God alone."

Day Sixteen
Quatna

As we rode beside the great black pillars of Quatna's huge palace, my neck hurt from craning. Their sun-god, Simige, had no mercy on that blistering day, so I used up most of my mulberry-bark salve to nurse the raw faces of the camel-boys. And when we finally loaded up all the copper, cloth, and wine the city had to offer, Eli'ezer smiled down at me in thanks for using the ointment to care for the men. Smiling too, I remembered my secret sage-scented encounter with the Presence on the pot-bellied hill. Was the One perhaps a God of mercy? Is that why the secret of the mulberry bark was whispered in my ear?

Day Twenty-Two
Dammesek

Eli'ezer broke his customary silence when we entered the gates of Dammesek—the city of his father. He told a long story of how Avraham found his father slaving in a date grove and paid a great price to redeem the boy from an owner who beat him cruelly. I glanced at Shabar, my broken twig—she and I were similarly redeemed.

Day Twenty-Four
Mount Hermon

We rested for a day in the shade of Mount Hermon, and bathed in the springs that gushed from the rocks. By then I paid no attention at all to the local talk of fierce storm deities and bearded bull-gods. By then, I was sure the Almighty would allow no interference with our progress. My head spun with stories of wicked gods and goddesses that filled the world. They were a parade of threat and wished to reap destruction if we refused to pay their dues. But Eli'ezer went placidly among these dangers. His face was unchanged when angry storms gathered or people muttered curses. He said the Almighty One was not intimidated by the gods and goddesses that surrounded us. And I felt secure.

Shabar began to regain her strength as the days went on. But she remained silent.

D'vorah spent her time fretting over my wedding attire. Too proud to ask Eli'ezer for help with this quest, she pulled me to bazaars in every town, looking for just the right garment. It had to be red, the colour of fertility. It had to be adorned with silver, the metal of faithfulness. I offered to trade my golden bracelets for some of the beautiful crimson veils we saw, but she would hear none of it. I was impatient with her constant chatter about weddings and veils and feast dishes. Her fussing frazzled my soul as we entered the land I would soon call home.

Day Twenty-Eight
Sh'khem

A lone guardian on the hillside, watching over the town, Sh'khem's Oak of Moreh stood in the distance. We had journeyed for weeks by that time and I was glad to dismount my bony camel. She was an ornery beast who could land a gob of spittle in a person's face from at least ten paces away. My beautiful fringed saddle was caked with the dust of the road and my mood was as black as the bells on my camel's bridle. So, Eli'ezer escorted me to the shade of the Oak and let the evening breezes soothe my spirit while he unfolded a story. His face began to glow in the setting sun. He seemed to grow taller as the telling progressed. The groans of the camels and shouts of the servants felt remote as Eli'ezer's words began to penetrate my spirit.

"It was on this very spot that Adonai came to Master Avraham and said, 'I will give this land to your offspring.' The land spread before you will belong to your children, Mistress Rivkah. The One heard your cries and saw your captivity. The price has been paid. You were redeemed from your people. You are a Woman of the Promise."

As seeds of faith sown long ago began to germinate, stirrings moved in my heart. I knew God chose Avraham and Sarah to fulfill a divine purpose, but had never considered that I could be chosen. Was it true? Did the God of Avraham notice the downtrodden? Did this strange deity heed the prayers of a captive girl? Did this God snatch me from bondage and deposit me on this mountaintop, a freed woman?

Overwhelmed, I released a flow of tears that spilled down my cheeks to water my faith. Embarrassed, I turned away from Eli'ezer to see Shabar striding up the path holding a bundle wrapped in fine white linen. She placed the package in my hands and knelt at my feet. Then she bent her face to the ground in a posture of homage.

"You are chosen by God to receive The Cloth of Redemption," said Eli'ezer.

Taken aback, I looked into his eyes and saw deep compassion there. Untying the string that bound the parcel, I folded back the fine wrapping and fingered the newly exposed cloth. I drew in a breath. Never before had I felt anything like it—so cool and smooth—like a mountain spring. I glanced questioningly at Eli'ezer. He smiled and helped Shabar to her feet. Stepping forward, she helped me unfurl the cloth. Bright red, and shimmering silver in the sun, it danced for joy in the breeze. Light as air, it took on a life of its own and soared up to God in a song of worship. Had I not anchored it in my grasp it would have escaped to the clouds. The camel-boys looked up with fascination. D'vorah, entranced, rose from her cooking fire to watch.

"It came to Egypt long ago from a land in the east, as a gift for queen Neferu," said Eli'ezer. "Before she died, she bid her servant to keep watch for a woman who would one day be redeemed from the court of the pharaoh. The price was paid by the pharaoh himself, and Sarah was redeemed."

Gathering the crimson cloth from the sky, I folded its great length back into the linen casing while it gleamed and bubbled like a water-brook in the sun. Then, sensing he had more to say, I turned back toward Eli'ezer.

"Before she died, Mistress Sarah bid me keep watch for the woman who would be redeemed to marry her son. She requested that I give her this cloth as a wedding veil."

For the first time in my life, I had no words.

Day Twenty-Nine
Biet-El

The next day, while collecting almonds in Biet-El's sacred wood, Eli'ezer poured more stories of faith into my ears. He told me the history of the world, and said ancient stories were written in the stars, stories of a Redeemer who would one day come to set our broken world aright. He admitted that the details of those tales were buried with those who knew them best. But despite this sad fact, I was glad to know that the God of the universe had a plan to heal the world. It said much about the intentions of my new God. And there, under the cool almond-tree archways, I put my arm around D'vorah. She still fretted about the silver adornment for my wedding veil and about finding spices for the traditional keskek meal. "If the God of Avraham is powerful enough to write a story in the stars, and loving enough to provide me with a wedding garment, this God will provide all our needs," I said.

Day Thirty
Biet-Lechem

After a day of trading in the sparkling hilltop city of Shalem, we set up camp in an open field on the edge of Biet-Lechem—a strange little town with plenty of scrub brush for our camels to eat and a cave for us to shelter in. An unearthly feeling came upon me there, almost a feeling of home. But of course, it was only a way-stop to our destination.

Shabar and D'vorah acted strangely that day. They disappeared into the depths of the cave with new wine and lemons and a collection of cloth and tools. I was happy to leave them with their secret task, and went to gather wild olives on the fertile slopes. The Land of the Promise is rich and abundant. In all my travels I have seen no place so covered with blessings. As I began to labour back up the hill with my bounty, I saw D'vorah and Shabar running down the hill toward me. My wedding veil was streaming out behind them, its edge twinkling with silver.

As they got closer, I saw that the black bells from my camel's bridle had been polished to a high shine and sewn onto the edge of the veil. "We found the silver, the silver for your wedding day," shouted D'vorah. "It was hiding in plain sight, on your camel's bridle." She and Shabar were jubilant as they spun me around in laughter. I dropped my olives to join their dance but tripped on the wedding cloth's great length and collapsed upon a field of flowers.

Winded, we lay watching perfect little heads of red and yellow lilies bob above us. Even the fabled king of Shalem, in all his glory, was not as beautifully clothed as the flowers of the field. "Did I not tell you, D'vorah, that the Almighty would provide? Avraham's God is the faithful One, the silver in our lives."

Later, I drifted off to sleep and realized that Shabar had laughed out loud. I heard her voice for the first time — in laughter. Her spirit was blooming like a flower. But something about her seemed familiar. Whose face did I glimpse in her joy?

THE WEDDING

The day began like many others as I lay in my small travel-tent, savoring the sounds and smells of camp. Midway between Biet-Lechem and my future home in Hevron, the day had dawned. Camels groaned in disapproval while their packs were being loaded. D'vorah and Shabar were baking bread. Their movements were soft and reassuring but my stomach was twisted in a knot and my heart refused to lay still. Through the tent flap, I watched the sun begin to dominate the sky. Sleepy thoughts cocooned me but they soon unraveled to release the day—my wedding day.

As we moved ever closer to our destination, D'vorah chattered on and on about plans for the wedding supper and the wedding breakfast and the wedding ceremonies and the wedding night. Anticipation also mounted among the camel-boys, who had not seen their families in months. Even the dromedaries seemed to pick up their feet and sniff the air with renewed energy. Jokes darted around my ears like swallows. Yitz'chak and I were usually the brunt of them, so I fixed my eyes on the ground in front of my mount's padded feet.

I did not notice the grazing flocks of sheep, or the sinking sun, or the lush barley field that spread out before us like a fleece—until a hush descended. A lark warbled in the distance and goat bells clanked but no one spoke. I looked up to see what caused the change. A man was walking in the field a short distance away. He was richly dressed, of medium height, and his beard was brown. He was staring at the sky—which was unremarkable and cloudless. A worshiper? My heart jumped. Was it him? What was he doing in the field? I was far from ready to meet him.

Not waiting for my camel-boy to make my stubborn beast kneel, I slid to the ground and landed in an ungainly heap of twisted robes. Frantically untangling myself, I ran to the front of the caravan where Eli'ezer stood looking toward the man in the distance. Breathless, I asked, "Who is that man walking in the field to meet us?"

A wide grin graced Eli'ezer's placid face. "He is my master."

At that moment, D'vorah came puffing up behind me and Shabar appeared bearing a linen bundle. While I sputtered like a small child, they beat the dust off my robes, dragged a wooden comb through my tousled hair, and washed smudges of dirt off my cheeks with their spit.

Shabar's silent pleading eyes penetrated my resistance as she held up the bundle — the veil. I allowed D'vorah to tie one corner of the cloth to my belt, then wrap its great length around me in delicate folds of crimson. It shimmered like a waterfall, pouring gently over my body and cooling my flushed skin. While the silver bells sang a blessing, D'vorah draped the edge of the cloth over my head and around my face. She tied a golden cord around my temples to fasten the veil in place. Then she stepped back to view her work. Only my eyes were showing.

"A true bride," she declared.

Meanwhile, Eli'ezer had moved across the field to greet my betrothed. They embraced and talked and gestured and nodded while Yitz'chak stole glances in my direction. He seemed impatient with Eli'ezer's long explanations of our journey, and finally broke away. But I was busy fending off the ministrations of my servants and had lost sight of how close he was while I batted at their hands and protested at their clucking. "Let me be. What will he think when he sees you fussing over me like a baby?"

"I will think my bride is being readied for her wedding." Startled, I looked up into laughing eyes of green and gold.

When our eyes met, I think I heard him gasp.

"You have her eyes." he said.

"Then so do you." My eyes, reflected in his, were astonishingly similar. We laughed as music exploded around us with pipes and drums and tambourines. Flowing over the hill from nearby Hevron, dancers appeared on the horizon — all dressed in wedding finery and singing joyous songs:

"How lovely you are, my darling, how lovely! Your eyes are doves behind your veil. Your temple is like a slice of pomegranate behind your veil."

A boisterous procession led us around the shoulder of a hill and down into a pleasant valley where a enormous grove of oak trees shaded a group of tents. The aroma of roasting meat filled the air and people were busy with preparations for the feast. I had not expected to see so many people among the tents of Avraham. And I had never seen such tents. They were settled sedately under The Oaks of Mamre, black and massive and richly decorated with banners of every colour.

As we drew close, the throbbing crowd parted to let an elderly man pass through its midst. He was as tall as an obelisk and his beard glowed white in the setting sun. Yitz'chak became tense and wary in the presence of the man.

When the ancient one's eyes met mine, I saw him startle. But he did not gasp like Yitz'chak had. "Greetings, Rivkah of Nachor. Welcome to the family of Avraham. From this day on you are my daughter." Those were Avraham's first words to me and I learned their full significance later.

The women of Hevron whisked me away in a wind of laughter. They painted my hands and feet with henna and baptized me in song. Then D'vorah proudly led me to my groom.

She placed my hand in his and I fell headlong into the deep whirlpool of his green and gold gaze. I was completely captivated when he recited the ritual wedding psalm of his people and broke open a ripe pomegranate—its abundant seeds promising many children.

Then Yitz'chak's eyes flickered away from mine and fastened on a large tent in the middle of the clearing. For a moment he seemed sad, as if reliving a grief. He swallowed painfully. Then he recovered his composure to chant a poem in a dreamlike state as he guided me toward the tent.

> *"I would lead you and bring you into my mother's house — she who has taught me. I would give you spiced wine to drink, from the nectar of my pomegranates."*

The walls of our nuptial chamber were lined with patterned sheets and hung with embroidered ribbons. Multicoloured floor-cushions lined the edges of the tent, but an elaborately carved wooden bed dominated the space. As we stood awkwardly together in the gathering dusk, an oil lamp spontaneously flickered to life and a soundless wind flowed over us. Yitz'chak reached out to protect me. Who was there? The Presence was deep and vast. We knew it could wipe out our lives. But it did not. We felt it pass through the tent, linger a moment, then dissolve into the night. Scarcely daring to breathe, we waited, tense and expectant.

When the tension dissolved, Yitz'chak turned my face to his with a gentle hand. His eyes shone with desire as he unclasped my veil and released my gown to flow around my feet. In a fragrant gust of frankincense, his lips claimed mine. And his tender fingers explored all my warm places.

THE RIFT

In the early days of our marriage, we lived in harmony with each other and with the earth that nurtured us. In each of our three home-places, I planted a garden. And I was grateful to have good company in those labours. In addition to D'vorah and Shabar, two male servants were appointed to do the more strenuous tasks. My days of harsh servitude were over. In this new country I was mistress of all.

So, I buried the wounds of my youth in the deep recesses of my soul and embraced my new life. For twenty years we contentedly travelled between our home-places. Those years were a journey of discovery for me as I leaned to love my husband and tend my gardens. Yitz'chak and my plants seemed to thrive when I catered to their likes and dislikes.

We waited out winter on Be'er-Lachi-Ro'i's warm plain. Yishma'el, Yitz'chak's wild half-brother, lived on nearby Mount Se'ir. He was a mighty hunter and traded venison for the hardy desert herbs I grew there.

Throughout the busy grape and pomegranate harvest, we summered with Avraham and his wife K'turah, in Hevron. Yitz'chak was always somewhat uneasy in the place of his birth, but his half-brothers eased our stay by entertaining us with pranks and jests.

In the fall we travelled down to Be'er-Sheva. There, we reaped lentils and grains to sustain us throughout the year. In those times of peace, I often felt the Presence as I wandered through my beautiful gardens.

I cannot tell you when it began to change.

෨෬

The horns of the crescent-moon pierced the sky. The restless tamarisks waved their branches in the wind. And I tossed and turned on my sleeping-pallet. Though weary from the labour of the day, I sighed, threw back the thin wool coverlet, and stepped into the night.

Standing in the dark, I lifted my face to the breeze and breathed in the scent of sheep, soil, and the fennel fragrance of olive blossoms. I felt uneasy. Gloom had settled on my soul. After years of marriage, no seed had germinated in my womb to start the promised nation. Was the Holy One angry? Was God displeased with our sacrifices? Was the Adonai dissatisfied with the ministrations of Yitz'chak who dwelt in the great black chieftain's tent next to mine? Or was it I who had failed?

Looking back at my luxurious pavilion, I sighed again. Twenty years in this bountiful land had delivered no child. Twenty years had only produced a drought of waterless promises — and famine in my soul. Though Yitz'chak's patience with God's promised plan seemed undiminished, dogged doubt was drying up my faith. If this unnamed God was truly the Almighty . . .

"What do you ask of the One, in the darkness of the night?"

My heart jumped. "Yitz'chak?"

"I came to join your prayer," he said from the shadows.

"I did not come out to pray."

"Then what do you seek?"

My heart began to throb at Yitz'chak's uncustomary probing and I released the truth we were trying so hard to ignore. "I have come out to mourn my empty womb. Perhaps my mother was right. I was too hasty to leave the worship of Inanna. I should have insisted on the full ceremonial wedding season to play itself out."

"You dare speak this way, under the watchful eye of the One?"

"What have I to lose? We have not felt the Presence together since our wedding night. The God of Avraham does not visit you as he visited your father. Perhaps the One has moved on to favour another man. We have heard of the goodness of Iyov in the far-off land of Uz. God blessed him with many children."

Yitz'chak stepped out of the shadow and into the

pale glow of the crescent-moon. His face was dressed in sadness but his eyes flickered with resolve. "It is enough for me that God spoke the Promise to my father and my mother. I do not need to hear the Voice."

A memory flashed. It felt like a lifetime ago. Did it truly happen? I had not shared the moment with anyone, not even Yitz'chak. Perhaps it was time. "Once, I think I heard the Voice — though only in my heart. I heard it in the land of 'Eden, giving me the mulberry-bark remedy for burns."

When he reached for me, his smile — kind but condescending — was lit by moonlight. "Do you believe me?" His face said it all and I backed away. "So, I am not worthy to hear the Voice? Was I not an answer to the prayer of Eli'ezer? Am I not redeemed to be the Woman of the Promise? Did the Presence not come back to Sarah's tent the day I entered it?"

"Yes. And the tent-lamp flickered to life and your bread dough is blessed as hers once was, but you are not Sarah."

His voice was gentle but I bristled with indignation. "No. I am not Sarah. And it seems the Promised child will never come through me. You should take a second wife. Take Shabar. I saw you looking at her."

I had done the unthinkable. Like Mother Havah, I abandoned the wisdom of waiting and offered an act of impatience to my husband. But unlike Father Adam, Yitz'chak backed away and we stood beside the Tamarisk of Be'er-Sheva watching the gulf between us grow. Yitz'chak suddenly seemed a stranger. All familiarity fled. We tried, at first, to reach for each other, but the chasm between us was too wide. Our hands hung limply at our sides while the abyss between us broadened.

"I will not take another wife," Yitz'chak said. "I am not Avram."

※

The next day began like many others as I lay in my tent, taking in the sounds and smells of morning. D'vorah and

Shabar were baking bread. Their movements were soft and reassuring but my stomach was twisted in a knot. I longed to close the gap between me and Yitz'chak, but had no idea how to go about it. Through the tent flap, I watched the sun break through the crust of the dark horizon and paint the rosy colours of dawn on my husband's troubled face. He was up and loading his donkey. He had cut enough wood for a burnt offering. Was he preparing to offer a sacrifice? Where was he going?

    I slipped a day-robe over my head and stood at the entrance of my tent. Something was amiss. Why was Yitz'chak leaving home to offer sacrifices? Why was he going without the company of family or servants? And where was the offering he would burn upon the wood that was loaded on his donkey's back? Wordlessly, I gestured for my man-servants to ready my donkey. D'vorah and Shabar wrapped the morning's bread in a cloth and tied it to my waist. Without a backward glance or a word to each other, Yitz'chak and I mounted our donkeys and rode toward the eastern hill-pass.

THE CAVE

I reached into the homespun bread-bag and drew out a jar of olive oil, a few small spice pouches, and a knife. I was relieved that D'vorah had included more than bare necessities when she packed for our journey. I stirred sumac, marjoram, cayenne, and a pinch of salt into the oil. I took comfort in the familiar task of spreading the savory mixture onto the bread.

When I offered Yitz'chak the meal, I looked into his eyes and saw fear in their depths. "Where are we going?" I asked. They were the first words either of us had uttered since we began our journey. I had no confidence he would answer.

"We are going to Mount Moriyyah, a place of prayer," he said. "My father took me there when I was young."

By nightfall we reached the fields of Biet-Lechem, and made our silent way to the cave where the camel caravan of my youth had camped long ago. I gathered sticks and made a fire that warmed my body—but my heart was cold with dread. Yitz'chak sat in the mouth of the cave, staring into the gathering murk of night. I sat down beside him but could not close the gap between us.   As we watched the stars appear, I wondered about the legend I heard long ago. Eli'ezer said the constellations told a story of redemption. It was something about a Saviour who would rescue the whole world from destruction. I could not remember the details of his story, and grieved the loss. Perhaps, in remembering it, I could have brought hope to my husband's anxious heart.

Yitz'chak turned to me, trembling as he spoke. "This is the place where my father made the first covenant with the Holy One. Here in this field, he divided a heifer, a female goat, a ram, a turtledove and a young pigeon." Yitz'chak's unsteady words stopped, and I waited for him to gather strength. "When the sun went down, a great darkness fell, a burning torch as hot as a furnace, passed between the animals—and Avram heard the Voice."

Though I already knew what God had said, I dared not interrupt Yitz'chak's telling. Every summer, Abba Avraham recounted the story—in great detail—around the cig kofte tray. We practically had it memorized. Everyone knew about the Promise of the Covenant. Everyone knew that Avraham's descendants were given this land forever.

My heart began to pound as understanding dawned. If we were on our way to Avraham's place of prayer, would Yitz'chak also hear Adonai's voice there? On that sacred mountain, would Yitz'chak petition God for the Promised child? Would my womb finally wake? I turned to Yitz'chak in wonder but he got up and shuffled into the cave, his back hunched with fear.

I followed Yitz'chak into his darkness and gave him the comforts of my body throughout the night. It was the only way I knew to calm the terror he wrestled with.

THE PRAYER

Though King Malki-Tzedek no longer lived in Shalem, Yitz'chak paused to leave a tithe of grain and oil on his ancient threshold. And while ascending the mountain, Yitz'chak found the courage to blurt out the terrible event his family had kept secret for years. I listened in awe to the horror that shaped Yitz'chak's fear — and his faith.

Avraham had proved his great love for God, by binding his only son to an altar on the very mountain we ascended that day. The patriarch was committed to slaying his son if God commanded it. But God stayed Avraham's hand at the last moment, and miraculously provided a ram for the sacrifice.

Yitz'chak had obviously never recovered from the trauma of facing death at the hand of his father. He was still tormented by the memory of it! Was that part of the reason his mother insisted on establishing a separate home-place? Was it a retreat for her son, a haven from the memory of Avraham's raised knife?

I thought back through the years, recalling the tension in Yitz'chak's shoulders whenever he entered his father's presence. We walked a while in silence and I realized that our journey to the mountain of Yitz'chak's terror might somehow be his way of proving his sacrificial love for me — and for his God. It would take great courage for Yitz'chak to face his fear and offer prayers upon this mountain. But . . . was it only prayer he wished to offer?

"Yitz'chak?" Deep in thought, my husband seemed oblivious to my voice. I cleared my throat and persisted. "Here is the fire and the wood," I said, pointing to these items, "but where is the lamb for a burnt offering?"

Yitz'chak stopped and stared at me as if I were an apparition and not a flesh and blood woman standing right in front of him. Then he broke the silence between us with hoarse cracking words. "Perhaps God will provide the lamb for the burnt offering."

I looked away from the torment in his eyes and desperately concentrated on the last few steps to the top of the hill. My mind was full of horror at what Avraham had purposed to do as he trudged along this very path. And we had no lamb for the sacrifice either. What was Yitz'chak thinking?

The stains of former sacrifices soaked the summit rock. Boulders and charred branches littered the area. The scent of sage drifted to us on the breeze. And though the air was warm, I shivered. Frightened and numb, I watched Yitz'chak roll and lift large stones into place to form a rough altar. Then he motioned for me to arrange the wood on top. What would happen next? Would he dare to bind me like his father had bound him? Or, would he wait for the One to act? How long would he wait? I trembled while he unraveled a rope and opened a pouch containing the fire-flint.

Just then, a shepherd boy crested the hill, carrying a lamb over his shoulders. "May I buy your lamb for my sacrifice?" asked Yitz'chak.

The boy's face split into a grin. "It would be a pleasure my Lord! I was just fetching this rascal from his latest adventure. He has a mind of his own and often strays from the flock. He would be honoured to be your sacrifice."

We burst out laughing and completed the ceremony with songs of thanksgiving. Yitz'chak's faith was revived as he sang out the Promise of God, claiming it as his own. Joy was reborn, as he lifted the lamb onto the altar and offered it back to its Creator. Hope was renewed, as he sought the Almighty's blessing on my womb.

Later, we sent the shepherd boy happily home with a mutton supper for his family. Then we stood together on the mountain and felt the Presence flutter down upon us like a dove, enveloping us in peace.

And while the stars of the Lion began to appear in the heavens, the seed inside me came to life.

THE PROPHECY

Father Avraham was thrilled at our news and began to make plans for the future. He built trusts for K'turah's sons by sending Eli'ezer to purchase land in far flung places and appointing servants to begin cultivation there. He asked my advice about what kind of crops to plant in the remote corners of our world. My knowledge, gleaned from the caravans of my youth and the gardens of my marriage, lent great prosperity to K'turah's boys. One by one, Avraham settled each son into a remote holding so there would be no competition for his heir. The patriarchal birthright and the spiritual blessing would belong to my son alone — the child of the Promise.

My abdomen grew with our joy as we anticipated the birth of the child. And proud as I was of my blessed state, I was impatient with my expanding girth. It made me even more clumsy than usual and hindered my ability to tend the gardens. By the seventh moon I would have dearly loved to carry my growing belly around in a cart. Yitz'chak laughed at my suggestion and said he would commission the carpenter to build one designed especially for that purpose. It was fine for him to be amused.

Like a relentless rain, fatigue and sleeplessness eroded my good humour. By nightfall I would collapse, exhausted, onto Sarah's great carved bed, only to toss about on its cushions and furs. It felt like a war waged within me. Lumps and bumps from inside my belly often surfaced to bruise my skin. None of my servants had seen anything like it. The child's wild thrashing constantly broke my sleep. Though tired from the labour of the day, I pushed back the thin wool coverlet and stepped into the night. I hoped a walk in the garden would sooth my restlessness and calm my tossing child. While breathing in the scent of soil and sage, I lifted my head to storied stars and longed to know their messages. Could those ancient tales have calmed my mind and soothed my fears? In deep frustration, I cried out to the Creator of the stars, "Why is this happening to me? How can I go without sleep night after night? If it is going to be like this, why go on living?"

Suddenly, the earth spun and the sky flashed brass. Breath laboured in my chest and my heart raced. I fell to the ground on my face, powerless over my limbs. My nose pressed into the herb-scented earth and I lay overwhelmed by the Presence. Then I heard the Voice.

"Two nations are in your womb, and two peoples from your body will be separated. One people will be stronger than the other, but the older will serve the younger." I did not know if the Voice came from without or within my body and dared not look up. I could not tell how long I lay on the ground, helpless.

"Rivkah?" D'vorah's voice was soft and distant. With great effort, I opened my eyes and peered up at her. She was concerned, her hand outstretched. I let her help me to my feet but said nothing as I returned to my tent, unsteady and overcome. Any hope for sleep was gone. I could scarcely believe that I heard the Voice. But I had heard it even as Sarah had. And I heard it while walking in a garden like Mother Havah had.

Yitz'chak would not believe me. As was his nature, he smiled kindly and said that surely God would have come to Avraham or to his heir with news of that importance. And since he and his father did not hear the prophecy, it must be a pregnant woman's fancy. At first, I let his comments rest. It made sense that the One would talk to Avraham, or to Yitz'chak. And it is true that pregnant women are known for their fancies.

Then I changed my mind and could not let it go. "But God came and spoke to your mother about your birth. We all know the story. The Almighty even laughed with her when she finally believed. You told me all about it."

He smiled gently, "You are not Sarah."

I did not smile back. Somewhere in the shadows, I thought I glimpsed a black snake slither under the edge of the tent as past resentments spread their venomous poison.

THE BIRTH

"You will see, Yitz'chak! You will see! Inferior woman though I am, the One spoke to me!" Women in labour often lash out at their husbands and my servants knew the repercussions of gossip in our small clan. They were trying to prevent me later embarrassment, but I would not have it. I screamed out my pain, heedless of D'vorah and Shabar who did their best to shush me. The foundation flaps of the birthing tent were lifted for ventilation, and with each cresting contraction I flooded the compound with my anger.

"Mistress, drink this. It will help speed the birth." I knew D'vorah's strategy. While I was busy drinking the birthing tea, I could not berate my husband. Good, kind, Yitz'chak — always so gentle and pleasant but never willing to acknowledge that his wife could ever rise to the status of his mother and hear the Voice of God.

Scowling at D'vorah, I sipped from her cup until another wave of pain took over. Then I spat out the tea and screeched, "You will see, Yitz'chak. Two nations are in my womb and the older will serve the younger. God decreed it!"

I could feel my sons struggle inside me while I panted and groaned, fighting to expel them from my body. Soon, all my energy was needed to push those nations into the world. They slid out in a rush — children born into envy and competition.

'Esav (Red) came first, his body covered in crimson fuzz. There was no need to bind him with the traditional scarlet chord of the firstborn. God had already marked him. While I watched in fascination, D'vorah scooped him up to wash him with warmed wine. His wide eyes fastened on mine and his little nose wrinkled at all the new smells. "Esav," laughed D'vorah as she rubbed olive oil into his skin, "our rough little red man."

Clutching 'Esav's heel, Ya'akov (Supplanter)

followed his brother into the world. Shabar scooped him up before he tumbled onto the mud floor of the tent. "A heel-catcher!" she exclaimed. "Did you see how his hand grasped his brother's heel?"

"And he will supplant him," I declared. "It is part of the prophecy that will come true despite my husband's unbelief."

Busy with the advent of the twins, there were two things I did not notice right away. The first was that I heard Shabar speak for the first time. Her voice, when I thought about it later, sounded familiar. A memory stirred, then dissolved in the demands of caring for newborn twins. The second thing I remembered, was a shadow at the tent door just as I declared Ya'akov's destiny. It hovered for a moment, then disappeared in a waft of frankincense. Yitz'chak.

As always, avoiding conflict.

THE TWINS

"Abba, watch this!" 'Esav was entertaining us with his toy bow, and we laughed as the tip of his blunt little arrow bounced off the flank of an annoyed camel. Yitz'chak and I did not live in the harmony we once enjoyed, but the antics of our sons often drew us together.

Ya'akov, not to be outdone, went around to the front of the camel to comfort the beast by stroking his nose. Instead of lashing out, the grumpy dromedary calmed almost instantly. Yitz'chak and I glanced at each other, awed at our second-born's way with creatures. So different our sons were. One hunted any animal that moved, while the other cared for their needs.

The rhythms of life continued. And to 'Esav's delight, we spent winters at Be'er-Lachai-Ro'i where he revelled in the visits of his rough uncle Yishma'el. He was intrigued by stories of Yishma'el's bold hunting exploits on the fabled Mount Se'ir. Yitz'chak sat by the fire with them. He was not a hunting man, but did love the venison Yishma'el traded for our produce. Yitz'chak ran his hand through 'Esav's curly red hair and I could tell he was hoping to raise a second-generation hunter.

Yitz'chak's and 'Esav's attachment to Yishma'el distressed me. Avraham and Sarah had cast him out of their camp. Why was Yishma'el now so free to come and go? How would that shape 'Esav's future? Would the smoldering resentment in Yishmael's eyes catch fire and spread?

Ya'akov was restless at Be'er-Lachai-Ro'i, preferring Hevron's luxurious tents and the stories told around Avraham's campfire. In Hevron, Ya'akov ran Avraham's errands and learned the business of shepherding, but 'Esav was bored and moody in such a domesticated place. I could see why the One chose Ya'akov to fulfill the Promise. He was more responsible than the adventurous 'Esav. I wished Yitz'chak could see it too. But he was deaf to my opinions and the years passed uneasily between us while the boys grew.

"Ima, how many days will it be until we go to Hevron?"

"Are you missing Saba (Grandfather)?" I looked into the smoldering eyes of my second son. His sun-bronzed arms were crossed in anger as he stared at his brother, father, and uncle. He was often shut out of their tight circle.

I put an arm around his waist and drew him to me. "I think Shabar is ready to take the bread out of the oven. If you hurry, she may give you a nice warm piece with honey on it." Ya'akov ran off, appeased for the moment, and I was left wondering what would become of my sons in their differences.

So time passed as one year folded into another until the plans of Adonai were revealed.

THE BIRTHRIGHT

"Saba! Saba!" As we rounded the curve of the trail that hid Hevron from view, Ya'akov's stricken cry rose over the noise of the caravan. Forsaking his fledgling manhood, Ya'akov ran down the road, sobbing like a child, his dark hair streaming behind him. This return to Hevron would change all our lives.

    We heard the shrill lament long before we saw the tragic truth. With their cries tearing the air, raven-like mourners surrounded a newly erected death-tent. K'turah stood in the middle of the road facing our arrival. Her face was bleak.

    Sent off to establish their distant kingdoms, her sons were not there to comfort her. They could never be summoned in time for their father's burial. Ya'akov brushed past K'turah and burst into the tent of Avraham. Even from a distance I could feel his disbelief. Had he thought his grandfather would live forever?

    Yitz'chak enfolded K'turah in a long embrace. She had tended him as a child. He had known her all his life. Entwined in grief, they rocked from side to side, their tears dropping onto the dust. And I stood alone on the road, wishing it was me my husband was drawn to for comfort.

    'Esav did not dismount his camel. He faced the scene before him like an unseeing statue. He was not close to his grandfather, at least not in the same way Ya'akov was, but Avraham was the root of all our lives and every branch feels the blow when the tree is cut down.

    I was so preoccupied with Ya'akov's shock and Yitz'chak's sorrow that I hardly noticed when 'Esav turned his camel around and fled the chaos of mourning. Later, I would regret not summoning him back to the family.

    "Saba!" Ya'akov's adolescent voice screamed and broke like his heart. It brought me back from my mental rambling and fractured my heart too. I strode past Yitz'chak and K'turah, past the assembled mourners, past the coloured rug at the entrance of Avraham's empty tent and crossed a threshold that had always been forbidden to women. I heard gasps and a sharp pause in the wailing ritual. I did not care. My son was in pain and I was determined to enfold him in a mother's love. I would cry with him as his father cried with K'turah. Our tears would mingle on the rich rugs of Avraham's empty tent. We would comfort each other. We both loved Father Avraham. "Ya'akov, my son, my son, how I wish I could spare you this loss but I cannot."

Darkness fell as we mourned there, spending all our strength on grief. When we had no more energy to cry, I broke the silence. "Are you hungry? D'vorah and Shabar are making red lentil stew in preparation for the burial ceremony tomorrow. Perhaps they need help with the stirring. Should we go assist them?"

Every young man is eventually obedient to his appetite, so Ya'akov uncurled himself from sorrow and followed me out of Avraham's tent. After we had eaten, we wandered into the courtyard and picked up two large wooden paddles to stir the massive pot of stew. Though there were many urgent tasks that needed doing, I could not think of anything else to occupy myself with, and I was relieved when I heard Shabar take charge.

"Who is free to go to the Cave of Machpelah and see that proper preparations have been made there for Father Avraham? Old Eli'ezer probably saw to everything, but he may have missed something in his grief. Did he send a messenger to Yishma'el? D'vorah, were the herbs and spices fetched from storage? Mistress Rivkah will need them to dress the body of our lord. See to it that one of the girls goes to collect them. There is much to do before the funeral. Everyone must help."

Shabar only spoke aloud when pressed by some extreme. It was unusual to hear her issuing instructions, but someone needed to override the paralysis of grief. Something in Shabar's voice and the tone of her commands, stirred childhood memories of Ima's bustling orders when a caravan approached.

And she was right. There was much to be done.

According to our custom, Avraham's body needed to be buried before sundown the next day. And as Avraham's only daughter, adopted on the day of my wedding, it was my duty to visit the tent of preparation and dress his body with myrrh and aloes then wrap him in fine linen. I left Ya'akov to stir the stew while I tended to that task. I did not notice 'Esav's return, and would have altogether missed the interaction between my sons if I had not gone back to the kitchen to fetch more spices.

I was relieved to see 'Esav back from his wanderings, and paused my labour to take in the sight of my sons huddled over the cooking fire. In contrast to Ya'akov's dark colouring, 'Esav was red from a day in the sun, red from the reflection of the fire, and his eyes were focused on the red pottage that Ya'akov stirred.

As for Ya'akov, he had momentarily laid his grief aside. He was sharp-eyed and calculating as he picked up a bowl and ladled stew into it. I knew that look. Was he plotting something?

The dull fog of sorrow clouded 'Esav's face. The gazelle he brought back for the funeral feast lay dead at his feet. Disheveled and weary, I could see that 'Esav made his contribution to the feast with great physical sacrifice, not stopping to eat or rest during the hunt.

What were my sons talking about? I edged closer but kept to the shadows, not wanting my presence to be known.

"Please feed me some of this red stuff, because I am exhausted!"

"First sell me your rights as the firstborn."

"Look, I am about to die. Of what use is it to me — a birthright?"

"Make a pledge to me now."

"Fine — may the God of Avraham curse me forever if I claim the birthright."

My heart stopped. Then it raced again when I saw Ya'akov calmly hand 'Esav a bowl of lentil pottage. Both faces were blank. They worked at pretending nothing momentous was taking place while 'Esav ate, drank, got up, and left his birthright behind to walk in the steps of Yishma'el.

I was rooted to the spot. What had they done?

Ya'akov, yearning to be his grandfather's heir, had stooped to treachery. And 'Esav, lost in the stupor of sorrow, had despised his birthright—while I stood by and did nothing. What would come of this? My first thought was to tell Yitz'chak. But what would he do? In the haze of grief, he would not be able to think this through. He hated dealing with conflict at the best of times. He would most likely tell me I imagined or exaggerated it. Then he would kiss my forehead and go to the fields to meditate. With Avraham's body only half-prepared, there was no time to ponder further so I hurried on to the kitchen to look for the spices I still needed.

༺༻

After laying Avraham to rest beside Sarah, Yitz'chak was unapproachable and I retreated to my herb garden. It was as dry and withered as my soul. Still disturbed by the transaction I witnessed between my sons, I rubbed feverfew leaves into my temples to quiet the thunder in my head. The rains had not come and I feared for my plants. I feared for us all and hoped the physical labour of tending my struggling garden would soothe me. I hoped the Presence would descend and the Voice would tell me how to go on after the death of Avraham. I hoped it would tell me how to heal the estrangement in my marriage and the enmity between my sons. I made countless trips to the well and back, trying, somehow, to survive the drought in our lives.

THE VISITATION

"But Potnia, the queen-mother herself, your mother's good friend, invited us to wait out the drought in G'rar. She talked to me about it at Avraham's funeral. Why do you say we should go down to Egypt instead? I hate to think what would happen to our sons in that evil land. They would be vulnerable to all its temptations — the multitudes of gods — and the women."

Yitz'chak and I stood on a hill above Hevron, lamenting the parched landscape. The sheep had eaten the grass down to the root and the wind played with the exposed topsoil, whirling it into eddies that even set the desert-hardy camels to coughing. We wrapped ourselves in layers and looked for ways to keep the dirt from penetrating our defenses. Our eyes and teeth constantly chafed with flying grit, and my garden was beyond hope.

"There are multiple gods and women in G'rar too," said Yitz'chak.

Knowing further pleas would go nowhere, I dropped my entreaty in the dust. After all, Potnia had extended the invitation to me and had not formally extended it to him, so it was not a matter Yitz'chak would consider. As usual, my opinion meant nothing and we had less and less to say to each other. Yitz'chak walked away from me, past the foraging sheep, past the guard tower, past the well, past the Hitti village. It was his way of dealing with conflict so I let him go. And I descended the hill to salvage seeds from my dying garden.

As evening approached, a shadow passed between the rows of plants and interrupted my solitude. I startled, then turned to face the intruder. Outlined against the sky, Yitz'chak's frame wavered in the heat. Lit by the setting sun, his face blazed with light. "Rivkah." His voice sliced through sparkling air and his eyes of green and gold were luminous in his sun-lit face. "Rivkah, I heard the Voice. The One spoke to me. The God of Avraham spoke to me and said to make preparations to go to G'rar."

So great was Yitz'chak's joy as we arranged to move to G'rar, you would think we were attending a festival instead of fleeing a drought. As we packed our dusty belongings, Yitz'chak's words reverberated throughout the camp. He told and retold the tale of his visitation. "And, the Voice said to me, 'I will be with you and will bless you—for to you and your seed I will give all these lands—and will confirm my pledge that I swore to Avraham your father.' And then the One said to me, 'I will multiply your seed like the stars of the sky, and in your seed all the nations of the earth will continually be blessed.' 'Esav! What do you think of that? Your father was visited just like Avraham was. Perhaps someday you will hear the Voice as well."

THE LIE

They came out to meet us on swift P'lishtim horses. Coloured banners and high-pitched shouts of welcome joined the cloud of dust that announced our arrival in the land of G'rar. With pomp and ceremony, the royal escort ushered us into the presence of the king. Inside the wildly painted palace, nobles were assembled in a red-pillared portico. We bowed before the Queen-Mother, Potnia, and her son, King Avimelekh. We were lifted from our knees with smiles and kind words while Avimelekh crossed the tiled courtyard to embrace Yitz'chak.

"Welcome, son of Avraham and Sarah. Welcome to you and to your people. We are honoured to give you shelter in this time of distress. Please make yourselves comfortable in our land. There is room for your herds and flocks on the outskirts of the city—where Avraham himself, dug a well long ago. Your servants and their households may set up tents on the plateau above the river that flows beside the city walls. We invite the family of Yitz'chak to dwell in our royal palace. You will no doubt enjoy our cool stone corridors after suffering the heat of the sun on your black tents during drought-time. My servants will show you to your rooms."

In response to this greeting, Yitz'chak drew himself up to his full height and said, "Great King Avimelekh, I pour out the blessings of my God upon you and your household. We accept your hospitality in honour of the friendship between our mothers. Allow me to introduce you to my family. This is my firstborn son 'Esav, his brother Ya'akov, and my sister Rivkah."

My eyebrows shot up and my mouth went slack behind my veil. Then I inhaled a breath of dusty air that sent me into a coughing fit. Doubled over with choking spasms, I beckoned to D'vorah. She obligingly came to fuss over me. I am sure she was glad to have something to do to hide her own surprise. What did Yitz'chak say?

Had he introduced me as his sister? Did I hear him say that? It was true in a way. In keeping with the customs of his people, Avraham adopted me as a daughter on the day of my wedding. And I performed all the traditions of a daughter at his funeral. I thought back to the day when Potnia and her servants attended that event. Did they assume I was Yitz'chak's sister, not his wife? Who, pray tell, did they think was Yitz'chak's wife and the mother of his sons?

I glanced at Yitz'chak, but he would not meet my eyes as we were escorted toward a distant passageway. My throat tightened and breathing felt difficult. I longed for a drink of water to clear my throat. What had our lives come to? Yitz'chak had never, even in our strongest disagreements, confronted me with anger. But perhaps he secretly boiled with it. Perhaps he assigned me the role of sister in order to detach himself from me — to ensure that his rooms were disconnected from mine.

Perhaps he wanted nothing more to do with me as a wife. Was this lie his escape? Truth be told, our rift had widened over the years. We now, indeed, lived more like brother and sister. Was this his way of confronting the fissure? We should have talked about it long since, but neither of us wanted to make the first move.

What had Sarah felt as she walked down this same vivid hallway after Avraham declared she was his sister? And he did it twice, with two separate kings. That must have caused a rift between them. Did they find a way to bridge it? Who spoke first? My stomach churned and my thoughts spun while servants ushered us into luxurious, but separate, rooms in a gaudily painted wing of the Hitti palace.

Yitz'chak kept his distance in G'rar. Apparently, the sheep needed more attention than his 'sister'. And, because he and our sons travelled daily to tend the flocks on the hills outside the city, I was left alone most of the time. But I am not created to be enclosed within the walls of a palace, surrounded by elaborately painted snakes. I need physical labour to smooth the rough edges of my life. So, I sent a message to Yitz'chak and asked him to buy me a field.

 Due to the drought, land was being sold for a good price—especially the fields farther away from a water source. I purchased an unwanted piece of land situated on a little cliff above the river. My man-servants built chadoufs like the ones I saw on my travels years before. The amazing machines swung gourds of water up out of the river and onto the parched earth above it. King Avimelekh watched from his palace window as Shabar and I planted the seeds I rescued from my drought-stricken gardens. And D'vorah hired the children of our servants to work the chadoufs—which were positioned at intervals along the river. We set a shelter over each chadouf to shield the youngsters from the sun. And while they laboured, I entertained them with songs and stories I heard around the cig kofte trays of my childhood. We had such a merry time that all the P'lishtim children begged their mothers to allow them to help as well.

 In due course, we turned the drought into a festival of story and song that enriched the land and our souls. Potnia and Avimelekh often joined our merriment, and the earth rewarded us a hundredfold. After the harvest, my little helpers sat beside a trade route that passed by the palace, proudly peddling our produce to the caravans. The herbs and spices of G'rar soon became famous. And Yitz'chak became a very wealthy man.

೮ഠ೧ഇ

In the cool of the day, when secrets drift on the breeze, my soul is caressed with the scent of life and the Presence often hovers over my gardens. One evening in G'rar, while I was grieving lost understandings of bygone gardeners and longing to gather up the vanished mysteries, I breathed in the aroma of rosemary, thyme and all their sisters, immersed in the musical rustle of grass, dreaming of that first garden where God walked with Mother Havah.

 Suddenly, all was quiet and I looked up to see

what caused the change. A man was walking in the field a short distance away. Yitz'chak.

After all our time in G'rar, did he seek me out? Why would he do that? Wary of his motives and annoyed that he would interrupt my meditations, I decided not to make the first move. Father Adam and Mother Havah also met in their garden after the first great breach that changed everything. Who was the first to break their silence?

"I have come into my garden, my sister, my bride."

Did he say sister? Again? But he said it with that old familiar smile. It was self-depreciating and apologetic. It melted me a bit but I still had no words for him after all that had passed between us.

"A locked garden is my sister, my bride, an enclosed spring, a sealed fountain." His words were as sad as a mourning dove's call, an aching contrast to the joy we once knew. And it was true, I had shut him out. After all, if I was merely a sister to him, how could he expect me to do otherwise?

He walked to a chadouf perched on the cliff above the river, and lowered its pole to the water below. We watched the hollowed gourd on the end of the pole fill to the brim with dripping hope. Then he swung it over the bank and guided it toward the roots of a pomegranate sapling. When the gourd emptied in a gush of life, I remembered the pomegranates of our wedding day, and the seeds of love that were sown in my heart. They lay dormant now. Was he somehow watering them too?

"Your garden is full of choice fruits . . ." As he spoke, Yitz'chak walked between the rows of plants, tenderly caressing the leaves and calling my herbs by name. ". . . henna, nard, saffron, calamus . . ." He turned to face me, his eyes of green and gold were filled with longing. A lump formed in my throat and unexpected tears spilled over my cheeks to water my withered yearnings. He smiled. "You are my treasure, a garden fountain, a well of flowing water. I long to drink from its depths."

Stubbornly, I did my best to hold on to my anger. But I never could resist his sweet poetic tongue. I dried a sudden flow of tears with the edge of my veil. I had not realized that he knew the names of my beloved plants—or noticed their progress. I had never heard him honour my life's work and cannot tell you how much this validation drew me back to him. So, I adjusted my veil and looked into his eyes before releasing the last dregs of my pent-up spite—though laced with hope. "Oh that you were like a brother to me . . . if I found you outside, I would kiss you and no one would despise me."

He laughed in surprise at my sarcastic retort and decided it was an invitation. I smiled in confirmation and we met among the fragrant herbs to kiss in thirsty passion beneath the setting sun.

Our long drought was over.

But trouble was brewing.

ಸಿಂ

The court of G'rar was in a tumult. Yitz'chak and I were summoned to appear before the ivory throne of Avimelekh. Dressing with great care, I trembled with anticipation as rumors buzzed through the corridors like hornets. Women gathered impatiently between the red pillars, and officials stood uneasily around the throne. Trying not to stare at the agitated assembly or at the transparent hangings that billowed in the breeze like flowing streams, I focused my eyes on the man who sat on the throne.

Avimelekh called Yitz'chak into the room and bellowed, "So, she is your wife after all! I saw you from the palace window. You caressed her in the spice-field. How come you said, 'She is my sister'?"

Yitz'chak looked at me for support, but I shrugged. Was I supposed to respond to this discussion among men? Obviously, the Almighty is able to defend my honour without intervention—just as the One did for Sarah a generation ago—in that very room. After all, I too am a Woman of the Promise. I was given the Cloth of

Redemption. The price for my freedom was paid, and I was released from the bondage I was born into.

Yitz'chak glanced from the king to me and to the gathered court, his face as crimson as the painted pillars. "I . . . uh . . . because she is a beautiful woman, I thought . . ."

Avimelekh scorned Yitz'chak's feeble excuse with a dismissive gesture. Then he frowned at the court women who, highly entertained, were suppressing snickers. The king leaned forward and continued in a booming voice, "What is it that you have done to us? One of the people could easily have slept with your wife and you would have brought guilt on us."

Yitz'chak glanced from the king, to me, to the gathered court . . . "I . . . I thought I might lose my life on account of her."

Avimelekh crossed his arms and glowered at Yitz'chak but said an eloquent nothing. He ended the awkward silence by lifting his arms in a royal decree. "Whoever touches this man or his wife will surely die." Then he stormed from the room in a rage, his entourage flowing behind him.

We left G'rar soon after that, and I sold my spice-field to Potnia for a good profit. It was time to go anyway. Our flocks and herds were too large to share pasture with the P'lishtim—who were jealous of Yitz'chak's wealth. As we moved from place to place, they repeatedly stopped up the wells we dug to sustain our lives. Yitz'chak, true to his nature, wanted no war, and we were chased all the way back to Be'er-Sheva. The water there was plentiful again, so we rested at last from conflict with our neighbours. But as the years marched on, the conflict in our home was not as easily remedied.

THE BLESSING

In the light of the oil lamps, the large brass cig kofte tray shone like gold and Yitz'chak's voice rose authoritatively over the murmur of the supper gathering. "... then I heard the Voice say, 'I am the God of your father Avraham. Do not be afraid for I am with you and I will bless you and multiply your seed for the sake of Avraham my servant.'"

Yitz'chak was telling the story of his second visitation—the one that happened years before—after the battle for the wells—on the night we returned to Be'er-Sheva from G'rar. 'Esav's disrespectful wives whispered to each other behind their ringed fingers. Bangles jingled as they gestured and smirked beneath their veils. Judith and Basemath had no regard for the visitations of God. They wantonly displayed their Hitti idols in front of their tents and fed the ugly things with produce pilfered from my gardens. Irritating plumes of pagan incense continuously billowed in our courtyard—inflaming Yitz'chak's eyes. And though he was slowly going blind from the hovering smoke, he would not confront the women. But I knew their idol worship filled him with disgust.

"'Esav, did you hear that? The One has blessed me with two visitations. As my firstborn, you may receive a visitation as well. Prepare your heart for it." Ignoring the antics of his silly wives, 'Esav smiled dutifully and reached for another loaf of bread. Yitz'chak refused to see it, but I knew 'Esav was much too focused on the immediate needs of his flesh to prepare for a divine visitation.

Ya'akov's dark eyes smoldered in the firelight. He longed for a visitation. But Yitz'chak made it out to be the sole privilege of the firstborn. Avraham was not Terach's first born nor was Yitz'chak Avraham's—yet they were both visited. The urge to recount God's message to me was almost overwhelming. But I choked back the words I longed to say and went about the task of collecting cast-off nut shells while marveling again at my husband's ability to discount the words of Adonai—if they were given to me. The next day began much like any other. I guided Yitz'chak to the rugs in front of his tent and settled him against the cushions. "Your wine is here." I guided his hand to the tray beside him and placed his fingers on the earthen cup. Then I guided his hand again. "And here is a bowl of figs and nuts. I will be tending the breakfast fire with D'vorah. Call if you need anything." Yitz'chak dismissed me with a kiss and a smile.

"My son . . ." Yitz'chak called his summons out into the courtyard and both sons raised their heads, though both knew he called for 'Esav.

"Here I am," answered 'Esav.

Ya'akov wrapped his mantle around his shoulders and walked toward the corrals to soothe his father-wound with work. Heartsick, I pulled my attention back to the pot I stirred, and to the conversation between 'Esav and Yitz'chak.

"Look, I am old. I do not know the day of my death. So now, please take your weapons—your quiver arrows and your bow, and go out to the field and hunt me some game. Then prepare a delicious meal that I love and bring it to me that I may eat, so that my soul may bless you before I die."

Seething, I ladled out some pottage, 'Esav's sustenance for his day of hunting. Boiling with anger, I helped 'Esav to gather his equipment and ordered a servant to bring him a camel. I went back to stirring the pot of lentil stew, hoping to spend my fury on it. But like my fury, the stew bubbled up and overflowed. There was too much to fuel it. Yitz'chak, after all these years, still refused to acknowledge my visitation. He was determined to override the words of God, to ignore them, discount them, dismiss them. He was preparing at this moment, to give his patriarchal blessing to 'Esav and make him the head of our people. It was too much to bear.

D'vorah jumped back in surprise when I slammed down my stirring paddle, almost scalding her with a splash of hot stew. She laughed uncomfortably. "Rivkah!

I thought you left your impetuous childhood behind. Remember the poor camel-boy you . . ." I stormed off in the direction of the sheep pens before she could finish her sentence.

Ya'akov, searching the sheep for parasites, was lost in his labours. I watched him for a moment, a little regretful to peel him away from the pain-numbing task. He looked up when my shadow darkened his work. His eyes were full of hurt and questions.

"I heard your father speaking to your brother 'Esav, saying, 'Bring me game and prepare me a delicious meal that I may eat and bless you in Adonai's presence before my death.'"

We both knew what that would mean to our people. 'Esav was a hunter, a man of the wilderness. In this role, he supplied the clan with game and wild tales of adventure, but he would never be a successful shepherd or overseer. Our flocks and herds would suffer and dwindle under 'Esav's leadership. Yitz'chak had to be stopped. It was obvious to everyone but him that Ya'akov was the true chieftain among us. He cared tenderly for our herds. He was an able administrator. And according to the words of my visitation, he was chosen to rule.

"So now, my son, listen to my voice, to what I am commanding you. Go now to the flock and bring me two young goats so I may prepare a meal for your father that he may bless you before his death."

Ya'akov wiped his hands on his tunic and frowned. He carefully closed the paddock gate and secured it with a hemp rope. He was a deliberate man and usually made no hasty decisions. But now, he was sharp-eyed and calculating. I knew that look.

"Look, my brother 'Esav is hairy man, but I am a smooth man. Perhaps my father will touch me—he will know I am trying to trick him. And I will bring a curse upon myself, not a blessing."

"Let your curse be on me, my son. Just listen to me and go get me the kids." How could I know the consequence of those words?

Ya'akov chose well. The first goat was a gamey

little thing from a high mountain pasture. With the right seasoning, it would taste just like venison. The second was a kid with curly red hair. We laughed at its texture. It only took small preparations to thin out the red kid's pelt to resemble 'Esav's arms and chest. I hummed with excitement as I prepared Yitz'chak's favourite meal and baked a fresh loaf of caraway bread to go with it. How could I know that my deception would sour all our stomachs?

My heart leaped in triumph when I remembered that 'Esav had left a torn hunting tunic in my keeping. Repairing it was a task beneath the dignity of his wives so I had promised to mend it. The garment smelled like fields and the blood of the hunt. It would be convincing when Ya'akov wore it. We chuckled when he put on 'Esav's tunic and I bound the goat skins to his neck and hands. How could we know it would be the last time we shared laughter?

Ya'akov winked at me as I pulled back my tent flap to signal that the way was clear. As I watched my son enter Yitz'chak's tent to deceive his father, I thought I was serving God. I thought I was fulfilling the Promise. I thought I was putting a stop to Yitz'chak's disobedience. How could I know that Ya'akov would walk into decades of deceit that robbed him of his greatest joys?

A few hours later, 'Esav's cries were loud and bitter. The whole camp heard them. "Bless me too, my father!" From deep inside the tent, Yitz'chak murmured an answer that no one heard clearly. Then 'Esav's voice rose again. "Is this why he was named Ya'akov — since he has tricked me twice already? He took my birthright and now he has taken my blessing!"

The walls of Yitz'chak's tent shook with the violence of 'Esav's pounding fists. His screams filled the evening air, releasing bitter hatred. The side-wall of the tent bulged as 'Esav's body slid to the ground in grief. "Have you not saved a blessing for me? Do you have just one blessing, my father? Bless me too, my father!" Again, a softly murmured reply rumbled in the recesses of the dark tent.

A few moments later, 'Esav burst into the central

courtyard. Not even his wives could console him as he saddled his camel and rode into the desert.

※

The next day began like no other. Shabar shook me awake. "Rivkah! Rivkah, wake up." In groggy confusion, I opened my eyes and saw Shabar leaning over me in the half-light.

"Why do you sound like my mother?" I asked.

Shabar froze. She receded into the shadows of the tent—the purpose she came for unstated.

"Shabar," I said more gently, "I did not mean to frighten you. Why did you wake me?"

"I heard the wives talking. 'Esav plans to kill his brother. When the days of mourning Yitz'chak come to an end, he will kill Ya'akov."

I shivered in the draft from the open doorway. What had I done? What horror had I set in motion? We could lose everything if 'Esav went the way of Kayin. How could we recover from that grief? It had to be stopped. But if I tried to alert Yitz'chak, he would dismiss the information. He would never believe 'Esav capable of killing his brother. He would do nothing. An idea came to mind so I rose and pulled a day-robe over my head.

Hurrying to the corrals, I found Ya'akov giving the shepherds their orders for the day. I interrupted his work without apology, and took him aside to whisper the warning. "Your brother 'Esav is consoling himself with the thought of killing you. So now, my son, listen to my voice. Flee to Lavan my brother, in Harran. Stay with him a few days—until your brother's rage subsides, until your brother's rage turns away from you and he forgets what you have done to him. Then I will send for you and bring you back from there."

Ya'akov's coppery skin turned pale and he stopped breathing for a moment. "Ima, you know 'Esav will never forget. He will always be angry. If I leave now, I may never return."

I reached up to touch the face of my son.

"Ya'akov, child of my heart, if he kills you, your servants

will rise up against him. They love you and would take revenge. Why should I lose both sons in one day? I have a plan for your safety. I will talk to your father and make an arrangement. He will call for you shortly."

A brief time later, I led Yitz'chak to the rugs in front of his tent and settled him against the cushions. "Your wine is here." Guiding his hand to the tray beside him, I placed his fingers on the earthen cup. Again, I guided his hand. "Here is a bowl of figs and nuts." Then I hesitated, grieved to carry out yet another deception. Then I hardened myself against my conscience and gathered strength to fulfill my plan. Getting to my feet, I bustled around, angrily fluffing pillows and straightening rugs. When I felt the time was right, I burst out, "I am disgusted with life because of the daughters of Het that 'Esav has married. If Ya'akov takes a wife from the daughter of Het—what is life to me?"

Yitz'chak beckoned me to him and bid me sit down. He lifted his gnarled hand to my face and touched the tears I had somehow managed to press out. And Yitz'chak, whose heart was always able to ignore a tumult of words, was often softened by my tears. "Call Ya'akov to me," he said.

The walk to the corrals seemed to take forever, as did the walk back to Yitz'chak's tent with Ya'akov by my side. Ya'akov sat down on the rug at his father's feet, while I arranged a tray of fruit for them. Then Yitz'chak said, "Do not take a wife from the daughters of the Kena'ani. Get up. Go to Paddan-Aram, to the house of B'tu'el, your mother's father, and take a wife from there, from the daughters of Lavan your mother's brother."

Yitz'chak leaned forward and stared intently into the face of his second born. He placed his hand on Ya'akov's thigh and gathered strength for a proclamation. Startled by the intimate gesture, Ya'akov tensed, expecting a rebuke for stealing 'Esav's birthright and blessing. Instead, Yitz'chak declared, "May El Shaddai bless you, and make you fruitful and multiply you so that you will become an assembly of peoples. And may Adonai give you the blessing of Avraham, that you may take possession of the land of your sojourn."

My busy hands stopped, and my head bowed. Genuine tears blurred my vision this time. Yitz'chak, after being tricked into giving away the first-born's blessing, freely gave Ya'akov the sacred blessing of Avraham — the possession of the land — the blessing 'Esav had pleaded for. In doing so, though there was no acknowledgment that I had been right all along, Yitz'chak finally bowed to the message of my visitation. Yitz'chak's repentance would now allow Ya'akov to rule our people. Overwhelmed, I collapsed to the ground in sorrow — for my husband, for my sons, and for myself. This was no victory. We were all broken by our sin and would scatter on bitter winds.

※※

Preparation for Ya'akov's departure was accompanied by a thin facade of feasting and song. The day before, 'Esav had packed up his wives and tents and I knew he would not return. If anyone thought it strange that both the brothers were leaving, no one said anything. Through one day's folly I lost both my sons — though not in death — a small mercy.

The next day I watched Ya'akov set out for Paddan-Aram. In his broken state he refused the company of servants or a camel train. He insisted on making the journey alone, wanting only solitude for companionship.

THE GARDEN

After Ya'akov's departure, I retreated to my garden in hopes that labour would soothe my anguished soul. Instead, my thoughts circled like angry crows—accusing and accusing. My hoe chopped down on tenacious weeds that grew up between the plants. And though I vented my anger on them, I really wanted to hack at myself and Yitz'chak for the damage our drive for supremacy did to our sons.

While wiping sweat from my brow with the edge of my veil, I looked toward the northern horizon. Ya'akov was no longer visible in the distance. Before he left, I gave him my most precious possession and he laid The Cloth of Redemption at the bottom of his pack before kissing me farewell.

After completing this final task for my son, many questions plagued me. Who would be the next Woman of the Promise? What price would be paid for her redemption? What kind of wife would a daughter of Lavan be? What kind of husband would Ya'akov be? Would the competition for God's favour continue into the next generation? Yitz'chak and I had not set a good example.

I pulled on a stubborn weed and cursed Yitz'chak's resistance to the words of my visitation. He had fallen into Father Adam's error when he insisted on ruling over me. If a husband denies his wife equality, the painful root of the wound runs deep. I threw the weed on the refuse pile in disgust—at myself. I had walked Mother Havah's path. When a wife demands equality, her husband feels diminished and discord grows. Yitz'chak and I wasted years, each insisting on the recognition of our worth. And now I knew, beyond a doubt, that victory achieved through bitter rivalry holds no satisfaction.

When did the noxious weed of competition

germinate in my soul? The pain of being devalued was sown in childhood, but the plant would have withered and died if not watered by my pride. It was only when we lost both sons that I saw what we had done.

Attacking another weedy growth, I bent and pulled at the stubborn root. Sweat trickled down my back and my hands were stripped raw by thorns. It was not this way in the beginning. We are created for the Garden of God — not for these aching struggles. When Mother Havah reached for that fateful fruit in her haste to gain its knowledge first, did she know what she would set in motion? Would it ever be possible, as daughters of Havah, to make peace with the result of our grasping? Could we find forgiveness for what we set in motion? Doubled over in agony, I sank to my knees, pleading for mercy.

Suddenly, the earth began to spin and the sky flashed brass. Breath laboured in my chest and my heart raced. I fell to the ground on my face, powerless over my limbs. My nose pressed against the hot earth and I dared not look up. Knowing I deserved to die in my wickedness I lay there — waiting for the judgment of the Holy One.

But a Presence, deep and vast, descended on the garden. Bearing no malice, it flowed over and around me like a nourishing flood — and I knew. I knew the One had seen my sorrow, graciously accepted my repentance, and restored my peace. It was the bright peace of a child on her abba's knee. And as I relaxed into it, my tears flowed onto the earth, cleansing the wounds of my heart.

I cannot tell you how I knew I was forgiven, nor how I knew the Creator would someday restore us to an Eternal Garden — where Yitz'chak and I would live in harmony, equals in every way, as Havah and Adam were in the very beginning. And in that sacred moment, I cannot tell you how I knew that cineraria leaves would heal Yitz'chak's eyes.

"Rivkah?" D'vorah's voice was soft and distant.

With a great effort I opened my eyes and peered at her. Concerned, her hand stretched out to help me up. Then a memory triggered and I had to know.

"D'vorah, why does Shabar's voice sound like my mother's? Why do her eyes and the tilt of her chin remind me so much of her?"

D'vorah sighed and looked like she would turn away, then she reconsidered. "Shabar did not want you to know. She swore us to silence. She was grateful for her rescue and wanted to serve you. She was afraid that you would make her an equal and not let her serve in the same way—once you knew."

"Once I knew what, D'vorah?"

"Once you knew she is your mother's daughter, your half-sister, conceived in the House of Joys."

I gasped, remembering closeted conversations between my parents, arguments about casting off a child, of leaving her in slavery. I stared at D'vorah in shock. Shabar was the child of those shadows. Shabar was conceived at the ritual that every newly married woman must perform. The tall stranger threw coins into Ima's lap and she cried for days. Shabar. My sister. I knew she had suffered before I found her but I had no idea . . .

As if reading my thoughts, D'vorah said, "Because your father refused to admit her into your family, she became a slave in the Ziggurat and gave sexual services to men who worshiped there. She was forced to service your brother and father even though the priests knew who she was."

"My sister! My Shabar!"

"Yes. She knows her rightful place in the family but wants to take the role of a servant—in gratitude for her redemption."

I whirled away from D'vorah and ran from the garden, determined to find Shabar. From that day on, the dark serpents of secret sin would shrivel in the light and mysteries would die. From now on we would live in truth while we walked the earth.

And, in a profound way, Shabar had shown me how to shoulder injustice with grace. I also determined to rest in the knowledge of who I am—a Woman of the Promise, chosen by God, a treasured child on her father's lap. And while resting in that knowledge, I too would be able to respond with acts of service. I too would take the lower place in gratitude to the One who redeemed me.

Leaning on his staff, Yitz'chak made his hesitant way to the edge of the garden. He heard me calling for Shabar and ran in urgent stumbling steps to intercept me on the path. Clothed with the setting sun, his glowing face was dressed in concern. Did he know the secret was revealed? How did he know? D'vorah was behind me in the garden. She had no time to give him a message of any kind. Only she and I and the Almighty One knew the secret was out. Oh. The Almighty knew.

Yitz'chak threw down his staff and opened his arms. Running into them, I soaked his robe with tears. "Yitz'chak, I have sinned against Heaven and against you. I am not worthy to be called your wife. From this day on, I will lay myself at your feet. I have no need to be your equal. I will be your servant, heart and soul. Shabar has shown the way."

Yitz'chak gathered me to him and I guided him home while he called out to D'vorah and Shabar, "Bring a lamb from the field and prepare a feast! From this day forward we will put away strife and competition. From this day forward we will live in Heaven's harmony. From this day forward we will prepare for the time when all will live as equals in the beautiful Garden of God."

Philippians 2:6,7
[Yeshua], though existing in the form of God, did not consider being equal to God a thing to be grasped. But he emptied himself—taking on the form of a slave.

Galatians 3:26-29
For you are all children of God through trusting Messiah Yeshua. For all of you who were immersed in Messiah . . . there is neither Jew nor Greek, there is neither slave nor free, there is neither male nor female—for you are all one in Messiah Yeshua.

Isaiah 51:3
For Adonai will comfort Zion, will comfort all her waste places, will make her wilderness like 'Eden, her desert like the garden of Adonai. Joy and gladness will be found in her, thanksgiving and a sound of melody.

Matthew 5:7
Blessed are the merciful, for they shall be shown mercy.

Le'ah

Woe to one who quarrels with their Maker, like a pot among the pots of the earth! Shall the clay say to the potter, "What have you made?

Isaiah 45:9

LE'AH

FAMILY

"Le'ah! Hide this somewhere."

"What is it, Rachel?"

"It is Shmuel's precious belt, the one he got from the traders. Hide it. Quick." I heard the snap of the door-curtain as she fled.

A few moments later it opened again, letting in a draft of air. "Le'ah. Have you seen Rachel? She took my belt."

"Shmuel. What are you doing in my kumbet? You know it is forbidden to men."

"I am looking for my belt. That pest, Rachel, stole it."

"Shmuel! I can hear you rummaging in my belongings. What will Father say when he finds out you have been in my room?"

"I know the belt is here. Rachel always goes to you for help. Where is it? Get up and let me look under your rug."

"Uh . . . but . . . the rug is unclean, brother. I have been hit by the weapon. You dare not touch a rug defiled by my monthly blood."

I could not see his expression but I felt his mortification as my brother backed away. I struggled to keep the smirk off my face. Young men are so easily foiled by womanly mysteries.

That night we laughed around the cig kofte tray when Rachel and I told the story to Bilhah and Zilpah. Ours was a merry home, full of pranks and mischief.

We eventually returned Shmuel's belt, tied around the neck of his favourite donkey. We chased it into our brothers' kumbet and the rascal dropped a few unsavoury deposits on the floor before he was discovered.

A day later, Rachel's best veil went missing and was found flying from the rooftop like a banner. My sisters and I retrieved it by standing on each other's shoulders. Rachel stood on mine, Zilpah on hers, and tiny Bilhah stood on top, stretching as far as she could to catch the flapping cloth. She barely managed to grab it before we toppled to the ground in gales of laughter — until Abba intervened.

"Le'ah, get back to your pottery wheel. With the harvest near, we need more grain jars. Rachel, what are you doing rolling around with your sisters like so many puppies? Go take the sheep to the well. And hurry. If those sons of Hamar get there first, my sheep will be drinking bottom sludge again. Bilhah and Zilpah, surely you have something better to do. I did not birth girls so they could loll around like so many Egyptian princesses."

Giggling, we dusted each other off and went our separate ways.

෨෬

My dim eyesight forces me to recognize people by their familiar odors. For example, my brother Shmuel smells like the salted fish he buys from passing traders. Brother Nahor reeks like a swamp weed. My half-sister Zilpah smells like clean linen. Maybe it has to do with her long hours at the loom. Little half-sister Bilhah's scent is of the herbs she tends in the garden that Aunt Rivkah abandoned when she married Yitz'chak. And my sister Rachel? She came back from the well that day, smelling as usual, like wool and milk — and prattling on about an encounter she had there.

"Le'ah, I met a man at the well. He is so strong that he moved the cover-stone all by himself. And he gave our flock a drink before the other shepherds could push me away. He knows much about sheep and saw right off that our flock suffers with tick fever. He says he knows a cure. And Le'ah, he is our kinsman, the son of Rivkah and Yitz'chak. Can you believe it?"

"Is he handsome? Young? Unmarried?"

"Are you wanting a husband, Le'ah? Shall I describe him to you? Shall I begin with how he smells? Or should I tell you about his eyes of green and gold or how soft his kisses are..."

"He kissed you?"

"Of course, he did. He is a kinsman so he kissed me. It was very chaste even though he cried when he did it. He is not young but he is not married. Maybe he is the man for you."

"Yes, if he is truly as ancient as you say, and his eyesight is failing like his father's, perhaps he will consider me."

"O Le'ah, stop joking. There is nothing wrong with you. You are beautiful. Abba is with him now. I wonder what they are talking about. If his father is as rich as they say, I wonder why he came all the way here without an entourage. Do you suppose he committed a crime or is fleeing a jealous husband or...?"

"All your wondering will not get the evening fire started and I am catching a deathly chill while you babble on. I have gathered the dung into a pile, will you strike the flint? Zilpah is on her way with the stew pot and needs a fire to cook on. Bilhah! Bring our shawls when you come. The night air is cool."

I stood in the darkening courtyard, reflecting on Rachel's news. A marriageable kinsman showing up on our doorstep was truly astonishing, but it would probably not change my life a great deal. Like other potential suitors, he would take one look at my squinty eyes and move on to other prospects. My defect was considered a liability to the running of a home, and the fear of passing it on to my offspring was doubly off-putting. So, I pushed matrimonial dreams aside and moved toward my sisters to joined their banter.

※

My thoughts whirled round and round with the rhythm of my pottery wheel. Sisters, brothers, our new lodger and the approaching bridal auction spun around my mind. Because of my eyes, I do not exactly know what my sisters look like. Rachel's skin is soft as silk and her hair looks to me like ripples of honey. I like to stroke it when we tell stories around the fire. Zilpah's skin is pale like our father's and she is as tall as an obelisk. They say her silky hair is the colour of ripe barley. Perhaps her mother was from the north. Bilhah's limbs are delicate as a gazelle's and as dark as Abba's mahogany walking stick. Her hair, when I comb it, is impossibly full of kinks and coils. We think her mother came from the lands of the south, below Egypt. Both Bilhah and Zilpah were purchased from the Ziggurat in Harran. They are a result of Abba's worship practices among the sacred prostitutes. When Mother died, Abba brought the little girls home and threw them into our room, saying something about not wanting to make his father's mistakes. They are our sisters, but they are slaves, bought by Abba to serve me and Rachel.

With satisfying roundness, the contours of a new grain jar emerge upon my pottery wheel. Soon I will need to ask someone if there are any flaws my fingers missed. Will Ya'akov admire my skill enough to save me from the bridal auction? Mysteriously, despite Yitz'chak's legendary wealth, Ya'akov came to us with no possessions at all—no bride-price to secure a wife.

While this disqualifies him to seek the hand of beautiful and perfectly formed Rachel, perhaps Abba will allow Ya'akov to look in my direction. But, will Ya'akov's impeccable bloodline be enough on its own, to influence my greedy father? Probably not. So, off to the bridal auction it is.

BRIDAL AUCTION

"In our tradition the eldest daughter always marries first. Though, who will have you is a mystery. Be sure to wrap your veil low upon your forehead to hide your weak eyes. And stand up straight. Perhaps someone equally as blind will pay the bride-price."

My sisters squealed with laughter while I exaggerated the nasal voice of our father. Then I snatched up Rachel's veil and wrapped it tightly around my body, covering my eyes completely and accentuating every curve below that. "Do you think this will fool the auctioneer or my future husband?" I tried to walk around in the tightly wound cloth but tripped on the edge of a rug and fell headlong into the laps of Bilhah and Zilpah who covered me with laughter and kisses.

"Le'ah, who could resist your noble nose and pomegranate breasts and the graceful way you walk?" they exclaimed. We dissolved again into helpless mirth but Rachel stood in the shadows of the kumbet and I could not tell what she thought. She had been distant since our kinsman arrived. I had not seen much of him, but Rachel, a shepherdess, spent long hours with Ya'akov and the sheep. A flash of light penetrated the room and I heard the door-cloth snap against the wall as she left.

When morning came, I washed myself in preparation for the auction. Then Zilpah coiled my heavy hair into an elaborate arrangement that she could only wish for. "As smooth and soft as a raven's wing," she sighed. "Look how it shines—like obsidian in the sun."

Bilhah smoothed out the creases on my gown. As a slave, she would never have an embroidered dress like mine and I ached for her. What did I care for embroidery I could not see? "I feel like a lamb prepared for sacrifice," I joked. But no one else laughed.

It was not a happy time as Abba and I mounted

camels at dawn. If a man bought me at the auction, I would immediately go to the house of my new family. Would I ever see my sisters again? I straightened in the saddle and stifled sad thoughts as I breathed in the familiar aroma of milk and wool drifting toward me. Was Rachel coming to see me off? I understood why she had not helped me dress. I had cared for her like a mother since ours died while birthing her. We had been inseparable until the last few weeks — and the coming of Ya'akov.

"Abba, I would speak with you for a moment."

"Not now Rachel. We are ready to go. Do you want the auction to begin without us? What hope would Le'ah have then?"

"Please Abba, I need to ask you something. It is urgent. It will only take a moment. It involves a money-matter." At those two magic words, money-matter, Father dismounted and disappeared into his kumbet with Rachel.

So, we waited while the rising sun warmed the earth, and flies buzzed around my tender eyes, and my camel spit a gob of gore onto a servant's clean turban — making him say unmentionable things.

When they finally emerged from the kumbet into the glaring light of mid-morning, Father ordered me, without explanation, to dismount my camel. Then he told everyone to get back to work. "I do not run a household that is free loll around like so many lazy Yishma'elites," he said.

Although the urgent 'money-matter' altered the course of my life, no amount of pleading, cajoling, bribery, or threats would drag the full content of the conversation from Rachel. All she would say is, "I could not bear for you to leave us Le'ah. I reminded Abba of how much money he would forfeit if he could not sell your pots in the markets of Harran. I said another suitor should be found who will bring commerce into our family instead of taking it away."

I am sure it was the partial truth, but I knew there was more. If I pressed Rachel, would I find out that Abba thought he might have to pay a man to take me as a wife? Some humiliations are hard to face so I left them to their secrets.

BETROTHAL

As she bent down to whisper the news, Zilpah's corn silk hair brushed my forehead. "Ya'akov is in negotiations with Father. Are they having betrothal-talks?"

Bilhah's giggle from the direction of the grinding-stone interrupted her rhythmic work, but I would not give my sisters the satisfaction of even a tiny pause in my labour, so the pottery wheel kept spinning while I answered. "Do you know our father? Is he not the same man who can sell sand to an Egyptian and make a profit? Is he not the same man who was talked out of sending me to the bridal auction so he could continue selling my pots? Will he now make marriage arrangements with Ya'akov who came to us with no bride-gift at all? What was Uncle Yitz'chak thinking? He must be in his dotage to believe that Abba would give his son a wife without the proper financial transactions."

A wave of milky warmth announced Rachel's arrival. After dropping a kiss on the top of my head she stooped to examine my new pot for tiny flaws my eyes might miss. "And what do you suppose Abba would give Ya'akov for a dowry?" she asked. "Is our father not the same man who rushed Aunt Rivkah into the world with only one handmaid to her name? He did not part with much of a dowry that time! And none of the proper rituals were held. Is it any wonder that Rivkah struggled to bear a child? When I get married, I will insist that all the fertility rights be carried out — starting with the betrothal ceremonies. Abba cannot treat us like so many worthless slave girls."

There was a quick intake of breath as Rachel realized what she had said. Bilhah's grinding wheel stopped. Zilpah's clacking loom stilled. "Come now girls," I said, "We know how things stand in our kumbet. We are equals here. Lavan will give all his daughters exactly the same dowry. Absolutely nothing!"

Tension dissolved into laughter and we went back to our tasks while the mysterious negotiations in Lavan's kumbet continued. I tried to talk myself out of the notion that I was the bride under consideration, but hope does not die easily. After all, as the oldest daughter, I should marry first. And, my pottery was gaining a decent reputation in local markets. And, according to my sisters, I was not hopelessly ugly.

Next morning, braying donkeys announced the dawn and I rolled over to touch the little shoulder on the next pallet. "Bilhah. It is your turn to feed them. Please get up and make that racket stop!" Then I joined the stretches and yawns of my sisters as we willed our bodies to face an uncertain day. One by one we pulled our day-robes over our heads, combed our hair, and walked toward our morning tasks.

We knew, without question, that Abba would not make any kind of announcement until we sat around the cig kofte tray that evening. All that day, my thoughts spun around like my pottery wheel. Would this be the day of my betrothal? Surely it would. Abba would arrange my marriage first—especially since Ya'akov had no bride-price and Rachel could fetch a good one at the auction.

An order came for a fresh clay tablet to be delivered to Abba's tent, and I knew it would be used for writing up a marriage contract. What kind of husband would Ya'akov be? I had not spoken more than two words to him since his arrival. I closed my eyes and remembered his scent . . . the fresh meadows of spring. I liked it. It spoke of plenty and beauty. Would he find me beautiful when I shed my robe on our wedding night? Embarrassed by my thoughts, I bent my head to my work.

As daylight dimmed, the spicy aroma of lentil soup and pungent cheese permeated the air. A fire blazed in our midst, illuminating a circle of waiting kindred. Ale cups clicked softly as Zilpah filled them with her wooden ladle. I gratefully accepted my portion and slid my hands around the circle of clay. It was good to have somewhere to put my hands. They had taken on a life of their own, touching my hair, smoothing my robe, wandering over my face, and drumming the ground before me. Taut with tension, we all jumped when Abba and Ya'akov entered the light of the fire. I could not see their faces but their bodies radiated victory. Family resemblance was apparent in their stance.

I strained to see if Ya'akov held the fresh clay tablet I made that day. Was it newly covered with the sharp indentations of a cuneiform contract? With a typical showy flourish, Abba removed his cylindrical silver seal from where it hung on a leather thong around his neck. It flashed in the firelight at the edge of my vision.

"We are gathered here to sign a marriage contract between the house of Ya'akov, son of Yitz'chak, son of Avraham, son of Terach—and the house of Lavan, son of B'tuel, son of Nachor, son of Terach," said Abba.

Then Ya'akov spoke confidently to the crowd. "I, Ya'akov, son of Yitz'chak, son of Avraham, son of Terach, pledge a bride-price of seven years labour for the daughter of Lavan, son of B'tuel, son of Nachor, son of Terach."

I hoped my face did not display my cynicism. Abba drove a hard bargain. Seven years labour was nothing to sneeze at. Would the seven years be served before the marriage took place? That would give me sufficient time to get to know my betrothed. But what on earth would my tight-fisted father give up as a dowry? The dung fire crackled and snapped as we listened with bated breath.

"I, Lavan, son of B'tuel, son of Nachor, son of Terach, pledge a dowry to Ya'akov, son of Yitz'chak, son of Avraham, son of Terach. I pledge to transfer the ownership of Bilhah my slave, as a dowry and legal handmaid of my daughter Rachel."

Rachel? Did he say Rachel? Did he pledge Bilhah as Rachel's dowry? Did he go against all tradition and arrange Rachel's marriage before mine? I could not hide the shock on my face and sat in a daze as I heard the squelch of Father's seal close the contract. I barely registered hearing Rachel go forward to kiss Father's hands and then Ya'akov's. I blocked out the sound of the golden bracelets Ya'akov slid onto Rachel's wrist. I refused to imagine the red woollen cord of unity that bound them together. And for once, I was glad I could not see the faces of my kindred as I went through the motions of eating the red lentil soup that would guarantee Rachel's fertility. As soon as I could, I backed out of the fire circle and escaped to the cool darkness of my kumbet. Humiliated and devastated, I wanted to be alone. But not much later, I heard the door-curtain snap against the kumbet wall.

"I am so sorry Le'ah," whispered Rachel. "I am so sorry, but Ya'akov loves me and I love him." She stroked my hair as I lay facing the wall, my arms wound around my tucked-up limbs—trying to reach into my fetal past for comfort.

"You should have let me go to the auction," I said.

She curled her wool-scented body around mine and sweet milky tears dripped down the back of my neck. "I could not live without you Le'ah. If I let you go to a new family, I would never see you again. I love Ya'akov but I am afraid of him too. He is so serious about everything. I need your laughter to balance my days. Who would help me play tricks on our brothers?"

"Ya'akov would do just fine in that role," I said. "The two of you are good at hatching plots while in the fields with the sheep."

She went absolutely still. Then, finally, she spoke. "I could not bear to let you go so I convinced Abba to keep you here. We will find you a husband, Le'ah. I promise."

I snorted in disbelief. "And exactly how will you do that? How many times in a person's lifetime does a man wander into our midst looking for a wife? And even if it should happen again, the suitor will take one look at me—the unmarried older sister, blind as a mole and covered in clay—then he will jump into the well, pulling the cover-stone over the opening."

Rachel tried to hold it in, but she started to laugh. Her breath hit the back of my neck with tiny blasts of warm air. I could not help it either. My body began to shake with mirth at the thought of the unfortunate man cowering in the depths of the well trying to escape me. *Both the mythical suitor and I, would eventually have to face the world as it is,* I thought. *At least, I will have the love of my sisters to cushion the crash of my dreams.*

WAITING

Seven years flew by while Ya'akov worked off Rachel's bride-price. When Shmuel and Nahor came of age they both found suitable brides at the auction. Shmuel's wife is a pepper-scented woman who spits fire at him if he crosses her. Nahor's wife smells like a spring of water and has given him three children already. The brothers are so busy with their wives that they now pay us little attention. And every year they move their camps farther from home to search out better pastureland.

Zilpah is still calm and serene but I feel a sadness seeping out of her when we talk about Rachel's wedding. In those times she sits close to me and gathers her long legs into her arms, so I hug her in solidarity. Little Bilhah seems unaffected while she bounces around like a spring kid, serving us with joy. I wonder if she will change when her monthly bleeding begins. Will she, like Zilpah, long for a husband and children? I know I do.

Rachel has changed the most. She is now as tall as me and her breasts have rounded into the firm pomegranate shape so typical in our family. She was finally hit by the weapon last month. At last, she is truly ready for marriage, coming of age just in time. She loves Ya'akov like a daughter loves a kind and doting abba — the one we never had. But I wonder if she is ready for the other kind of love. I know Ya'akov is. I smell his musk when Rachel is near him.

As for me, I spin through the years like my potter's wheel. The bridal auction comes and goes but Rachel makes it clear she does not want me to leave home — so I humour her. Maybe when Rachel is married, I will look to my own future. In the meantime, there is a wedding to plan and the arrangements have fallen to me.

Rachel's wedding veil is causing most of the tension. Since her monthly bleed began, she is moodier than she used to be and nothing seems to satisfy. Zilpah added red embroidery to the beautiful piece of linen that our mother wore as a bride, but that was not enough. Apparently, the whole veil needs to be red to meet the requirements of the all-important fertility rites. So, we bought a large sack of those insects that make their home in the scrubby oaks of Mount Ararat. We crushed up the disgusting things and boiled them in water along with a white cloth. But the deep crimson result was far too itchy for our princess. In frustration, I left her in tears and did something uncharacteristic.

Striding out of the courtyard, I headed toward the pens where Ya'akov and the hired men were checking the sheep for tics. I could tell Ya'akov apart from the others by the compassionate way he bent over the ewes, and by the smell of the fields that wafted off him as he exerted himself.

"Brother-in-law, I am sorry to bring you the troubles of women. But Rachel is beside herself with anxiety over her wedding veil. Our mother's veil does not suit her fancy because it is not red. Furthermore, linen is stiff and wool is itchy. And apparently, her veil must be light enough to flow around her like a breeze. You know Father forbids his women to go into Harran, and I would never trust my brothers with such a task, but is it possible for you to go to the city on market day and search for such a wonder?" It was the longest speech I had ever made to my sister's betrothed.

Ya'akov chuckled and straightened his back. "My mother gave me her wedding veil before I left Hevron. I think it will do quite nicely," She bid me give it to the one I would marry and I have been looking for the right moment. I will take it to Rachel this evening."

"No. You cannot. She is unclean. Her moon-flow is upon her and no man can go near her without being defiled. Her bleeding will stop in a few days and you can give it to her then. But alas, I will not be alive to welcome you to our doorway. I will be lying in my grave, slain by the effort of trying to fulfill all Rachel's wedding demands." The laughter of Ya'akov and the hirelings followed me as I walked back to the kumbet.

"Le'ah!"

I had never heard Ya'akov speak my name and

it stopped me mid-step. My heart fluttered wildly as I pushed aside the desire to hear him speak it again. I waited for him to continue.

"I will go to fetch the veil. I know well the risk of delaying her gratification." I could hear a smile in his voice. "But first, I need time to wash the sheep-grime off my hands. I would not dare to soil the veil."

Regaining my composure, I turned to face in his direction. "Surely, there is no need to keep Rachel waiting. I will send Bilhah to your kumbet. Show her where the veil is and she will handle it for you." He laughed again and walked toward his kumbet while I called for Bilhah.

As I waited in the courtyard for Bilhah to emerge from Ya'akov's kumbet, that contrary god Enlil sent one of his hot winds to twist my robe around my legs. So, I prayed to Gala (god of the sun) to keep Enlil and Enki (the rain gods) far away for another week. We did not want one of their famous storms to make an appearance at the wedding. Rachel was not the only contrary force I had to appease in my efforts to plan the event.

While wrestling with my robes, Bilhah's herbal essence floated to me from the direction of Ya'akov's kumbet and came to a stop in front of me. I looked up and made out the shape of a pale bundle in her arms. Placing the parcel in my hands, she knelt at my feet. Then she bent, with her face to the ground in a posture of homage. Squatting down to observe her better, I felt her forehead. Was she feeling unwell? What on earth possessed her to bow like that? I did not notice Ya'akov's presence until the wind shifted direction and his meadow-scent wafted toward me.

"You hold The Cloth of Redemption in your hands," he said.

Taken aback I looked toward him and rose to my feet. "The what? Is it red? Will it flow around her like a river? I fear to show it to Rachel if it does not."

"Open the bindings and judge for yourself."

Untying the string that bound the parcel, I folded back the wrapping and touched the newly exposed cloth. I drew in my breath. I had never felt anything like it—so cool and smooth—like a mountain spring.

I glanced questioningly at Ya'akov while Bilhah rose to her feet. Stepping forward, she helped me unfurl the cloth. Then a puff of wind snatched it from my hand. Flashing red and silver in the sun, it bubbled through my fingers. Taking on a life of its own it rose up to the heavens and the bells on its fringe sang a song of worship. Had I not anchored it in my grasp it would have escaped into the fields. My brother's wives paused their chores to clap with delight. Zilpah, entranced, left her weaving and ran to join me.

"It came to Egypt long ago as a gift for queen Neferu," said Ya'akov. "Before she died, she bid her servant to keep watch for a woman who would one day be redeemed from the court of the pharaoh. The price was paid by the pharaoh himself and Sarah was redeemed."

Gathering the cloth in from the sky, Bilhah, Zilpah, and I folded its great length into the linen casing. I turned back toward Ya'akov, sensing he had more to say. "It was given to my mother when she was redeemed from the house of B'tuel. It was her wedding veil. When I left home, she bid me to give it as a wedding garment—to the woman who would be redeemed to marry me."

For the first time in my life, I had no response. So, I turned and walked across the courtyard to tell Rachel the story. She loved the veil, but I never felt she appreciated its history.

NUPTIALS

Musicians were booked and due to arrive. We had been preparing the feast for a week. Zilpah made all the traditional delicacies to feed the crowd of kinsman and neighbours who travelled to join us. Bilhah baked mountains of bread and went through the fields picking flowers to arranging in the clay pots I created for that purpose.

Shmuel and Nahor were showing guests to their quarters and entertaining early arrivals. Would we have room for all of them? Some guests would need to stay in the livestock shelters. Ya'akov assured us the camels and donkeys would be fine hobbled in the sheep pasture for a while. My brother's wives were busy putting final touches on the garments Rachel would wear under her veil. I sent Rachel to check on them and fretted over a hundred more details. Had I forgotten anything?

Next morning, our quiet kumbet village exploded with sounds and smells. The aroma of roasting lamb and spicy wedding soup filled the air. Wine and beer flowed freely. Musicians and drummers pounded out rhythms. Even I got caught up in the dance as we sang the amorous songs of Inanna, the goddess of fertility.

Rachel was readied for the day, fully veiled, as blind as me. She needed guidance to navigate the crowded courtyard. If my brothers played their role well, they would guard her purity in her last few hours as a virgin—not letting her out of their sight for a moment. But where were they? Where was Rachel?

Abba strutted around like a rooster. You would think he had paid for the whole feast. I was thankful, for Rachel's sake, that Ya'akov had seven years to save up for the extravaganza. The long wait also provided Yitz'chak time to send a caravan of bridal gifts for us all. Even Zilpah and Bilhah were dressed in beautiful Egyptian linen. Zilpah floated like a cloud as she went about her tasks, but Bilhah hiked her expensive gown around her little brown stick legs so she could run more easily to complete her errands. Would she ever grow up? I hoped not.

"Le'ah."

Why did Nahor call for me? Did the dolmas burn? I told Bilhah to keep a watch on them. Did she get distracted?

"Le'ah. Over here."

I stood staring in the direction of Nahor's voice, hesitating. Then suddenly, I was pushed from behind and guided roughly toward the kumbets. "Nahor, what is wrong? Where are you taking me? Why have you left Rachel's side?"

"She is with Shmuel and Father. They told me to come get you."

"Very mysterious, Are you up to your old tricks? Let me go. I need to supervise the feast."

I was led to the prayer room of my father's kumbet, a room I avoided since the day I heard snakes scuttering under the door-cloth. It was dark, and smelled of sour ale. I gagged and tried to determine how many of us were crowded into the tiny space. Nahor stayed outside by the door, and the fishy smell of Shmuel brushed past me to join him. The dusty odor of my father filled the space to my left, and Rachel's warm woollen scent was on my right.

"What is happening? What is this about? I need to be out in the courtyard with the guests. There is a lot of drinking. Things could get out of control."

They said nothing. They just stood there. Finally, Father spoke. "Rachel, give your veil to your sister."

The silver bells tinkled as Rachel unwound the fluid cloth. "What are you saying Abba?" I asked.

"You will marry Ya'akov in place of Rachel. He is drinking enough wine and ale that he will not know it is you. He will see the veil and think it is Rachel. Do this quickly. He has gone to the latrine but will re-enter the feast soon."

"He will know it is me. I smell different from Rachel. A man like Ya'akov will not be fooled."

"I brought some wool residue to rub into your skin, Le'ah." Rachel's voice was tight with tears. I slept in my undergarments for a week so you will smell like me when you put them on. And our bodies are the same size now, so are our breasts." Then she began to sob.

"Enough talk!" said father. "Exchange your garments and get back to the feast. We have no time to stand around haggling, like so many market traders." Then Father stalked out of the room.

Shocked to silence, I waited a moment before speaking. "Was this your idea Rachel?"

"I planned it with Abba long ago so you would not need to go to the auction. He was overjoyed to keep earning profits from your pottery, and he will get two bride-prices eventually — for I will marry Ya'akov in time. We will be sister-wives, never to be parted." She recited this as if from memory, her voice vacant of joy.

My mind was numb but I should have protested when she peeled off my robes and massaged greasy wool residue into my skin. I should have prevented her as she helped me into her clothes and wound the jingling veil around my body. I should have run out the door before the wedding garments bound me, covering everything, even my face. But I stood in stunned silence, breathing in an ancient desert scents and a faded hint of almond blossoms. Somewhere in my heart, I think I did want to marry Ya'akov — but not that way.

"Are you finished? We have no time to wait around for lengthy rituals, like so many temple worshipers."

The open door-cloth let in the jumbled odors of my male relatives. A firm hand grabbed my right wrist, another clasped my left. Before I had time to blink, I was ushered into the uproar of the wedding feast. The sun had set while we were in the prayer room and the crowd was unruly. I smelled wine-soaked breath and felt the leers. Dancers swirled around me, calling for the consummation, calling for Ya'akov. Laughter and lewd hooting mounted in volume as the guests chanted for the bridegroom to join me. Where was he? I needed to tell him what was going on. Perhaps he could stop the madness before we all succumbed to it.

Suddenly he was there, his familiar scent mingling with the wine and ale he drank. I tried to talk to him but the revelers drowned us out. He put his arm around me and tenderly drew me to him. Placing his mouth near my veiled ear he said, "Don't be afraid my lamb, I will be gentle tonight and I will care for you the rest of my days."

My brothers blessed my temples with frankincense, and declared my purity to the crowd. Ya'akov anointed my hands with myrrh to pledge his life-long love. My soul recoiled at the deception and I leaned toward Ya'akov in panic—trying to reach his ear. He thought I was leaning in to embrace him and held me closer, whispering endearments meant for Rachel.

Why was I speechless while my eyes poured tears? I should have said something but I was as dumb as a sheep being shorn. Perhaps it was his tenderness that broke me. In my secret thoughts I longed for a man like him. Was that why I said nothing?

Still gathered to his side, I moved with Ya'akov toward his kumbet and felt his body tense as we stood before the door. For a moment he seemed sad and pensive. Or, was it anger that flowed from him? I could not tell. His grip tightened and I felt him sway drunkenly. Recovering his balance, he chanted in a dreamlike state. "I would lead you and bring you to my mother's house—she who has taught me. I would give you spiced wine to drink, the nectar of my pomegranates."

No lamps were lit in the windowless kumbet as we staggered together through the doorway and fell clumsily onto the floor cushions. He disrobed me in feverish need and I tried to protest. He shushed my mouth with urgent kisses and fell upon me with burning power. He forgot his promise to be gentle and I gasped in pain when he drove in. I panted with the pressure of his thrusts, and I remember thinking that Rachel, at least, was spared this drunken horror. Then he collapsed.

Pushing him onto the cushions beside me, I pulled a blanket over us both. He was already fast asleep, snoring in sozzled oblivion. But I lay awake, dreading the dawn.

DAWN

Cold morning air seeped under the door-cloth of Ya'akov's kumbet, and all the celebrants of the previous evening were silent. Donkeys brayed in distant fields but no one moved to tend them. Ya'akov stirred when a sliver of light from the doorway began to pass over his face. Then he groaned in pain and covered his head with the blanket. Gradually, I felt him come to consciousness — and the realization that it was his wedding morning.

"Rachel, my lamb." He nuzzled the back of my neck and drew my body toward his. We slid together and I melted into the comfort of his warmth — though knowing the truth would dawn on him soon. "Arise, my darling," he said. "Our keskek (wedding breakfast) is waiting at the door." His arm reached around me, caressing my breast, waking sensations I had never felt. "Daylight has come. It is a morning of love."

While my tears fell onto the pillow, I felt him swell behind me and his kisses became more passionate. "Arise, come my darling, come to me. Show me your face." Playfully, he pulled the blanket away from my shoulders. Then his breathing stopped. Gasping, he grabbed a handful of my hair and held it up in the half-light. He dropped it as if he held a serpent, then leaped out of bed and vomited in the shadows of the kumbet. It was not the effect I hoped to have on my husband the morning of my wedding — but who could blame him.

Ya'akov wasted no time in pulling a robe over his naked body. And a flash of light announced his departure as the door-cloth snapped against the wall.

"Lavan! What is this you have done to me? Was it not for Rachel that I worked for you? So why have you deceived me? Lavan! Wake up supplanter! Wake up and face me with what you have done!" Ya'akov's voice faded as he strode across the courtyard to my father's kumbet and our guests' voices rose in protest of their abrupt awakening.

My father was up for the challenge. After all, he had a full seven years to prepare for it. I could hear sounds of a struggle as Ya'akov was pushed into the middle of the courtyard where witnesses could hold back the level of violence. The shuffle of many feet and the wine-soaked stench of people's clothing, told me of a gathering crowd. This was not quite the wedding drama they expected but no one wanted to miss the show.

When enough protection was assembled, Father answered Ya'akov's accusation. His voice was soft and persuasive but chiselled hard in its undertones. It was the same manner he used when bargaining with the traders that frequented our village. "It is not done so in our land—to give the younger before the first-born. Complete the bridal week for this one. Then I will also give you the other—in exchange for work that you will do for me—another seven year more."

Ya'akov knew our laws, and he knew our guests affirmed our customs. If he openly opposed Lavan, it would diminish his chances of good business relationships in the future. Besides, he had obviously spent the night with me. If he backed out of the marriage at this point, he would have to pay the required fine and be banished from our midst— leaving Rachel behind forever. When he and Rachel hatched the plot, crafty Lavan most certainly accounted for Ya'akov's financial ambitions as well as our family dynamic.

Livid that Father outwitted him, Ya'akov stomped off to the fields while I ate my wedding keskek, alone, on the threshold of his kumbet. For once, I was thankful I could not see the expressions on the faces of the people around me. I straightened my backbone to feign dignity. I knew the guests assumed I was part of the deception. Many, I am sure, watched me with amusement as I slowly and deliberately finished my portion of keskek then ate Ya'akov's portion as well.

While licking the savory meal off each finger, and leisurely sipping my bowl of tangy ayran, I decided not to humiliate myself with either denials or explanations. I had fully expected to be engaged in the supervision of the feast so Rachel and Ya'akov could lounge in front of their kumbet, making eyes at each other all day before retreating inside for the night. But all that had changed and Rachel now served me. She brought me a washbowl, combed my hair, and perfumed me in preparation for the evening tryst with my husband—though Ya'akov was nowhere in sight.

The guests overcame their surprise by getting down to the business of eating and drinking all that was available. Zilpah and Bilhah spent their spare moments sitting companionably on the rug beside me. We talked about everything but what had happened, while secretly wondering how the changed circumstance would affect our lives. I supposed that Zilpah would be given to me as my dowry. It would only be fair. And so, the day wore on while I concentrated on eating my delectable wedding delicacies to avoid thinking of nightfall.

COUPLINGS

Ya'akov did his duty, every night of my bridal week. He would appear in the kumbet after dark to breed me from behind — quick and businesslike. Then he promptly fell asleep, or pretended to. The only time I talked with him was in the morning as he dressed for the day.

The second morning I said, "It was not my idea."

"I know," he said, "Rachel told me." Then the door-cloth snapped against the wall and he was gone.

The following morning, since men are interested in their work above all else — well, almost all else — I tried a different approach. "How are the animals faring with the changes they have to endure these days?"

"Fine," he said. Then the door-cloth snapped against the wall and he was gone for the day.

While I sat in the sun in Rachel's wedding finery, eating delicacies on the threshold of Ya'akov's kumbet, I had plenty of time to ponder the problem of my husband's unwillingness to converse with me. I confess I had not paid much attention to him during the seven years he lived in our midst, and I had no idea where to start a conversation with him. I knew he loved animals, business deals, and Rachel. But I had already found those topics to be unproductive, or awkward.

Around the evening kofte tray, I sometimes heard him disparage our gods, so I tried the topic of his religion the following day. We all knew the Legends of Avraham and the singular god he worshiped, but Ya'akov never said much about the rituals of this god, and I was genuinely curious.

"Ya'akov, now that we are married, would you teach me how to worship your god? You have no prayer room and no idol in your kumbet. What object do you pray to and how do you petition your god?"

Ya'akov stopped rummaging for his robe and turned toward me in the half-light. I could feel his penetrating stare but it was some time before he answered. "Adonai's image cannot be created by human hands. Worship of the Almighty is not confined to a room. I also worship in the open fields, on mountain tops and under the stars that speak of God's redemption."

"What form does your worship take out there? How do you appease your god in a place so far removed from the trappings of man-made temples and chanting priests?"

Ya'akov found his clothes and put them on before answering me. "My father taught me to sacrifice an unblemished lamb upon an altar made with unhewn stones, then to listen for the Voice."

"Does this god speak to you?" By now I was thoroughly interested. Our clay idols had never seemed real. They were so easily made and even more easily crushed to pieces that I failed to believe they had any life or power.

"The heavens declare God's glory night and day, but I have only heard the Voice once. On my way here, I had a dream while I slept in the almond grove of Beit-El. I saw the heavens open and angel spirits ascending and descending a ladder. Then the Voice made me the same promise that was made to my father and his father before him. I will someday return to the land of my birth, and my children will inherit it for all generations."

"Ha! Try telling that to Lavan! I believe he intends to keep you right here, working off bride-price after bride-price for the rest of your life!"

The door-cloth snapped against the wall and I was alone, cursing my careless joking. But I congratulated myself on learning the secret of coaxing conversation out of Ya'akov. So, I ate a double portion of keskek to celebrate my victory.

The next morning, I asked, "Does your god have a companion goddess? All our gods have female consorts who influenced them."

Ya'akov stood in the doorway, the curtain drawn back, dawn outlining his frame. He pushed his hair away from his face and sighed. "The Breath of Life is both Father and Mother. And by that very nature, humankind is created in the image of God. Both man and woman are made in equal likeness to our Creator, two facets of the One. But we are not God. We are created beings. The One is not created. All those that you call gods and goddesses are myths or demons. They are either useless pieces of clay or jealous spirits that try to destroy God's good handiwork. No good will come of worshiping them."

I was astonished at this mystery. "Where did you learn this wisdom?" I asked.

"Avraham taught me as a child. He learned it from his grandfather who learned it from his grandfather. This ancient knowledge goes back to the time of Noach and beyond. But only a remnant believes. It is hard for people to trust a God they cannot see."

When the door-cloth snapped against the wall, I sat in the cool darkness of the kumbet pondering the wonders I had heard.

On the last morning of my bridal week, I asked my husband to tell me the story of the time when God spoke to Sarah. He sat on the floor cushions and patiently recounted how God and Sarah laughed together. Ya'akov's God then worked a miracle and Ya'akov's father, Yitz'chak, was born to his ancient parents. I had heard the story many times around the kofte tray, and loved the thought of a deity who spoke kindly to women about the birth of their children. Our gods and goddesses harboured cruel intentions regarding childbirth. Unless we appeased them with sacrifices and rituals, they kill our children before birth or steal their breath afterward. I knew the mating of my bridal week would bear fruit, and I longed to know more about this god who would nurture my children, not harm them. So, I questioned my husband again.

"Where was Sarah when she heard the Voice? What was she doing at the time?"

"She was preparing food for her guests in the tent of Avraham. She was going about her daily business when the Almighty called for her."

"Did your mother, Rivkah, hear the Voice?"

Abruptly, Ya'akov rose from our bed and walked toward the door. He pulled back the curtain and gazed out at the day. His shoulders sagged in the soft morning light. With sorrow? With anger? I could never discern his emotions if his mother was mentioned. When his feelings were under control, he answered me. "She was distressed by the war in her womb so God told her she would birth two nations and the elder would serve the younger."

"Where was she when she heard the Voice?"

"In her garden, among the herbs and flowers she loves."

By that time Ya'akov was far away in his memories so I let him walk into the morning while I absorbed the new information. Not only did the God of Avraham, Yitz'chak, and Ya'akov speak to their women, but they heard the Voice in the common places of their lives.

That night I moved out of Ya'akov's kumbet and Zilpah brought in clean linens for Rachel's bridal week. Truth be told, it was a relief to move back into my familiar kumbet with Bilhah and Zilpah. Their embraces were a comfort after the cold coupling I endured.

Next morning, we feasted again on rich wedding food while Father swaggered around in triumph. Again, Rachel was veiled and paraded about by my brothers. This time Ya'akov did not leave her side, and he was careful not to over imbibe in the liquor that still flowed in our courtyard like a river. Did he expect Rachel to be exchanged for Zilpah this time? I smiled at the thought. I was sure Lavan had considered it.

Finally, the hour came for the couple to disappear into their nuptial chamber and everyone retired, exhausted after eight full days of feasting. But I lay awake on my pallet wondering how we would ever endure another week of wedding revelry. How would we pay for such an extravagance? How would our livestock, hobbled away from their shelters, fare for another week? Where would we find the time to prepare another week's worth of food? Who could I appeal to with these concerns? Abba was too proud to send his guests away, and Ya'akov would never deprive Rachel of her wedding week.

Then I thought of Rivkah who had been so exasperated with the war in her womb that she ran into the night and called out to the One. As Ya'akov's wife, would I have the ear of God?

Tossing back the thin wool coverlet, I stepped into the night. I stood in the empty courtyard sampling the scent of earth and grass and flower blossoms. I spoke aloud the trials of my life. I poured out my disappointment about my disabling eyesight and my humiliating marriage. Then I begged the Almighty to do something about the financial consequences of Abba's decision to have two weddings at the same time. I stood silent after saying my piece. I listened, but heard no Voice. The night was perfectly still. Not a breath of wind stirred through my clothing or my hair. Even the night creatures were silent. So, I went back to bed.

Braying donkeys announced the dawn but they sounded different, more urgent. I pulled my day-robe over my head and combed my hair before stepping out of the kumbet to help Zilpah prepare the morning meal. The air was breathless and cloying. The scent of the flowers was more pungent than usual but no insects buzzed around them. No birds chirped. No banners or door-cloths snapped in the wind.

Our guests were scurrying back and forth between the kumbet village and the fields beyond. Then the aroma of linen and freshly baked bread glided by. "What is happening, Zilpah?" What is everyone doing?"

"Preparing to leave," was Zilpah's hasty reply. "Ya'akov says a storm is coming, perhaps a haboob. He says the clouds above and the air below are moving in opposite directions and the guests need to seek shelter." Then she hurried off to deliver bread and hummus to departing visitors.

I followed at her heels, eager to do my part in saying the traditional farewells, and giving gifts. Bilhah bounced along beside us, concerned for her herb garden. As she chattered on and on about the coming dust storm, my mind was on the astounding turn of events. The Creator may not have answered my petition with words, but this intervention was as clear as a Voice. I was amazed that my prayer was listened to, then acted on. It felt like a holy seal on my marriage. I felt accepted into Avraham's clan despite the indifference of my husband.

    The storm raged as we huddled in our kumbets with the livestock, enduring their stink and filth. And, while Bilhah fretted for her garden, Zilpah and I giggled about Ya'akov and Rachel's first week of wedded bliss being observed by their wide-eyed sheep. At the first sign of the storm's passing, Bilhah bolted from the kumbet to survey the damage. I was not so eager to walk into my storm ravished world.

BIRTHINGS

After her wedding, Rachel took up residence in Ya'akov's kumbet and I continued to share mine with our sisters. My premonition was correct. Signs of pregnancy soon showed up in my body, and I found I could stave off nausea by eating bread and drinking tart ayran, so I kept a big stash beside my bed. The more I ate the better I felt.

    I did not know how to react to Ya'akov and Rachel's obsession with each other. I missed Rachel's soft laugh and her warm scent on the night cushions we used to share, but I do not think she missed me. We never seemed to have time anymore, to tell our secret little stories or to laugh at ourselves. Yet, in so many ways our lives went on as usual, me with my pottery and Rachel in the fields with Ya'akov and the sheep. She did come to stay with us during her monthly flow. And she radiated joy as she told us stories of her beloved. They were like The Epic of Gilgamesh—in her mind. Zilpah and I would tap each other's arms at Rachel's exaggerations, but Bilhah hung on every word, fascinated with the mysteries of marriage and men. I suppose both could be palatable if you were adored like Rachel was.

    I consoled myself by hugging the knowledge of my child to my heart. Zilpah's sharp eyes noticed the changes in my body and also kept my secret. Neither of us knew what to say while a babe grew in me and there was no sign of the same thing happening in Rachel's body. It is best to keep life peaceful as long as possible.

ℰᴏᴄℛ

"Sit still or the scorpion in your hair will crawl down your back." Bilhah screamed and stripped naked on the spot. Her robe landed on my head and knocked the comb from my hand. She danced around in the dim light of the kumbet, shaking everything that might be a resting place for a stinging insect. Zilpah and I convulsed with laughter while I threw Bilhah's robe in the direction of her screeches. "Put that back on. You are not such a tiny child that you can prance around without clothes. Come sit on my knee and I will finish combing your hair. It is like a scorpion nest you must admit."

I could not see Bilhah's face but I heard her checking her tangled tresses, making sure they were scorpion free. Then, in spite, she plunked herself down, hard—on my lap. "Oomph," I exhaled loudly when she bumped into my huge protruding belly. I laughed. But my laugh was cut short by a cramp so severe I pushed Bilhah away and clutched at the child inside me. Zilpah rushed to my side. Bilhah ran out the door. She returned several contractions later with Rachel in tow. Her wool and milk scent penetrated my hazy veil of pain and soothed me.

Rachel lay her animosity aside to tend me like one of her ewes. She massaged my belly to hasten the birth, and anointed my underparts with olive oil so the skin would not tear. She sought to calm me by singing low pleas for mercy to the goddesses.

"Stop singing those songs!" I yelled. "I am not in the care of your worthless idols. I am in the care of the God of Ya'akov." My sisters backed away and the air grew stale with fear. They were warned by the old women of the land to expect angry outbursts from a labouring mother—but they lived in terror of the goddesses—especially in the hour of birth.

I took advantage of a break between contractions to grab Rachel's robe and pull her close. "No good thing will come from worshiping idols. Call upon Adonai to deliver me. Sing songs to the Breath of Life. Call upon the God of our husband. Did Ya'akov teach you nothing out there in the fields? Did he not show you how to worship the Creator of the heavens and the earth?" My lecture was cut short by a strong need to push, and Rachel grasped my hand while she urged me through the last few contractions.

With a shout of triumph, she caught my firstborn in

her arms and cleared the mucus from his mouth. Zilpah washed him with wine and Bilhah rubbed his little body with herbs and olive oil—which made him so indignant that we wept and laughed together.

༺༻

Proud of my accomplishment, I looked up toward the face of my husband and said, "See? A son!"

Ya'akov's body held no enthusiasm as he bent to examine the newborn. "Yes, call him Re'uven (Behold a son)," said Ya'akov. Then he turned and left the kumbet in a field-scented gust of indifference.

I stared in disbelief at the silver light around the door-cloth. Had Ya'akov gone without congratulating the mother of his son? Had he gone without holding his child and giving him the blessing of the firstborn? Rachel followed him out the door, but Bilhah and Zilpah were plastered against the walls, not wanting to believe the dishonour they had witnessed. Stunned to silence, we did not speak until the baby's grunts released us from our stupor. His needs compelled us to quiet ministrations while trying to comprehend Ya'akov's reaction.

A few minutes later, Re'uven suckling peacefully at my breast, startled when the door-cloth opened and Rachel entered. I soothed Re'uven and coaxed him to latch on again, then turned eagerly toward her. "Look at him Rachel! He is nursing already, a hungry little hyena, greedy and strong!"

Rachael stood in the entryway of the kumbet, holding the door-cloth aside as if she sought a quick escape. I was puzzled by her hesitancy. Then she spoke. "Ya'akov asked me to give you this." Something dangled from her outstretched hand and Zilpah reached for it. "He purchased it for the birth of my firstborn, not yours." Rachel spat out the bitter words and left. Once again, my sisters and I were stunned.

Wordlessly, Zilpah dropped a small object into my hand. I could see very little in the dim light, but I knew the smooth presence in my palm was a stone.

"What is it, Zilpah? What kind of birthstone did he give his son?"

Zilpah picked up the orb and carried it to the doorway. She raised it toward the sun and drew a breath. "How beautiful! Look at it, Bilhah! It is lapis lazuli, as bold and blue as a drop of water! What a fitting gift for a son born beneath the stars of the Water-Bearer constellation. I am sure there is a message in the stars and the stone, a message from our Almighty Creator. The One is our Water-Bearer, the giver of life. It is the One who made all things, the One who pours life-giving water onto the world."

Bilhah held the blue gem to the light of the doorway. Then she came back to the bed and peered into the sleeping face of my child. Deep tenderness emanated from her as she stroked his downy little head. "Bilhah! Stop mooning over my child and fetch me a bowl of that pottage simmering in the courtyard. The work of birthing has made me as ravenous as a jackal." Bilhah scurried off and left Zilpah to tend me and the babe. Something unsettled me when Bilhah bent over Re'uven, but food was sure to restore my calm.

ଽଠଓ

After the birth of Re'uven, Rachel spent even more time with Ya'akov and his blessed sheep. He only summoned me to his kumbet during the time of Rachel's flow. She and I barely saw each other, and when she did seek me out, Rachel would gather her garments around her and lift her chin in disdain while she relayed whatever message she was bidden to give. Could she not see that she had the better part of Ya'akov? She had his heart. I was merely a means of procreation. Other than that, Ya'akov wanted no part of me—and neither did my sister. My heart was slowly breaking.

Some consolation lay in the camaraderie of my other sisters and the recounting of the wondrous stories I was able to coax out of Ya'akov during my nights with him. They were tales of a benevolent God who dwelt among us as a friend. I learned that Adam and Havah, our first parents, were fashioned from clay — like the vessels I love to create. And in the time before the great breach, husband and wife lived in perfect harmony. As a daughter of Havah my desire is also for my husband. I long for a similar union. So, I pleaded that God would make Ya'akov love me. I also asked that somehow, the gulf between Rachel and I would be bridged. I had no idea how to go about achieving those desires. The Almighty was my only hope. But God did not answer those petitions as promptly as my first request was answered after my wedding week. There are many mysteries in a relationship with Adonai.

༺༻

Shim'on arrived a year later, under the constellation of the Sea-Goat. He screamed his way into the world, squalling and red-faced. I laughed at his angry cries and called him Shim'on (Hearing). I was sure that God had finally heard my prayers. For how could Ya'akov fail to love me after giving him two healthy sons?

But on the day of Shim'on's birth, Rachel let me know that Ya'akov would not stop by to see his new son. He was in Harran hiring field workers so he could turn his attention more fully to the care of the sheep. Then Rachel dropped Shim'on's birthstone on my pillow and left the kumbet. I watched her go, grieved that both my prayers remained unanswered. I also grieved Rachel's empty womb. There were many things I wished to say, many comforts I wanted to give, but she left no opening.

"Shim'on's birthstone is a sea-blue quartz," mused Zilpah. "And it has a bolt of lightning flashing through it." She held the quartz closer to my eyes in the hope that I could see it. "The message of the Sea-Goat constellation seems clear. The Divine Water-Bearer pours the living water on all life, both on the earth and under the sea. And the flashing bolt in Shim'on's birthstone repeats that message. The Water-Bearer's life-giving power reaches from the highest heavens and penetrates the depths of the sea. All life is within the dominion of the One."

I ignored Zilpah's words. Stories of stars and stones gave me no pleasure. Disappointment with Rachel and Ya'akov overshadowed everything. "Where is Bilhah?" I asked, "tell her to fetch me some of that lamb I smell roasting in the courtyard. I am hungry after the work of giving birth."

Zilpah adjusted the pillows behind my head and lifted Shim'on into her arms. "Bilhah is in Ya'akov's kumbet," she said. "She will stay there until Rachel gives her leave."

"Rachel?"

"She has given Bilhah to Ya'akov. As Rachel's handmaid, Bilhah will bear a child . . ."

"Yes, yes, I interrupted . . . on Rachel's knees. That is how she will start her family. I know the custom." I mourned the news. It seemed my sister was not content with monopolizing the total devotion of our husband. She now schemed to steal my rank as tribal mother. I was recognized in our community as the First Wife, the mother of Ya'akov's heir. But Rachel's child, through Bilhah, would be pampered, doted on and elevated to a station above my sons. Rachel would insist on it. And poor little Bilhah would have no say while Rachel reared her offspring in jealous discord. I feared for Bilhah and her children. Even though he bowed to them, Ya'akov was bound to be angry with Rachel's demands. Would Bilhah and her sprouts bear the brunt of his anger?

Facing the wall, I wept and prayed, "My God! Do you see our sorrow? Our conflicts now control our lives. Be gracious, Almighty God. Send us a judge to mediate the affairs of your people. How we need a Saviour."

෨෧෬

Bilhah's son was born before mine, arriving as the sun journeyed through the stars of the Scorpion constellation. I remembered Bilhah's fear of the creatures and smiled a little. Then I cringed. Our family certainly felt a poisonous sting when Rachel triumphantly named the baby Dan (The Judge). In her opinion, God had judged her worthy to mother a son before the birth of my next child. And while I celebrated the arrival of Bilhah's child by feasting on smoky baba ghanoush, I begged God to be the judge between me and my sister. What had I ever done but fall into her schemes—and the schemes of my father? Why should my husband resent me because of their deceit?

Zilpah described the dark red garnet that commemorated Dan's arrival. It was a life-giving fertility stone and Zilpah felt it meant that God would someday birth an antidote to the scorpion's miserable sting of discord and death. But Rachel had other ideas about garnet's meaning. She mounted it in gold filigree and hung it on a chain around her neck—to boost her fertility.

In a fit of spite, I sent Shmuel to Harran with the birthstones Ya'akov had given me. I had them placed on a chain to grace my neck. As enmity's poison infected us all, our spirits died little by little, as each bitter day passed.

Bilhah returned to our kumbet after the birth of her son. She was allowed to nurse him but that was all. Officially, Dan was Rachel's son and she took over his care. Crestfallen Bilhah immersed herself in caring for my children, spending especially long hours in her garden with little Re'uven. He proved to be a quick and ready student, repeating the names of her plants in his sweet baby voice. Bilhah found some comfort in that, but I was disturbed by their bond.

෨෬

A few months later, Levi slipped into life—serenely unaware that conflict swirled around him. From his very first breath he seemed to assure me that all would be well. But my obsession with being first in the eyes of Ya'akov, kept me from taking comfort from Levi's gentle spirit. Instead, I named him Levi (Joining), hoping Ya'akov would acknowledge that it was I, not Rachel, who would populate his nation. Surely, my husband could finally see that it was *I* whom God chose to bless, *I* whom he should join—body and soul.

A few hours after Levi's birth, that hope lay smashed on the kumbet floor—along with the amethyst Ya'akov gave me. When he arrived by my bedside and peered into the swaddling linen, he asked if the babe was whole and healthy. That affirmed, he made some comment about the financial value of raising a future workforce. Then he dropped a jagged stone into my hand and left the kumbet. Once again, there was no praise at all for the mother of his sons.

The amethyst, the so-called stone of peace, filled me with such rage that I screamed with all my might and threw the thing across the room. Bilhah gathered up the pieces of broken gem and remarked how they looked like the two Fish of the constellation Levi was born under. She and Zilpah began to question why there were two fish. And why did star-chains bind them? Would the poison of conflict split our people in two? Would chains still bind us together somehow? And, would Adonai bring the peace that the jewel embodied? We longed for peace.

Taking no pleasure in signs and stars and grudging gifts, I put my face toward the wall and let my tears soak the pillows. Deep despondency gripped me. Not even Zilpah's soft assurances penetrated my despair. She drew my attention to Levi's calm essence that remained unbroken even when I wept and carried on. She thought Levi was the prayed for priest and mediator. I let Zilpah chatter on. Ya'akov had made it very clear. Apart from the job of birthing a 'workforce' he wanted no part of me. My heart was crushed and my sadness knew no measure.

༄༅༅

Cycles of sacrifice and feasting continued as they always had. Winter rains gave relief from the relentless summer sun but left a cloud of gloom on my soul. My life held no joy. Only pottery-making gave me comfort. The whirling wheel soothed my spirit and allowed flashes of unity with my Creator who, from the very beginning, enjoyed making things from clay. When my dark thoughts spun out of control, my pots turned into shapeless gourds. It then felt good to smash the rebellious clay into submission and start again. It felt good to vent my anger on useless brown blobs that dared to resist my guidance. Did they think they could dictate a purpose apart from their creator's vision? Can a pot say to the potter why have you made me this way?

    I suppose we are all vessels of clay, created for a purpose we do not choose. If we balk, does the Divine Potter's hand smash us down then build us up to satisfy our original design? Bitterly, I smacked at the base of an unformed bowl, trying to stretch a little further. It resisted but I pressed it wider — wide enough to hold a whole harvest of pomegranates. There! Finally! I slowed the wheel and touched the beautiful contours of the vessel while thinking about people not pots.

    Some of us wish to live out the purpose of others, even though we do not suit their soul's mandate. I drew a surprised breath as I saw myself in that state. Was I demanding to fulfill Rachel's purpose, not mine? Ya'akov's purpose was to father a nation. And that could not be done without the womb of a woman — my womb — and now Bilhah's. None of us choose our path. After all, like vessels of clay, we are formed by the Creator's will, not ours.

    To courtyard bystanders, one lump of clay may look the same as another. But from the moment my fingers begin to explore nuances of texture and elasticity, I start to form a plan for each glob of earth. Some clay does well when fashioned into water pitchers, and some is best for making pots that need to withstand heat. I sigh with pleasure when an especially smooth slice of earth slides through my searching fingers. I love to make that rare clay into delicate vessels. On those, I create a small irregularity, an owner's mark, so others know that I will keep them for myself. They are cherished.

    My wandering thoughts produced tears that etched dark patterns into the raw clay bowl in my hands. And while my fingers searched out tiny flaws and fissures in the clay, a new thought was born. Perhaps my weak eyes are an owner's mark of sorts. Perhaps God marked me to keep me close. Did Adonai cherish me enough to mark me? Did the One want my heart like I wanted Ya'akov's? Grief gave way to awe as I sat among my pots, running my hands over their contours, enjoying their silent praise.

"Le'ah, I need you to make three more jars for the anointing oil. Make the ones with the little spouts. It is almost tic season. When can you have them ready?"

"Shalom Ya'akov. I can begin work on the oil pots tomorrow—or the day after if I am interrupted by the needs of your sons." I smiled up at Ya'akov and he gave a grudging grunt before going back to the sheep—and Rachel. I followed his retreating form as far as my eyesight allowed. "At least my pots praise my worth." I said this quietly in the stifling air of mid-afternoon and reached into the bowl of dried grapes that were always at my side.

How we long for praise. I always obeyed Ya'akov, with no encouragement at all. But what would I be motivated to do if I was complimented once or twice? Would it be so hard for him to improve both our lives? I ate the grapes as I pondered the thought. Praise. I considered its power as the potter's wheel spun back to life. I pondered the influence it could have over me if I was ever lavished with it. The word 'praise' went around in my head to the rhythm of the wheel. We were never praised by our father. It was Ima who delighted in our achievements and touted them out in front of everybody. After she died, we practiced her ways in the women's kumbet. We were happy in our mutual admiration of each other—until the weddings. I sighed. Much had been sucked into the cesspool of that disaster. Could the simple act of praise restore some of the loss?

Levi looked up from his play. He was sitting at my feet, stacking up potsherds to form wobbly towers then gleefully toppling them. But now he wanted something else and my breasts filled in response. He was almost weaned but another babe would soon take his place at my breast. I was not a mother like Bilhah who fended off pregnancy until her child was completely weaned. In fact, I had not been hit by the weapon since the time before my marriage. In my mind, this was one of my greatest blessings. I had not missed the cramps, the mess, and the days of inactivity our tribe required during a woman's flow. Smiling into the sapphire sky, I praised the One for the fruitfulness of my womb and a hiatus from my monthly flow.

I scooped Levi onto my lap. "You are a good tower builder, my son."

Levi chuckled with joy—the first fruit of my praise.

"Bilhah, bring me some of the savory herb-bread you baked today. It is the best I have ever tasted. I thank the Creator that you have both Sarah's blessing with bread and Rivkah's skill with herbs." Bilhah appeared with the bread, and a vessel of mint tea I had not even asked for. When Zilpah left her weaving to join us for tea, I asked, "What are you working on?"

"A new rug for the entrance of Abba's kumbet. It is red and orange with yellow leaves woven through it."

"I wish I could see how beautiful it is. Bring it to me when you finish. I love to feel the skill of your handiwork. It fills our lives with richness."

I could not see their tears at the unexpected praise, but joy and sorrow flowed among us in a beautiful blend. So, healing began in our courtyard, with praise as the ointment for our ills. And our laughter gradually returned.

෨෬

"What will you name this robust son?" laughed Zilpah as she washed my squirming newborn and wrestled him into a swaddling cloth. "He is fighting me, determined to get back to you. Look at him straining. He knows what he wants from his very first moment of life."

Later, while settled on my breast, the babe relaxed. He was as content in my arms as I was in the embrace of God. Zilpah, Bilhah, and I, lived in harmony in the kumbet of women. It was an island of peace in a hostile world, a world in which I no longer fretted about my purpose. Instead, I was full of gratitude for joys that surpassed sorrows. The One had become more precious to me than ten husbands. And I was chosen to mother a nation.

My determined new son all but roared when he lost his latch on my breast. I was not surprised at his confident nature. He was born under the royal stars of the Lion. Zilpah was sure a great King would someday spring from his loins, an Eternal King who would rule the world with justice and mercy, restoring the balance our conflicts had destroyed. I resettled the baby on my breast and looked up at my sisters. In a clear strong voice I said, "This time I will praise Adonai. I will name him Y'hudah (Praise)." The babe had drifted off to sleep but Zilpah said he smiled when I declared his name.

To mark Y'hudah's arrival, Ya'akov sent me a magnificent carnelian, the healing stone. The servant who brought it said that Ya'akov and Rachel were leading the sheep to higher pastures—away from the summer drought. They took little Dan with them and planned to return when the weather cooled.

I felt Bilhah's silent sorrow when Dan was mentioned. She had never recovered from losing her son—who lived close but out of her reach. Again, I silently asked the Almighty to heal the wounds in all our souls, and to restore Dan to his mother.

"Bilhah, take the gem and hold it in the light of the doorway. Perhaps, if the sun is just right, I can see it." In the blaze of midday, the carnelian between Bilhah's fingers glowed red, like a drop of blood. I wondered about that. Would the blood of the coming King heal us somehow? There were so many mysteries for the future to reveal.

ೞಃಥ

When my moon-blood returned, I was astonished. What was the Creator saying with this new sign? Were my praises insufficient? Or, was this a test to see if I could be satisfied without the monthly visits to the kumbet of my husband? As a daughter of Havah, fashioned from the rib of a man, could I transfer all my desire to God? Was that my task?

When I left off bearing, Ya'akov turned again to Bilhah's fresh young womb, hoping to give Rachel another child. In truth, it was a secret relief not to endure the awkward coupling that existed between me and Ya'akov. I missed the stories though. I loved repeating them around the cig kofte tray before the children went to bed. I loved acting out each scene and feeling the anticipation ripple when my little boys heard the mighty acts of God. I longed to know more about Sarah's laugh, Avram's journey, Noach's boat, and Hanokh who walked with God. There had to be a way.

ಸಂಬ

When Bilhah's second son was born, Rachel named him Naftali (My Wrestling). She snatched him up from the birthing bed and paraded him around the courtyard, proclaiming that she had wrestled with her sister and won.

Born when the sun passed through the stars of the Virgin constellation, Bilhah's babe was dark-skinned like his mother and as delicate as a girl. According to the servants he would be best suited to scrambling up mountains like an Ibex. "I suppose he will be useful in the hill pastures during the summer drought," Ya'akov mused. Then he pressed a gem into Bilhah's hand and left.

"What is it?" Zilpah and I asked in unison. Bilhah shrugged her thin little shoulders and handed the stone to Zilpah who held it to the light. "It is a sky-blue chalcedony . . . the gem of goodwill . . . the betrothal pledge-stone. We sighed in wonder at the unfolding story of the stars and stones. Did they predict that a betrothed virgin would someday bear the Eternal King who would pledge goodwill to all?

I held back tears when dutiful Bilhah took the

stone to Rachel who wound it about with gold cording and put it on the chain around her neck.

※

When my moon-blood began appearing at regular intervals, I was puzzled by my barrenness—but Zilpah's plight did not escape my notice. She was quiet and kind in her care of the children. A little too quiet I thought. It seemed unjust that she should not experience the joy of children birthed from her own body. And she also enjoyed Ya'akov's stories so I wondered if . . .

I knew that Bilhah's usefulness to Rachel was at an end. Rachel was very possessive of Ya'akov's body and content enough with two healthy sons. What if . . .

"Zilpah," I whispered.

Silent as a cloud, she stole across the dark kumbet so as not to wake our sleeping family. I breathed in her clean linen scent and reached out to feel the expression on her face. She was wide awake, her brow full of questions. I drew her ear toward my mouth. "Do you want your own child?" I asked.

At first, she backed away. Was it shock, or alarm? Then her shoulders relaxed and a deep sigh escaped. Moments later, warm tears splashed onto my upturned face and I had my answer. "I will offer you to Ya'akov as a wife. A wife in your own rite, not a slave. I want you to have full access to your child. Ya'akov knows I have stopped bearing. And Rachel's body cannot build his nation. Rachel will end Ya'akov's conjugal arrangement with Bilhah now that she has birthed two sons. But Ya'akov wants a large tribe. He will see practicality in my suggestion. But I would not demand it, my sister. It must be something you want."

Instead of answering me in words, Zilpah lay down, slipped her long arms around my body and rocked me to and fro like a child. I wrapped my arms around her and we cried together until sleep claimed us.

In the morning, I approached Abba to make arrangements. It was a complicated circumstance. Zilpah was Lavan's daughter and my slave. I had a legal right to suggest her as Ya'akov's concubine, but if she was to be a true wife, Abba must provide a dowry that Ya'akov agreed with. Her lack of worth to Lavan proved to be an advantage in the bargaining. And to my delight, Zilpah's marriage was secured with nothing more than a dowry pledge of extra pottery.

Ya'akov was extremely pleased with the drinking troughs I proposed. I invented a unique design that would cater to the needs of sheep and lambs at the same time — a two-tiered marvel. And what could Rachel say in the face of her beloved's obvious excitement to put the troughs to immediate use? I am sure he was convincing when he explained that the transaction was about the drinking troughs — not the extra wife. And, it was also about lightening his beloved Rachel's heavy labours at the well. At least, I assume those were the arguments he used to persuade her.

ଛଓର

"He is piercing me with arrows," screamed Zilpah. "He is attacking me! Pull him out! After three days of trying to push out the babe, Zilpah's travail was excruciating. She writhed in pain and fear, knowing both she and the child were in danger.

I prayed frantically for the mercy of God. While Rachel, ever calm during the chaos of birth, massaged Zilpah's belly, trying to discern the position of the child. "Roll over onto your back. Good. Now raise your hips up just a little. Alright. I will turn him now. It will only take a moment. Do not fear."

"AAAAAAAHHHHH!" Zilpah screamed the child into the world and he lay on the floor of the kumbet squirming, ready for a fight. "My child!" gasped Zilpah in relief. "My child is here! He is finally here."

Bilhah gathered up the boy and began to clean him while Rachel cut the cord. I hugged Zilpah to me — grateful she was alive. "We will call him Gad (Good Fortune) and we will praise the Almighty for sparing both your lives."

Zilpah groaned as she pushed out the afterbirth. "Good fortune? The babe has pierced me with many arrows in his fight to escape my womb. I suppose I should have expected that from a son born beneath the stars of the Archer constellation."

"And the Star Archer has his bow aimed at the evil Scorpion," said Bilhah, smugly. "Will God someday slay that creature and end its sting of death and discord? That will be the world's good fortune. What birth-stone did Gad's father give him?"

"A fire jasper," said Rachel as she prepared the placenta for burial. "It is in the little pouch on your pillow, Zilpah. Ya'akov gave it to me last night before leaving for Harran. I am sure it will look lovely, Le'ah, next to all the other gems around your neck. Be careful not to strain your back with the weight of them."

Sadness hid behind Rachel's hard words. She suffered deeply as she helped child after child come to birth. I longed to tell her I saw her sorrow. I wanted to relieve it, not add to it. I yearned to take her in my arms and hold her to my heart. I wanted to melt away her pain with the hugs and laughter of our youth. But the wall she built around herself was impenetrable.

"A fire-jasper!" I exclaimed, "It is the symbol of enduring protection. What a beautiful message. Our God burns with a desire to protect us from destruction. What a fitting stone for our little archer. But this gem will rest on Zilpah's breast, not mine. She deserves a reward for her labours. Bless you Rachel for saving our sister and her son from certain death. Your faithfulness will surely bring the favour of God upon you. I pray for your happiness."

My words were gentle but Rachel jolted to her feet and whirled out of the kumbet in a fury. You would think that I had slapped her. I guess I said the wrong thing.

೫೦ഌ

Afraid for Zilpah's life, I tried to dissuade her from the monthly visits with Ya'akov, but Zilpah would not listen. She loved the stories as much as I did, and hungered for more. "Well then, ask him about his mother. Whenever I ask, he leaves the kumbet under a cloud. There is a mystery there. I cannot tell if he is angry or sad or both. Perhaps you will have better success. Start by asking him about her gardening. That should be a neutral topic. Tell him Bilhah wants to know. You know she does. And tell him his firstborn is taking a keen interest in growing things. Re'uven is almost at an age to send him over to dwell in the men's kumbets. Perhaps if Ya'akov can see a lucrative future in it, he will finally show an interest in the boy.

So, we learned about Rivkah's gardens in her three home-places, and of her success in the land of G'rar because of how she irrigated the fields during a drought. Bilhah put this method into practice right away. Re'uven loved dipping the gourd at the end of the long chadouf pole into the water, then swinging the pole up over the plants and dousing them.

Zilpah's second son, Asher (Blessed), was born when the sun passed through the Weigh-Scale stars. Zilpah looked into the eyes of her babe and proclaimed that God weighs all our actions on a balanced scale of justice and mercy. And, when Ya'akov presented Asher with a yellow crystallite, the harmony stone, we prayed that God would someday restore the harmony of 'Eden to our family and our world.

So, two golden stones hung around Zilpah's neck, reflecting the light of her beautiful soul. And though I was grateful to God for weighing her worthy to bear a second son, I forbade her to put her life at risk to try for another. Instead, I begged the Almighty for a new way of coaxing stories out of Ya'akov.

༄༅

This time, the Almighty came to my aid sooner than expected. It happened at the time of the wheat harvest when Re'uven made his first foray into the world of men. After seven winters, he moved into my father's kumbet. By rights, he should have lived with Ya'akov, but Rachel would not abide it. He was a bright and curious child, but uncertain of his father's love. I hoped Lavan could, in some ways, make up for that loss—though I had my doubts.

Re'uven, a child of the fields, was always searching for wild herbs and eagerly showing them to Bilhah to see what they were and how they could be used. I knew he would like being a part of the wheat harvest, so I sent him out with joy, then settled down to make my pots. I did not see him again until we gathered around the kofte tray that evening.

"Bilhah says I should bring these to you," said Re'uven.

"What are they?" Strands of leaves and roots were outlined in the light of the evening fire but I could not see them in detail.

"She called them mandrakes. I found them in the wheat field when I was harvesting. She says you will know what to do with them."

I laughed and reached out to accept my son's gift. "Yes, I know how to use them but I doubt I will have the opportunity to see if they work." Re'uven was puzzled and I heard Zilpah walk away—perhaps to hide a smile.

Rachel, alerted by my laugh, edged closer, curious about our conversation. I heard her gasp when she saw the plants in my hand. Then, in an intense whisper she said, "Please give me some of your son's mandrakes so I can be fertile."

To my shame, I replied in anger instead of grace. This woman was the reason my husband rejected me and my sons. She had it in her power to encourage Ya'akov to love me, or at least to be civil in his dealings with me, but she forbade even that—so I lashed out. "Is it not enough that you have taken away my husband? Do you have to take away my son's mandrakes too?"

It probably never occurred to Rachel that the mandrakes would be useless to me while she prevented my access to Ya'akov's kumbet. In my heart, I was already amused by that irony. And as ever, I had started softening toward her. She still longed for her own children and I did not ever wish on her the curse of barrenness. I was almost ready to offer her the mandrakes when she said, "Very well, in exchange for your son's mandrakes, sleep with him tonight." Her voice had become shrill. It echoed in the evening air. Everyone around the supper fire tensed as they tried to come to terms with what they heard.

And Ya'akov, who had stayed late at the sheep pens with a sick ewe, chose that exact moment to enter the courtyard. On hearing Rachel's outburst, he stopped in mid-stride. Swiftly, I gathered up my robes and rose to meet him. I caught him by the arm and laughed, "You have to come and sleep with me because I have hired you with my son's mandrakes." Then I addressed Zilpah with all the dignity I could muster. "Zilpah, prepare a plate of the choicest food and bring it to our master's kumbet. Bring my plate also, I will join him there." Ya'akov was too stunned to refuse.

ଌଠଠଣ

Beneath the stars of the Scarab constellation—and their promise of eternal reward—Yissakhar (God's Reward) was born. And I did count Yissakhar's birth a reward for allowing Zilpah the joys of motherhood during my barren years. A glorious topaz joined the gems around my neck. It spoke of Adonai's royal pledge to reward us, and rested next to my heart as a guarantee.

I praise God that Ya'akov did change somewhat, after the event with the mandrakes. For the first time since our wedding, he seemed to treat me with respect. It was communicated in the way he leaned in and talked about the pots he wanted. And when he told me stories about the Almighty, there was something new in his voice. It was not quite love—perhaps it was more akin to trust. He kept it hidden from Rachel though. The old walls would go up when she was around. However, when she was hit by the weapon, he defied her and called me to his kumbet. Had he finally seen Rachel's unjust treatment of me? Or was he longing for his far away home and comforted by our mutual love of the old stories? He eventually began to tell me how his father favoured the fierce impulsive

'Esav while abandoning him to Rivkah's care. It was clear to me then, why he had no way of knowing how to bond with his sons.

๛

Z'vulun and Dinah made their appearance when the sun passed through the stars of the Ram constellation. It was the high season of sacrifice, when we celebrated Avraham's ram that was caught by his horns in the thicket and sacrificed instead of Yitz'chak. We rejoiced that our God would accept the death of a ram as a substitute atonement for our wrongdoings. And we looked forward to a time when God would provide a permanent sacrifice. So, we welcomed the new babes, two horns of the ram, male and female equally created in the image of God.

When Rachel finished her birthing chores, Ya'akov stopped by to examine both newborns with a shepherd's careful eye. Z'vulun was hairy and red. "Just like 'Esav," mused Ya'akov. Dinah was smooth and petite and Ya'akov spoke tenderly when he held her. "She will enjoy her position as the only girl in your kumbet. What should we name them?"

"I will name our son Z'vulun (To Dwell), for my husband truly dwells with me now."

I felt Ya'akov's smile. "And call the girl, Dinah (Vindicated), for the One has judged you worthy to mother a nation. I brought only one birthstone though. It is a peridot. I did not expect twins."

I laughed and held out my hand for the jewel, the evening stone, God's glowing promise of guidance on night's dark paths. "It is a good stone to mark Z'vulun's birth," I said. "As for Dinah, her worth is far above pearls and the One will bless her future."

Truthfully, I did not expect a reward or inheritance for a daughter. It had never been the way of our people. And I was beginning to understand that God rewards worshipers regardless of gender. So, I prayed that my daughter would join me in worship. But I could not have imagined the dark direction her path would take.

"Rachel's child is almost due," said Ya'akov. "She is fearful and anxious. I hope you will be recovered enough from the birth of the twins to help her through her labour. Unlike you, she is sickly when she carries a child. I am afraid for her."

"Her child is the answer to our prayers, Ya'akov. And God will bring to completion that which has begun. Remember Sarah. Remember Rivkah. Both suffered to bring a child to birth, but the Almighty spared them — and their babes."

"You are a blessing to me, Le'ah." Ya'akov's voice was tight with emotion.

I laughed again and gave him a chance to regain his composure. "You really have no need for concern. You have given the women of our kumbet years of practice in the skill of birthing children. We are ready now to take on the challenge of Rachel's labour. Perhaps God was wise to delay her time until we knew what we were doing."

He chuckled and left, snapping the door-cloth in the old familiar way. And I lay down with my babies, to rest in the arms of God.

※

Rachel's son was born beneath the stars of the charging Bull. And Bilhah pointed out that the Bull in the constellation was trampling the evil beast that kept the two fish bound in chains. Despite this warlike sign, Yosef slipped quietly into life, his newborn mewling muffled by Rachel's screams and obscenities.

To mark Yosef's arrival, Ya'akov gave Rachel a brilliant diamond, a token of everlasting love, the strongest of all stones. Zilpah was sure it meant that the everlasting love of God would triumph over evil and free us from the chains of iniquity that keep us bound.

Rachel hung the diamond on the chain around her neck, proclaiming that God had lifted the curse of barrenness and would surely give her another son. I hoped she was right, but I wondered how we would ever endure another emotionally charged pregnancy and birth.

    Ya'akov's smiles knew no end as he paraded Yosef around like a prize lamb. Nothing was too good for the little prince. The best clothes and the choicest morsels were lavished on the favoured son, his slightest whimper catered to.

    Our other sons, already troubled by lack of attention from Ya'akov, began to respond according to their characters. Re'uven retreated further into his world of plants and herbs, trying to shut out the pain. Shim'on and Levi fed off each other's anger, looking for ways to annoy Yosef. Y'hudah stood apart from his brothers, silently brooding, not wanting to inflame the conflicts.

    After Yosef's birth, Dan and Naftali were returned to Bilhah, Rachel no longer felt any need of them. So, God answered my prayer of years before, and Bilhah was wreathed in happiness. Zilpah too, was content with her two boys who bonded with Bilhah's to become a foursome of little warriors.

    We set Zilpah and Bilhah up in their own kumbet. Mine was overcrowded with boys rolling about on the floor, knocking over storage jars and ripping curtains apart like a litter of naughty puppies.

    Shim'on, like Re'uven, came of an age to live in my father's kumbet and I was glad they had each other there. Lavan had bullied my brothers and I was uneasy about what he would teach his grandsons through talk and example. So, I gathered them around the evening kofte tray, telling them stories of God's dealings with their ancestors, hoping to offset the dark worship practices of their grandfather. During the day, I busied myself with my younger sons and watched Dinah grow into a beautiful laughing child who delighted her brothers with an infectious spirit.

FLOCKS

With the seven years of labour for Rachel's bride-price finally complete, Ya'akov began building up a flock for himself. He talked Abba into giving him the spotted and dark rams as wages. Then, in a conjuring trick of some sort, involving my clay water troughs and peeled sticks, he made sure the rams born to his flock were strong enough to be the first to mount Abba's ewes when they came in heat.

    Ya'akov grew wealthy, purchasing many donkeys and camels. And he harvested the pelts of all our black goats then paid a band of nomads to sew them into tents. I wondered why we would need tents, but Ya'akov was tight lipped about his purposes—like God often is.

    Abba seemed oblivious to Ya'akov's activities, and arranged for my brothers and their families to live a three-day journey away, saying, "Our flocks need more room. We cannot have them packed together like so many city dwellers." So, Lavan was often on the road between my brother's village and ours. Re'uven and Shim'on went with him, taking care of their aging grandfather who only came back home to steal some of Ya'akov's strongest rams. Lavan always insisted he had not agreed to give up the brown ones or the striped ones or whatever struck his fancy at the time. For seven years, Ya'akov seethed with anger and I prayed that Adonai, as the stars foretold, would somehow mediate the brewing conflict.

FLIGHT

During shearing season, when the sun is merciless, workers often take a break in the shade of our kumbet doorways. They call greetings to me as they pass, then forget that I am there, part of the furniture of the courtyard, turning my pottery wheel. Praise the One that my ears work well, even if my eyes do not, so I keep my hand on the pulse of our community and glean information from conversations that no one expects me to hear. It was at such a time that my brothers took refuge in the doorway of our father's kumbet—forgetting how an archway magnifies sound.

"Did you see the size of that ram?" asked Shmuel.

"Yes," replied Nahor. "His fleece weighs almost as much again as he does. By the power of Dumuzi, I would love to have that big boy in my flock."

"That ram is not even the best or the biggest of Ya'akov's sheep. A servant told me he secrets the choicest of his flock into the hills so Father cannot take them when he comes here."

"*His* flock?" growled Nahor. "Ya'akov came to us empty handed, seeking refuge from whatever it was he did in Kena'an. And look at the size of his herds now. Then, look at our puny holdings. Ya'akov has taken away everything our father once had. It is from what used to belong to our father that he has become so rich."

"You are right brother," said Shmuel, slapping his thigh in disgust. "Ya'akov has cheated our family and prospered. Perhaps it is time to do something. We should talk to Father. He has been muttering about that supplanter for a while. Perhaps he is ready to do more than curse him."

"Yissakhar!" I pulled my thoughts away from my brother's plotting to call across the courtyard where the younger children played. "Yissakhar, come get this jug and fetch me some water from the well."

My son, reluctant to stop playing, protested. "But there is plenty of water in the jug."

"Go offer it to your uncles over there. I want *fresh* water. Ask Rachel to draw it and bid her bring it to me." Yissakhar guided my hand to his muscles. "I am strong enough to bring the water all by myself."

I felt around in the pile of vessels beside the kiln, found one the right size and handed it to Yissakhar. "Take this jug too. The day is hot and the little ones are thirsty. Fill this one and bring it back to me, but ask Rachel to bring the other one."

Having rescued Yissakhar's budding manhood, I sent him off. I knew Rachel would be intrigued if I asked her to fetch water rather than asking Bilhah, Zilpah or one of the servants to do it. Satisfied with my plotting, I chose a few nuts from my meze bowls and munched on them until Rachel arrived. Foiling our siblings' plans had been a great joy since childhood. It still brought us together as women so I did not wait long.

"Your water?" asked Rachel.

"Yes, thank you."

I ladled a drink for myself and for the children who now played close to my feet. I also offered them some treats from my meze bowls. Their noisy competition muffled the sound of my voice just as I thought it would.

"Our brothers were very talkative today." I spoke quietly, not facing Rachel directly. "They had a lot to say about their brother-in-law. They plan to find the sheep hidden in the hills. I hope Ya'akov's shepherds are not taken by surprise."

"I will make sure they are not." Rachel's voice sparkled with humour and she squatted down to reorganize the meze bowls on the rug beside me. "Last night Ya'akov had another visitation from the One." Her voice was serious. "He is very troubled by it. He is sure his god said to return to the land of his ancestors—to his kinsmen there. What will become of us if he does that Le'ah? How can we go on such a long journey? The children are too young."

Calmly, I joined my sister in the ruse of redistributing food in the bowls. "Perhaps this is the best way out for him," I said. "Perhaps his own family will be kinder to him than ours has been."

"He is afraid, Le'ah. For some reason, he dreads going back. Something happened between him and his brother. It involves his mother too. He trembles when I ask about it."

"I know, I have never been able to understand how he feels about his mother, but his fear of 'Esav is written on every line of his body. We will see who he fears most, our family, his, or Adoani."

Rachel nodded and stood up. While she acknowledged Ya'akov's fear, her own overshadowed it. "Who are the gods of Kena'an? Will our gods be strong enough to protect us? Yosef is so young."

"What would Ya'akov say?" I asked dryly.

Rachel shrugged. "He would talk on and on about the Almighty who protects us from all threats," she said. Then she left the courtyard in a wool-scented huff.

I watched her to the outer limits of my vision, perplexed about Ya'akov's confidence that God would protect him from menacing gods, while he lacked faith that God would protect him from 'Esav.

∞○○

After the shearing, everyone gathered to praise the gods for a successful season, and to pray for blessings in the year to come. My brothers and father were noticeably drunk when Ya'akov tapped Rachel and me on the shoulders, signaling for us to follow him. We left the children with Zilpah and Bilhah, puzzled, unused to being summoned at the same time—for any reason. As Ya'akov and Rachel guided me through the moonlit fields, the sounds of revelling began to fade and soft breezes played with our clothes. I lifted my face to sample the scent of sheep, and grass, and the fennel fragrance of olive blossoms. Being away from our kumbet village was a novel experience. Being alone in the night with my husband and my rival was even more novel. I wondered what urgency brought us to that place.

Ya'akov soon enlightened us. "I can see by your father's face that his expression is not the same as it was just a day or two ago."

I replied first. "We are ashamed that our family is not treating you as they should." Rachel made an affirmative sound that encouraged Ya'akov to continue.

"But the God of my father has been with me."

In unison, Rachel and I blessed God's goodness.

"You know that I have served your father with all my strength. Yet your father has changed my salary ten times. But God has not allowed him to harm me. If Lavan said, 'the spotted sheep will be your salary,' then the flocks would give birth to spotted young. Or if he would say, 'the striped ones will be your salary,' then all the flocks would give birth to striped young. So God has taken away your father's livestock and has given them to me."

Already well familiar with Ya'akov's grievances, I wondered about his motivation for this big speech. It seemed to me that he, himself, had laboured to grow his flocks these past seven years. I also remembered the conjuring trick Ya'akov had employed to increase them. Was he trying to convince us, or himself, that it was really God who brought about the result? Adonai alone knew the truth. I had no need for fancy explanations, but Ya'akov continued.

"Once, when the animals were mating, I had a dream. The angel of God said to me in the dream, 'lift up your eyes and see — all the males going up to the flock are striped, spotted and speckled. For I have seen everything Lavan has done to you. I am the God of Beit-El where you anointed a memorial-stone with oil, where you made a vow to me. Get up now, leave this land and return to the land of your father's.'"

Ya'akov suddenly had my full attention. It would be a good tale to tell the children. The land of his fathers? Did he say he intended to take us there? Yes! That is exactly what he said. Excitement gripped me at the thought of the new stories I could draw from his mother and father. I was ready for such a journey. I was ready to shed the disdain and suspicion of my family and meet my husband's clan.

Rachel interrupted my thoughts with a petulant whine. "You are right in thinking Lavan and my brothers are against you. Is there still a portion or inheritance left in our father's house for us? Are we not considered foreigners to him? For he has sold us and also completely used up our bridal price."

I nodded. It was true. Like many daughters, once the bride-price was paid and consumed, we were worthless in our father's eyes. My mind flickered to Dinah's future and determination slid through my belly. If we stayed in our homeland, would Ya'akov view her the same way Lavan did his daughters? Would my hopes and prayers for Dinah's future be better met in the Promised Land, under the protection of a God who favoured women? I took a step closer to Ya'akov and said, "Whatever God has told you to do, do it."

Rachel was hesitant. She was afraid to let Ya'akov take her and Yosef away from everything familiar. On the other hand, she was loath to seem less supportive than me. So, she nodded and our course was settled.

※※

We were a noisy company as we set out for the Promised Land. Animals bawled, children shrieked, and servants shouted to each other. We stopped in Harran to buy more carts for the younger children to ride in, and extra pack animals to carry the load of all our possessions. A piercing call to prayer sounded from the Ziggurat, and a dark, suffocating hush fell. Even the beasts were silent. From the moment we left home, Rachel sat on the camel beside mine, pouring titillating stories of the mystical Ziggurat into my ear. I knew the tales from childhood but let her prattle on about the sacred marriage of Inanna and Dumuzi. Her stories came to a sudden stop, hushed by the blast of the worship horns. What a relief.

I was disgusted by the fertility practices of my country, and glad to embrace the faith of Avraham. The One had proved more than capable of making our wombs fertile. Why could Rachel not see that too? She bore the evidence in her own body — as did our relatives, Sarah and Rivkah.

We made camp the first night, in the shade of a hill that rose from the ground beside us. We laughed when Rachel said it looked like Abba's pot belly. Three days later we forded the Euphrates River at Carchemish and Ya'akov refused to pay a crossing tax to their goddess. "We pay homage to the God of Avraham alone," he said. The ford-keepers frowned but let him pass and I asked why they did not argue. "The God of Avraham does not bow to their goddess, not to a common alewife like Kubaba, not to anyone," said Ya'akov.

A few days later, while camping in the hills of Mizpah, Ya'akov's scouts let us know that Lavan had discovered our flight and summoned our brothers to pursue us. Ya'akov wanted to press on but the children were languishing in the heat and the livestock needed a rest. So we made a circle-fortress of carts and wagons, pitched our tents in the middle, and waited for Lavan. My nerves were frayed and I longed for the numbing whirr of my pottery wheel but it was packed beneath a heavy load of garden tools. I turned instead to my stash of nuts and olives for comfort.

In the dim light of dawn, a commotion erupted outside my tent. Someone was yelling. I sat up in bed, straining to hear the voice that was cutting in and out with the gusty wind. It sounded distinctly like Abba.

"What have you done? You have carried my daughters off like so many prisoners of war! Why did you secretly flee away and steal from me?"

Then I heard a lower, softer voice. Ya'akov was trying to talk sense into Lavan.

"Why did you not tell me so I could send you away with joy and with songs, with tambourines and with lyres? You did not even let me kiss my sons and my daughters good-by!"

My heart lurched with regret. It was true. We had not said the proper farewells my oldest sons deserved. They had grown close to their grandfather during the years they lived in his kumbet. Would Ya'akov have compassion on them in this matter?

I learned the answer to that question when Lavan's

next outburst rose to a feverish pitch. "I have it in my power to do you harm!" The wind carried Lavan's screeching away and a long silence followed. My heart skipped a beat. Had my aging father collapsed from the strain of the confrontation? With relief, I heard him continue, his tone more subdued. "But yesterday, the God of your father's spoke to me, saying, 'Watch yourself—least you say anything to Ya'akov good or bad.'"

Again, there was a low rumble I could not catch. But Lavan's high pitched reply carried clearly. "Granted that you had to leave because you longed so deeply for your father's house, but why did you steal my gods?"

Goaded by that accusation, Ya'akov's voice rose to match Lavan's. "Anyone with whom you find your gods shall not live! In front of our people, identify whatever is yours that is with me and take it back!"

"The gods!" I gasped. "Yissakhar. Quickly. Run to Rachel's tent and tell her to hide the gods. Lavan has come looking for them and your father vowed to kill the person who took them. Run! Warn her! Your father knows nothing about Rachel and those gods."

Yissakhar sped off to do my bidding while I hurriedly dressed. I felt my way around the back of our tents, trying to reach Rachel's dwelling without being seen. I heard Lavan storm into Ya'akov's tent, sure the idols were there. Silly man. Why would Ya'akov steal gods that he despised? Which way would Lavan's search lead next? Would he go to Rachel's tent on Ya'akov's right or mine on his left? "Please God, guide him to my tent. Give us time."

I arrived at Rachel's tent to find her in a panic, gathering gods into her arms, dropping them on the floor and picking them up, her breathing ragged . . . "Rachel, put them under your camel saddle. Good. Are there more? Put them with the others. Now lay a rug over the saddle and sit on it. When Abba comes, tell him you have been hit by the weapon and the saddle is defiled with your blood. You know how squeamish he is about the moon-flow. He will not look under it."

Rachel giggled despite her fear, and did as I

suggested while Yissakhar and I disappeared around the back of the tent to listen. Praise God that Lavan searched other tents first, giving Rachel time to compose herself before he burst in on her without so much as a morning greeting. I felt the goatskin bulge as Abba rummaged through Rachel's belongings that were stacked around the sides of the tent.

Rachel greeted Father politely and asked what he was doing. She sounded shocked when he explained. I could hear Lavan's search getting closer to Rachel and held my breath until she said, "Please do not be angry that I cannot rise before you, for I am having the way of women."

At that, Abba left Rachel's dwelling. "With a face as red as a sunburned northerner," said Yissakhar later.

There were a few negotiations afterward, and the two men came to a peaceable agreement. A celebration followed, involving the tambourines and lyres Lavan first suggested. The next morning, we kissed Abba a final goodbye and my heart sat heavy in my chest. Father's ways were often hurtful, but his bluster had always been a part of my life. It felt strange to face a future without it.

BROTHERS

As our journey continued, we visited the ancient city of Hallab. There, I retold the famous story of Avram giving milk to the poor during his stay. The familiar tale came to life as we walked the streets where it happened. At Hamath we visited the legendary chadoufs that made Yitz'chak such a wealthy man in the land of G'rar. Re'uven especially enjoyed seeing the place where the story originated. Days later, Quanta's huge palace awed the children as we squinted up at its towers. They talked about it for days, imagining the lives of the people who lived behind the walls. We traded at Dammesek, birthplace of Eli'ezer, the servant of Avraham who journeyed to our kumbet village in search of a wife for Yitz'chak—our own Aunt Rivkah. Then, sun scorched and travel weary, we arrived at the base of Mount Hermon to bathe in the bubbling springs and rest from our adventures. The only blight on our journey was Ya'akov's growing anxiety.

We speculated about the trouble between him and his brother, but Ya'akov told us nothing. He sent daily scouts to see if 'Esav was in the area. He rested very little, becoming gaunt and surly. Even Rachel avoided him.

While camping by a brook one night, one of Ya'akov's scouts trotted a haggard little donkey right into our supper circle. The man slipped off the heaving sides of the beast and knelt in the dirt at Ya'akov's feet. "Esav is camped beyond the next mountain," he said. "I told him you want to win his favour. He is coming to meet you and with him are four hundred men."

Ya'akov sprang to his feet and divided his people and herds in two. Like a locust cloud, the air buzzed with alarm. "If 'Esav comes to comes to one camp and strikes it, the camp that is left will escape," he said. Then he climbed the hill above the river and lifted his arms to the emerging stars. "Deliver me please, from my brother's hand, for I am afraid of him that he will come and strike me and the mothers with the children." His hoarse prayers bounced off the hills until the morning broke. Then Ya'akov instructed servants to drive a huge peace offering of flocks and herds toward his brother.

In hopes of tempting him back to our morning meal, Zilpah took Ya'akov a ladle of ale and a few olives. He joined us reluctantly, not knowing what else to do. He did not look at us. His gaze followed the disappearing livestock. Then he got to his feet and insisted we all ford the brook with the best of our possessions.

Did he think the tiny brook would protect us from 'Esav and four hundred warriors? There was nothing to do but go along with our husband's wild panic, so we left Ya'akov on the opposite bank of the stream, alone all night with his fears.

Limping toward us and doubled in pain, Ya'akov appeared at our pottage circle next morning. Rachel jumped up and ran to support him. "What happened? How were you injured? Did a beast attack you in the night?" We were riveted to his reply, wanting to know if the danger he faced would affect our little ones. Ya'akov sank onto the rugs, his body weary and broken but his spirit surprisingly buoyant. Amazed at the change in his demeanor we asked again, "What happened?"

"I have seen God face to face, yet my life was spared. I wrestled with a Man until daybreak, not willing to stop until he blessed me. He told me my name is changed from this day forward. I am to be called Yisra'el (He Wrestles). I asked the Man's name but he declared none—though he gave me the blessing of God." After relaying this amazing news, Ya'akov refreshed himself with a morning meal and slept away the rest of the day as soundly as a newborn babe.

Groggy from sleep, I woke the next morning with a scratching of grit in my throat. I assumed it was a sandstorm coming in from the desert, but Ya'akov's frantic commands woke us to the realization that it was the day he feared. A cloud of dust was stirred up by an army of four hundred men—and 'Esav.

The glaring sun we assembled under, allowed me to observe Ya'akov, limping in pain as he led us straight toward a choking wall of dust. It almost swallowed him up before he held up his hands, stopped our march, and prostrated himself on the ground seven times.

'Esav's army came to a halt that threw the dust cloud even higher. Then it settled all around us, and on us, on everything. A huge, ruddy man emerged from the cloud and dismounted his camel in a flurry of flowing robes. He ran toward Ya'akov and we all froze—suspended in dread. 'Esav almost knocked Ya'akov off his feet and threw huge arms around his neck. The brothers, locked tightly together, kissing and weeping and rocking back and forth.

"How is Father?"

"He is well. Rich as ever and full of years. Mother found a remedy for his eyes and he has regained much of his sight."

"That is good. How are D'vorah and Shabar? Still alive?"

"Yes, as always, the faithful servants. They will be glad to welcome you home."

"And Eli'ezer?"

"He sleeps with his fathers now. Hevron is not the same without him."

With questions answered, 'Esav looked up and saw us staring at him like so many cows. "Who are these with you?"

"The wives and children God has graciously given to your servant," Ya'akov said. Then he beckoned us forward and we prostrated ourselves while Ya'akov introduced us in turns. After the introductions, we rose self-consciously and began to beat the dust off each other, valiantly trying not to choke or sneeze as we did so.

"What do you mean by this whole caravan that I have met?" asked 'Esav. He was still looking intently at us while his massive arm remained around Ya'akov.

"To find favour in your eyes, my lord." replied Ya'akov, still hesitant to believe that 'Esav was so friendly.

'Esav laughed and slapped his brother on the back. The force of the blow made Ya'akov stagger but

'Esav seemed not to notice Ya'akov's wince of pain. "I have plenty already my brother, keep your possessions for yourself."

Ya'akov regained his footing and straightened his robes, "No. Please! If I have found favour in your eyes, then you will take my offering from my hand."

After much feasting and celebration, 'Esav returned to his home near Se'ir and we departed for Sukkot. Ya'akov promised Rachel he would build a house for her there, to give relief from life on the move. There was much to ponder on the way to Sukkot. For example, why did Ya'akov decide to build a dwelling in Sukkot after God told him to return to his birthplace? And, why did Ya'akov not ask 'Esav about the well-being of their mother?

REST

While Yisra'el ignored God's command to reconnect with his kinsmen, the refuge of Sukkot served us well. And while our older sons grew into young men, Dinah romped among the younger ones. Yosef and Dinah were especially close, sharing secrets and dreams, each feeding off the lively imagination of the other.

Dinah overflowed with the essence of honey. She was sweet and spirited with smooth copper coloured skin and hair as red as Z'vulun's. It was thick and curly as a sheep's winter wool. No one could tame it—or her. I was determined as ever to direct her future, and began by giving her the same freedoms and privileges as my sons. Ya'akov looked on with disapproval but did not contest my decisions. Those were blessed days. I was finally at peace with the limitations and disappointments of life, fulfilled in Adonai's plan to build a nation through my offspring, and confident that future prayers would be answered just as past prayers had been. Rachel still possessed the better part of Ya'akov's love, but the Almighty's favour was enough for me.

Ya'akov grew more restless as the years passed—especially during the season of high sacrifice when he renewed his vows to follow the God of his fathers. I pondered the patience of God in allowing Ya'akov's procrastination. And I marveled at the fickleness of Ya'akov who wavered between Rachel's fears and the commands of the One. But finally, the Almighty's Voice was heeded and we packed our belongings to journey south.

VIOLATION

If I squinted, I could see the outline of an ancient tree, a lone guardian on the hillside, watching over the town of Sh'khem. After days of travelling, I longed to dismount the grand camel Ya'akov assigned me. She turned out to be an impolite beast who roared and groaned under my considerable weight.

"Le'ah, organize the women and set up camp. We will stay on the plateau."

I gave my husband a long and speculative look. I knew the story of the tree and Sarai's plea for a house and Avram's refusal to settle in Sh'khem. According to legend, the city was full of evil gods who tempted men to do reprehensible things. The acts themselves were shrouded in mystery, but I knew Ya'akov's family abhorred the place. I drew a breath to say so when Rachel raced up to us. The silver bells on the neck of her pretty white camel jingled, her voice was alight with hope. "Ya'akov, she said, "take no notice of my sister's opinion. Look at that tree. The Oak of Moreh is the most beautiful tree in the land and the Almighty visited your grandfather here. He built an altar and sacrificed a lamb on it. Why would we leave this place? Is this not part of the land your God has promised? We could build a fine house here in the shade of the Oak. You know I long for a home, and the Kena'ani . . ."

"No," I said. "Sh'khem is the city of Ba'al—a storm-god who demands infant sacrifice and leads men to do things only whispered about. How can we bear to gaze down upon this grievous place?"

Ya'akov slumped in his saddle, caught again between the opinions of his wives. And we all knew he would favour Rachel.

༄༅

"Hold still! Unless I tame your flaming tresses, the daughters of Sh'khem will mistake you for a burning bush and run away yelling, 'Fire!'"

"Here," laughed Zilpah, "bind her hair in this ribbon I bought at the market last week. It is the same colour green as her eyes."

Dinah squirmed under the painful tug of the comb, but I persevered to wind the ribbon around the masses of curls. "Did you pay attention when Zilpah taught you how to walk like a proper young lady? Does she need to give you another lesson?"

"Why do you make such a fuss?" pouted Dinah. "Why is it so important how my hair is dressed and how I walk? None of my brothers care about that."

"Of course not," said Zilpah, as she adjusted the laces on Dinah's new robe. "They are your brothers and will love you as you are, but the girls of the town are different. They will see how you look and decide whether they want you among them."

Dinah was quiet as she digested this new information. She was curious about the world beyond our encampment and had worn us down with begging to accompany Zilpah and Bilhah on their weekly trip to the market. She longed to meet girls her age, so I set aside generations of tradition that kept our maidens safely in their homes and I let her go to Sh'khem. I remember praying fervently for her safety while Dinah's buoyant little form faded from the outer limits of my vision.

※

"Lulululululululululululululululululululululululu . . ." Looking up from my potter's wheel, I tried to determine the source of a mourner's wail. It approached our tents from the direction of Sh'khem. It sounded like . . . could it be . . . Bilhah? What had happened?

On a nearby cloth, I cleaned my clay encrusted hands and rose to face the lament. It came closer and louder, shutting out all other sounds. "Bilhah?" She fell at my feet, hugging my legs and trembling, her hot tears splashing onto my toes. Zilpah arrived, panting from her run up the hill. She joined Bilhah at my feet, her grief silent. I touched Bilhah on the top of her head, quieting her so Zilpah could speak.

"Dinah was taken. We were in the market, looking at the melons. We turned away for a moment and she was gone. We heard her scream but the people of Sh'khem blocked our way. She was taken by the prince of the city. They said he has a right to bed a virgin—a tax levied on traders." Zilpah could say no more and fell on her face in the dust while Bilhah's sharp keening declared our heartbreak.

Drawn by the high-pitched wail, Ya'akov, Rachel and Yosef ran from the sheep pens begging Zilpah to repeat her story. They stood in the middle of the courtyard, as motionless as standing-stones, all thoughts of sheep and cattle erased from their minds. Time stopped for all of us. Frozen in horror, no one said a word while the burning sun marched across the arc of the sky to complete the day.

My mind was whirling with the realization that the Almighty had ignored my prayers for Dinah's protection. Paralyzing agony and the sound of Bilhah's wailing held our bodies immobile until our sons came home from the fields and Zilpah once again repeated her story. Though gathered into strong young arms, I was numb to all comfort. The servants made quiet preparations to bed down the livestock, but no one lit the cooking fires.

In the gathering darkness, a group of men, led by Hamor the father of Sh'khem's prince, climbed the hill and drew Ya'akov aside to speak with him. Bristling with outrage, our sons joined their father and the stench of their violent intentions drifted toward me.

Hamor's words were proud and clear as he kissed Ya'akov on both cheeks and slapped his shoulder in a familiar way. "My son, Sh'khem, is very attached to your daughter. Please give her to him for a wife. Intermarry with us. You can give your daughters to us and take our daughter for yourselves."

Hamor must have thought it was a generous offer. And he seemed to ignore the menace of our sons who stood by Ya'akov's side with clubs and staves in full display. His voice only cracked a little as he sweetened the pot in an attempt to avoid an armed clash. "You can live with us and the land will be open to you. Live in it, move about freely in it and settle down in it."

Dumbfounded, Ya'akov stood silent while his sons, weapons ready, formed a barrier between him and the Kena'ani. In response, the men of Sh'khem rustled among themselves, drawing weapons from the folds of their garments. The metallic stink of war filled the air.

Then a hearty young voice filled the space between the two groups. "Would that I find favour in your eyes! Whatever you say to me I will give. Set the dowry as high as you like, but give me your daughter as a wife." It was the prince himself.

My sons muttered among themselves. What were they plotting? When they turned to face the Sh'khemites, Re'uven stepped forward. "We cannot do this thing — give our sister to a man who is uncircumcised — for this is a disgrace to us."

The uneasy Kena'ani adjusted their positions and anxiety heightened as our sons stirred up sinister puffs of dust, forming a solid line of defense. Then Y'hudah's voice sliced through the tension like a sword. "Only on this condition will we consent to what you are asking — that you become like us by having every male among you circumcised."

Levi added, "Then we will give you our daughters and take your daughters for ourselves, and live with you and become one people."

"But," said Shim'on, waving his club for emphasis, "if you do not listen to us and be circumcised, we will take our sister and leave."

No one asked how the brothers planned to accomplish that. After all, they were men of the fields and hills, used to confronting threats from man or beast. And the men of Sh'khem were gatekeepers and traders, softened by town living. I suppose they saw wisdom in complying with our sons' requirements.

Hamor's men hurried back to the city and convinced its citizens to circumcise every male. I do not know exactly how they managed that. I heard later that Sh'khem made himself the first example and put on a very brave show—strutting around as if the procedure was painless. How much poppy juice did he have to consume to carry that off?

As reports of the town's compliance filtered in, our sons laughed. They had lied about making peace with the Kena'ani and I did not care. How could Dinah be abandoned? How could we buy, sell, and intermarry with a people who consider children fair game for the ravishes of adult men? For two days and two nights we kept to our tents without food, turning our faces to the wall while imagining Dinah in that evil place. How I longed to hold her in my arms and comfort her.

Lost in misery, we did not notice when Shim'on and Levi mustered their servants to attack the disabled men in the town below. We barely heard the cries for mercy that drifted up from the valley and mingled with our tears. As we rocked to and fro in grief, we were oblivious that the rest of our sons had joined the plundering of Sh'khem.

ಸಂ∞

In the morning, thick smoke and a growing commotion brought us, choking, from our tents. "What is the meaning of this outrage?" Ya'akov's voice could barely be heard over bawling animals, moaning women, and screaming babies. The smell of blood and excrement was overpowering. Flames from the burning city below, shot sparks onto our plateau, igniting fires and shrieks.

Then I caught their scent. Dinah stood in front of my tent with Y'hudah. I went to the doorway and opened my woollen cloak. She ran inside, enveloped. She did not move or say a word while Ya'akov projected his fear for our safety onto her brothers.

"What have you done? You have brought trouble on me, making me a stench among the inhabitants of the land, the Kena'ani and the P'rizi. They will gather about me and strike me—then I will be destroyed."

I could not see the surprise on our son's faces, but I felt their confusion. They had expected their father's approval. They thought he would hail them as heroes when they rescued his only daughter. Devastated, they drew together in solidarity while Re'uven yelled back at Ya'akov, "Should he treat our sister like a prostitute?"

Intervention was sorely needed at that point, so I voiced an order. "Stop arguing and form a water brigade to put out these fires. Soon, there will be nothing left for the Kena'ani and P'rizi to pillage." Then I guided Dinah into my tent.

I have no idea where the refugees of Sh'khem bedded down that night. My only thought was for Dinah, who clung to me in terror. I coaxed her to eat, but she would not speak, so I gathered her under my cloak like a hen gathers her chicks. Why did God let it happen? Was it punishment for camping in a forbidden place? My anger boiled toward Rachel and Ya'akov. Did they bring this judgement down on us? Then my anger turned on myself. Why did I allow Dinah to go to Sh'khem?

No one slept that night.

The blast of a ram's horn trumpet announced the morning. Yisra'el was summoning us to a sacred assembly. I emerged from my tent with Dinah cowering under my woollen wing. The captured women and children of Sh'khem also gathered silently, Dinah's fear mingling with theirs. They too had suffered a great trauma in witnessing the death of their husbands, fathers, brothers, and sons. And now, their lives depended on the will of Yisra'el.

Our sons, unmarried at that time, stood together, clothed with a new tension. Their lust hung hot and pungent in the air. And though I could not see the women of Sh'khem clearly, I assumed there were pretty ones among them. My anger boiled up again. How could my sons have thoughts of mating after what happened to their sister? Dinah felt my rage and tightened her hold around my waist. Apprehension grew while dawn brightened the sky.

Yisra'el claimed the center courtyard, hands lifted to Heaven in a posture of prayer. Loud and hoarse, he cried out to God in repentance and remorse. He pleaded for mercy. He begged for protection. He fell on his face in tears. Moved by our leader's anguish, our tears joined his and we pressed our faces into the dirt. The Kena'ani women huddled together, sobbing. Only Dinah remained dry eyed in the circle of my arm.

Finally, Ya'akov rose to his feet. He dusted off his robes and waited for the crowd to feel his change of demeanor. Much shuffling and snuffling followed as we stood to face the head of our clan. What would his judgement be? What fate would he proclaim for the women of Sh'khem—and for our sons?

Yisra'el's voice rang out, echoing off the hills and filling the razed valley with sound. "In our midst, there is no god but the One. Divide the plunder of Sh'khem accordingly. Get rid of the foreign gods that are among you. Cleanse yourselves and change your clothes. We are going to move on and go up to Beit-El so that I can make and altar there to God, who answered me in the day of my distress, and has been with me in the way that I have gone."

Without a word, our sons and the women of Sh'khem, moved toward the pile of plunder that had accumulated beside the livestock pens the night before. With quiet discussion back and forth, they sorted out objects of spiritual meaning. Foreign gods and symbolic jewelry amassed at the feet of Ya'akov. And while the heap of idolatrous filth grew in our courtyard, no one noticed Rachel steal back to her tent. I cannot imagine the war in her soul as she fought to lay bare the secret she had kept from our husband for years. Defeat radiated from her as she prostrated herself before Ya'akov and lay our family idols at his feet.

Without a word of rebuke to his favourite wife, Ya'akov attacked his father-in-law's gods with his shepherd's club, smashing them, crushing them, grinding them into dust. Then he dug a hole with his own hands and buried the abominable things beside the Oak of Moreh.

    Straightening from his task, Yisra'el turned to me, "Le'ah, begin this very day, to instruct these women and children. Teach them our ways and tell them the stories of the One."

    Without acknowledging his request, I turned and took Dinah to my tent. Apparently, Yisra'el would serve Adonai despite everything. But after what had happened to Dinah, I was not sure I would. My prayers had been ignored. My daughter had not been protected. And yet, who else could I serve—the filthy gods of the land who condone the murder and rape of children?

MOURNING

"Is it true that your god does not require the sacrifice of children?"

On the hot and dusty road to Beit-El, as Yisra'el instructed me to do, I told stories of the One. Up on a camel, with Dinah cradled in my arms, my answer to that question floated down to the women and children of Sh'khem. "No. Adonai does not demand the death of children. In our community, we never throw our infants into the fire."

"Come now, we know the legend. Your God told Avraham to take Yitz'chak to Mount Moriyya and sacrifice him there."

I understood their skepticism. I also struggled with the mysterious God who protected children sometimes—but not always. Pressing Dinah to me, I grieved her wall of silence. It seemed similar to the wall I was building between myself and the Almighty. To tell the truth, I was furious with God and done with prayer. But Ya'akov had commanded me to explain the unexplainable to these women, so I controlled my anger and carried on, declaring Ya'akov's beliefs.

"Avraham's journey to Moriyya proclaimed his dedication to the One. He displayed the same courage and devotion your menfolk did when they sacrificed your children to Ba'al. But the One stopped Avraham's raised knife and provided a ram, making it clear that the sacrifice of children is not required.

But please understand. The shedding of blood is necessary for the atonement of our wrongdoings. We heedlessly destroy life every time we harm others. Justice demands atonement for our harmful actions. We deserve to die when we hurt those around us. But our God permits a substitute. We sacrifice the best of our flocks for that purpose. We do it to remember that our God of love and forgiveness would become a man and sacrifice himself, if need be."

I felt like a hypocrite. Did I even believe what I said? How could a God of love let my daughter sustain such damage? With tears sliding down my face, I ignored the Sh'khemite women until their sobs gained a momentum I could not disregard. "What is the matter?" I asked. "What has disturbed you?"

There was a wrenching stretch of time while the women reigned in their sorrow enough to speak. Finally, a tight voice choked out some words. "We have lost so many children to the fires. And our souls are crushed by ritual copulation. Our men, afraid to defy the gods of our land, were deaf to our pleas for mercy — so we cried to the heavens for rescue. Did your God of love hear us? Did your God rescue us?"

I was rebuked by the depth of their anguish. Their loss was so much greater than mine. Finally, I managed to say, "Yes, your cries for deliverance were heard, God has rescued you. While you live among us you will never sacrifice your children or be violated by ritual sex."

Their weeping rose to swirl around me like a mighty wind. And prayers of thanksgiving joined their searing pain. Dinah's suffering still stabbed at my heart, but the women's tears opened my inner being to new thoughts. My daughter's ordeal had released these women from unspeakable wickedness. And they were somehow freed from an unbearable future through the angry vengeance of my sons. How could that be? I was unsettled. On that hot and dusty day, the ways of the Almighty almost seemed repulsive — but hope awoke as well. Could there also be a plan to release Dinah from her suffering? Was she being crushed by the Potter so she could be molded into a more beautiful vessel? While I pressed my broken daughter to my heart, I could barely comprehend such a thing. But the question stayed in my soul.

As the force of the Kena'ani women's sorrow began to wane, another woman asked. "In the community of Yisra'el, what rituals do men command of their women? How do your men force their women's subservience?"

"Force subservience? Do not bow to that old lie! Women and men are equal in the eyes of God! Each should work for the other's well-being. No one is subservient. We serve each other." I shuddered, recalling how often we failed to live out that ideal. Then I went on. "The Breath of Life formed Father Adam from the dust of the ground, infusing him with the Divine image. Then God put Adam in a beautiful garden and asked him to tend it. Though he loved his work, Father Adam longed for a companion to help him fulfill his mandate, someone to share his dreams and plans. So, God told the animals and birds to present themselves to Adam, who named each one in turn. But Adam found no mate among them. Then, the Creator put a deep sleep on Adam, took out one of his ribs and formed Mother Havah from a bone fully infused with the image of God. So . . . how can we question our equality?"

The women of Sh'khem trudged along in silence, pondering new things. Then a boy-child spoke up. "If women are so important, why did God wait so long to make one?"

I laughed at the age-old question and gave him my answer. "Father Adam needed time. After being left to cope on his own for a while, he realized how indispensable women are." The Kena'ani women joined my laughter as we rounded a curve in the road. Then Yisra'el bid us stop and make camp on a large field under a single oak. Its deep shade cooled and comforted us as we set up camp.

༄༅

We set up a circle of tents around the solitary tree, and I began making pots beneath its canopy. Being in the middle of the community gave me an advantage. When I heard my boys sniffing around the tents of the Kena'ani women, I was able to interrupt unhealthy liaisons by sending offenders off on random errands. Ya'akov had warned his sons to be moral and chaste with the women, but where was he during these courtyard intrigues? I was also able, from my central position, to observe the new women in our midst. I directed the choice ones toward my sons, and the rest to the hirelings. Re'uven seemed uninterested though, he preferred to spend his time in the large grove above our encampment, helping Bilhah cultivate almonds in the beautiful grove there.

Acute hearing also helped me sound an alert when visitors approached our tents. Detecting a rumble in the distance one day, I called out to Yosef. "Run to the fields and tell your father a caravan approaches from the south. He will want to greet it."

Yosef looked up from his studies, his eyes were unfocused as he tore his mind away from the tablet Yisra'el gave him to read. Dinah looked up also. She had not spoken a word since the horror of Sh'khem. But she found Yosef's company, and the challenge of learning to read, a distraction from her pain. Alarmed by the news, she left her scroll on the bench and sat down by my feet, pressing into my robes while Yosef ran to the fields and I called out orders.

"Zilpah, a caravan is on its way. Prepare for guests tonight. Yissakhar, go get Bilhah. She is in the almond grove. We will need her to bake more bread. Z'vulun, stop tormenting that poor goat and climb a palm tree on the hill to see if you can give us any idea how big the caravan is." In a flurry of activity, we prepared for the travelers: cooking, cleaning, erecting guest tents, and spreading extra rugs on the ground.

They arrived at dusk, outlined against the fading sky. The lead camel collapsed to unload its burden and I strained to see what manner of person would greet us. The chatter of the travelers sounded vaguely familiar. It was an accent like Ya'akov's, so I knew they had come from the south lands. Did they know his kindred? I looked toward Ya'akov, trying to read his reaction. He seemed transfixed for a time, then he limped as fast as he could toward a she-camel.

"D'vorah? Do my eyes deceive me? Is it you? Is it really you?" Their sobs shook us all as they clung to each other and night descended. When their emotions were spent, Ya'akov guided D'vorah to the seat of honour at the cig kofte tray. He helped her settle onto the rugs and sent Yosef for more cushions to support her back. "This is my old nurse, D'vorah. She is also the one who nursed my mother, Rivkah."

We were shocked to silence for we had never, before that day, heard Ya'akov say the name of his mother. I snapped my fingers to signal for food, then we took our places around the tray while gesturing to the newcomers where to sit. We waited politely, serving our guests first and wondering who would begin the conversation.

"How is my father?"

"He is well, and waiting for you to join him in Hevron."

"Is that why he sent you — to ask me to come home?"

"He did not send me. I came on my own errand."

I could smell Ya'akov's tension. In desperation to avoid D'vorah's next words, he gave Re'uven and Shim'on some unnecessary instructions about the gate of the sheep pen, then issued more useless orders to various servants while D'vorah waited patiently.

"Your mother sent me here with a message. It was her last wish that I deliver it."

Ya'akov muffled a groan and his supper-bowl clattered to the ground.

"She begs forgiveness for her part in the plotting. She lived in deep sorrow for the pain she caused. She wants you to know she has died and you can go home. Yitz'chak needs you there."

Seeing his distress, Rachel went to Ya'akov and helped him rise from the rugs. Without a word, they moved toward their tent and disappeared inside.

D'vorah let them go, then leaned over and touched my hand. Her ancient voice trembled as she asked me to take her to the tent prepared for her. I bid Dinah bring some tea and food to D'vorah's tent. She gathered up the things I asked for, and silent as a shadow, she followed us inside.

❧◯☙

D'vorah was buried under our solitary oak. Yisra'el named it the Oak of Weeping. The old servant had used the last of her strength to bring Rivkah's message to Ya'akov. After that, there was nothing Dinah and I could do to staunch the flow of life that seeped from her.

Ya'akov also withdrew from life on hearing the news of his mother's death. He retreated to his tent, sending Yosef back and forth with business messages. Yosef felt important while shouldering this responsibility. But our older sons treated him like a pesky fly.

When not running errands, Yosef spent his time listening to the stories D'vorah told as she journeyed toward eternity. The boyhood antics of Ya'akov and 'Esav made us laugh. And we were saddened by the story of Shabar's terrible childhood. Then the tale of her restored speech held us in awe. Just before she died, D'vorah told us the terrible account of the stolen birthright and blessing—and how the family was fractured as a result. Then she brightened as she described Rivkah and Yitz'chak's home that was wondrously transformed by repentance and servant-hood.

I finally understood Ya'akov's conflicted feelings about his mother. I also saw why he played favourites with his sons. And I decided to break my silence with the One, praying fervently that Ya'akov's heart could be healed like Rivkah's had been, and that Dinah's speech would be restored like Shabar's had.

A short time after D'vorah died, God opened Rachel's womb. In those dark days it was a spark of light for us all. She was ill but triumphant as her belly filled with child. And while she escorted Ya'akov to D'vorah's graveside every day, the two of them hatched a plan as well as a child. I was not invited into their plans. I was merely a bystander, a vigil keeper beside the grave of D'vorah—busy spinning pots.

It was Yosef who broke the news. "We are going on a journey, Dinah. We are travelling south to meet our Saba Yitz'chak. We will leave when the year of mourning for Rivkah and D'vorah is complete. What sights we will see! Do you think Father will let us ride on camels this time? I think we are beyond needing to ride in a cart like babies." Dinah's reading-tablet was suddenly forgotten and my heart jumped into my throat at the news. Shabar's speech had been restored on the journey south to Hevron. Would the same happen to Dinah?

PARTINGS

Determined to arrive before the birth of her child, Rachel set her face toward Hevron. Not even Ya'akov could persuade her to stay safely in Beit-El until the baby came. So, we prepared for our journey with grave misgivings and grimly set a pace moderated for Rachel's swollen body. She rode a sturdy little donkey instead of lurching along on the back of a camel. That, at least, was a good decision.

"How are you feeling?" I asked, as we stopped beside a brook for the noon meal. "Eat these almonds. They will strengthen you. The camel-boys say that the journey from here to Biet-Lechem is mountainous and taxing. We should rest for the night and climb the hills in the cool of the morning."

"Le'ah, do not try to dissuade me. I need to escape the territory of our old gods. They know their likenesses were smashed into dust at Sh'khem, and I fear their retribution. Perhaps in Hevron, my child will be safely under the protection of Avraham's God."

I sighed and shook my head. There was no arguing with Rachel when her mind was made up. I gave a nod to Zilpah. We gathered up the dishes, rolled up the rugs, then straddled our donkeys to face the mountains ahead.

※

"Dinah. Run to Biet-Lechem and fetch a midwife. Do not stand there. Run!" Wide eyed and terrified, Dinah made no move to go. "Take Yosef with you. He will speak for you and keep you safe. Run! Now!"

They flew off like arrows and I was relieved they would not witness Rachel's rising agony. My sisters and I had no experience at all with such a birth. Bilhah gave Rachel soothing herbs but she vomited them onto the ground. Zilpah rubbed her back and stomach but was swatted off and screamed at. My fingers were blue from gripping Rachel's hand and I begged God for mercy. Early that morning the men had taken the flocks into the hills to find pasture. The rest of us had stayed at our camp beside the road on the way to the town of Biet-Lechem. I dispatched one of the camel-boys to tell Ya'akov what was happening, and pleaded with the Almighty to help Dinah and Yosef find a midwife.

The children returned with an unveiled woman who broke into our circle and barked out commands. "Light a fire and heat more water. Bring a larger vat of olive oil if you have one. Does anyone have clean linen? Good. Dip it in the brook and press it to her forehead." The orders went on and on . . .

"Le'ah? Are you there?"

"I am here Rachel, holding your hand. I will not leave you."

"Le'ah, I am sorry for grieving you these many years. Jealousy overpowered my love. I am so sorry."

"All is forgiven Rachel. I am happy another child is on the way. Are you feeling the urge to push?"

"Le'ah . . ." A spasm ripped through Rachel's body. She went rigid and pushed with all her might then fell back in my arms. "Le'ah . . . take the gems from my neck. Take them and put them around yours. Promise that you will mother Yosef. Promise me." Another contraction racked her body and she cried out. "Take care of Yosef. Promise me!"

"Do not be afraid," consoled the midwife as she wrestled the child from Rachel's womb,"for this is also a son for you. What will you name him?"

"Bin-Oni (Son of My Grief)," said Rachel, as tears rolled down her face. "He was conceived in a time of grief and will live in the shadow of grief."

And, from that moment on, my beloved sister slipped slowly away, her earthly labours complete.

We stayed by her side until the Twin constellation melted into the pale light of dawn and disappeared. Zilpah thought the Twin stars represented the twofold purpose of God. As the Twin with the harp, the Redeemer will come in peace to comfort us in sorrow. As the second Twin, the Redeemer will come with a weapon — to conquer the cause of our sorrow.

Later that night, Ya'akov pressed a lovely sardonyx into Rachel's cooling hand. Its red and white stripes echoed the twofold promise of the stars, assuring us that the God of Avraham was both our comforter and deliverer.

༺༻

Though grief dragged our spirits to the ground and would not let them rise, sorrow's heavy burden must be carried no matter the tasks at hand. Yisra'el set a standing stone on Rachel's grave but could not find nearby pastures for the flocks. So, we moved our camp to the other side of Migdalia Eder and made a pilgrimage to Rachel's graveside every evening for a year.

Our older sons fled from our grief, making the excuse to seek new pastures. Their youthful spirits could not endure another year of mourning—or their father's further withdrawal. Bilhah went to cook for the young men, and to escape our oppressive gloom. As Rachel's handmaid, she had been mistreated, so she did not grieve as deeply as Zilpah and I. And there was her attachment to Re'uven...

༺༻

"Keep this woman away from me! I cannot bear the sight of her! If I were Kena'ani she would die!" Without a further word, Ya'akov turned on his heel and left. The door-cloth snapped behind him while Bilhah collapsed on the floor of my tent.

"Bilhah, what happened? ... Bilhah?"

Daylight flashed into the tent when Zilpah entered. Stooping, she touched Bilhah's shoulder but got no response. She gathered little Bilhah into her arms and cradled her like a child, stroking her hair and murmuring comfort.

"What happened, Zilpah? What did she do? I have never seen Ya'akov so..."

"She defiled his bed. She lay with Re'uven. What will become of her? What will Ya'akov do?" Zilpah rocked Bilhah back and forth in agony.

I put my hand to my mouth to hold back the gorge that rose in my throat at the thought of what I heard. "Bilhah is this true? Did you do this wicked thing?"

Bilhah nodded and forced out a sobbing explanation. "R . . . Reu . . . Re'uven was so broken, so forlorn, so . . . so beaten down by . . . by Ya'akov's rejection . . . I saw him crying alone in the field and went to comfort him. It . . . it somehow happened. I have always loved him but now my love has ruined him." As Bilhah's small keening wail filled the dark tent, Zilpah and I said nothing but we knew our lives would never be the same.

JOURNEYS

We straggled into Hevron, a sorry company and much diminished in numbers. Ya'akov waited out Rachel's year of mourning but hurried to leave the vicinity of her grave after that. He all but banished Re'uven, Shim'on, Levi and Y'hudah to a region around Sh'khem, giving them charge of half the flock in compensation. Then he rounded up the rest of his family and his livestock to head south to The Oaks of Mamre.

I lost my sister and four sons that year. And though the rhythms of life continued, I felt detached from everything. Zilpah and I did the best we could for Bilhah and Dinah — our two shattered ones. In those dark days, it was a discipline to praise the One, but it was also the only act that gave me any hope.

When we arrived in Hevron, Yitz'chak gave us a chieftain's welcome. He hosted a great feast under The Oaks of Mamre, inviting neighbours and kindred from all around. Ya'akov commissioned Zilpah to weave Yosef a multicoloured coat for the occasion. And he introduced Yosef as his heir. He introduced Rachel's baby as Bin'yamin (Son of the South). Zilpah and Bilhah's sons were kept away from the feast, occupied in the outer fields. And Ya'akov only mentioned my children when someone specifically asked after them.

Bilhah, in disgrace, did only menial work while Zilpah, Dinah, and I ate with 'Esav's wives who gossiped about the news brought by passing caravans. The biggest story was about a man named Iyov, grandson of Yishma'el, a godly man who lost everything in a series of terrible disasters. 'Esav's disrespectful wives mocked the fellow mercilessly.

"That's what comes from thinking you only need to sacrifice to one god," cackled Adah.

"Yes," said Oholivamah as she reached for another helping of lentil stew. "I heard this god did not protect Iyov's children even though he made sacrifices on their behalf. What was Iyov thinking when he rejected the gods of Yishma'el? Does he not see our prosperity?"

"I heard it was sin that caused Iyov's god to abandon him," said Basmat. "But Elifaz told me the man would admit to no wrongdoing. What arrogance!"

"Is it true that he sits in the rubble of his life, scraping away at his boils?" asked Adah.

"Yes, Elifaz says Iyov's revolting sores ooze a putrid liquid that stinks to the heavens. He scrapes at them with broken pieces of pottery, crying out all the while for Adoani to save him. Please pass the dolmas, Le'ah, but help yourself first. In your time up north, did you hear of this Iyov? He was once the greatest man of the east but now is so disgusting his wife wants nothing to do with him. She told him to curse his god and die, then she walked out of his life to live in her brother's house."

"Who could blame the poor woman?" I said, "She lost everything . . . her children, her home, her possessions, everything. And this man, Iyov, still petitions God after all he lost?"

"Yes," snorted Adah. "Who but a madman would cling to his god after that?"

Who indeed? What manner of man was Iyov? I had experienced the pain of multiple losses but not on that vast scale. And like Iyov, I clung to faith, hoping for some small sign of better days. I longed to meet Iyov, but not to comfort him. I had no solace to offer. All I wanted was to sit with him and wait for rescue. And, I could make him some new pots . . .

What were those haughty women laughing at now? What did they whisper behind their hands while they looked Dinah up and down? Did we come all the way to Hevron just to be derided by silly women with nothing better to do?

"Dinah, guide me to our tent. Then look for Yosef and bring him to our door. I have a proposal to make to your father. If I ask Yosef to explain my petition, Ya'akov will back our cause. Your father refuses him nothing. Go find him now. I will put some thought into my plan while I wait for you."

We were almost ready for our journey. Shabar had packed samples of all the healing potions Rivkah discovered over the years. A patient little donkey was laden with them and their containers clinked musically when he shifted position. Dinah had packed meticulously copied instructions for all of Rivkah's cures and ointments. I was proud of her skill as a scribe. It was an unusual occupation for a woman—born from the need to communicate. In a way, the One had answered my prayer. Dinah's speech was restored through the skill of writing.

Zilpah had worked for months, weaving beautiful tapestries, rugs, and all manner of household linens to replenish Iyov's supply. They were neatly folded into camel packs now. Bilhah was ready to go on our journey but counted her bags of seed one more time. She included every variety she had cultivated over the years.

As gifts for Iyov, Yisra'el and Yitz'chak had separated out portions of their herds and flocks. True to their natures, the patriarchs gave generously of their best. And my youngest sons, Yissakhar and Z'vulun were filled with the spirit of adventure, proud to represent the sons of Yisra'el as they escorted us to the land of Utz.

In leaving Hevron to bless Iyov, I admit my motives were somewhat selfish. I sought a place for Dinah to start a new life—away from wagging tongues and crippling memories. And I hoped the company of someone who also suffered deeply, would help her heal. And ... I wanted to shelter my two youngest sons from patriarchal favouritism. However, I did pray that our bountiful gifts would truly encourage Iyov.

Ya'akov stood apart from us, watching our preparations. He knew the expedition was partially my attempt to get some distance from the hurt of our past. But he bore no grudge. My departure from Hevron would also distance him from painful memories. And then there was Bilhah ... the separation would be best for both of them.

As we made our final arrangements, we were a

noisy company charged with purpose and excitement. We were feasted, blessed, instructed, warned and embraced as we prepared to leave. I looked around for Yosef and spotted his colourful coat. I knew he would miss us deeply and was glad Zilpah would stay to mother him. He was still young enough to need it.

"Yosef, come here. You are not too old for a farewell kiss, are you?"

Yosef closed the distance between us and I heard the smile in his voice. "I will never be too old for a kiss Mother Le'ah, but I do not like farewells."

"And it hurts to be left out of an adventure?"

He laughed, then became serious. "I am glad of your chance to escape," he said. "Your life in the family has been difficult. I have seen the pain you carry."

I pressed Yosef to my breast, grieved for the pain he carried. Being the favourite is not a blessing. It is isolating and lonely, perhaps even dangerous considering his brothers' hot tempers. "The Almighty gives a way of escape when the right time comes," I said. "You will have your own journey in time, Yosef. No eye has seen, no ear has heard, and no one's heart has imagined all the things that God has prepared for you."

Yosef led me safely around the piles of luggage being loaded into carts. He helped me mount my waiting camel and adjusted her bridle. He handed me the reins before he spoke. "I fear that the journeys of God are not always as joyful as the one you embark on today, Mother Le'ah."

"No, they are not, Yosef." I reached down to touch his cheek, sad to leave this boy who was wise beyond his years. "The purposes of God are most often fulfilled through suffering. And every sorrow is redeemed through praise. When you are called to suffer, praise God in the midst of it and wait for deliverance. It will come."

Yosef took my hand from his cheek and tenderly kissed my palm. "I will follow your example, Mother Le'ah. I will keep my hope in the Almighty."

Isaiah 54:5

For your Maker is your husband. Adonai-Tzva'ot is his name. The Holy One of Yisra'el is your Redeemer. He will be called the God of all the earth.

Psalm 71:18,21

So even until I am old, and gray, O God do not forsake me, God, till I tell of your strong arm to the next generation, your might to all who are to come. For your righteousness O God, reaches to high heaven. You have done great things—O God. Who is like you? You made me see many troubles and evils—You will revive me again—from the depths of the earth you will bring me up again. You will increase my greatness and comfort me once again.

Matthew 5:4

Blessed are those who mourn, for they shall be comforted.

Tamar

The heavens declare the glory of God,
and the sky shows his handiwork.
Day to day they speak, night to night
they reveal knowledge.

> Psalm 19:1, 2

TAMAR

ACCUSED AND CONVICTED

I told Mother I was visiting the latrine, knowing full well she would ply me with constipation remedies when I got back. Her disgusting remedies were a small price to pay for sneaking away from my chores and climbing the hill above our village to soak in the glory of the golden time.

When the sun begins its descent, our village dwells in shadow. But if the sky is right, I climb the hill that divides our village from Y'hudah's. I love to see the sun gild the world, especially when no one knows I am watching—except the Creator—who enjoys the wonder with me.

That day, Y'hudah's people were scurrying about like ants whose hill had been disturbed. Sharp evening shadows followed busy servants carrying armloads of bedding and supplies. Several tents were erected on the outskirts of the village and beautiful woven rugs were spread at the entrances. Y'hudah was expecting guests, important guests who merited more than a hastily constructed shelter in the central courtyard. It was not a trading caravan then, but who could it be?

Shelah stood on top of the far hill, looking intently toward the eastern trade route. He had recently grown from a pup to a man, his body filling out to match the size of his feet and hands. If Y'hudah kept his word, I would soon be summoned to consummate a marriage with his youngest son.

What would marriage to Shelah be like? Would he accept me and love me and give me a child? Would I finally find a place to belong? Or would Shelah treat me like his older brothers had? I shuddered as terrible memories flashed and flared. My last two marriages were complete failures ending in the death of both husbands — Y'hudah's older sons. Y'hudah then promised me to Shelah when he grew up — so I could bear an heir for 'Er, his first born. Not that 'Er deserved an heir.

    I focused again on Shelah as he stood on the distant hilltop across the valley from me. Y'hudah's family lived in the south, but Shelah faced due east as he waited for the expected visitors to come into view. Who could the travellers be? They had obviously sent a messenger ahead to let Y'hudah's family know of their coming, so it had to be a company known to the tribe. Who would be arriving from the east? I searched my memory for family or acquaintances who might arrive from that direction but could think of no one that would cause such a commotion. Everyone in the village was dressed in their best and delicious aromas drifted to the top of my hill. It was not the smell of the usual lentil pottage, but a complex mix of many dishes — a feast.

    "They are here!" Shelah shouted. "They are here!" A reckless descent declared his youth and I winced as his body tumbled past his feet, sending him plummeting down the hill, smudging his multi-coloured cloak with dirt. If his mother Bat-Shua were still alive, she would be livid at the mess he made of it.

    As the caravan emerged from behind the eastern hills, sunlight flowed over and around them. It sparkled through the dust and danced on man and beast. It lit their forms in sharp relief while glinting off the daggers that hung at the sides of the guards who led and followed the caravan. Judging by the colourful blankets and ornate leather saddles gracing the camels' backs, it was a wealthy group.

    A rusty-haired man on the lead camel flashed a wide grin, jumped off his beast, and ran toward Y'hudah — who stood on the road facing the newcomers. They embraced, rocking from side to side and talking over each other in loud exclamations of greeting. Another man, dark and swarthy, trotted his camel up to them before jumping down to join their embrace. Who were they? They had the look of Y'hudah's kindred.

Were they perhaps, Y'hudah's brothers? Why had they come from the east, not the south?

In unison, the three men turned toward a she-camel that pulled away from the line and drew up beside them. Y'hudah caught the creature's bridle, gave it the command to kneel down and helped a large veiled woman dismount. He put his hands on her shoulders and stared into her eyes for a long moment. Then he lay his head on her breast and wept. She wrapped her generous arms around him and stroked his hair like a child. She had to be his mother.

I knew all about her. Le'ah was the one who tricked Ya'akov into marriage. On the day of her sister Rachel's wedding, Le'ah impersonated the rightful bride and usurped the place of the first wife. That despicable act set a crooked course. It birthed great conflict between the sisters and their sons.

Y'hudah pulled away from his mother's embrace and wiped his tears on his sleeve while beckoning for Shelah to come closer. When Le'ah reached out to feel the contours of Shelah's face, I remembered hearing about her weak eyes. Le'ah's exploring fingers suddenly stopped. She lowered her chin to her breast and I could not read her emotions. Was she sad? Angry? Surprised? Her sons stood uneasily around her. And Shelah, awkward youth that he was, froze in place with his arms dangling to his knees like an ape. They always said he was the exact image of his grandfather Ya'akov, who had banished Le'ah's six sons from his presence, favouring Rachel's boys.

I rubbed my neck. It was sore from the strain of trying to understand the scene that played out below. After all that Le'ah had done to destroy his family, I could not grasp why Y'hudah would welcome her to his village. And how could Y'hudah embrace her while he shunned me? Though I had not acted deceitfully in any way, I was thrown out of Y'hudah's village after the death of Onan. And no one cared to hear my side of the story.

Y'hudah guided Le'ah to the cig kofte tray and gave her the seat of honour, a place no woman had occupied as long as I had known the clan. Even the esteemed Bat-Shua was relegated to the women's section on the other side of the tray.

It was a quiet gathering as they all leaned in to catch up on family news—most of which was not good. Y'hudah played absently with his food while he talked, and Le'ah stroked his knee in comfort. I ducked into the tall grass when Y'hudah gestured toward the hill between our villages. The brothers who arrived with Le'ah, glared in my direction until she gathered their attention back to the kofte tray and somehow got them laughing—probably at me. So I slithered backward on my stomach, leaving them to their speculation that I was responsible for bringing a curse of death on their family. I sighed and rose to my feet. It was time to go home and face Mother's constipation remedies.

STORIES AND STARS

Wildly whirling above my head, a canopy of silver leaves spun in an azure sky. Woven together with wonder, the revolving leaves were interlaced with dark, delicate branches and dotted with pale green olives. Lost in the beauty of the moment, I ignored the sound of a donkey walking along the trail to my village. I hoped the beast and its the rider would pass me by without a tiresome comment on the weather, or the harvest, or something else I had no wish to discuss. I was irritated when the donkey's clopping slowed to a stop and its rider asked, "Why have you confused Metushelach?"

This was not the conversation starter I expected so I stopped twirling around, and waited for the rotating earth and sky to slow enough to reveal a large woman on a rattled donkey. It was Le'ah. What was she doing on the path to my village? "Who is Metushelach?" I asked.

"He is my ancient donkey who takes me from place to place. If he comes across a suspicious activity, he stops until he feels safe to proceed. What were you doing?"

Annoyed at being questioned, I considered making up a wild story for Le'ah to take home to her judgmental family. Then I remembered her weak eyesight. Perhaps she could not see what I was doing. What would she say if she knew?

"I was twirling."

"Twirling? Well, that explains Metushelach's confusion. Why were you twirling?"

Again, I considered making something up to spare my reputation, but that was already in tatters so I told the truth. "When I twirl around, the world blends into beautiful patterns and I forget my troubles."

"Yes, I can see how that might work. But now, will you be so kind as to walk over here and stroke my donkey's nose so he knows you have stopped twirling?"

I had no intention of stroking that filthy old nose, so I stood beside the road with my arms crossed over my chest.

"Please, I need to take this path to the village of Hirah. Do you know it?"

"What is your business there?"

"I seek a young woman named Tamar. I have some embroidery I want done, and I hear she is very skilled."

"Tamar's family keeps her busy day and night with all manner of chores. What makes you think they would release her to embroider something for you?"

"I will make the embroidery very profitable for Hirah. I will sit beside Tamar as she works, and I will spin pots for his household. We will trade our labour. I am also very skilled."

My resistance dissolved. Le'ah's pottery was a great treasure in the household of Y'hudah. For years I had wondered how she spun such delicate shapes without the benefit of good eyesight. So, I stroked the old donkey's nose, grabbed his bridle, and led him down the path to my home. I did not need to tell Le'ah who I was. She already knew.

ଛୋର

The next morning, I did not pause to marvel at the inky black branches of the gnarled terebinth that shaded our courtyard. I did not revel in its sharp medicinal scent or notice the oval patterns the leaves made in the red dust at my feet. Le'ah was on her way, and orders were given to prepare a spot for her pottery wheel and kiln. For some reason our equipment was not good enough, and pitiful little Anat was assigned to help me clear a place for Le'ah's. Anat, a lowly latrine slave was assigned to this task! This measured the disdain my family had for me — and for Le'ah.

What was Anat doing? She would need to work harder than that if we were to be ready for Le'ah's arrival. "Anat, pick up the broom and make it useful on the pile of rotten fruit over there. And put those rocks by the wall. When you finish, fetch me a ladle of water, it is hotter than the fires of Molech in this courtyard." Perverse little Anat moved sluggishly to the rock pile.

She knew my parents would not insist that she obey my directives. Since I had returned from Y'hudah's village in shame, I was nothing to them but a problem, a blot on their reputations, a constant reminder of the disapproval of our closest neighbours. But did Anat think herself to be a princess instead of a slave? "Anat, before you deal with those rocks, come back and finish cleaning up the fruit. Concentrate on your task, girl. What are you staring at now?"

Anat's eyes had widened as she focused on a spot behind my shoulder. I turned to follow her gaze. Le'ah had arrived, accompanied by Shelah who carried a bundle wrapped in linen. He avoided my eyes and shuffled from foot to foot awaiting his grandmother's instructions. Le'ah ignored Shelah for the moment and directed her attention to my slave. "Anat . . . did I hear your name correctly? Anat? Kindly take Metushelach over to a shady spot beside the wall. He is old enough that you do not need to tie him up, but he should not be allowed to make deposits on our workspace. Shelah, help me dismount, then go fetch Metushelach a bucket of water. And hurry back, I will need you over here."

I picked up the broom to finish the task my slave had abandoned. Muttering under my breath about being reduced to a slave's labour must have distracted me from what was happening. For when I looked up, Anat was striding importantly toward me with Shelah's bundle in her arms. Shelah stepped forward and took the broom from me, and Anat placed the parcel in my hands then knelt at my feet. She bent, with her face to the ground in a posture of homage. What on earth possessed a surly little slave like her to bow down like that? I certainly had no standing in our household that would warrant it. I was so puzzled that I hardly noticed Le'ah's presence until her shadow fell on us.

"You hold The Cloth of Redemption in your hands," she said.

"The what?"

"Open the bindings and see for yourself."

Untying the string that bound the parcel, I folded back the fine white wrapping and touched the newly exposed cloth. I drew in my breath. Never before had I felt anything like it—so cool and smooth—like a mountain spring.

I glanced questioningly at Le'ah while Anat got to her feet. Stepping forward, my servant helped me unfurl the cloth. Flashing red and silver in the sun, it danced for joy in a sudden breeze that tumbled off the hills. Light as air, the cloth played in the wind and the bells on its edge sang out a song of joy. Had I not anchored it in my grasp, it would have escaped to the hills. Shelah's face softened at the sight, and the village children ran to join us.

"It came to Egypt long ago as a gift for queen Neferu," said Le'ah. "Before she died, she bid her servant to keep watch for a woman who would be redeemed from the court of the pharaoh. The price was paid by the pharaoh himself and Sarah was redeemed."

Gathering the cloth in from the sky, Anat and I folded its great length into the linen casing while it bubbled through our fingers like a water-brook in the sun. Then I turned back toward Le'ah, sensing she had more to say.

"It was given to Rivkah when she was redeemed from bondage to the house of B'tuel. She wore it as a wedding veil. When Ya'akov left home, she bid him keep watch for the woman who would one day be redeemed to marry him. She requested that he give her this cloth as a wedding garment. Both Rachel and I wore it when we were redeemed from the idolatry of our father."

The breeze deserted us as suddenly as it had arrived, and my voice sounded small in the vacuum left behind. "Is this the garment you wish me to embroider?"

"Yes. But first you need to know about the birth of Ya'akov's sons so you can sew their constellations and birthstones onto the cloth. Shelah, go get the rugs from Metushelach's saddle packs and spread them out in the shade of this lovely tree. Anat, you may finish clearing away the rocks and debris so we can sit here comfortably. And Tamar, go fetch your aged grandmother a ladle of cool water and a few bowls of raisins or almonds. On second thought, bring enough water and meze for everyone who wants to hear the stories."

༄༅

Stars bloomed, one by one, in the silent meadows of the sky. I like the darkness. Unless the sky grew dark, we would never see the stars. That night I sat alone on the top of my hill and sloughed off the gloom of my soul to ponder their mysteries. Y'hudah's Lion roared across the heavens, flanked by Naftali's Virgin and Yissakhar's Scarab, the symbol of eternity. Le'ah's stories flamed and flared through my mind . . . from the Virgin . . . would come a Ruler who would usher in an Eternal Kingdom. How could those things be? I jumped to my feet, frightened by my thoughts and questions. It was all just legend anyway, tall tales that Le'ah heard on her travels. She said the knowledge was preserved since ancient times, but how could I believe a deceiver like her?

Then I remembered Le'ah weak eyes. Had she never seen the stars? If I embroidered the family constellations on The Cloth of Redemption, could her fingers see what her eyes could not? Suddenly, my mind flowed with ideas and I was lost in the thrill of creation.

༄༅

One with the earth, she settled under our terebinth, her contours echoing the shape of her earthen jars. To her, the smell of clay was as lovely as the smell of flowers, and she spun elaborate pots and tales together, exuberant under the dappled light of the tree. Glowing with concentration, her face unlined despite her age, was mesmerizing as she talked.

I vented my anger at her joy by stabbing the delicate weave of the magnificent veil with my embroidery needle. How dare she pretend that all was well? How dare she tell stories of hope and love when injustice and rejection ruled our world? How dare she fill the village children's heads with tales of Adonai, while the furnace of Molech loomed on the hill above, waiting to devour them?

Despite dark thoughts, I skillfully pulled the golden thread up through the crimson cloth. Then I pushed it down to begin a journey toward each neighbouring star. Naftali's sky-blue chalcedony, the betrothal stone, was placed in the Virgin's hand. Y'hudah's blood-red carnelian was fastened on the heart of the Lion. And while I sewed, Le'ah's stories continued. They were stories of hope I could never feel, stories of joy that made me bitter, stories of belonging that excluded me. In and out I pierced and pulled my mounting anger through the weave. Finally, I could take no more and interrupted the tale of Yosef's birth with a wrathful outburst.

"I know the other stories—the ones whispered in dark corners—the ones you would never tell in the presence of children. How can you sit here spinning marvels when your suffering hangs in the air like carrion birds?"

Le'ah's face remained placid while her hands caressed the vessel in front of her. She did not miss a turn of the wheel while she answered. "Yes, little Tamar, what you say is true. Life is full of suffering, and I am no stranger to its blows. I am a broken pot, fractured by conflict and hardship. But God poured silver into the cracks of my life. And joy now shines from the empty places—the places where I once bled."

Le'ah sent the children to refill the meze bowls and asked Anat to put the cast pots in the sun to dry. Leaning toward me, she said, "Like you, my daughter Dinah suffered from heedless lust. She was also damaged by what happened to her."

Snorting in outrage, I jumped up from my work. Pretending to need a drink from the water jar, I bent over the ladle and spit out the words, "Bat-Shua told me how Dinah seduced the prince of Sh'khem so your sons could start a war where the men were murdered, the city looted, and all their women forced into slavery. How dare you compare me with her."

"Bat-Shua told you that?"

I looked over at Le'ah, shocked at the change in her

voice. The pottery wheel stopped and she sat upright. Her dark eyes emptied of life and tears made tiny rivulets on her dusty cheeks.

Anat hurried back to Le'ah's side and dipped a clean linen cloth in the water jar. Tenderly, she wiped the dust and clay from Le'ah's face and hands. Then she helped Le'ah to her feet and led her toward Metushelach. Just before Le'ah mounted the little beast, she turned toward me and her voice filled the courtyard. "I have always blamed myself. I was the one who let Dinah go into Sh'khem that day. She was snatched away from my sisters in the middle of the marketplace—a tax on traders they said. She was taken to the prince and he defiled her, a little girl who had not even bled."

Looking old and stooped, Le'ah mounted Metushelach. She took up his reigns and pointed his nose toward Y'hudah's village. Then she turned in her saddle and spoke to me again. "My sons began the war to get Dinah back. It was Y'hudah who took her from the dead prince and placed her in my arms. Y'hudah held Dinah's hand all the way from Sh'khem to our tents. And from that day on, she never spoke again."

TRUTH AND LIES

A storm built up outside while I passed a sleepless night, wrestling with an ominous knowledge that had entered my soul. My life was built on lies. Dawn brought a heavy rain that hung a thick liquid curtain across my open doorway. I was mesmerized by the silvery striations that trapped me inside my crudely built hut. My hand disappeared when I pushed it through the veil of water. Turning my palm upward, I cupped the falling liquid. My people prayed for this rain. They petitioned Molech for it by mutilating their bodies and throwing their children into his fire. The screams of the mothers still lived in my ears. And they surely would have been my screams if 'Er had given me a son. Despite Y'hudah's disapproval, 'Er would have secreted our child to the furnace at night and sacrificed him. Perhaps that is why Y'hudah's God had killed him.

    I pulled my cupped hand back through the wall of water and poured the crystal liquid onto the floor. Jagged patterns spread on the hard-packed earth. My husband's family was in their luxurious tent-village, smugly living off the blessings of my people's prayers, allowing us to sacrifice our children while theirs lived. How many babies had been burned alive to produce this life-giving downpour? Everyone knew the sacrifice of an innocent child was the only way to replenish the earth.

    Or . . . was that another lie? If I had been misled about Dinah, was there more?

    Many years before, I had stopped praying to my vicious village gods. And Y'hudah knew I had forsaken them. That is why he chose me to marry his son. He knew I abhorred gods who devoured children and consigned disobedient wives to shrine prostitution while their husbands strutted around doing whatever they pleased. I preferred to save my worship for the Creator—not for the created. But if Y'hudah thought I could entice 'Er away from Bat-Shua's beliefs, he was wrong.

As the deluge slowed, I surveyed the soggy courtyard beyond my doorway. It was a brown lake filled with scum and debris. I sighed. Under the terebinth today, no pottery would be made, no embroidery done. But I wanted to find out more about Dinah.

Turning toward my storage chest, I opened the lid and took out threads, needles, thimbles, and finally, The Cloth of Redemption. Running my fingers lightly over my work, I traced the paths of the stars. Le'ah knew all their stories. She and her sisters had wondered about their mysteries, and she said she learned more about them from Iyov — whose fortunes were replenished by the One.

His was an amazing tale of vindication. Dinah had travelled to Utz from Hevron to meet the man. But she did not come back with Le'ah and I needed to know why. So, I packed The Cloth of Redemption and all my tools, into a sheepskin bag. Then I strapped the bundle onto my back and pulled a woollen cloak over everything. A little rainstorm would not stop me from seeking the truth.

༄༅

I stood on the threshold of Le'ah's tent, dripping wet, making puddles on the ground while marveling how a goat hair dwelling breathes freely in hot weather and is waterproof when it rains. Le'ah sat on a raised platform covered with rugs and cushions. And though she faced in my direction I knew she could not see me clearly — so I spoke. "Savta (Grandmother), I came here to embroider the cloth. It is too wet under the terebinth today."

Despondency sat in the room like a stone and lamplight flickered over Le'ah's sagging features. It exposed dark shadows beneath her eyes. This was a Le'ah I had not seen, and I felt uncomfortable in her presence. I took off my soggy shoes, shook out my cloak, and hung it on a line next to other wet items of clothing. I was at a loss as to how to begin my quest.

Without speaking, I unstrapped my bundle and felt it all over to make sure the rain had not soaked through. Then I carefully took out my embroidery tools, and the precious cloth.

"Pass me the cloth and get a dry robe from my storage chest. I do not want you dripping on everything." Le'ah had no welcome in her voice.

Obediently, I handed the cloth to Le'ah and opened the chest. Pulling a warm woollen garment over my rain-chilled body somehow gave me the courage to ask questions. "Where is Dinah? Did you leave her in the land of Utz?"

Le'ah poured fragrant tea into delicate clay cups that were decorated with intricate designs. White as a waterfall, her unbound hair flowed over her bosom and her eyes pierced my soul as she held out a steaming cup. "All the daughters of Havah are entrusted with a cup of suffering. We must be willing to drink it, all of it, if we are to find our purpose on this earth."

Puzzled by this pronouncement, I took the cup in my hands. Its warmth restored feeling to my cold fingers but I was not ready to drink it. "Savta, where is Dinah? Did she find her purpose on this earth?"

"We send out our children to bless others with the love they have received from us. It is painful to let them go, but it is the mission of life."

I frowned in frustration. Why did Le'ah talk in such riddles? "Who, exactly, is Dinah blessing with the love you gave her, Savta? And where is she?"

Le'ah leaned back against a large cushion, and casually plucked an almond or two from her ever-present meze bowls. She narrowed her eyes and stared at my face as she considered my question. "So, you are not as well informed as you think you are, little Palm Tree. You admit then, that you do not know everything that happens in this family?"

I hung my head as she referenced my name, Tamar (Palm Tree). I pretended to sip the tea because I could not look into eyes that saw so little and saw so much. My name is a symbol of knowledge. Palms stand tall in the midst of a village so a scout can climb up and inform those below of approaching visitors or threats. Palms bring information and safety through the knowledge gleaned from their waving tops. But, as Le'ah pointed out, I lived in ignorance. "Forgive me Savta, I have believed many lies but now I want to hear the truth. Will you tell me Dinah's story?"

"I told you about her mistreatment in Sh'khem. And you of all people will understand her despair and the suffering she bore. Afterward, I kept her close to me, and suggested that her father should hire a tutor for his favourite son—Yosef. Dinah took the lessons too. Ya'akov never guessed that my true intention was to restore Dinah's speech through learning to read and write. Ya'akov would never have considered hiring a tutor for a girl-child.

I took her to the land of Utz to escape the tongues and stares of people who thought, as you did, that she seduced the prince. She found purpose there, in recording an accurate story of Iyov's trials. A permanent record of Iyov's suffering can now be passed to future generations. His children, and ours, deserve to know the truth. As you know, many false rumors fly about on the wings of malicious words. We have all been their victims."

Le'ah stopped to sip her tea. She plucked another almond or two from the meze bowl and lost herself in memories. When she looked up, the years had once more melted from her face and she continued. "Though older than Dinah, Iyov became her heart's companion. Each had suffered deeply so they found comfort in each other—and they married."

I gasped and leaned forward, not wanting to miss a word. My marriages had only brought abuse and rejection. And no one in my life could ever be called a heart's companion. I had always struggled to understand acceptance and love—but I longed for it. Oh, how I longed for it. "She is happy there with him?" I asked.

Le'ah smiled for the first time that day and leaned toward me, her nose almost touching mine. "You and I know nothing of that kind of union. It is a foretaste of the Eternal Kingdom that the stars speak of. I am glad to have witnessed it at least once in my lifetime. It prepares me for a time when I will be fully immersed in the Love of God and the chains of hate and distrust among God's people will be broken asunder by the One.

"Yes. Dinah is happy there with him. Iyov loves her tenderly. And he wrote a contract promising that she and her daughters, not just her sons, will have an equal share in any inheritance he leaves. So, you see, Dinah's cup of suffering has led her to salvation."

I gasped again—shocked at such a wonder. I had never heard of a woman being so elevated in a marriage. Scenes from my marriages marched across my mind and pain bowed my head while tears dripped into my tea. Both my husbands had set themselves against me. Then, when 'Er and Onan both died, I was branded a husband killer and returned to my father's household, shaming my parents, shaming my village. Unwanted and shunned by everyone, I could never hope for a future like Dinah's.

Le'ah's finger lifted my chin compelling me to look into her eyes. "Every daughter of Havah is crushed in spirit if her husband sets himself against her. And you will only live a half-life if you continue in that shame. Do not despair. Our suffering is the pressure of God's hand. If we do not resist its pressure, suffering will mold us into useful vessels. Can you find the courage to drink the cup of suffering God has put before you? As daughters of Havah our purpose springs from its depths. If you drink the cup, all of it, shame will be washed from your soul and joy will return."

DISHONOUR AND DESTINY

I sat on the top of my hill, watching spring shrug off its winter cloak. Fresh green leaves danced on their branches, crocuses broke through dry brown grass, lambs played beside wool-heavy ewes that were being led away to give up their bulky coats. The shearing would be held at Timnah this year. There would be days of hot, dusty work, followed by nights of unbound revelry. Even pious Y'hudah participated in the debauchery of the shearing festival.

In past years, he had been content to drink himself to oblivion in the arms of his wife. What would he do this year? With the time of mourning Bat-Shua at an end, he had every right to choose a new woman to warm his bed. Or, would he indulge himself with one of the veiled prostitutes who frequented the shearing shrines?

'Er often accused me of sneaking off to whore at the festival. In his mind, that accusation justified many a beating. Onan, too, accused me of harlotry while he spilled his seed on the ground—rather than impregnating me. But that was just an excuse to keep from providing 'Er with an heir. Onan wanted to prove me barren so his first wife's son would inherit the rights of Y'hudah's firstborn.

Snatches of song drifted up from the valley below. It was a children's chant, amplified by the hillside. It came from the direction of my village. Did I hear my name in the chant? I turned around to look and listen. The village children were in a circle holding hands and mimicking a festival song but making up their own words . . . what were they singing?

"Tamar, Tamar, twice defiled, you will never hold a child. Tamar, Tamar, in widow's weeds, with no future and no seed."

I sprang to my feet in indignation. How dare they make up cruel songs about me? Where were the adults who were supposed to keep their behaviour in check? Did they sanction the heartless song? Probably! Then

I may as well make truth-tellers out of them all and go whoring at the festival! In a rage, I stormed down the hill, burst through the circle of stunned children and stomped into my hut. I took The Cloth of Redemption from the storage chest and walked away from the village without a backward glance. I told no one where I was going.

☙❧

'Einayim is a hilltop shrine beside the road to Timnah. It is named for the spring that splashes out of a rocky outcrop and flows down the hill like a wedding veil. In ancient times, an almond grove took root beside the bubbling spring. It is in full bloom at shearing time and it seemed like a good place to set a trap for young Shelah.

After shedding my widow's robe and stowing it under a sheltering bush, I carefully unfolded The Cloth of Redemption and attached one end of the fabric to a belt around my waist. The silver bells jingled as I wound the shining ruby cloth around my body and positioned the gemstones so they would catch the sunlight. It took some time to adjust everything properly. Finally, everything but my eyes were hidden behind the dazzling veil. And I was ready to act the part of an ornately-clothed shrine prostitute.

I had no intention of becoming a temple harlot. I only thought to trap Shelah in a sexual liaison that might shame Y'hudah into keeping the law of his people. After all, in the eyes of Y'hudah's God, the act of consummation is a sacred seal on a union between man and woman. If I lured Shelah into such and act, what could Y'hudah do but recognize the marriage? The possibility of motherhood drew me to this strange venture. I felt alone in the world. I longed for a child to love — and a child to love me.

While hiding in the almond grove to avoid other passers-by, I soon recognized the voices of Shelah and Y'hudah as they herded their sheep toward 'Einayim's water-pool at the base of the hill. I stepped from behind a tree and turned my body toward the sun. The glinting jewels on the cloth, caught Y'hudah's attention. But Shelah was distracted by a ram who caught his foot in a bramble bush. To my dismay, he focused on rescuing the ram and began to pick burrs from its fleece. Then Y'hudah spoke.

"Shelah, stay with the sheep while they quench their thirst at the pool. I will be back soon." Still searching for burrs, Shelah mumbled a reply. And Y'hudah walked up the hill toward me. Suddenly I panicked. This was not going according to plan. What was I to do?

"How charming, how delightful!" Y'hudah reached the top of the hill and assessed me like a prized ewe. "Your appearance is as stately as a palm tree, and your breasts, its fruit clusters. Perhaps I can climb up and take hold of them." His smile was lecherous.

I could not believe my ears at the lewd way my father-in-law addressed me. And I gasped when he said my name, Palm Tree. Did he recognize me? Did he recognize the veil? Had Le'ah described it to him? With its new gold embroidery and sparkling gems, the original look of the cloth was much changed. No one in Y'hudah's family had seen it since the day I took it into my keeping — had they?

Weak with shock and fright, I sat down on a stone beside the fountain. What would be my fate if Y'hudah guessed who I was? What scorn would he heap upon me? What punishment would he mete out? Then his voice broke into my thoughts and I resorted to playing the part of a harlot in an attempt to delay exposure.

"Please, let me sleep with you," said Y'hudah.

"What will you pay to sleep with me?"

"I will send you a young goat from my flock."

"Will you also give me something as a guarantee until you send it?"

"What kind of pledge shall I give you?" The fog in my mind lifted somewhat and I glanced around, considering how to answer. Y'hudah leaned on a distinctive almond-wood staff. And, in preparation for business transactions he hoped to make at the festival, he wore his seal on a cord around his neck. "Your seal, and your cord, and your staff in your hand." I thought if I asked for items that were so much needed for the business of the next few days, it would cool Y'hudah's lust and I could escape. But the look in my father-in-law's eye dashed that hope. Where would the madness end?

In disbelief at how quickly he gave up those precious things, I was led to the middle of the grove where Y'hudah spread his cloak on the ground to protect my beautiful garment from the dirt.

Moments later I lay on my back, gazing up at a ceiling of pink and white blossoms. I breathed in their bitter-sweet scent and concentrated on the music of the bees that fertilized the flowers. Y'hudah was silent as he moved in and out to expel his seed. Just as he finished, a breeze whispered in the treetops and a fragrant shower of pink and white petals floated onto the floor of the glade.

Y'hudah left me without a word, and I wept as I folded the veil into its casing. I sobbed as I reclaimed the robes of my widowhood while remembering the stories of Sarah, Rivkah, Le'ah and Rachel, who wore the same veil in a variety of circumstances. We were a strange sisterhood.

JUDGEMENT AND MERCY

After that, there was nothing to do but wait—and to finish embroidering the constellations on The Cloth of Redemption. As Yissakhar's Scarab stars took shape, Le'ah reminded me that they were a sign of God's indelible promise to grant eternal life to all believers in the One. While fastening Yissakhar's topaz onto the Scarab's claw, she bid me remember that the stone is worn by royalty—to honour such a pledge. Though I felt unworthy in every way to inherit that pledged promise, I did beg to receive eternal life after death. For if I now fell pregnant, and my people punished me according to their customs, my life on earth would certainly end.

While sewing Bin'yamin's red and white banded sardonyx onto the cloth, I puzzled at the affinity I felt while working on the Twin constellation. Twins are common in Avraham's family line. And Le'ah said there are mysteries to be explored concerning the Twin stars. The possibility of actually birthing twins excited me somehow. Secretly, I prayed for such a happiness—if I did fall pregnant—and survive.

Yosef's diamond fit perfectly between the horns of his charging Bull and I meditated on the legendary strength of the beautiful gem. I pleaded for strength to withstand the pressure I was under. And I hoped the evil Molech would be trampled under the Bull's sharp hooves, just as the star-beast was, under Yosef's Bull constellation.

Z'vulun's Ram constellation reminded me that a sacrifice is needed to cover our wrongdoings. So, I nestled Z'vulun's peridot into the curl of the ram's horn and decided to make an offering for my failures. And because the peridot's inner light is said to guide those in darkness, I asked God's guidance for my dark looking future.

After that, I began to embroider the stars of Levi's Fish constellation. I attached the broken pieces of amethyst to the eye of each chained fish. It seemed that the family of Avraham was very much like the amethyst and the fish. Both were broken apart by divisions that seemed impossible to mend. I beseeched Adonai to come into our midst—like the Morning Star did when it entered the fish constellation. Without a Saviour to break our chains of discord, how could we find a way to live in peace?

As the constellation of the Water-Bearer took shape, the story of Re'uven and Bilhah brought me sorrow. I knew all too well how a moment's rash decision could change the course of a life. Le'ah wept with me when Re'uven's lapis lazuli dripped from the Water-Bearer's cup like a tear. Together, we implored God to restore and refresh all our souls with Heaven's Living Water.

I had finally decided to do as Le'ah recommended, to drink my cup of suffering—all of it—even the suffering I brought on myself by my own foolish deeds. She seemed to think the Almighty One had the power to turn our worst mistakes into something good. I had my doubts, but her stories were convincing. It did seem like the One had turned many people's blunders into blessings. Le'ah's stories gave me courage to beg God that I might join that company. Though undeserving, I prayed that God's redeeming power would over-ride my foolishness, and save me from destruction. Then I sewed Shim'on's flashing green quartz to the forehead of the Sea-Goat. It is a symbol of life's resurrection and I took hope in that thought.

When I placed Gad's fiery jasper on the tip of the Heavenly Archer's arrow, I requested protection from the conflict my blunder with Y'hudah could cause. I fastened Dan's deep red garnet to the tip of the Scorpion's tail, and hoped the consequence of my sin would somehow lose its sting. Asher's yellow chrysolite was the final stone. And when it balanced securely on the Weight-Scales of his stars, I pleaded with God to weigh my actions mercifully.

All that praying was unnatural to me. Usually, I just sat in the presence of the Creator and we enjoyed the world together. I had never considered petitioning God for anything, and wondered if I would hear an answer. Perhaps Le'ah knew. How could I start the conversation?

"Savta, do you ever hear the Voice like Sarah and Rivkah did? When you talk to God, do you hear answers?"

Le'ah laughed softly and shook her head at my question. "We need no words. We are like an old married couple. We have understandings. How does God speak with you?"

For a long time, I pulled embroidery thread in and out of the cloth in my hand, journeying through the scenes of my life, pondering Le'ah's question. Finally, I said, "Once, I think I felt God's love bubble up in the sound of a water-spring. And I think I heard a still small Voice in the music of the bees. It said I was accepted in the Beloved, and bid me rest in mercy."

It was a soothing memory, but by the time I put the final stitch in the last constellation, I knew I was pregnant. And I was terrified. Unmarried women in my position were most often sentenced to burn in Molech's furnace. After all the shame I brought on them, my parents would be glad for that to happen. And who knows if Y'hudah would intervene. Probably not.

I looked toward the hilltop shrine behind my home and saw the iron statue of Molech—the bull god—glaring down at me. His pointed metal horns glinted in the harsh sunlight. The furnace in his belly was open and hungry and roaring. That fiery belly would be my final end if I was found out. Miscarriage was now my only hope.

Weeks later, that hope dwindled. It had been three months since my last bleed—and Anat knew. As latrine slave she was in charge of washing our moon-rags. Lately, she had been staring at me and glancing away when I caught her at it. What could I do? If Anat did not expose me, my secret would show itself anyway.

෩෬

Dread gripped my soul while the glare of the malevolent moon-god poured into the window of the hovel I shared with the servants. I tossed on my pallet, wondering if I should tell Y'hudah the child was his. Would he save me if I told him? If he did not, what would become of me? The pointed horns of the crescent-moon pierced the sky and drew me toward their menace. With a sigh, I threw back the thin wool coverlet, submitted to Molech's evil power and stepped outside. What could the vile moon-god want?

Standing in the dark, I lifted my face to the breeze and sampled the clove-powder fragrance of acacia blossoms. I raised my head to the god on the hill. Molech seemed angry again, unappeased by the sacrifices the village had offered. My heart began to pound in time with the throb of the drums on the hilltop shrine. Growing up with that sound did not dull its threat. On the hill above, shrieking priests were dancing themselves into a frenzy. My heart constricted with fear. There would be bloodshed tonight. Some poor soul who offended the gods would be offered as placation.

The screeching worship grew louder and more frantic as priests abandoned the shrine to search out their prey. Who would it be? A thin line of fire-torches writhed down the hill, a flaming serpent intent on a kill. I watched, spellbound by the vertical flow of light, unable to think or move. I must have known they were coming for me but I pushed the thought away. Only when I saw the reptilian eyes of the priests, and smelled their wicked stench, did I run into the slave-hut and shake Anat by the shoulders. "Did you tell them? Did you betray me?"

Flames threw leaping shadows onto the walls of the room. Bloodthirsty chants rose to a crescendo. Anat's eyes were wide with terror. There was no escape. Then Y'hudah's voice pierced the din. "Bring her out! And let her be burned alive!"

Screams filled the air as filthy hands gripped my arms. "Anat! Bring the things that are hidden behind my storage chest. Hurry! Bring them! Please Anat!" Then the tumult drowned my words while the torches pushed me, stumbling, up the hill. Evil Molech belched his foul-smelling flames while his priests leered at my fear — and Y'hudah led them.

We locked eyes in the hideous glow of the furnace that spewed sparks onto my hair and clothes. Sweat beaded on Y'hudah's brow and glistened on his beard while priests lifted me onto their shoulders and began the final procession. Soon they would throw me into the red-hot arms of Molech—who would drop me into the devouring flames of his open belly.

    I held Y'hudah captive with my eyes until Anat came panting up the hill. His belongings were in her hand. "I am pregnant by the man to whom these things belong." My voice was hoarse and broken from screaming. My strength to fight was spent. But I still held Y'hudah's eyes in an iron grip. "Do you recognize whose these are—the seal, the cord, and the staff?" He finally broke away from my gaze and looked at the things Anat held up. His eyes darted from them, to me, and back to them as understanding dawned. It seemed an eternity before he raised his hands to stop the priests.

    Under the stars of the Lion, we walked away from the stunned worshipers. Saved from death, I went with Y'hudah, down through my village, around the breast of the hill, taking the path to Le'ah's tent. Y'hudah was weeping when we arrived.

    Lamplight lay upon Le'ah's shoulders like a blessing and I knew she was expecting us. Falling into her outstretched arms, I pressed my face into her soft bosom and shivered violently while she stroked my scorched hair. I did not see the look that passed between mother and son, but I felt a mighty river of rage and love flow toward Y'hudah.

    He spoke with the voice of a chastened child. "She is more righteous than I."

    "Because you sentenced her to death for an act you committed with her?" Because you condemned her for a practice you participated in?"

    "Yes, and because I did not give her to my son Shelah." Then Y'hudah left and I heard the door-cloth snap.

AQUITTED AND ACCEPTED

I told Le'ah I wanted to go to the top of the hill and soak in the glory of the golden time. Her smile was wistful as she gave me leave. And I grieved that she could not see the Creator's handiwork for herself. At the base of the hill, barley fields, white and gold, waved restlessly in the wind. Did the distant sea look as splendid? While climbing the hill, my heavily swollen middle almost touched the dry summer grasses and I wondered if my long-ago premonition of twins was true. I laughed out loud, remembering Le'ah's story about Yitz'chak promising to make Rivkah a cart to support her pregnant belly. I could use one of those!

On the night of the fire, Le'ah's tent became my permanent home and I seldom left her side after that. After years of wondering who would have me, I was accepted at last. Le'ah's words were true. It was through suffering that I found my place in the world. And I was glad to serve a woman who loved me like a daughter and protected me like a warrior. Still, it was good to get away at times and sit on the top of my hill with the Creator, watching wonders unfold.

On that particular evening, Y'hudah's people scurried about like ants whose hill had been disturbed. Long shadows followed busy servants carrying armloads of bedding and supplies. Travel tents were being loaded onto carts, and piles of cooking supplies collected in the courtyard. All but two of Y'hudah's brothers had gathered for the evening meal, but their faces were not celebratory.

For some time, while Le'ah and I sat in the courtyard spinning pots and embellishing clothing, trouble had been festering. Le'ah could not see her sons' faces as they grouped in tight knots of intense conversation. And though they knew to stay well away from the range of their mother's sharp ears, I was sure she felt the mounting tension. Now, it looked like the festering boil had come to a head. What were those men up to? Perhaps it would be best to descend the hill and talk with Le'ah.

She sat on the floor of her tent with The Cloth of Redemption spread out before her. Slanted shafts of evening sunlight penetrated the doorway and glinted off the golden threads that outlined the constellations her sons were born under. Her fingers traced their paths and her face glowed with pleasure as she read the story of the stars. I hated to interrupt.

"Savta, something is stirring. The sons of Yisra'el are keeping secrets and making plans. I know you sense it too. What are your understandings?"

She unrolled the cloth a little further and followed the threads to Yosef's Bull stars. Her face clouded when she touched his diamond, then it lit with joy as knowledge dawned. "The One who sits in the Heavens will laugh. Justice will flow like a mighty flood and their wayward plans will bring it about. Divine purpose is accomplished through rebellion as easily as it is through obedience."

"Ima!" Y'hudah burst into the tent unannounced. His face was stricken and his hands held a multicoloured cloak dripping with blood. My first thought was for Shelah. He had a cloak like that—but the colours were wrong. "It is Yosef's cloak, Ima. We found it in a field, soaked with his life-blood. The beast must have dragged his body away. A man from Sh'khem said Yosef was looking for us so he could give a report to our father. What should we do?"

All the brothers poured into the tent, some wailing, some silent, some shuffling in discomfort. The putrid jumble of male odours threatened to turn my sensitive stomach inside-out. I had not met Yosef, but knew the brothers hated their father's favourite son. What had they done? I knew what they were capable of. So did Le'ah.

As she carefully folded up The Cloth of Redemption and returned it to its casing, she would not look in the direction of Yosef's bloody cloak. When her task was complete, she settled back onto her luxurious cushions, plucked an almond or two from her meze bowl, and looked at her sons with narrowed eyes. "Well then, we will all leave for Hevron at dawn. When we get there, you will tell your story to Ya'akov—and his heart will break."

BIRTHS AND BEGINNINGS

On the first night of our journey, we stopped on the outskirts of Biet-Lechem—a strange little town near the ancient city of Shalem. We set up camp in an open field at the top edge of the village. There was plenty of grass for the animals, and a cave for us to shelter in.

The sun set in glory that day. And as I stood on the threshold of the cave to watch it ignite the hills and houses below with fiery splendor, an unearthly feeling came upon me—a feeling of home, a sense of belonging. But Biet-Lechem was only a way-stop to our destination so I shrugged off the feeling and went inside to help Le'ah and Anat with supper.

Later that night as I stood again on the cave's threshold, enjoying the indigo world, the twinges in my back that began on our early morning climb into the hills, increased in strength.

"Are you well, Tamar?"

I paused to let a twinge pass. They were sharper now, closer together, and cutting off my breath. "You startled me Anat." I expelled my breath, amazed that the girl I once held in such disdain, had become a heart's companion. No one said a word when she followed me into Le'ah's tent and took up residence there. She was a different girl after the horror that changed everything. We were all different.

"Are the pains close together?"

"They are not severe."

I was making my way back to my sleeping pallet when a contraction coursed through my body, bending me double. Anat helped me straighten, then led me to Le'ah's bedside. I paused to breathe through another pain while my eyes adjusted to the darkness. Then I exhaled slowly.

Le'ah lit a little lamp that sat nearby, and smiled. The flame flared up to bathe her face in light. "As you know, I brought many babes into this world. I will help Anat know what to do. It will be quiet here, and away from prying eyes." She smiled again and I clung to the love in her eyes while a cramp built up. Then I exhaled.

"What is this place?" I whispered.

"There are stories about it," she answered. "They say Sarah and Rivkah stayed here on their journeys to Hevron. Rachel and I would have stayed here but she..."

Noticing my growing distress, Le'ah rose and began issuing orders. "Anat, warm some wine and find the swaddling linens. They are in the casket under my saddle. I will also need a vial of olive oil, a jug of warmed wine, and a jar of clean water. Tamar, come lean against me, we will do this work together."

I looked around at the rugged walls and wondered what they would say if they had the power to talk. Le'ah would tell me all the stories in time. For now, it was enough to remember the courage of the women who went before me... and ... AAAHHHH ... and push my child into the arms of their faith.

"Le'ah! I think there are two!" Anat's voice was frantic. "One has his hand out already. And feel this ... there is another child inside."

Le'ah remained calm. "Go snip a length from Tamar's red embroidery thread, then take hold of that little hand and tie the cord around it. We need to mark the firstborn." That done, we waited for my next contraction so I could push my firstborn onto Le'ah's lap. But when it came, it was not the child with the scarlet cord around his wrist!

"How did you manage to break out first?" exclaimed Anat as she scooped up the baby to make room for another.

Despite my confusion and my pain, I laughed out loud. "We will have to call him Peretz (Breaking Out). Do the sons of Avraham always fight for the place of the firstborn?" Then, another spasm engulfed me and Zerach (Scarlet) was born with the red thread around his arm. Exhausted but exhilarated, I pulled myself upright and stretched out my arms for my sons. Their eyes met mine and I kissed their little upturned faces. Finally, after all my troubles, I had not one but two children. And I would give them all the love and acceptance I had been denied.

GRIEF AND GROWTH

From Biet-Lechem we journeyed on. A sorry company and full of trepidation, we straggled into Hevron. The sky was burdened with heavy clouds that roofed the land with a mantle of grey. Sadness dripped from the cloudy ceiling, dampening our spirits as well as our clothes. Though relieved to end an exhausting day of slogging through damp and colourless hills, I feared what lay ahead. Beneath the Oaks of Mamre — would I be accepted or rejected? Would my twins be honoured as Y'hudah's sons, or shunned because of their questionable conception? Le'ah assured me Mother Zilpah would welcome us with open arms. Similar promises regarding Ya'akov were absent.

As the last day of travel wore on, Le'ah, like the hovering sky, descended into gloom. Throughout our journey she was stoic and calm as she swayed atop her camel, telling stories of past events that had happened along the way. But as we approached Hevron, she gathered her woollen veils around her, cocooned in thoughts she would not share.

He met us on the road, a lone figure in the mist, searching our eyes for answers. As silent as the murky drizzle, his sons dismounted one by one and bowed before him in the mud. Only Le'ah remained on her camel. "Your sons have something to show you," she said.

The earth held its breath while Y'hudah pulled the blood-stained garment from under his cloak and spread it out before his father. "We found this. Do you recognize whether or not it is your son's tunic?"

Ya'akov grasped the robe in his hands and pressed it to his heart. His face crumpled as he fell to his knees and buried his face in the folds of the ravished garment. "It is my son's tunic!" he cried. "An evil animal has devoured him! Yosef must be torn to pieces!"

No one had noticed Leah dismount her camel.

And we all gasped when she appeared at Ya'akov's side. She helped him to his feet and led him down the sodden road toward Hevron. We trudged behind them, a sorry procession of mixed emotions, entering the circle of Hevron's tents with heads bowed and feelings muddled with angst and guilt and curiosity.

Leah was right. The news about Yosef broke Ya'akov's heart. His sobs filled the air as he tore his robes and put on sackcloth. Refusing to be comforted, he was determined to go down to the grave in mourning. He would not acknowledge our coming with a traditional feast of welcome. He did not cast a glance at my sons when Y'hudah introduced them as his. He ignored everyone's attempt to offer condolences for the loss of Yosef.

Eventually, we let him be.

※※

Though the rhythms of life continued, I felt detached from everything. As Le'ah foretold, Mother Zilpah welcomed me to Hevron. Her loving arms were a comfort while all around me people drifted to and fro in a fog of grief and guilt, doing their duties without laughter or song. Le'ah spent much time with Ya'akov, coaxing him to eat. Zilpah dedicated her time to me and the twins, making sure we thrived.

The sons of Yisra'el, one by one, slunk away to their homes. Y'hudah acknowledged my boys as his, but wanted no part in fathering them and departed Hevron in deep disgrace. The shame he left behind, clothed me like a shroud. The people of Hevron did not know how to place me. I was neither wife nor concubine to Y'hudah, neither daughter nor servant to Le'ah, neither kin nor foreigner to Ya'akov. I lived between all roles while Ya'akov grieved and Hevron languished. I was a woman with no standing.

In those dark days it was difficult to praise God — but Le'ah insisted on it. So, we praised Adonai for the fruit of the ground and the health of my twins and the comfort of our companionship. And I must admit that the sacrifice of praise was the only act that gave us any hope for the future. That, and my growing boys—who cajoled us into laughter and awe with their race to best each other.

They were as different as night and day. Peretz was dark, moody, and always on the lookout to rescue a human or an animal in trouble. Zerach was bright and sunny with curly red hair and a face wreathed in mischievous grins. He hankered for adventure and urged his brother to try outdoing him at every turn. Their rivalry was as fierce as their love for each other. And though each wanted to be first—the first to roll over, the first to sit up, the first to crawl, to walk, to run—they were also quick to applaud their brother's victory if they lost the competition.

As they grew, their escapades began to lift the spirits of Ya'akov's people, giving them a focus beyond their master's grief. At the end of each day, as the exploits of my sons were recounted, the talk around the Kofte trays began again to buzz with humour.

As the twins grew, Ya'akov's youngest son volunteered to watch out for them. This was not as much of a blessing as it might seem. Bin'yamin was a wild wolf of a boy, and if they were together, I feared to let the three of them out of my sight. They terrorized the whole of Hevron by weaving in and out of the tents like swarming wasps. Was it any wonder they were swatted at now and then? If a commotion ever broke out in the camp, I always hurried in that direction hoping to arrive in time to save my children and their foolhardy young uncle from serious harm.

On one such day I flew across the courtyard in a panic, trying to reach the sheep paddock before it was too late. A cloud of dust churned above a crowd of cheering onlookers who blocked my view. I wedged myself between some watching shepherds and shoved aside a servant or two. What were those boys up to? The dust became so thick we choked on it and waved our hands in front of our eyes. We were barely able to see the terrified ewe that bolted from the midst of the haze with Zerach clinging to her back, his fiery hair floating above him like a banner. Bin'yamin ran behind, shouting encouragement.

But Peretz emerged from the dust-cloud, cross and frowning. I had no time to yell at them before the ewe gave a final frantic kick and Zerach flew through the air to land at my feet with a thud. Bin'yamin all but bowled me over before he came to a stop. And Peretz, still in a huff, marched off to calm the traumatized ewe.

The laughter began while I was trying to make sense of what had happened. It was deep and throaty and rose in volume as we turned to determine its source. Ya'akov stood in our midst, hands on hips, bellowing mirth. We were dumbfounded. I had lived in Hevron for years by then. I had never heard him laugh. We were even more surprised by what he said next.

"Peretz, Zerah, give that poor ewe a drink from the trough and join me at my tent door. For a moment, while watching the two of you, I thought I was back in my childhood. Would you like to hear the stories of my adventures with my twin brother 'Esav? You should come hear the stories too, Bin'yamin."

The three boys nodded in unison, shocked that the aging patriarch had offered them such an honour. With business-like attention, they watered the ewe, returned her to the paddock and ran across the compound toward Ya'akov's huge black tent. Little puffs of dust followed them all the way.

And so began a happier time under the Oaks of Mamre. Ya'akov still grieved Yosef, but my boys were taken under his wing and we all breathed easier in the gladdened air.

FAMINE AND FAREWELLS

As I climbed the hill above Hevron, fatigue compelled me to stop near the top. Panting, I surveyed the drought-stricken land spread out below. It looked for all the world like the pale flesh of a naked woman, stripped of her dignity. The withered leaves of Mamre's oaks, were caked with layers of dust that turned them a gritty brown—giving scant shelter to Hevron's massive tents. And with their triumphant colours bleaching in the relentless sun, Yisra'el's magnificent tribal banners hung limp and dispirited in the stale air.

    A while ago, a deluge of rain had sent mountain soils sliding into the valleys, forming shallow lakes and marshes. For a time, the moisture resurrected dormant seeds and biting insects. But the earth lay cracked and broken again—as parched and dry as an old man's face. The crops were struggling to live and so were we.

    On the side of the hill above the tents of Yisra'el, I could see the massive cedar doors of the family burial cave of Makhpelah. They were worn smooth by wind-driven sands that beat upon them constantly. Le'ah had joined Avraham and Sarah there. And I was glad she did not have to watch the slow demise of our lands and people.

    During her lifetime, despite the sorrow she bore, Le'ah continued to praised the One for all her blessings. But toward her life's end, Yosef's disappearance lay as heavy upon her as a millstone. She grieved his loss but even more, she grieved her sons' part in it. Though she never breathed a word of her suspicions, Le'ah knew what they were capable of and carried that burden in her soul. Even while she lay dying, Le'ah assured me that the Almighty turns every evil deed around to work for the good of those who love God. But I sometimes find it hard to have her faith, especially while the land and its people languish.

    After resting a while to recover my strength, I climbed to the hill's summit and piled up stones to make a small platform. I mounted it and shaded my eyes against the glaring sun, hoping to catch a glimpse of the smoke from Peretz and Zerah's cooking fires. When they came of age, Ya'akov honoured them by digging a well in the next valley over and giving them charge of a large flock of sheep. They were proud to be trusted with their own enterprise, and I was proud of them too. I saw them several times a week when they came to discuss business with Ya'akov, but I missed their daily misadventures that filled me with worry — and with laughter.

My sons were now looked after by newly acquired and very long-suffering wives who were somehow able to take their antics in stride. The latest competition between my sons was a race to populate the earth. Peretz's dutiful wife had promptly produced a set of twins. Now, everyone waited to see how many children Zerah's wife held in her growing belly.

Since Le'ah's death, I did what I could to care for the needs of Ya'akov. Anat had taken old Mother Zilpah beyond Sh'khem, to live with Gad and Asher. I had hoped Zilpah would find contentment among her own, but heard she was denying herself so her grandchildren could eat and thrive. I feared she would not be long for this world.

Turning my head to scan the horizon, I was glad to see a dark cloud forming. My heartbeat quickened. Would the cloud produce enough rain to save the knee-high crops that withered in the drought? I followed Le'ah's example and started to pray.

As I watched, the cloud grew larger and darker, its ominous shadow flowing across the fields like a plague. If I had Le'ah's acute hearing I would have been forewarned. I would have run to tell the others. I would have helped to blunt the invasion by battening down the edges of our tents.

The air around me seethed with malice as the mighty swarm obscured the sun while calling out their battle cry. Rooted to the spot with shock, I was somehow unable to flee. But I finally took a leaden step and began to walk toward our tents — buffeted by millions of diminutive soldiers that did not break ranks as they descended onto Hevron with me. Defeated by dread, I climbed into Le'ah's carved wooden bed and pulled the covers over my body. I hid there for days while destruction reigned. The locusts devoured everything in their path. Like a crackling fire, they advanced through the fields, scaled our tent walls and invaded our storehouses. When they ran out of food, the unstoppable horde left to ravish other lands, moving toward Egypt. Who could save us?

❧☙

On their first return from Egypt, the sky was hard and crystal-blue, the sun a brazen disk. A sorry company and full of trepidation, Yisra'el's sons straggled into Hevron, their faces scorched and bleak. We counted their number and dreaded to ask why Shim'on was not among them. We eyed the donkeys' bulging packs with relief. At least they brought us food. The rumor must have been true. We heard there was grain being sold in Egypt so we traded all our camels for the silver to purchase it. Would it last until the crops grew again?

 We could not hold a feast for the brothers' safe return—unless dried locusts and brackish water counted. We frowned when we opened the grain sacks and found the silver. It looked like the same amount Ya'akov sent with them to Egypt. What had they done? Had they stolen the grain they had in their packs? Were they on the run from Egyptian soldiers sent to retrieve it? Where was Shim'on? Had he been captured? What would become of us?

 The brothers were obviously exhausted so we waited for them to speak while silently storing the grain safely away and urging them to eat their fill of fried locusts. Y'hudah was their usual spokesman but he seemed reluctant to begin the tale we were all so anxious to hear. Finally, he broke the silence. "The man, the lord of the land, spoke with us harshly, and took us as spies." Y'hudah spat a rotten locust onto the ground and rinsed his mouth with a long pull from his water-gourd. Then he continued. "But we said to him, 'We are upright. We have never been spies. We are twelve brothers, sons of our father. One is no more and the youngest is with our father today in the land of Kena'an.'"

Re'uven interrupted Y'hudah, eager as always to take his place as the first-born spokesman. "Then the man, the lord of the land, said to us, 'By this I will know if you are upright. Leave one of your brothers with me. As for the hunger in your homes, take grain and go! Then bring your youngest brother to me, so that I may know that you are not spies, but you are honest. Then I will give back your brother and you can move about freely in the land.'"

During Re'uven's speech, the other brothers slumped over their food, busying themselves with their meal, not wanting to meet their father's eyes — or Bin'yamin's.

Ya'akov uttered a groan of dismay. And with a force of anguish that rocked us all, he rose from the rugs and tore his robe from top to bottom. He kicked his tray of fried locust aside and yelled into the gathering gloom of night. "You made me childless! Yosef is no more! Shim'on is gone, and next you will take Bin'yamin! Everything is against me!"

Re'uven was the only one brave enough to fill the silence that followed. He rose and gripped his father by the arms. Looking deep into Ya'akov's tortured eyes, he said, "You can put my two sons to death if I do not bring him back to you! Put him in my care. I will return him to you."

We all cringed at Re'uven's attempt to gain Ya'akov's approval. It had been an obsession all his life. And after the incident with Bilhah, Re'uven's groveling was constant. We knew this last effort, like all the others, would fail. We averted our eyes, not wanting to witness Ya'akov's contempt.

As we expected, Ya'akov shook off Re'uven's grasping arms. His face was creased with loathing as he poured out a torrent of resentment. "Bin'yamin will not go down with you — for his brother is dead and he alone remains. If harm should happen to him along the way you are going, you will bring my grey hair down to Sh'ol in grief."

My hilltop refuge provided a temporary reprieve from the anxieties in the valley below. For days I had climbed to the top of the hill, trying to glimpse sight of the brothers' second return from Egypt. Our patriarch was frantic with worry that Bin'yamin would never come back. And there was nothing the rest of us could say to soothe his fear. The best I could do was assure him that I would be a daily lookout. True to my name, I scanned the earth and sky for dangers — or sheds of hope. A least I had some small purpose in the clan.

In the eastern sky, the moon was a faint white sphere in a dome of limitless blue. I smiled, remembering how Le'ah taught me not to fear the moon as my ancestors had. It was not an evil god, but an object the Almighty placed in the sky — not to menace or control us — but a light to mark the months. And the moon had gone through a full course since Ya'akov had grown so desperate for food that he allowed Bin'yamin go to Egypt — in Y'hudah's care, not Re'uven's.

Due to lack of food, the effort of climbing the hill was growing increasingly harder. Like Mother Zilpah, I gladly gave my ration to my pregnant and nursing daughters-in-law. After all, I had completed my life's work and they had not. I had birthed two fine sons so Y'hudah would have an heir — since Shelah seemed unable to succeed in that department. I had also embroidered the story of the stars onto the Cloth of Redemption, so Le'ah could pass on the knowledge of the Redeemer who would one day come to save us all.

But where was the promised Redeemer? Where was our Saviour? Without Le'ah and Zilpah near to bolster our faith, we were beginning to doubt the truth of those lofty tales. The details of their stories were becoming muddled in our minds. Famine was robbing us of more than our wealth.

As the day wore on, sharp evening shadows began their daily march toward the east, but the beauty of the golden time barely penetrated my thoughts. Family members in the valley below trudged two and fro like languid beasts of burden. Hoping to urge our sheep to live another day, they carried armloads of prickly desert brush to feed to the hungry flock. At the edge of the camp, dusty guest-tents were sad and empty without the brothers' quarrelsome presence. And the woven rugs of the supper-circle lay faded and desolate on the ground.

I shaded my eyes against the setting sun and looked toward the southern trade route. A brilliant cloud of dust or wind — or something — shimmered in the light along the horizon. What could it be? Surely not another locust swarm. A desert fire had recently ravaged everything that the locusts could eat. And trading caravans had long since ceased to cross the lands. What was arriving from the south? Could it be . . . ?

"They are here!" I shouted. "They are here!" A reckless descent declared my age and I winced as my body tumbled past my feet, sending me plummeting down the hill and smudging my robe with dirt. If Le'ah were still alive, she would laugh when I told her of it.

As the caravan emerged from the shadow of the hill, the golden light engulfed it. Sparkling through the dust, sunlight danced on man and beast. It lit their forms in sharp relief while glinting off the daggers that hung at the sides of guards who led and followed the caravan. Judging by the colourful blankets, multiple wagons, and the ornate leather packs that graced the donkey's backs, the brothers had come home wealthy. How could that be?

My piercing cry brought Ya'akov from his tent and he stood on the road to welcome his sons. Bin'yamin's hair gleamed like fire as he jumped off his beast and ran toward his father. Locked in a hard embrace, they rocked from side to side and talked over each other in loud exclamations of greeting. Then, Ya'akov embraced all his sons in turn, even Re'uven.

As they shouted their joy, the brothers' words tumbled out in ecstatic phrases. "The Redeemer saved us! He paid the price and saved us from death! The Saviour of the stars has come! Like Mother Le'ah said he would, he has delivered us! He who was dead is now alive! And he is our very own brother — Yosef!"

MEMORIES AND MOONLIGHT

Egypt. From our vantage point on a sandy dune, the fabled River Nile was a glinting silver cobra writhing through the plain. Its toxic hood-like delta was unfurled, ready to strike us.

Thanks to Yosef, our mysterious redeemer, the menacing land of Egypt was also the land of our salvation. And judging by the verdant valley below, the pastures of Goshen would ably nourish us despite the desperate drought in the rest of the world.

But what would happen to our souls? After everything Father Avraham had done to turn us to the One, would the venom of Egypt's multiple gods poison our hearts? I feared for my sons and grandsons.

The blazing sun had turned my body into a fountain of perspiration. I wiped my brow with the edge of my gritty sweat-streaked veil, then glanced at the stone-faced man by my side. When would he would start the conversation? Y'hudah kept his distance over the years. Since the birth of the twins, we seldom spoke. Even when the sons of Yisra'el reunited and we travelled together to Egypt, he barely cast a glance in my direction. So, his opening words shocked me.

"Soon I will accompany you to Avaris. Yosef has asked that our people and flocks stay in the land of Goshen, but he asks that you dwell with his family in Egypt's capital."

Y'hudah changed position to plant his feet more firmly on the shifting dune, then he continued. "We will enter the land of Goshen on the morrow. When my flocks are settled there, I will take you to my brother." Y'hudah pulled his cloak around him, intently searching the distant horizon. Then he continued. "Please prepare yourself. Yosef's palace is resplendent, and you are not used to such great riches. If you need to purchase clothing or cosmetics, I will buy them for you."

I turned to stare at him. And I am sure my mouth hung open most unattractively. In all the years I had known Y'hudah, he had never offered to buy me anything. Why was he doing so now? Yes, I was the mother of his heirs, but he had never given me special consideration. I knew I had no place in his heart. Everyone knew. Did his encounter with Yosef change him somehow? Or was he, in some way, forced to acknowledge me?

Y'hudah kept his eyes on the Nile, struggling with his thoughts, trying to find the right words. Finally, he continued. "In Avaris, the Egyptians need to see you as a Matriarch of Yisra'el . . . it is the desire of Yosef." I continued to stare at Y'hudah's face, trying to read it. His sun-bronzed skin had gone pale. Motionless, with arms crossed, he refused to look at me. What had he just said? 'It is the desire of Yosef'? Judging by Y'hudah's frown, it was obviously not *his* desire that I be elevated to the status of his mother and the other matriarchs before her. And I could not help but agree with him. I had never held any place of importance among the people of Yisra'el.

A blast of scorching wind threw sand against my perspiring skin, but my heart felt cold and bereft. I tightened my veil around myself and stared at Y'hudah. It seemed his regard for me was a shallow thing. It was only his regard for his rediscovered brother that motivated him to spend money on me. How insulting.

A lump formed in my throat and I blinked back tears. They were all ashamed of me. Yosef needed to pretend I was a Matriarch of Yisra'el so I would not soil his name when I entered his prestigious household as a servant of some kind. And I was sure Y'hudah was glad to get me out from under his feet, so as not to remind the others of his blunder.

I gazed down at the land of the pharaohs. If I felt a misfit in the land of my birth, among the tribes I lived with, how could I possibly find belonging in Egypt's capitol city? It would be far away from everything familiar. A whole day's journey would separate me from my sons and their families. The thought of living so far from them left me struggling for breath. How could I go on living if they were not nearby? What purpose would I have if I could not care for them? My head spun with choking thoughts of being torn away from those I loved. Overwhelmed and overcome, my heart quaked and the shallow trench of my heart-wound became a great crevasse of grief. For a moment I thought I would lose myself and fall in.

But in a rush that left me gasping, Le'ah's words of long ago flowed into the fissures of my heart. "All the daughters of Havah are entrusted with a cup of suffering. We must be willing to drink it, all of it, if we are to find our purpose on this earth."

A welcome breeze stirred my sweat-soaked veil and caressed my anguished face. It lifted my robes away from my body and cooled me with a gentle fluttering hand. It almost felt like the soothing touch of a mother's love—like Le'ah's. And in my heart of hearts, I heard her voice again. "Our suffering is the pressure of God's hand. If we do not resist that pressure, suffering will mold us into useful vessels."

Oblivious to the silently brooding presence of Y'hudah, I asked Adonai for the strength to endure pain's pressure. Leaving my children and grandchildren to go and live in Yosef's palace was the most bitter cup I had ever been offered. I swallowed with difficulty. The desert sun had dried my throat, but sorrow had dried my soul so I begged the One to restore and refresh me with the Water-Bearer's living water.

Then Le'ah's voice spoke softly again. "Can you find the courage to drink the cup of suffering God has put before you? As daughters of Havah, our purpose springs from its depths. If you drink it, all of it, shame will be washed from your soul and joy will replace it."

"But my children," screamed my broken heart, "How can I live so far from them?"

"We send out our children to bless others with love they received from us. It is painful to let them go, but it is the meaning of life." As I submitted to Le'ah's wisdom, a deluge of tears began to wash the desert's sandy grit from my face.

Y'hudah, discomforted by my sobs said nothing

as he busied himself with rearranging his robes and headdress. When my tears were spent, a tender wind came to dry them. Heavy of heart but resigned, I knew what I had to do.

"Very well my lord," I said. Then I turned away from Y'hudah and slid down the shifting dune to prepare for my future. If I was to be a servant in Yosef's household, I would accept my lot. I would not resist the pressure of God's hand. And, I would not shame my people by arriving at Yosef's palace looking like a famine-ravished pauper. A week of treatments would wipe the desert's damage from my skin. Then, when it was smoothed with honey and bathed in water scented with dried rose petals, I would ask my daughters-in-law to apply intricate henna designs to my feet and hands. And . . . oh yes, I would also rinse my hair with henna to cover the silver threads that appeared in recent years. On the morning of my departure, I would put on The Cloth of Redemption, the only garment I had that would be at home in a palace. If Yosef wanted me to appear to be a Matriarch of Yisra'el, I would do my best to look the part.

೫ා෬

When the boat docked, the great silver sheet of the river was utterly calm. I held the delicate folds of The Cloth of Redemption well away from the lapping water and stepped ashore. At the water's edge, an imposing gate was manned by two fearsome guards. Y'hudah confidently nodded to them and led me up a crunching path of small white stones that opened onto a vast courtyard.

Rose-gold and glowing in the evening light, a huge palace loomed ahead. At the front door, a heavily armed guard acknowledged our presence with a nod. When Y'hudah led me around the side of the building I followed him, assuming he was taking me to the servant's quarters, where I would be introduced to the steward in charge of my duties.

"Stay here and wait," Y'hudah said. "I will find

Yosef and bring him out to meet you."

I shrugged and nodded, surprised that the much-esteemed Yosef would meet me at the servant's entrance. Y'hudah walked away and I watched him disappear into the shadows of a pillared portico. Then I turned around to examine Yosef's expansive gardens.

With the golden time upon us, the palace grounds were lovely. Lavish plants of every height and shape, burst with vibrant colours and wafting perfumes. Feeling empty from the drab devastation of drought, I thirstily drank in the sights and scents, letting them dissolve in my soul.

The flames of the setting sun were painted on a pond of water. Entranced by the brilliant display of orange and red, I was mesmerized, lost in wonder—and in the companionship of the Creator. Drawn by the shimmering colours, I wandered to the pond's edge to watch the blaze of glory fade to yellow, then to mauves and deeper purples.

In time, an inky blackness crept over all, and night took over the world. Fascinated, I kept my eyes on the little lake as stars began to appear. They were tossed about on the moving surface as if they danced for joy.

PLONK! A large object hit the water in front of me. I gasped and jumped backward to rescue my delicate garment from the damaging splash. PLONK! It happened again, closer to me this time. What was happening? I could see nothing but the dark shapes of trees and bushes. Was I being attacked? Would anyone come to my aid if I cried out?

A torch-lamp flared to life and I followed the path toward it. Perhaps the gardener who lit the flame could usher me to safety. Or, was the torch lit by my attacker? I trembled in the pool of torchlight under a date palm, and steadied myself by leaning against its trunk. Should I call out? Should I be silent? All alone in this strange place, what should I do?

Plop. Plop. Plop. Blurred objects fell from the date palm's branches, onto the ground—hitting the earth before me with three soft thuds. They were the wrong shape and size to be dates and seemed to glow in the dark. What were they? As I leaned in closer, legs, pinchers and curved stingers unfurled. I backed away from the tree — away from the branches laden with scorpions. Fear crawled up my spine and I turned my head from side to side, trying to see through the darkness. Who was out there?

A sharp whistle split the air. Did it come from the branches above me? "YEOWWW!" A dark Egyptian cat ran across my path — low to the ground, ears back, eyes wide. I screamed and jumped away from a long-nosed dog that burst from the shadows, ears pointed, tongue lolling, enjoying the chase immensely.

And I started to laugh.

"I cannot see you but I know you are hiding in this tree. Stop sneaking around trying to scare me. Come down and introduce yourself. Lord Yosef wants to meet me in the garden but I strayed from where I was supposed to be and need help to find my way back."

Instead of scorpions, two sheepish boys dropped from the branches overhead and plopped onto the path. My head jerked back in surprise. In the torchlight, they could have been mistaken for Peretz and Zerach — when they were children. A pang of longing ripped through my heart and stole my breath.

"I see you have met my offspring, Mother Tamar."

I whirled around to see a man dressed in a knee-length linen kilt. Rimmed with kohl, in the Egyptian way, his eyes of green and gold sparkled with laughter. Yosef!

Heedless of my fragile gown, I knelt in homage.

"No, Mother Tamar, you are not a servant. You must not bow like that."

Perplexed by the urgency in his tone, I looked up and saw that his eyes were shining with tears. He did not staunch their flow while his sons quietly helped me to my feet. "But you are the Redeemer," I said. "You are the King of the stars, the Promised One — sent to save us all. That is what your brothers say."

Yosef shook his head and tried to rub away a smile that suddenly sprang to his face. "My brothers, as usual, are confused, Mother Tamar. The Redeemer the constellations foretell, will come from Y'hudah's seed, not mine. The Eternal Redeemer is from the tribe of the

Lion stars. And you are a Woman of that Promise. You are the mother of Yisra'el who bowed before me in my dream so long ago."

"The dream? The dream about the sun, the moon, and the eleven stars bowing down to you?"

"You know it then? They mocked me fiercely when I told them about it. Even my father rebuked me. And I cannot blame them, for I was also baffled." Merriment sprang again to Yosef's face. I could never have imagined a circumstance where my brothers or father would bow down to me." Then humour faded from him and he continued. "Then there was the problem of my mother. She was no longer with us when I had the dream, so I assumed Le'ah was the moon-mother I dreamt about. But . . ."

"Le'ah loved the moon," I said. "If the sky was clear she could sometimes see it."

Yosef turned away and bowed his head, his shoulders sagging. His sons threw their arms him, their upturned faces lit with tender concern. Yosef smiled down at them and pressed their small bodies to his heart. Then he turned back to me. "Come, Mother Tamar. Let us find a bench where we can sit and talk. I want to hear of Le'ah's last days. My brothers told me some of what she suffered, but I want to hear the story from you as well. M'nasheh and Ephraim, go find your mother and bring her to meet Mother Tamar."

Yosef gave his boys a gentle push in the direction of the palace, then guided me to a pale stone bench that rested under a fragrant jasmine tree. For a while we sat together under the tree, breathing its sweet perfume. "Le'ah would have loved it here," I said.

He bent his neck and rubbed his face while sorrow rose from his skin like steam. He looked up and turned his face toward me, his eyes pooling with silver that he did not blink away. "Yes. I planted jasmine and oleander, hoping she would enjoy their scent one day . . ."

"The grief you feel is the price of love," I said.

Again, he dropped his head to his chest and looked away. "I also grieve the wounds our family inflicted on you, Mother Tamar."

"And you have been deeply wounded by our clan, Yosef."

Yosef shrugged and rubbed his hands on his thighs while gathering in his sorrow. His voice was once again calm when he said, "They meant it for evil, but God meant it for good."

My eyes grew wide and I leaned in to see his face more clearly. He turned and looked into my eyes. "She said that all the time," I said.

Then Le'ah's familiar words sprang from both our mouths, "We must be willing to drink our cup of sorrow, all of it, if we are to find our purpose on this earth." We laughed with painful joy at the shared memory, then turned our heads toward the sound of a soft footfall.

From deep within the shadows she emerged, a whisper of a woman, beautiful and delicate. She held Yosef's sons by their hands and timidly approached. When she bowed at my feet I rose in protest.

"My wife, Osnat, the daughter of Potu-Fera, priest of On," said Yosef.

We were silent as we assessed each other. I could only imagine what she made of me. With my sparkling gem-studded garment, she probably thought I was dressed above my station. And I did not know what to make of her. She was just a slip of a girl. Her glossy black wig was adorned with bright beads of turquoise and gold that matched the jewelry on her arms and neck. Her face was kind though . . . open and pensive.

Yosef interrupted the awkward silence. "Osnat has forsaken the beliefs of her people. She now worships the One."

"I also forsook the gods of my youth," I said to her. "And the Mighty One has brought me more satisfaction than thousands of gods.

"Yes," she said, her voice as melodic as a flute, "My people have thousands of gods that predict many things. For example, they say the hereafter will be another cycle of life like this one, with all its potential for grief and pain, where only rulers have a place. But I would rather trust my husband's God who prepares a perfect city and garden for the afterlife where all are welcome. Yosef says that the One will banish sorrow there, and everyone will live in harmony."

Not knowing what to say, I turned my eyes to Yosef's lovely garden. It was hard to imagine a more perfect place. And yet, Osnat was right. The Redeemer, as the stars foretold, is preparing a better place for us, a place free from conflict and sorrow.

The little boys, bored with adult talk, had sauntered over to the pond. Kneeling on the shore and combing the water with their hands, they were bathed in the moonlight of childhood. I smiled. Were they looking for more creatures to do mischief with perhaps? I hoped so! In the Kingdom of Heaven will we all be as delightful as children?

Reluctantly, I turned my eyes away from Osnat's sons, and back to her. "Yes," I said, "The beauty of this earth is always marred by pain. In the Redeemer's Kingdom, it will not be so."

Yosef cleared his throat to break the spell between his wife and me and we turned to face him. His eyes were shining and the space around him seemed to glow with the intensity of his feelings. "Mother Tamar," he said, "we want you to live with us and teach us about the Kingdom of Heaven. But I know you would grieve to leave your sons and their families in Goshen. So, with the pharaoh's blessing, I will ask your sons to move their families to the outskirts of Avaris. They will become Royal Shepherds, keepers of the pharaoh's flocks. And your grandsons can be tutored here at the palace with my sons—if you approve."

I could not comprehend what Yosef was saying. I stared at him and could not utter a word. I was committed to following God, to leaving my children in Goshen if that was required. Was God now preventing that sorrow—as on Mount Moriyyah when the sacrifice of Yitz'chak was stayed? I could hardly take it in.

"I fear for the children of Yisra'el," Yosef continued passionately. "The seductions of Egypt's gods are strong. We need to combat them. We need you to teach us about the One."

I dragged my thoughts back to what Yosef was saying and somehow found my voice. "But I have no standing among the people of Yisra'el. Who would allow me to take such a role? I am neither wife nor sister, neither mistress nor servant. I am no one. I have no place among our kindred that would give me authority to teach them."

Yosef caught me by the shoulders and looked into my eyes. "Mother Tamar, in the Kingdom of God, the least among us is always the greatest. The Kingdom belongs to the poor in spirit."

A murmuring wind moved through the treetops. It rustled the branches of the palms and exposed the shining crescent of the new-moon. Osnat shivered when she saw it. She wrapped her arms around her body as if chilled. My compassion was stirred. Osnat's fear was a familiar reaction from my past—and I could not let her be bound by it. "Le'ah taught me not to fear the moon," I said. "It is not a malicious deity but a light to brighten our darkness. And like our people, it will wax and wane through the years, until the Great Redeemer comes to save us."

Tired of their play by the water, the boys ran to join us and we all stared up at the moon while the trees clapped their branches in the breeze. "Perhaps the people of Yisra'el should meet together at the time of the new-moon," said Yosef in a tentative voice. Then his words rose with power and excitement as the idea gripped his imagination. "On the first sighting of the new moon, we should put away our work and rejoice in our coming Salvation. On that night, we will make a festival of praise to the Mighty One—from generation to generation."

"A festival of praise!" I exclaimed in delight. "Le'ah would love it!" Caught up in the wonder of the thought, I laughed aloud and swirled around like a child, all my heaviness dropping away as I abandoned myself to dance. When I looked up, the stars in the sky were hung so low it seemed like God had flung them upward from the earth—thousands of sparkling gems to guide us all. And while I twirled through the indigo night and set my whole world spinning, I knew Le'ah was right. When I drank my cup of suffering, the One, the Morning Star, came to shatter my soul's darkness. In that instant, chains of shame fell away and I was free — free to teach Osnat and her children about the One — free to help our people praise the Almighty. Truly, our purpose flows from our suffering and our praise.

Osnat, quick to embrace my joy, eagerly ran to join my dance. She snatched up the edge of my veil and spread it wide. A playful breeze caught it and threw it heavenward, a flowing crimson banner sparkling in the torchlight, rejoicing with the stars. Osnat's smile blazed in the darkness and she held out her hand, drawing her family toward us. In her breathy voice she asked, "Will you tell us the story of the stars, Mother Tamar?"

Under the rippling ruby banner, I sang the song of the stars, a ballad of redemption Le'ah taught me. At first, the others joined in hesitantly, reaching out to try a strange new melody. But as their voices rose in confidence, I saw in their glowing faces, the future that the stars foretell.

As people of the Promise, our suffering prepares the way for a Saviour to come. Though the night of our sorrow is dark and fraught with struggle, our praise will usher in the day — the day of the Lion from the tribe of Y'hudah, the Eternal King, the Morning Star. On that day, our chains of hate and distrust will break asunder and we will be fully immersed in the Love of God — free to enjoy the glory of the golden time together.

Psalm 81:1-4,6
Sing for joy to our God our strength!
Shout to the God of Ya'akov!
Lift up a song and sound a tambourine,
a sweet lyre with a harp.
Bow the shofar at the New Moon . . .
. . . He set it up as a testimony in Yosef,
when he went throughout the land of Egypt.

Hebrews 11:1,2,13,16

Now faith is the substance of things hoped for, the evidence of realities not seen. By faith we understand that the universe was created by the Word of God, so that what is seen did not come from anything visible.

[Those who went before us] all died in faith without receiving the things promised—but they saw them and welcomed them from afar, and they confessed that they were strangers and sojourners on the earth... But as it is, they yearn for a better land—that is, a heavenly one. Therefore, God is not ashamed to be called their God, for he has prepared a city for them.

Matthew 5:3
Blessed are the poor in spirit,
for theirs is the kingdom of heaven.

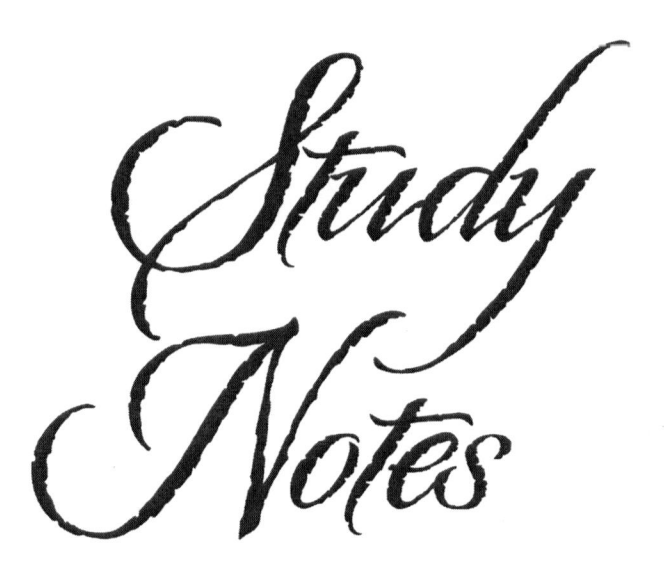

Study Notes

STUDY NOTES

SARAH

Read the Biblical account of Sarah's life in
Genesis 12:1 – 23:20

Let's explore Sarah's life as a daughter of Havah
- Describe the cultural differences between modern life and Sarai/Sarah's life—regarding marriage, slavery and the status or role of women?
- In *Daughters of Havah*, how did the One communicate with Sarai/Sarah?
- Does God visit people today in the same ways?
- Can you relate to her experiences?

Our Need for Redemption
The Oxford Dictionary of English Words defines the word redemption as:
1. The action of saving or being saved from sin, error, or evil.
2. The action of regaining or gaining possession of some thing in exchange for payment, or clearing a debt.
3. The action of buying one's freedom.
- What was Sarai redeemed or freed from?
- What price was paid for Sarai's redemption?

Our Inner Longings
Read: Genesis 3
- What inner longing(s) may have prompted Havah/Eve to disobey God? (Genesis 3:1-6)
- When Havah disobeyed God, what changed in her relationship with Adam? (Genesis 3:16)
- What possible common longings did Havah and Sarai/Sarah share?
- Are these longings common to all women?

Our Need for a Home
Read: Genesis 2 - In the beginning, God created a perfect garden as a home for Adam and Havah.

Read: Genesis 3:22-24, Genesis 4:1-16, 1 Chronicles 9:1, Ezra 5:12, Matthew 7:24-27 - People sometimes lose their homes due to natural causes, bad choices they make, or due to the oppression of others.
- In *Daughters of Havah*, why do you think Avraham didn't build a home for Sarah?
- Have you ever lost a home?

Read: Genesis 12:1-6, Exodus 6:8, Numbers 14:8, Jerimiah 29:4,5, Mark 10:29,30 - The Bible seems to indicate that it's always God's plan to settle his people in a home even if they are in exile for bad behaviour — or victims of the bad behaviour of others.
- In *Daughters of Havah*, what home did God give Sarah?
- Was it the home she wanted or expected?
- Describe your home. Is it the home of your dreams?

Read: Hebrews 11:8-10, John 14:1-3, Isaiah 11:6-9, Isaiah 65:17-25, Revelation 21:10-27 - God has promised to redeem the earth from the destruction of our bad choices, and to build a new home for us — where all will live in safety and harmony.
- In *Daughters of Havah*, how did this knowledge affect Avraham and Sarah's lives?
- How does this knowledge affect your life?

The Part Pride Plays
Read: James 4:6, James 4:10, Proverbs 11:2, Proverbs 16:5, Proverbs 6:18, Proverbs 29:23
- What part did pride play in the committing of the world's first act of disobedience?
- In *Daughters of Havah*, how did Havah show pride?
- How did Adam show pride?
- In *Daughters of Havah*, how did pride affect the lives of Avram, Sarai, and their community?
- When did Sarai recognize that she needed to repent of her pride?
- What was the result of Sarai's repentance?

Matthew 5:5
Blessed are the meek, for they shall inherit the earth.

Read: Psalm 37:11, Matthew 11:29, 1Timothy 6:11, Titus 3:1,2, James 3:13, 1Peter 3:1-6 - In Matthew 5:5 (see the verse above), the Greek word 'praus' (easy, mild) was translated into English as 'meek'. The Bible verses listed above, contain that same Greek word but are sometimes translated differently. The English word 'meek' is difficult to define and has many shades of meaning. Jesus described himself with this word, but it doesn't mean he was a pushover who didn't stand up for himself. Merriam-Webster's Dictionary defines the word 'meek' as "enduring injury with patience and without resentment."

- In *Daughters of Havah*, how did Sarai show meekness when she was sold into the pharaoh's harem?
- How did Sarah show meekness in the court of Avimelekh?
- How did Avram/Avraham live up to or fall short of the standard of behaviour in 1Peter 3:1-12?
- How did Sarah inherit the earth, due to her meekness?

FACT OR FICTION?

When we get to Heaven, I'm sure Avraham and Sarah will relish straightening out my mis-impressions of their lives. And we'll have a good laugh about the things I got wrong. Until then . . . we can only wonder . . .

What was the significance of moon worship in ancient Mesopotamia? The worship of heavenly bodies is one of the world's oldest religions. As the people of the earth fell away from worshiping the Creator, they began to worship the created. John 3:19 says that ". . . people loved darkness rather than light. Why? Because their actions were wicked." When people forsook the worship of God, they gravitated to the most prominent object in the darkness—the moon.

The story of Avraham and Sarah begins with Ziggurat worship in the city of Ur. Accounts of Ziggurat practices, the worship of Nanna, and the existence of the priestess Enheduanna, is factual. Avraham and Sarah came out of the moon-god religion and its horrific practices. I only grazed the surface of its abominations.

When was the story in the stars discovered? David writes in Psalm 19, "The heavens declare the glory of God, the dome of the sky speaks the work of his hands. Every day it utters speech, every night it reveals knowledge. Without speech, without a word, without their voices being heard, their line goes out through all the earth and their words to the end of the world."

The psalm begins with how God speaks in the heavens and goes on to extol how wonderful the Word of God is. What message did God speak when the heavens were created? What story was told? According to Jewish tradition, it was Havah and Adam's son Seth who first named the constellations. Obviously, the famous wisemen of the Christmas story knew the story of the stars. They came to Bethlehem to worship the King whose birth the stars revealed. If Chaldean stargazers centuries later, knew that the King of Kings would someday be born, did the first family on earth also know that truth? I think so!

How did we lose that knowledge? Was it perhaps a Satanic cover-up that involved demonic fortune telling — using the same constellations that God put in place to tell us about the plan of redemption through the coming Messiah?

Romans 1:18-22 seems to say just that, "What is revealed is God's anger from heaven against all the godlessness and wickedness of people who in their wickedness keep suppressing the truth; because what is known about God is plain to them, since God has made it plain to them. For ever since the creation of the universe his invisible qualities — both his eternal power and his divine nature — have been clearly seen, because they can be understood from what he has made. Therefore, they have no excuse; because, although they know who God is, they do not glorify him as God or thank him. On the contrary, they have become futile in their thinking; and their undiscerning hearts have become darkened."

Who was the pharaoh in Avram and Sarai's story?
Chronological events in both the Bible and Egyptology have been matters of debate for centuries. There are gaps galore in the records. Many scholars believe that Avram and Sarai went to Egypt in about 1975 BCE. Who was the pharaoh at that time? Could it have been Senusret 11 or his son Senusret 111? They are both muscular dudes with big ears. They look like harem builders to me.

Was the Cloth of Redemption Real? Of course not! When I was a child in Sunday School, I was intrigued by what my teachers taught about a scarlet cord of redemption that weaves throughout the entire Bible leading up to the great event of Jesus' death on the cross. In my stories, each woman in Jesus' lineage is given the fictional Cloth of Redemption when a price is paid to deliver her from bondage.

Once, when I was explaining my book to a literary agent, he asked if it seemed far-fetched that the cloth would be well-preserved enough to be passed on through hundreds of generations of women and end up with Miryam, Jesus' mother.

I shrugged and said, "We believe in the virgin birth, don't we? Would it be such a stretch for God to make a cloth last for thousands of years?"

You will need to read *Daughters of Havah, Volume Two*, to see how this fictional cloth is given to Rachav, Ruth, Bat-Sheva and Miryam—the next four women in Jesus' lineage.

What is the significance of Biet-El? Mentioned in Scripture many times, Biet-El is a place where many important things happened in Jewish history. It was originally called Luz, the almond tree (Genesis 28:19). It was later known to Avraham's descendants as Biet-El, The House of God. Inspired by the original name (Luz), I made up the presence of the mystical almond grove, and the birds (perhaps the Eurasian Nuthatch?) that fed on the almonds there. For more about Biet-El, read Genesis 12:5-8, Genesis 28:11-22, Joshua 16:1, Joshua 18:11-13,22, Judges 1:22-23, Judges 20:18-27, 1 Kings 12:28-29

Who is Malki-Tzedek? His name can be translated as "King of Righteousness," and he's referred to in many ancient texts. The Bible mentions him several times as a mysterious priest and king who serves God apart from the hereditary order of the Judaic priesthood that descends from Aaron. See: Genesis 14:18, Psalm 110:4, Hebrews 5:6-20, Hebrews 7:1-17. In the book of Hebrews, how was Jesus compared to Malki-Tzedek? And, in *Daughters of Havah*, did you figure out who Malki-Tzedek had a previous appointment with—when Sarai went to his home in Shalem to meet with him? See: Genesis 14

Did the conception of Yitz'chak and the destruction of S'dom happen at the same time? Maybe, maybe not. The chronology of Scripture is sometimes confusing to untangle. But when taken at face-value, it seems that the two events happened close together. The angelic messengers who gave Avraham and Sarah the news that Yitz'chak would be born in a year, were on their way to rescue Lot and his family from the destruction of S'dom. I get shivers thinking about how the holy judgment of sin, and the loving plan of redemption, spring from the heart of the same God.

Who was King Avimelekh? Avimelekh was the generic name given to all P'lishtim kings in the Hebrew Bible. See: Genesis 20:2-18, Genesis 21:22-32, Genesis 26:1-26, Judges 8:31, Judges 9:1. King Avimelekh of G'rar also appears in other ancient accounts as one of the twelve regional kings of Avraham's time. According to other accounts, he was a God-fearing king who is said to have built the city of Shalem for Malki-Tzedek. The Bible makes no mention of this though.

When did Avraham marry K'turah? In our modern way of looking at life, we'd prefer to think that Avraham married K'turah after Sarah died. But it was not uncommon, nor was it considered immoral, for men to take a wife or concubine when their first wife was old.

Given what we are told in Scripture, let's think this situation through. The Bible says Avraham was 137 years old when Sarah died, and 175 years old when he died (Genesis 25:7). If Avraham waited to marry K'turah until after Sarah died, the oldest of their six sons would only be, at the most, 38 years old when Avraham died. If a son was born every two years after that, the youngest boy would only be 26 years old when Avraham died. In those days, people lived so long that the age of 38 was considered to be very young. If you look at the Biblical genealogies, young men were just starting to marry and have children at that age. The Bible tells us that during his lifetime, Avraham established distant home places for K'turah's sons (Genesis 25:6).

Would Avraham have the heart to send very young sons away from their mother — permanently? I'd like to think not. So, I favour the view that Avraham and K'turah had their sons before Sarah died. I hope, as a compassionate father, Avraham established them in their distant homes when they were of reasonable age to be independent.

Did Avraham and Sarah really live separately in their old age? When Sarah died, Avraham was 137 years old, and was not likely travelling around the countryside on business like he did in his younger days. Sarah too, at age 127, was probably pretty much settled in one place when she died. Genesis 23:1 says, "Sarah lived to be 127 years old and died in Kiryat-Arba, also known as Hevron, in the land of Kena'an; and Avraham came to mourn Sarah and weep for her."

So ... Avraham wasn't with Sarah when she died. And the Bible doesn't say he 'came back' or 'came home' to mourn for her. Speculation on why they separated is mine, but it is also based on Jewish tradition.

RIVKAH

Read the Biblical account of Rivkah's life in Genesis 24, 25:21-28:5

Let's explore Rivkah's life as a daughter of Havah.

Work in Paradise
Read: Genesis 2:9, Revelation 2:7 - In partnership with Adam, Havah was Earth's first female gardener.
- What trees were planted in the Garden of 'Eden and will also be in the Paradise of God?

Read: Isaiah 65:17-25 - Work isn't a punishment. It's not a result of sin. But our struggles with work are a result of the deteriorating condition of the world brought on by sin. (Genesis 3:17-19)
- Can you imagine a new Heaven and Earth where the struggles of our labours are removed and work becomes pure joy?
- In that new world, what would you like your job to be?

Our Need for Redemption
The Oxford Dictionary of English Words defines redemption as:
1. The action of saving or being saved from sin, error, or evil.
2. The action of regaining or gaining possession of something in exchange for payment, or clearing a debt.
3. The action of buying one's freedom.
- What was Rivkah redeemed from?
- What price was paid for Rivkah's redemption?

Our Need for Equality and Validation
Read: Galatians 3:26-29, Psalm 68:11, Joel 2:28-29, Acts 2:14-18, Romans 6:3
- In *Daughters of Havah*, when Rivkah's story begins, what was the reason for her inner turmoil?
- How did the desire to be validated as a spiritual equal to Yitz'chak, affect Rivkah's life?
- Is this desire wrong?
- In *Daughters of Havah*, what was Rivkah redeemed from?
- What price was paid for Rivkah's redemption?
- When did Rivkah begin to turn from the gods of her culture?
- How did the One communicate with Rivkah?
- Does God visit people today in the same ways?
- How did Rivkah's desire to be validated affect her marriage?

- How did Yitz'chak's desire for validation affect his marriage?
- How much of a problem is this issue in today's marriages, families, churches, and workplace relationships?

Read: Mark 10: 45, Luke 22:24-30, Ephesians 2:4-10, Philippians 2:1-11, Colossians 3:1-4
- In *Daughters of Havah*, when did Rivkah realize she needed to repent of her prideful drive to spiritually compete with Yitz'chak?
- What was the result of Rivkah's repentance?
- What does the Bible say about taking the lower place as Shabar did?
- When do you take the lower place to serve God and others?

Matthew 5:7
Blessed are the merciful, for they shall be shown mercy.

Read: Matthew 9:13, Proverbs 11:17, Proverbs 12:10, Colossians 3:12,13, James 2:13 - The Oxford Dictionary of English Words defines 'mercy' as: compassion or forgiveness shown towards someone whom it is within one's power to punish or harm.
- In *Daughters of Havah*, how did Rivkah show mercy?
- How did other people show her mercy?

Read: Psalm 86:5, Daniel 9:9, Isaiah 30:18, Proverbs 28:13, 1 John 1:9, Titus 3:5 - Both Rivkah and Havah, devastated by bad decisions, met with God in the garden. And both experienced God's mercy in the garden.
- How has God shown mercy to you when you have made wrong choices?

FACT OR FICTION?
While researching the lives of the women in *Daughters of Havah*, I tried to stay as close as possible to the Biblical account of their lives. Much of the dialogue in Rivkah's story comes straight from Scripture (The Tree of Life Version). I also leaned heavily on ancient Mesopotamian texts. They were a treasure trove of information about the religion and way of life of the people of that time.

Who is King Nimrud the Evil? The story of King Nimrud vs Avram has been passed down for thousands of years and may (or may not) have some truth at its core. Also, King Nimrud may (or may not) be the same person as the Biblical Nimrod, mentioned in Genesis chapter 10.

What's cig kofte? The legend about it gave you some idea what this ancient staple is like. While the recipe varies from region to region, Cig Kofte is made by adding salt, chopped onions, tomato, isot pepper, mint, and parsley to kneaded bulgar wheat and raw ground meat. Cig kofte is still popular in the Middle East.

Was Rivkah's kumbet village real? While researching the ancient city of Harran in Turkey, I became fascinated with the historic dome houses of the area. We don't know if Rivkah and her family lived in a village like that, but it's fun to think they might have. Check out Harran's historic cupola houses. You'll be fascinated too.

Was The House of Joys real? I discovered many sad and horrifying truths about the worship system Avraham and his family left behind them. The House of Joys was just one of them. And yes, every newly married woman had to have sex there—with someone who paid her.

Where is The Pot Belly Hill? While researching the trade routes that Avraham and his family might have travelled as they criss-crossed the Biblical landscapes, I made the delightful discovery of Gobeklitepe (Pot Belly Hill) in Turkey. It's one of the oldest civilized places ever discovered, and is in the general location of where the Bible says the 'People of 'Eden' lived. See: 2 Kings 19:12, Isaiah 37:12, Ezekiel 27:23.

    It's just wild speculation on my part to think that there might be a link with this site and Rivkah's story or the Garden of 'Eden. But who knows? When Gobeklitepe was discovered in 1963, the whole site had been weirdly obscured, millenniums before, by filling in the whole place with dirt. See: Genesis 3:23,24. I wonder . . .

Are Rivkah's herbal remedies real? Jewish tradition says that Rivkah was a well-known healer. And while I don't know if she used the healing herbs mentioned in her story, the herbs cited were used in ancient medicine—and are still effective today.

Did Yitz'chak and Jesus look alike? Logically, because God the Father doesn't have a physical body, Jesus inherited his physical characteristics from the human part of his bloodline. In the Bible, it is often noted when a woman in a story is beautiful. But in the story of Jesus, his mother's looks are never mentioned. This leaves me to think she was an ordinary looking girl. The prophet Isaiah said of the Messiah, that "He had no stately form or majesty to attract us, no beauty that we should desire him." (Isaiah53:2)

Hmmmm . . . if Jesus, who probably looked a lot like his mom, was an ordinary looking man, who else in his lineage did he (and Mary) take after? Not King David! (1 Samuel 16:12)

It's just speculation on my part, but I'd like to think Yitz'chak may have passed down some physical characteristics to Jesus. After all, they were both beloved sons who were bound for sacrifice on the very same hill.

What does the Bible say about Yitz'chak's faith? When Avraham and Yitz'chak made the journey to Mount Moriyyah, there is no record that Yitz'chak protested or struggled when Avraham put him on the altar and bound him as a sacrifice. We are never told how this incident affected Yitz'chak's faith, but it must have left a deep impression—regarding Avraham and his God.

Is that why Yitz'chak's son, Ya'akov, describes his father's God as "The Fear of Yitz'chak? (Genesis 31:53) It's the only place in the Bible that name for God is used.

Who was the mysterious Ioav? Many Jewish scholars, and the early Christian leaders, hold to the view that Iyov/Job lived at the time of the Patriarchs and was a descendant of 'Esav/Esau through 'Esav/Esau's grandson Zerah. (See: Genesis 36)

Iyov/Job's three friends were thought to be Elifaz/Eliaphaz, king of Temen and descendant of 'Esav/Esau (maybe his uncle or cousin), Bildad, king of the Shuhites, and Zophar, king of the Naamites.

All three are thought to be contemporaries of the patriarchs. But both historical and Biblical genealogies are tricky to untangle because they sometimes omit generations and sons are often named after their fathers without making it clear who was who.

Job 1:1 says that Ioav/Job lived in the land of Utz/Uz which was thought to be east of the Promised Land in the territory of Edom—'Esau/Esav's territory.

Why a birthright and two blessings? The Birthright is the inherited right of the firstborn son. It's the right to rule the clan spiritually. It's also the inherited right to the judicial authority of the father. Along with this right comes a double portion of the father's material possessions.
- In the story of Ya'akov and 'Esav, blessing #1 was like a last will and testament that Yitz'chak originally wanted to give 'Esav. It included Yitz'chak's material riches as well as his political position in the land. Blessing #2 was the blessing that God gave Avraham and Yitz'chak—the possession of the Promised Land. In Genesis 28:13-15 God affirmed Ya'akov as the blessing's rightful recipient.

LE'AH

Read the Biblical account of Le'ah's life in Genesis 29-35

Let's explore Le'ah's life as a daughter of Havah

The Potter and the Clay
Read: Genesis 2:7, Job 33:6, Isaiah 64:8 - Beginning

with the very first human, the analogy of God as a potter and people as vessels of clay, is a common one in Scripture.
- What images come to mind when you think of this word picture?

Read: Isaiah 29:15-16, Isaiah 45:9, Romans 9:19-21 - The analogy of a clay vessel questioning the potter about how it was made, is also common throughout Scripture.
- What circumstances or handicaps could have caused Le'ah to question God?
- Have you ever questioned God in regard to allowing your flaws or handicaps?
-Or, have you wished you could have been born into or lived in different life circumstances?

Read: Jerimiah 18:1-4, Job 10:8,9 - I define 'sin' as a harmful/destructive thought or action. When sin's destructive influence entered the world, God's splendid vision for our lives was spoiled.
- How did sin spoil Le'ah's life?
- How has it spoiled yours?
- What do we need to do to break free from sin's destruction? See: 2Timothy 2:21

Read: Lamentations 4:2, Jeremiah 29:11, Ephesians 2:10, 2 Corinthians 4:7 - God, the Heavenly Potter, doesn't leave us in a sin-spoiled state. God plans to redeem us and remake us into useful and beautiful vessels.
- In *Daughters of Havah*, what was the price paid for Le'ah's redemption?
- Describe the change in Le'ah's life as God began to redeem her.
- Have you made peace with the way you are designed?
- If so, how is God redeeming your situation?

Our Need for Redemption
The Oxford Dictionary of English Words defines redemption as:

1. The action of saving or being saved from sin, error, or evil.
2. The action of regaining or gaining possession of something in exchange for payment, or clearing a debt.
3. The action of buying one's freedom.
- In *Daughters of Havah*, what was Le'ah redeemed from?
- What price was paid for Le'ah's redemption?

Our Need for Intimate Relationships
Read: Genesis 12-35 - The ancient Code of Hammurabi outlines rules of marriage and divorce during the time of the patriarchs. Under these laws, a woman could get a divorce. She could keep her dowry, property, children — and even get child support if she could prove her husband had 'degraded' her.
- In *Daughters of Havah*, what family dysfunction did Avraham and Sarah come out of?
- In the areas of marriage and parenting, did they do a better job than their parents?
- In what way did they follow in their parent's dysfunction?
- How did Avraham and Sarah's marriage affect Rivkah and Yitz'chak's marriage and parenting?
- What good decisions did Yitz'chak and Rivkah make?
- How were Ya'akov and his wives influenced (good or bad) by the example they had to follow?

God's Word to Husbands and Wives
Read: Proverbs 31:10-12, Malachi 2:14,15, Matthew 19:4-6, Ecclesiastes 4:9, John 5:12, 1Corinthians 13:2-7, Ephesians 4:2-3, Ephesians 5:22-33, Colossians 3:19, 1 Peter 3:7 - The men and women in *Daughters of Havah* didn't have the Scriptural encouragement and instruction that we have now.
- Would the lives of the Genesis patriarchs and matriarchs have been different if they had the written Word of God?
- Why do you think Le'ah did not seek the legal divorce settlement allowed in her culture?
- In *Daughters of Havah*, alternative to divorce did she choose, and why?
- What alternatives to divorce could be considered in

modern marriages?
Read: Psalm 133:1, Proverbs 12:26, Proverbs 17:17, Proverbs18:24, Proverbs 27:5-9, Ecclesiastes 4:9,10, John 15:12-13, Romans 12:10, Colossians 3:12-24, 1 Thessalonians 5:11 - God wants us to have fulfilling and intimate relationships—so the Bible is filled with advice on how to obtain and maintain them.
- In *Daughters of Havah*, what were the sustaining relationships in Le'ah's life?
- How did she maintain and nurture those relationships?
- How did she deal with difficult relationships?
- What are the relationships that sustain and nurture you?
- What are you doing to nurture them?

Matthew 5:4
Blessed are those who mourn, for they shall be comforted.

Read: Psalm 147:3, Isaiah 49:13, Isaiah 61:1,2, Jeremiah 31:13, 2 Corinthians 1:3,4
- List Le'ah's griefs.
- How many of them do you relate to personally?
- In the story of Le'ah, how did she 'self-medicate'?
- What is your favorite way to soothe yourself when you are grieved or stressed?
- Why did Le'ah choose to follow God though life was hard?
- How did others in *Daughters of Havah* comfort Le'ah?
- How did God comfort Le'ah?

Read: Matthew 16:27, Matthew 25:21, John 14:2, I Corinthians 2:9, Revelation 21:1-4
- How was Le'ah comforted in Heaven?
- What rewards did she receive there?
- How does the knowledge of future rewards, comfort you?

FACT OR FICTION?

Once again, much of the dialogue in Le'ah's story comes straight from Scripture. Throughout The *Daughters of Havah*, I predominately used the *The Tree of Life* Version's dialogue. And again, I leaned heavily on ancient Mesopotamian texts when writing about the religion, marriage customs/laws, and the way of life of the people of that time.

What was wrong with Le'ah's eyes? There's controversy in scholarly circles on what Genesis 29:17 exactly means when it comments on Le'ah's eyes. The Hebrew word referring to them is 'rak' which means "tender, timid, soft". After commenting on Le'ah's 'rak' eyes, the Bible contrasts Rachel with Le'ah as being perfectly formed and beautiful. So . . . how was Le'ah not perfectly formed? Were her eyes weak? That is how many scholars have translated 'rak'. When I wrote the story of Le'ah, based on the most common interpretation of the word 'rak', and on Le'ah's family medical history (Genesis 27:1, Genesis 48:10), I depicted her as nearsighted.

What are keskek, meze, baba ghanoush, and ayran? Keskek is a ceremonial meat and grain stew traditionally served at middle eastern weddings, funerals, and other religious festivals. Meze is a collection of small dishes with various treats in them—like nuts, fruit and olives. Baba Ghanoush is made from delicious smoked eggplant, olive oil, lemon juice and seasonings. It's used as a dip or spread. Ayran is a cold (savory/tangy) yogurt-based drink still popular in the ancient Middle East—as are all the dishes mentioned above.

How close together were Ya'akov's sons' births? There's more than one way to look at this question. See: Genesis 31:41—Ya'akov spent twenty years with Lavan. For fourteen years he worked off his wives' two bride-prices, for six years he worked for wages. Some scholars think Ya'akov first worked fourteen years to pay off Le'ah and Rachel's two bride-prices, then he married the women and had eleven sons in seven years. I (and other Biblical scholars) think that perhaps Ya'akov worked a seven-year term to pay off Rachel's bride-price, but mistakenly married Le'ah. Right after that, he married Rachel and pledged to work off another seven-year bride-price (after marrying her). That would mean, the eleven sons were born in fourteen years—still daunting, but if you spread the boy's births among four women, its doable.

Were Ya'akov's sons associated with the signs of the Zodiac? Yes! Jewish tradition is very sure about this—but opinions are divided about which son was born under what sign—or exactly what each constellation meant. So, on that issue, please take this part of the story with a grain of salt. And one more word of caution . . . the signs that Ya'akov's sons were born under, foretold the future Israel and its place in the world as it pertains to the coming of the Messiah and his future kingdom. **The signs of the Zodiac do not foretell our personal futures. Our modern understanding of astrology is not of God.**

What's with the birthstones Ya'akov gave his sons? From ancient times, jewels were given to mark baby's births. And the spiritual significance of precious stones is scattered throughout Scripture. See: Exodus 28:15-30, Ezekiel 28:13-16, Revelation 21:18-21. While the translation of the names of Biblical gems is debated, as is their meaning and what tribe of Israel each stone is associated with, great spiritual importance is given to these tribal jewels. I believe they display the wonder and splendor of God's character. So, in the story of Le'ah, I've used the gems and their very ancient meanings to illustrate the attributes of God. "For since the creation of the world, his invisible qualities, his eternal power and divine nature, have been clearly seen, being understood through what was made." Romans 1:20 (NIV)

How old was Dinah when she was violated? Dinah was Ya'akov's eleventh child, born between Z'vulun and Yosef (Genesis 30:21). If (as formerly discussed) Ya'akov waited fourteen years to marry Le'ah and Rachel, then sired twelve children in seven years, then left Lavan's employment to have ten or eleven years of experiences in the land of Kena'an/Canaan—Dinah may have been seven to ten years old when she was raped. But if, (as in theory number two) Dinah was born six years before her family fled from Lavan, she may have been twelve to sixteen years old when she was raped.

Where is Rachel's tomb? You can visit Rachel's tomb, located at the northern entrance to the Palestinian city of Bethlehem, just where the Bible says it is. (Genesis 35:19,20)

What does the Bible say about slavery? The Bible, if read carefully and taken in context, deals with slavery as an abhorrent practice that causes misery and suffering—an oppressive situation that people need to be rescued from. See: Genesis 15:13,14, Exodus 2:23,24, Exodus 3:7, 6:5. But because slavery was a sad fact of life in those days, laws were made to govern slavery and keep it humane. See: Exodus 20:8-11, 21:1-11, Leviticus 19:20-22, Deuteronomy 16:13,14, Job 31:13-15, Jerimiah 34, Joel 3:1,2, Ephesians 6:5-9. The Bible also has much to say about those in trapped in slavery. In God's sight, we are equals. See: Matthew 20:25-28, Mark 10:41-45, Luke12:35-38, John15:12-16, Acts 2:17,18, Galatians 3:26-28. Hopefully, God's people in ancient times, treated their slaves as equals, not purchases.

TAMAR

Read the Biblical account of Tamar's life in Genesis 38

Let's explore Tamar's life as a daughter of Havah

The Cup of Suffering
Read: Matthew 20:20-23, Matthew 26:36-39, John 18:10,11, Luke 14:27, Romans 8:14-23 - Jesus talked about the cup of suffering he was asked to drink, and also about the cup of suffering every one of his followers must drink.
- What was Tamar's cup of suffering?
- What is your cup of suffering?

- How have you fought against, or accepted, the suffering in your life?
- How did Tamar's cup of suffering lead her to her purpose in life?
- How is God using your suffering to lead you to your life's purpose?

Our Need for Justice
Read: Deuteronomy 32:4, Psalm 33:5, Psalm 37:28, Psalm 140:12, Ecclesiastes 3:7, Isaiah 1:17, Isaiah 30:18, Isaiah 61:8,9, Amos 5:24, Romans 12:19, Luke 18:6-8, Hebrews 10:30
- What injustice did Eve face? See: Genesis 3:12
- How did God show her justice? See: Genesis 3:15
- What injustice did Tamar face?
- How did God show justice? See: Genesis 38:26, Ruth 4:13-22
The name 'Tamar' means 'Palm Tree' (A place to climb up and look out for visitors, signs of rain, or dangers etc.)
- In *Daughters of Havah*, how did Tamar live up to her name?

Our Need for Truth
Read: Psalm 109:2-4, Jerimiah 7:8, Romans 16:17-18, Colossians 2:8, Proverbs 3:5,6 - Satan, The Father of Lies (See: John 8:44), holds us in bondage when we believe his lies.
- In *Daughters of Havah*, How were Le'ah and Dinah set free from rumors, lies, and the cultural oppression of women?
- What lies did Tamar believe?
- How did they affect her life?
- How did lies keep her in bondage? See: John 8:32.
- How was Tamar set free (redeemed) from the lies that kept her in bondage?
- What lies have you believed?
- How did they affect your life?
- How did they keep you in bondage?
- Is God still actively freeing women from lies and injustice? See: John 8:1-12, Psalm 89:14.

Our Need for Acceptance
Read: Psalm 9:10, Psalm 27:10, Psalm 34:18, John 16:33, Romans 8:15, Romans 8:37-39 - God has great

compassion for those who are rejected.
- In *Daughters of Havah*, who rejected Tamar?
- Who accepted her?
- How have you felt rejection from others?
- Do you believe God has a plan to turn the rejection you have experienced into acceptance?
- How is that happening in your life?

Our Need for Redemption
The Oxford Dictionary of English Words defines redemption as:
1. The action of saving or being saved from sin, error, or evil.
2. The action of regaining or gaining possession of something in exchange for payment, or clearing a debt.
3. The action of buying one's freedom.
- What was Tamar redeemed or freed from?
- What price was paid?
- Can you retell the story of redemption using the constellations and gems in *Daughters of Havah*?

When sin entered the world, so did the need for redemption from sin's destruction. Like Sarah, Rivkah, Le'ah and Tamar, we have no power to redeem ourselves. Through his death on the cross, Jesus paid the price for our eternal redemption.

Let's praise God like Tamar did!
Read: Psalm 107:2, Psalm 130:7, 8, Lamentations 3:55-60, John 3:16,17, Galatians 3:13,14, Colossians 1:13,14, 1 Peter 1:18-21,

Matthew 5:3
Blessed are the poor in spirit,
for theirs is the kingdom of heaven.

Read: Psalm 34:6,7, Psalm 107:41, Proverbs 22:4, Matthew 18:4, Romans 12:3, James 4:6 - Oswald Chambers said, "The bedrock in Jesus Christ's kingdom is poverty, not possession; nor decisions for Jesus Christ, but a sense of absolute futility—I cannot begin to do it. Then Jesus says—Blessed

are you." (My Utmost for His Highest, July 21st, The Gateway to the Kingdom, page 203)
- In *Daughters of Havah*, how did Tamar display poverty of spirit?
- How did her poverty of spirit help her embrace God's Kingdom?
- How did Tamar's poverty of spirit gain her a position in the Kingdom of God?

FACT OR FICTION?

In the book of Genesis, Tamar's story is told in one short chapter. So, I had to dig deep into my imagination when trying to build her life. When we hear Biblical stories told, we often disconnect them from the stories of other Biblical people from the same time-period. In telling Tamar's story, I tried to show her to relationship to other Bible characters, places and events of her time.

Have you noticed how much the Bible mentions constellations and stars? Job 9:9, 38:31, Amos 5:8, mention Pleiades, a cluster of stars in the constellation of Taurus (the Bull stars). These verses also mention the constellations of Orion and the Great and Little Bear. Also see: Genesis 1:6, Genesis 15:5, Genesis 37:9, Numbers 24:17, Deuteronomy 4:19, Nehemiah 9:6, Job 3:9, 9:7, 22:12, 25:5, 38:7, Psalm 8:3, 33:6, 136:9, 147:4, 148:3, Ecclesiastes 12:2, Song of Songs 6:10, Isaiah 13:10, 34:4, 40:26, 45:12, Jerimiah 31:35, Ezekiel 32:7, Daniel 8:10, 12:3, Joel 2:10, 3:15, Obadiah 1:4, Matthew 2:2-10, 24:29, Mark 13:25, Luke 21:25, 1 Corinthians 15:41, Philippians 2:15, 2 Peter 1:19, Revelation 2:28, 6:13, 8:10-12, 9:1, 12:4, 22:16 - WOW! That's a lot of verses—and not an exhaustive list either. Look them up. It's a fascinating study.

Does God mend the cracks of our lives with silver?
This metaphor in the story of Tamar was inspired by the Japanese art of Kintsugi. In this ancient art form, broken pottery is mended by pouring liquid gold into the cracks

of damaged vessels. I thought it was a beautiful metaphor for how God mends us. But in my stories, I used the metal silver—the ancient symbol of faithfulness.

Did Dinah marry Job? Was the book of Job written by Dinah? In the Apocryphal book, Testament of Job, Dinah is said to have married Job after the death of his first wife. Today, many Jewish traditions hold that Dinah married Job, and it was her daughters who shared the inheritance with her sons. I hope it's true. The authorship of the book of Job is the subject of much debate. Ancient stories were sometimes passed on orally for generations, so it's hard to say who wrote Job's story down for the first time. I just speculated\hoped that it might be Dinah.

What did Molech look like? This fearsome god's name was also spelled 'Moloch'. His image was fashioned as a huge bull, sitting on a throne. His arms were stretched out in front of him to hold the sacrifice that would then be dropped into the flames of a furnace at the base of the statue. Israel was often admonished for worshiping this God. See: Leviticus 20:3, 1 Kings 11:15, Acts7:43

Were the patriarch's marriages really that bad? A good friend suggested that I may have exaggerated the faults of the men in my stories. From the patchy information in the Biblical tales, it's hard to get a clear picture of people's relationships. All I could do was to try to put myself into the situations the Bible described. I don't know if I got it right but here's my thinking . . .

Avram - If I was Sarai, I would have been really angry when Avram sold me to the Pharaoh. And, she probably coped with the situation better than I would have, because she is commended for it in 1 Peter 3:6. There is no indication in Scripture that Avram ever apologized for what he did. But because God called him a 'friend' (Isaiah 41:8), I thought Avram would repent and apologize so I wrote it into the story.

Yitz'chak - The Bible clearly states that Yitz'chak loved Rivkah (Genesis 24:67). But he did seem to me like a man who habitually avoided conflict. In the Scriptural account, he never verbally acknowledged the validity of Rivkah's visitation from God. He didn't rebuke Esav for selling his birthright or marrying pagan women. He avoided conflict with the men who were stopping up the wells he dug. He didn't rebuke Rivkah or Ya'akov for their deception regarding the stolen blessing. It seemed to be a dysfunctional pattern to me. I hope he made everything right with Rivkah at some point, but there is nothing in Scripture that says he did.

Ya'akov - It's pretty clear from Scripture that Ya'akov struggled with being a husband and parent. A low point in his life was yelling at his sons for rescuing Dinah from Shek'hem. I think Le'ah did her best to cope with Ya'akov's favouritism toward Rachel and her sons, but his enduring attitude would have eroded any sense of intimacy in their relationship.

Y'hudah is a difficult character to come to terms with. The Scriptural accounts don't paint a positive picture of him. He was the one who came up with the idea of selling his own brother into slavery (Genesis 37:26). And, sadly, I didn't make up anything he did to Tamar. He was repentant after realizing that he was the one who impregnated Tamar (Genesis 38:26). I hope he treated her respectfully after that, but the Bible drops the story there, leaving us to wonder how and where the twins were raised.

When did Yosef live in Egypt? Again, controversy is rampant regarding the years that Yosef lived in Egypt. There are two main theories called 'the long sojourn theory' and 'the short sojourn theory'. I'll leave you to research them at your leisure. I chose 'the short sojourn theory' for my story because of an amazing 1960s discovery. In the area of Goshen, near the ancient Egyptian capital of

Avaris, British Egyptologist, David Rohl, may have found the palace, tomb, and statue of Yosef!

The storehouse city of Ramses (See: Genesis 47:11, Exodus 1:11) was also located in this area. Archaeologists concur that the land around Avaris was settled during Egypt's Middle Kingdom (the 12th Dynasty) by a Semite people from Kena'an and area. The population must have been friendly with the Egyptians because no fortifications were built. The architecture, pottery, and burial sites of this Semite population matched the Kena'an culture.

At the archaeological dig site called Tell el-Dab'a, the palace of a Semite official who worked for the Egyptians, was found just outside Avaris. It was built in the Egyptian style and is dated to the late 12th Dynasty or early 13th Dynasty of Egyptian Pharaohs. The palace entrance was supported by twelve pillars. And eleven Semite-style tombs were built in the gardens behind the palace. It also had a small pyramid grave in the garden. In a shrine in front of the pyramid-shaped tomb, the remains of a colossal statue of a Semite ruler was found—wearing a striped, multicoloured, Semite-style coat. The bones of the person buried there were missing (See: Genesis 50:24-26).

If those discoveries weren't exciting enough, in 1979, a cylindrical seal was found on the floor of the palace at Tell el-Dab'a. Seals like the one found, were commonly worn on a thong around the neck and used to press the owner's mark onto clay or papyrus documents. The seal was carved with the twelve symbols of the sons of Israel, based on Ya'akov's blessings, and possibly on their star signs. See: Genesis 49:1-27.

In the 1600s BCE, after a period of great prosperity in Egypt, a northern tribe called the Hyksos invaded Egypt and conquered the people of the land. Exodus 1:6-11 says a king rose up in Egypt who didn't know Yosef, and he pressed the descendants of Avraham into slavery. Was this a Hyksos king?

ABOUT THE AUTHOR

Born to missionary parents, Ellen Hooge was whisked off to Nigeria, at ten months of age, and spent a happy childhood exploring the land and culture she was immersed in.

Her mother's failing health took the family back to Canada where her father, Dr. Henry Budd, taught at Briercrest Bible College and later became the school's second president. So, Ellen finished growing up in a rich spiritual and academic environment.

After college, Ellen married Jack Hooge and joined North America Indigenous Ministries. Their experience with working alongside indigenous people has been full of adventure as they served God.

Ellen and her husband, Jack, now live in Calgary, Alberta, Canada. And she divides her time between publishing books for Indigenous Christian authors, publishing books for friends and family, writing and publishing her own books, and keeping tabs on ten growing grandchildren.

For more information about Ellen Hooge's work:
www.sparrowhousecollective.com
jehooge@shaw.ca

ACKNOWLEDGMENTS

The old proverb says, "It takes a village to raise a child." It also takes a village to write and publish a book. First of all I want to acknowledge those in my 'village' who opposed or disagreed with me while I wrote *Daughters of Havah*. I'm sincerely grateful for all the objections and warnings expressed. As I thought through each point of objection, my knowledge of human nature and our theological past was deepened in ways that couldn't have happened without listening to those who have a different view from mine. Keep the opinions coming! You know I love a good discussion.

I would also like to thank many who encouraged me on my writing journey. Helen Suk, my heart friend and prayer partner whom I lean on all the time. Alana He, Elyse Schindel, Lara Hogan and Joyelle Komierowski (my daughters), Sue Thiessen and CJ MacKinnon (my sisters). All the above-mentioned have been so patient with this long drawn out process of writing this book. And though I'm sure that all of you thought it, you never once said you doubted I would finish. Thank you for not giving up on me and my book.

And to my writer's group: Sandi Somers, Kim Clarke, Lorraine Boerchers, Diane Ablonczey, Linda Joncas, Tracy Francis, Jeanelle Derry, Liz Chua - how could I have written this book without your encouragement? I just couldn't have. I also want to thank the members of InScribe Christian Writer's Fellowship for all the great networking and friendship over the years.

Next, a very heartfelt thanks to Jean Barsness, Marilyn Elliott, Tracy Krauss, Dane Neufeld, and my amazing launch team who gave of their very valuable time to read advanced copies of *Daughters of Havah* and write such glowing reviews about it.

Last but definitely not least, thanks goes to my husband, Jack. I know my world of writing, books, and all things literary, has been a mystery to you for forty-seven years. Thank you for your faithful, enduring, encouragement and love.

BIBLIOGRAPHY

Beside the Bible, I used many secondary sources to help me understand and write about the lives of the women of Genesis. In addition to many on-line sources that informed me about the geography, language and culture of the people I was researching, the following titles had an important place in helping and inspiring me as I wrote the stories of Sarah, Rivkah, Le'ah and Tamar.

Robert Alter
The Five Books of Moses: A Translation with Commentary, 2004, W.W. Norton
ISBN: 0-393-01955-1

Henri J.M. Nouen
Can You Drink the Cup? 2006, Ave Maria Press,
ISBN: 978-1-59471-099-5

Aviya Kushner
The Grammar of God: A Journey into the Words and Worlds of the Bible, 2015, Random House
ISBN: 978-0-67964-526-9

Joe Amaral
Story in the Stars: Discovering God's Design and Plan for Our Universe, 2018, Faith Words
ISBN: 978-1-54601-074-6

Saint Ignatius of Loyola
The Spiritual Exercises of Saint Ignatius or Manresa
2010 Reprint edition, TAN Books and Publishers
ISBN: 978-0-89555-153-5

Flavius Josephus
The Life and Works of Josephus, translated by William Whiston, 1928, The John C. Winston Company.

Manufactured by Amazon.ca
Acheson, AB